THE TRIP

Speeding toward the cliff at the end of the world

THE TRIP

Speeding toward the cliff at the end of the world

A Novel

Armando García-Dávila

McCaa Books • Santa Rosa

McCaa Books

McCaa Books
1604 Deer Run
Santa Rosa, CA 95405

ISBN 978-0-692-81072-9

First published in 2017 by McCaa Books,
an imprint of McCaa Publications.
Revised edition published November 2017

Printed in the United States of America
Set in Minion Pro

Cover photograph by Robert McIntyre.
Map by Moira Hill, www.moirahilldesign.com.
Cover and book layout by Waights Taylor Jr.

www.mccaabooks.com

Dedication

I dedicate *The Trip* to any son who has
longed for his father's approval.

PROLOGUE

December 13, 1862 – Fredericksburg, Virginia

JOHN SHIVERED AS MUCH FROM THE COLD as from the ominous, dark feeling about the battle that lay ahead. His regiment, 1,200 rifles strong, was in one of five brigades that had marched to the battlefield. The percussion from cannon and musket fire, neighing horses, bugles, and officers screaming orders, previously muffled by distance, was now sharp and clear at the staging area where his brigade waited. "God be with us," he whispered. A bitingly cold breeze carried the sinister odors of war: exploded gunpowder, blood, burnt flesh.

"Fix bayonets!" yelled Devil McGhee, the first sergeant. Thousands of steel knives snapped into place.

A corn snake crawled from a weed patch toward a nearby stream. McGhee slid his sword from the scabbard to lead the advance and caught sight of the snake wriggling by at his feet. McGhee brought down his blade beheading the snake. Its body writhed violently, its head lying to one side still as a stone, eyes staring blankly toward heaven.

"Wasn't necessary to harm it," John whispered. Locks of his dark brown hair hung out from under his cap and fluttered in the icy December breeze. John nervously licked the ends of his moustache that hooked over the sides of his mouth.

McGhee raised his sword. "Shoulder arms!" Rifles thumped against shoulders. "Forward, march!" The sergeant led them up and over a knoll that had hidden them from the battlefield.

John's heart grew cold. Before him lay a field covered with the bodies of fallen soldiers, casualties from previous charges. A half-mile off across an open plain, thousands of enemy fighters were dug in behind a wall of fieldstones cutting down advancing troops. "Steady," he whispered tightening his grip on the rifle.

The brigades' mission was to do what previous brigades had failed to do: overrun the wall and take the enemy.

McGhee pointed his sword to the field. "Forward, double quick!" The brigade charged, its battle screams filling the air. John's only hope was a fool's luck to avoid the barrages of cannon fire and shrapnel. He jogged steadily forward, bayonet pointed at the enemy.

Smoke blasted from a string of cannon on the hillside behind the wall. Bodies flew in pieces as cannon balls found their marks. Hot shrapnel hit John's ear, a numbing blow. His blood flowed warm against the winter air.

The brigades pressed on, within range of the enemy's long rifles. A snake-like cloud of smoke rose along the wall. Men around John fell as musket balls cut through limbs, torsos, and skulls. A campmate running next to him caught a ball in the chest. He screamed. A second ball passed through his open mouth, exiting his neck and taking fragments of shattered teeth and splintered vertebrae.

"Charge, you bastards, charge!" McGhee screamed, his eyes aflame. The brigades weren't close enough for their return fire to reach the enemy. John leapt over the bodies of the dead and dying. Some had scarcely a wound and appeared to be lying asleep; others mutilated beyond recognition. A headless body lay with its arms at its sides as if at attention, blood pouring from the neck and forming a dark pool on the ground. Nearby, a leg from the knee down stood in its boot.

The air thick with smoke from continuous barrages along the wall clouded the enemy's view, and John's brigade began taking fewer losses. The enemy fired blindly in the direction of the advancing brigades. Seizing the moment McGhee raised his sword. "Make stand!" Soldiers lined up. "Shoulder arms, fire!" Sparks and plumes of smoke blasted from their muskets. Thirty of the enemy fell along the wall. Smoke thinned allowing them to see. They answered with a volley of hundreds of rounds. Dozens along McGhee's line fell, some piling on top of others.

John dropped a charge and ball into his rifle packing it with the ramrod.

McGhee screamed, "Ready, aim, fi…" The rage in his homicidal eyes turned stunned. A ball passed between his eyes. His bear-like body fell back and landed with a thud. McGhee stared blankly toward the heavens. A fountain of blood pulsated from the hole in his head.

Men surrounding John fell in rapid succession. The line broke. Someone screamed "Retreat!"

John ran praying that he wouldn't die running from a battle. A tremendous punch hit him from behind above the hip and knocked him to the ground. He pushed up dazed and looked behind him. Who had hit him? Not a man standing. John put a hand to his hip and brought it forward. Blood dripped from his hand. He put his hand to the front, next to his abdomen: more blood. A ball had torn through him.

The battlefield grew eerily quiet before cheers broke out along the wall. The enemy had held and won the day. Cries of the wounded, drowned out by the din and chaos of war, rose from the field.

John tore his handkerchief in half and stuffed a piece into each side of the wound. His head spun as if he had just shared a whiskey with a campmate.

John lay still. A grizzly lesson learned from war was to remain still until nightfall. Standing made one an easy target for snipers. He held, nauseous with pain, through the afternoon and into the cold dusk. The wounded cried, wailed and moaned. Their voices wove into a dirge of agony that rose from the field of misery to God's deaf ear. John shivered with cold but the frigid air slowed the flow of blood from his injury. Cries turned into pitiful pleas for water and calls for loved ones.

A man next to John spoke in his delirium, "Abram, do as your Ma says. Put on your coat lest you freeze, sonny boy."

John had hoped to make it back to camp under the cover of night, but he had lost the strength to lift himself. Was this the end for him? What would it be like to die, for his soul to extricate itself from his body? He took solace in knowing that he had sewn his name and town to the inside of his jacket. At least his family would learn what became of him. He wondered if the modest amount taken from his pay each month and sent to his mother and father would continue, or if it would die with him. He drifted in and out of restive sleep.

John dreamed he was inside his home, lying near the front door with a foot trapped between floorboards. The door stood ajar, the outdoors white with snow. Frozen air whistled through, chilling him to his marrow. He tried time and again to reach the door, but he couldn't free himself.

THE SUN ROSE OVER THE PLAIN. John awoke with fever despite the winter cold—tongue dry as leather. A lake of water could not satisfy his thirst. *I would give my arm for a taste of water.*

The day warmed and pleas from the field rose anew "Water! Water!"

Footsteps approached. The shadowy image of a man appeared, knelt at John's side, and lifted his head.

The voice of a young man. "Here you are, mister." He poured drops of water over John's lips. John opened his mouth and water trickled in.

John gulped. "Thank ye," he said in a parched whisper.

"I can't hear what you're saying, mister, but I'll figure it's to the good. Have a bit more."

John held the water in his mouth for a moment before he drank feeling the blessed moisture. "Who, are, you?" he said.

"Say again?" The man leaned into John's lips.

"Who, might, you be?"

"Regret to report that I'm with those you're fighting against."

Drained of strength, John could only mouth the words, "Lord, bless ye." His world evaporated into blackness.

The water bearer put an ear to John's chest, listened and said. "You're better off leaving this wicked war."

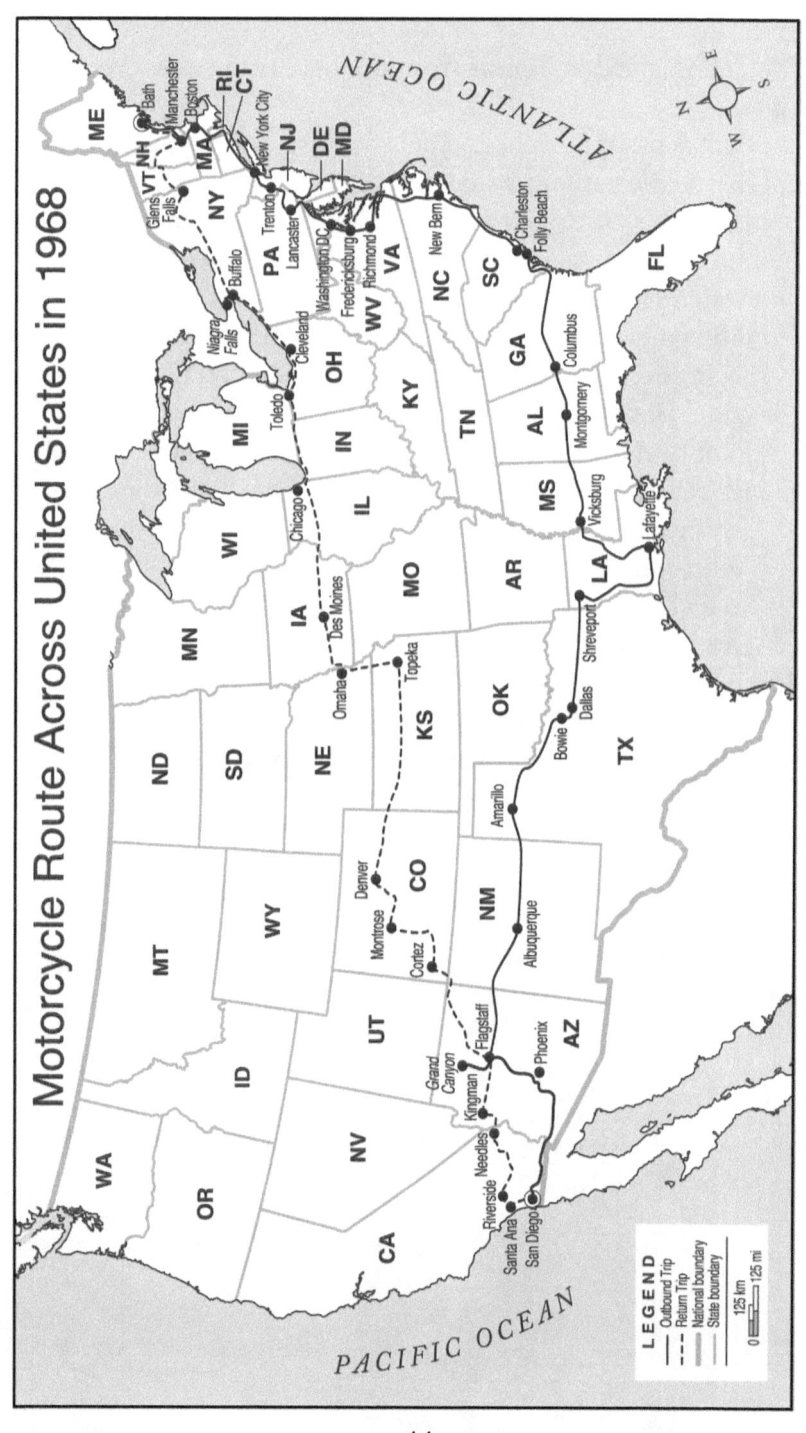

Motorcycle Route Across United States in 1968

LEGEND
Outbound Trip
Return Trip
National boundary
State boundary
0 125 km
0 125 mi

Part 1

Taking Flight

1.

Freedom

San Diego, California – Saturday, August 3, 1968

"*¡Á* NNNDALE! (CHARGE!)," SCREAMED Tino Caballero, speeding out of the driveway on his powerful new motorcycle. He bolted up Euclid Avenue and glanced into the rearview mirror. Standing at the curb seeing him off were his identical twin brother Val, his pregnant sister Carolyn, and his mother Concepción. She raised a hand and made the sign of the cross giving Tino her blessing.

Tino shook his head thinking it pathetic at how much faith she put in that invisible world of hers. Did her countless blessings and invocations to God, the saints, and her ancestors ever do any good?

He reached the Highway 94 on-ramp, narrowed his deep brown eyes, and raced down the incline toward the highway.

Trees and shrubbery on either side of the on-ramp formed a darkened tunnel around him. He emerged into the light feeling as if he had just opened his eyes for the first time and could truly see—as if an entirely new world had just opened before him. Exhilarated, he gunned the engine. The bike jumped with a burst of speed.

He wove in and out of highway lanes, effortlessly passing car after car.

A teenage boy sitting in the rear seat of a white American Motors Rambler stared at Tino on his bike loaded down with gear. *That's right kid, I'm on the trip of a lifetime!*

The sun lay low behind him casting his shadow long to his front. For the first time, he was leading, no one to tell him where to go; no one to tell him what to do. Warm summer air streamed gloriously through his thick dark wavy brown hair and whipped the sleeves of his nylon jacket. If he spread his arms, he'd surely fly.

Tino blasted through Lemon Grove, merged onto Highway 80 in La Mesa, and rocketed past hot and dry El Cajon.

He had never gone on a trip without his family. Not even his twin, Val was along. Tino had shared everything with Val: bedrooms, circle of friends, ball teams, even their underwear. For eight years they'd made a daily mile-long trek to Saint Rita's Catholic Grammar School. Their teachers, the nuns, referred to them as "the bookends."

"Where's Val?" people asked Tino when he was alone.

Val, whom Pa called *el abusado* (the sharp one), had made the responsible choice to register for junior college instead of taking this month-long cross-country motorcycle odyssey from San Diego to New York and back.

His father had said, "No trip for you. You're registering for school with Val." But Tino made his escape from his life with too many rules and responsibilities: chores, school, studies and church services, when Pa went to bed that afternoon to sleep before his graveyard shift at work.

Undoubtedly, Tino would pay a heavy price for his transgression when he returned, maybe a beating. But he had planned this trip for a year with his older brother and friends, Gary and Patrick, and he was not going to miss out.

Fuck the consequences, I'll pay 'em.

Tino and his bike ascended into the Laguna Mountains in East County and entered the Cleveland National Forest. The multilane highway had narrowed to a two-lane road. Traffic, except for an occasional car or long haul truck, was nonexistent. The air, cool with altitude and impregnated by the scent of pine forests, soothed him from the summer heat. Smooth round boulders nestled into the landscape looked like eggs from a prehistoric age.

By the time he reached the foot of the eastern slope, night had folded over the land. He tripped the headlight switch and began the trek across the furnace-like Anza-Borrego Desert. He checked the odometer. Tino had only traveled seventy miles. This was just too cool. He had barely started—the month of freedom still lay ahead.

2.

Rocinante

A N HOUR INTO THE RIDE, Tino rolled out of the dark into a Chevron gas station in El Centro. His body tingled from the vibration of the engine and felt rousingly good between his legs. Without the air fanning his sweat, the full intensity of the desert heat engulfed him. He took off his jacket and stashed it in his gear.

An attendant close to Tino's age stepped up to the gas pump. His white uniform shirt and navy blue pants were smudged with engine grime, shirt stretched taut over his paunch.

"It's a hit!" A play-by-play announcer's voice emanated from a transistor radio tucked into the attendant's shirt pocket. He turned down the volume on the electric buzz of cheering fans. "Must be nice riding that Honda."

Tino set the gas nozzle into the tank. "It's bitchen. I bought it today from an old guy who hardly ever rode it. Sat in his garage most of the time."

"No shit," the attendant said. "Looks like it's fresh off the showroom floor. You sure it wasn't an old lady who just rode it to church on Sundays?"

Tino laughed, proud.

The attendant stepped back to get a good look at the bike. "450 cc's, that's plenty of power."

"It carried me and my gear over the mountains without so much as a hiccup. If it were a horse, it wouldn't have even broken a sweat."

He lifted the nozzle and held it over the tank, allowing the last of the gasoline to drip in, and hung the hose. He reached for his wallet, opening it wide enough to show off the stack of bills amounting to over $150—more money than he had ever carried. He peeled out a dollar and handed it over.

The attendant inserted a key, hanging from a chain hooked to a belt loop, into a cash drawer. "You been riding long?"

"Not really. I've ridden my big brother's bike a few times, and I just bought this bike today. I'm taking a trip around the whole country."

"Jesus, that's an awful long way for just starting to ride."

"I can handle it," Tino said.

The attendant fingered coins from slots in the drawer. "I tried a cross-country trip on a motorcycle last year."

"Right on, man! How'd it go?"

"Fell." The attendant extended his arm showing a long scar. "Compound fracture and I wound up with this zipper." He pointed to suture points on either side of the scar that ran from palm to elbow.

Tino winced.

"Ended my trip right there."

A green dust-coated Chrysler station wagon, its windshield splattered with insects, pulled into the adjacent pump island. The car was packed with an adult couple and kids of all ages, roof rack loaded with baggage.

The attendant grabbed paper towels and a squeegee and made for the car. "Lotsa luck, just be careful," he said with a backward glance.

"Yeah, sure," Tino said, disappointed he couldn't say more about the adventure he'd just embarked on. And who was this clown to say "be careful." Tino swung a leg mounting the bike and gave the kick-starter a hearty jump. The engine roared deep and loud. He gave it gas and let go of the clutch lever. The bike reared back, its front tire lifted a foot off of the ground. The rear tire screeched, leaving a black line of pulverized rubber on the concrete.

"Whoa! Easy, boy!" Tino said. He and his powerful bike sprinted into the night. Miles and time passed allowing time for reflection. It wasn't fair that Tino's Pa didn't want him to take this trip. Pa had always let his brothers have anything they wanted. Sure, Tino had gotten into a little more trouble at school for fooling around, and his grades weren't the best, but did it give Pa the right to treat him like crap? Pa called Tino *Chato,* a Spanish term referencing one's nose. Tino had broken it as a child and although minor, the disfigurement was magnified a hundredfold in his mind. He looked at himself in a mirror and wondered, *Who could ever love this face?* He felt a blow to his confidence each time that Pa called him Chato.

Hot gusts of wind rolled large, round tumbleweeds across the road. Tino leaned side to side adroitly dodging them like a skillful rider on an obstacle course.

His bike needed a proper name, but what? Aha, Rocinante! what the knight, Don Quixote named his horse. Sal, Tino's older brother by ten years, had read epic stories like Don Quixote in school and related many of the adventurous and funny passages to his twin brothers.

Tino leaned left dodging one tumbleweed and then right dodging a second.

He laughed with delight, skillfully zigzagging on the road. Tino felt the same way about his mount as the Spanish knight had felt about his: "A finer and more valiant steed has never been known."

Blink! The world turned black. The headlight without warning turned off. Panicked, Tino hit the brakes. Rocinante skidded off of the road into the desert and ran head on into a spindly creosote bush, stopping him dead.

Tino kept going. "*¡Ay!*" he yelled, flying over the handlebars and through the bush, its stiff branches raked hard against Tino's face. He slammed against the ground, tumbled over the grit of the desert floor and came to a dusty stop.

No hard pain anywhere but a wet sensation on his cheek. He put a hand to it. Blood. He walked unsteadily to his bike pressing a handkerchief against his cheek.

Rocinante stood in the bush, held up by its branches, engine softly puttering. Tino tugged on the bumper. Stuck. He pulled harder; scarcely an inch of movement.

A coyote's howl echoed in the night. Tino had heard of Javelinas that can slice a man open with their razor tusks, and God only knows what man-eaters could be on the prowl for an easy meal. He pulled with adrenaline-fueled strength, ripping Rocinante from the entanglement. He pushed on the handlebars and jogged the bike to the road.

He hit the light switch—nothing. Lights from a distant town formed a faint domed halo on the horizon. His eyes had adjusted to the dark allowing him to differentiate between the black asphalt and the desert floor along the side of the road. He rode off slowly, pitched forward eyeing the road for objects that might cause him another fall. He looked up at the dome of light, down to the road, checked his mirror for vehicles coming from behind. He looked up, down, checked the mirror.

Feeling confident, he gave it a little more gas. The air pressed harder against him as he accelerated.

Bam! A hard jolt. He lost and regained control in a beat. *What the hell was that? Rock? Dead animal?* He slowed to a nervous crawl.

Lights from approaching vehicles shimmered through waves of heat rising off the baked earth. A set of headlights riding high off the road closed in from behind. Tino pulled to the side. A Greyhound bus sped past. He hit the gas, caught up, and followed in a wake of hot diesel exhaust, resting his hand and foot on the brakes should the bus suddenly stop.

The bus slowed when they reached a town. A sign read WELCOME TO HOLTVILLE – CARROT CAPITAL OF THE WORLD.

3.

The Wrath of Carrots

TINO PULLED INTO A TEXACO GAS STATION that serviced long-haul trucks. Small clouds of insects hovered around the overhead fluorescent lights. He dismounted and dropped to a knee to inspect the wiring but found nothing obvious. Better to wait until tomorrow when he would meet up with Sal.

Tino closed and opened his hands, flexing his fingers, stiff from gripping the handlebars. His neck muscles ached from keeping his head up against the constant push of air. He stretched, yawned, and made for the bathroom where he washed the threads of dark dry blood from across his cheek. The cold water felt good against the heat. He then asked a clerk in the station office for directions to the town jail.

The route ran through a district of produce packinghouses. A strange shimmering appeared under a streetlamp at the end of the block. It looked to be some kind of liquid glistening in the night. Tino came upon it to find hundreds of crickets crawling up and over and around each other, each shiny little back a facet reflecting the streetlight. Collectively they looked like some type of horror movie alien life form on the prowl for flesh. Tino stared transfixed at the eerie spectacle. He rode off in a daze.

Tino parked at the Holtville Police Station and Detention Center, an aging, single-story concrete block building, slightly bigger than a two-car garage. Rocinante's engine fins and exhaust pipes pinged and popped as they cooled. He ran a steel cable through the front and rear wheel spokes securing the ends with a padlock, and patted Rocinante. "*Hasta mañana compa.*"

He opened the station door. The policeman's swivel chair squeaked when he swung around.

"Excuse me, sir. I'm on a trip and wonder if I could sleep in a cell."

Sgt. Wood, read the officer's nameplate. His dark hair was neatly combed, mustache trimmed, uniform, starched flat. An ancient black fan on his desk begrudgingly oscillated side to side.

"Think we're running a motel here?"

"No, sir. But my older brother told me that sometimes police will let a guy who's traveling sleep in a cell if it's not being used."

"Where's your brother?"

"He and two of my friends left yesterday on this motorcycle trip. I'm catching up with them tomorrow in Flagstaff."

Wood narrowed his eyes. "Well why didn't everyone leave together?"

"I was short on the money I needed to make the trip, but I got a loan today."

"And you're going where?"

"Around the country, sir."

"Around the whole U.S. of A.? Ballsy. Where'd you start?"

"Today in San Diego."

"Jay-sus kee-ryst! You barely started."

Wood looked to a cop standing on the opposite side of the room and pouring cream into a coffee mug. "What do you think, Flattop? Let him stay?"

"I don't know, Bobby. Doesn't he fit the description on the guy that there's an APB on?"

"Pardon me, sir, but I've never been in that kind of trouble in my life."

Flattop sank a spoon into the cup. "That's what they all say. It's your call, Bobby. You're in charge. Just don't blame me if you wind up with a slit throat in the morning."

"Tell you what," Wood said. "I'm going to lock you up. You know, just in case."

"Thank you, sir. You won't have any trouble with me."

"That's what they all say," Flattop said.

Wood took a clasp envelope from a desk drawer. "Empty your pockets." A large patch riding high on the arm of his uniform had a graphic of the earth skewered by a carrot.

Tino handed over the bike key and his coins, but hesitated to let go of his wallet, fat with bills. Wood tugged it away.

"Relax, it'll be safe with me." He placed Tino's items in the envelope and into a file cabinet. "If you find an IOU in the morning, don't worry. I'll be good for it, right, Flattop?"

"You betcha. Bobby always makes good."

Tino smiled weakly hoping that they were kidding, but neither smiled.

A tall, broad-chested policeman with beefy arms entered the station and pointed his chin toward Tino. "Whadda we got here?"

Wood took a heavy black skeleton key off a hook on the wall behind his desk. "He's on the road, wants to stay the night."

Wood led Tino to a cell with bunk beds and banged the door shut behind him.

"Hey, Bobby," Flattop said. "Now that the kid's in the slammer, what do you say we borrow a little of his dough and get some lunch."

"Turkey, on a soft roll," said the new policeman.

"Pastrami on rye, hold the mayo," Flattop said.

Tino sat on the lower bunk fretting. He leaned over to unlace his boots and jumped with a start when a black cockroach the size of his thumb scurried out between his feet.

"Don't step on Fido!" Wood said.

Laughter.

Tino looked out the wire-mesh window and took comfort in seeing Rocinante parked alongside a police cruiser. A mutt meandering by stopped, sniffed Rocinante's rear tire, and lifted a leg. Tino sighed and climbed to the upper bunk, leaving the lower one for someone who might be arrested later and brought in a drunk or, God forbid, something worse.

The two-inch thick, cotton-stuffed mat of the cot smelled of mold and had nasty dark stains in the middle. The wall radiated the day's heat like an oven. Tino's T-shirt was damp with sweat and peppered with tiny winged insects.

The cops played cards at the sergeant's desk under a blue haze of cigarette smoke. On a radio, Johnny Cash sang about falling into a ring of fire.

He faced the wall and laid an arm over his eyes to shield them from the light thinking the cops terribly rude.

What sleep he managed to get came in sporadic naps through a string of disturbances: ringing phones, doors slamming shut, the acrid odor of tobacco smoke.

Tino awoke deep into the night confused over his surroundings before remembering where he was. Except for the hum of the fan, the office was quiet.

A different cop, alone, was lying back in Wood's chair—feet on desk, hands on chest, hat over face. Tino rolled to his side and fell asleep; he dreamed that he and Rocinante were speeding down a foreign road. It ended at a cliff; no ordinary cliff, but the one that existed in a tale that his old Mexican uncle Nene had told Tino as a boy, a mythological cliff found at the end of the world. Children who disobeyed their parents were thrown over it into the abyss. Tino hit the brakes in his dream, the cliff drew nearer and nearer, but Rocinante raced on. He awoke with a pounding heart.

Sharp spikes of sunlight pierced the gray dawn over the hills and onto the cell wall. Relief, the long, hot night had come to an end, and the air was pleasantly cool.

He'd be back on the road soon. Tino hopped off the bunk, catching the eye of the cop at the desk.

"Good morning," he said.

The cop stared stone-faced.

Tino pulled on his boots and laced them. "I'm ready to leave sir. The sergeant put my stuff in an envelope last night and—"

"You think I don't know the drill?"

"Yes, sir. I mean no, sir. I'm sure you do."

The cop took the envelope out of the file cabinet and walked in a deliberate gait toward Tino, waving the envelope in a tease. "Is this what you want, August?"

"Y-yes, sir," he said, afraid and confused over the cop's attitude. "But maybe that's somebody else's. My name is Augustino."

The cop slapped the envelope against the bars. "Not here, it ain't, boy. You're in America, Seenor Augustino Cabalero. I'll let you out, but only because I have to. But first you become an American. We're going to start by getting your name right. Say, 'My name is August, August Wetback.' He laughed ugly. "Got a nice ring to it, don't it?"

Beads of sweat formed on Tino's brow.

"You chicken? No. Not chicken, a yellowbellied taco bender. Ha! Ha!" The cop took the wallet from the envelope and peeled out a twenty. "City ordinance to cover costs." He dropped the wallet into the envelope, reached for the key hanging on the wall, went to the cell, and unlocked the door. He tossed the envelope bouncing off of Tino's chest. Tino snagged it.

"Time to pick carrots."

Tino walked a wide arc around the cop to the door.

"If you people just came and worked and went back, but no. You got to bring your fucking music, and put your kids in our schools, spreading their head lice. Now that greaser, Chávez, is organizing. Organizing my ass, he's nothing but a goddamn Commie agitator. Go on, get outta here before I cite you for vagrancy."

Tino quick stepped it to Rocinante, unlocked the padlock, stashed it in his gear, kick-started the engine, and took off, checking his mirror as he rode. Would the cop come after him? He raced onto the highway afraid, angry, and confused.

He passed acreage, once hard desert, now transformed into soft green blankets of farmland. Mexican men and women, wearing wide-brimmed straw hats and long-sleeve shirts were hard at it, stooped over, pulling bright orange sticks from the rich earth. A red flag with the geometric black eagle, the emblem of the United Farm Workers Union, hung from a pole.

4.

Flagstaff

THE GREEN FARMLAND soon gave way to the tough gray bush of the desert. Tino crossed into Arizona an hour after leaving Holtville. He rode through Yuma, an island of activity in the hard and silent Sonora Desert. He passed towering saguaros, their thick spiny arms reaching up to welcome visitors. Mesquite, *palo fierro, chollas,* and gentle *palo verde* trees with jade-green bark and soft wispy foliage rose above the chaparral of sage, greasewood and creosote. *Opuntia* cacti, their flat, round pads looking like Mickey Mouse ears. Bowling-ball sized barrel cacti, with their long thick spines, dotted the desert floor. Distant hills rose sharply and then abruptly became flat plains, *mesas,* (tables) to the Spanish explorers.

Tino headed north at Gila Bend, toward Flagstaff, where Sal was to be waiting for him. A length of thick rope lying on the road caught his eye, except that it was moving. A sidewinder rattlesnake was crossing Tino's path. He leaned hard to avoid the sidewinder and nearly ran off the road.

He rode through Phoenix and onto highway I-17. The temperature reading on a bank wall abutting the highway was

110 degrees. The aching at the base of his neck had intensified. It hurt keeping his head up against the push of air.

The temperature had dropped considerably when he reached the desert plateau at Camp Verde. He passed signs for Flagstaff 30 Miles, 5 miles, 2 miles.

What if Sal wasn't at the gas station waiting for Tino? His brother was absent minded, always losing his wallet. He lost his car key and had Ma, Pa, Val, and Tino looking frantically through the house because he had an appointment for a physical for a new job. The key turned up in his pants coin pocket. It'd be just like him to forget his own instructions and not be at the gas station. Or what if he'd be in the bathroom and Tino drove by and they missed each other. How would Tino ever find him?

The yellow logo of a Shell gas station, mounted on poles, stood a half-mile off. On the road next to a motorcycle loaded with gear, was a short, brown-skinned, man with kinky black hair wearing a faded gray sweatshirt with the sleeves cut to the elbow, shorts, and boots. Sal!

Sal peeled off his wire-rim sunglasses and danced a jig. Tino pulled up laughing and had to shoot out a foot to keep from toppling over when Sal lunged giving him a bear hug.

"You made it, *Chico!* (kid) You made it!" Sal said. He stepped back and gestured at the lines of scabs on Tino's face. "*¿Qué te pasó?*"

"Tripped. Fell on Ma's rosebush yesterday," he said, not about to admit to a fall so early in the trip.

"*¡Hijo!* (Wow)" Sal said, taking in Rocinante. "That's a big bike!"

"The only thing wrong with it is that the electric push-button starter doesn't work, so I have to kick-start it every time."

Sal patted his Honda 305-cc Super Hawk. "I don't use the electric starter either. Buttons are for wimps. How'd you manage to get it? I thought it was over for you when you couldn't leave with us yesterday."

"Me too," Tino said. "I about cried seeing you guys go without me. I went to church to pray on it and ran into Father Mooney. He asked what I was doing there, since it wasn't Sunday. I told him what happened and he gladly lent me the money."

"You're living a charmed life," Sal said. "By the way, did you bring everything I told you to?"

"Yup, at the surplus store, I got a canteen, a toolkit, helmet for the states where we have to use 'em, and extra clothes wrapped in an old sleeping bag I found in Pa's garage. Ma even sent along some *burritos de frijoles* for us."

"*¡Bien hecho!* (Well done!)," Sal said with a laugh.

"Hey, where're Gary and Pat?" Tino said looking around.

"I told them to go on and we'd catch up to them. Let's gas up."

They rode from the roadside to the Shell station. A tall, lanky attendant ambled over. A mountain chain of red acne with white caps ran across his forehead. He took the cigarette pressed between his ear and head, a lighter from his pocket and lit up. A sign behind him read, NO SMOKING. "Lotsa pussy out there in California," he said. His Adam's apple, the size of a walnut, bounced as he gabbed.

Sal grabbed the gas nozzle and laughed. "You don't have girls here?"

The attendant tilted his head back and blew a smoke ring into the air. "Not like there. You got beaches, Hollywood, and all kinda good shit. I'm going to save me some money, buy a big-ass chopper, and ride with the Hell's Angels in L. A. Chicks dig bikers."

"Sounds like you've got quite a life planned out for yourself."

"Fuckin' A right, man."

Tino ignored the future Hells Angel. "I suppose that you want to press on, Sal."

"Why wouldn't we?"

"I need to get my headlight fixed. I was really hauling last night when it cut out. One second light, next black." Tino snapped his fingers. "And my neck's killing me. I'm not used to doing so much riding, like you."

"I'm on a tight schedule," Sal said. "I've only got a month's vacation time. But *ni modo* (no choice), we'll have to make up for the lost time tomorrow. I'll buy rubbing alcohol and give you a rubdown. I passed a Honda dealership on my way in where we can get the headlight checked out. We'll find a laundromat after and wash clothes to save time from having to do it later. Somewhere along the line, we'll stop at the jail and see if we can spend the night to give your neck a rest."

"I don't want to stay in another jail," Tino said and recounted his episode in Holtville.

"How could he get away with that? Weren't there other cops around?"

"A few the night before, but just him this morning."

"Why'd you let him steal from you like that?"

"He was big and mean. I really want to stay somewhere else."

"Relax, Chico, I'll be with you."

"But—"

"I'm going to be with you," Sal said sharply.

"Okay," Tino said in submission.

"That's the spirit. It's Sunday, so we'll need to find an evening Mass."

They learned at the dealership that Rocinante had a burned-out fuse. Next stop; the Flagstaff Jail, it was a good deal larger than the jail in Holtville.

A woman sitting at a desk, a cigarette between her lips, said, "Officer Wolfe, the night sergeant, is the only one who can give the okay."

"May we speak with him?" Sal asked.

Her telephone rang. She raised a hand to hold off Sal and stubbed the cigarette in a glass ashtray filled with lipstick-smudged cigarette butts. She tapped a button on the phone.

"Dispatch. Un-huh, Un-huh, sure Joe. I'll send someone right away." She flipped a switch on the microphone of a short wave radio on her desk. "Unit 12, disturbance at the Little Big Horn Bar. Unit 12, a 10-15, at the Horn."

"I'm on it, Claire," came over the radio.

She switched off the mic, opened a desk drawer and took out a half empty pack of L&M cigarettes. "Officer Wolfe's shift starts at 7:00," she said, lighting up. "Come back then."

Sal nodded. "Thank you, ma'am," he said, and asked her for directions to a Catholic Church.

The church was a meek adobe block structure, styled after a Spanish mission. A modest wooden sign read "Evening Mass 7:00 p.m."

"Hmmm," Sal said. "Same time as when we're supposed to ask for permission to stay at the jail. What do we do, get a place to sleep in a cell or go to Mass?"

"I'd rather go to jail."

"Look," Sal said laughing. "It was because you went to church that you were able to get the bike, right?"

Tino rolled his eyes. "Yes."

"If we hurry, I think we can do both."

The night sergeant arrived late for his shift at the jail but gave the okay. Tino rode Sal's tail as he raced to the church. They tiptoed in when the sermon ended.

Sal whispered, "Half over, no sense in going in now."

"Isn't missing Mass on Sunday a sin?" Tino said on their way back to the bikes.

"There're exceptions. We're traveling, so this is a special circumstance, and we don't have to abide fully with church canon. What do you say we get an ice cream at that shop we passed on our way here?"

"*¡Simón que sí!* (Absolutely!)"

A small bell over the door tinkled happily as they entered. A young woman stood behind a counter serving cones. Her copper-colored skin was smooth as a windless lake, and her thick, black hair, reflecting the lights, hung to her waist. Her eyes shone black as obsidian.

What a fox! Tino thought.

Sal rubbed his hands together playfully. "I'll take the biggest scoops of strawberry you can make."

She smiled shyly. "Would you like a double scoop?"

"How about a double-double and stack 'em four high."

She laughed with her eyes.

Tino melted. If he would ever actually make love to a woman, was it too much to hope for one just like her?

"I'm sorry, sir, but two scoops is the limit."

Sal feigned annoyance. "Well, all right. Start with two and we'll see after that. Deal?"

Tino envied Sal for his ability to engage with strangers, be it a tough looking guy or a beautiful young woman.

"Do you go to school?" Sal asked.

"I just graduated from Flagstaff High," she said rolling a fat pink-red ball. Tino stared at her every move that flowed with grace.

"I registered at Arizona State for the fall."

"Terrific!"

Tino shook his head at Sal. Why did he always have to talk excitedly with young people?

"What's your major?"

"Geology."

"Fantastic!"

Even if his enthusiasm was suspect, Sal was genuinely interested in people's lives, especially students. "Why geology?"

She reached over the counter and handed Sal the cone. "Father took me to the Grand Canyon for a ceremony when I was little. I was taken by its beauty. Father said that all of creation has spirit: trees, animals, even water and stones. I've come to understand the canyon's spirit. I want to learn of its science and structure."

"Wow! You're on a terrific path. Your father must be proud of you."

"He says our people need education, not only in our ways, but in the ways of the white man."

"Your father is very wise, and you're a fine example to anyone."

She seemed ill at ease by his praise. She turned to Tino, raised an eyebrow, and gestured to the tubs of ice cream. But he was lost admiring her breasts.

"Excuse me, sir. What would you like?"

"Huh? Oh, two round ones."

"What, sir?"

Tino flushed with embarrassment. "Uh, two scoops of chocolate."

He couldn't help but ogle as she rolled them out. She held the cone over the counter. Tino gazed into her gleaming eyes and grabbed the ice cream instead of the cone.

"I meant to do that." Even as the words stumbled out of his mouth, he realized how idiotic he sounded.

She looked away, eyes shining with amusement.

He hurried for the door, wiping his hand on his pants. "Nice meeting you."

He sat on the curb licking his fingers. "What a dork! I couldn't stop staring at her. Everything about her was so beautiful."

"Maybe you could go to college with her after the trip."

"No kidding, Pa'd sure like that. He told me to register with Val instead of coming on this trip. But I'm so tired of school."

Sal turned the cone on his tongue. "Can't blame you for wanting a break, but Pa doesn't want our lives to be as hard as his. All he's ever known is work. He's not young anymore and he's still hard at it. Education's a way out."

"I know that he wants what's best for us, but I wish he wasn't so tough on me."

"You think he is?"

"Yes, much as I've tried, I've never done as well as Val or you."

"In what?"

"Anything—holding down jobs, schoolwork, behaving. Ma and Pa have no faith in me. Ma tells me, '¿Por que no puedes hacer como tus hermanos?' (Why can't you be like your brothers?) Sometimes I'm afraid that I'll wind up a bum and a shame to the family. I'd be better off dead."

"You're being awfully tough on yourself."

"When Pa found out that I got fired from my last job, he shook his head and said 'I just don't know about you.' I think that he's given up on me."

"Did he see you off when you left yesterday?"

"No, I snuck out when he was sleeping before his night shift."

"He's not going to like that."

"Boy, no kidding. I'm afraid he's going to really let me have it when I get back. He smacked me around good when I was a kid. I've been afraid of him ever since."

"You're nineteen," Sal said. "He shouldn't be treating you like a child."

"'You live under my roof, you live by my rules,' Pa tells me." The opening Tino needed to tell Sal of his plan to join the Marine Corps after the trip had just presented itself.

Tino had played the scene in his mind many times. He standing at attention in his Marine dress uniform, complete with white hat and gloves; Pa putting his hands on his shoulders saying, "I'm proud of you, *mijo*."

But Sal would most likely not like the idea because of how many American casualties were mounting in Vietnam. Thousands of young men were returning home missing limbs or in coffins to be buried. But Tino needed Sal as an ally when it came to dealing with Pa.

"I'm going to do something that's going to make Pa proud of me."

Sal glanced at his watch. "Hold the thought. We got to go! I don't want to miss out on getting a cell."

"I GET THE TOP BUNK," Tino whispered into Sal's ear when they entered the Flagstaff Jail.

5.

All Part of the Adventure

OFFICER WOLFE, THE FLAGSTAFF JAIL night sergeant, possessed the tired facial lines of middle age. His long, slender arms seemed at odds with his heavy chest and belly. The protruding bones of his eyebrows and the bulging bridge of his nose reminded Tino of the profile on an Indian-head nickel.

The sergeant placed their wallets, coins, and keys in well-worn manila clasp envelopes, and set them into one of fifty numbered slots cut into a wall behind his desk. He hit a button on his phone. "Charlie, would you come out? Thanks."

A portly staffer a head taller than Sal and dressed in white shirt and pants appeared through a door. His hair was gray fuzz, his nose and cheeks, fat, and a mosaic of tiny red veins stood out against his pasty-white skin.

"They asked to spend the night," Sergeant Wolfe said. "Still should be a few bunks left in D-unit."

Charlie looked Sal and Tino up and down and muttered, "C'mon." He led them through a door and down a hallway. "Don't know why free men would want to do time in jail."

Unlike Charlie's soft-soled shoes, the sound of Tino and Sal's boots against the floor echoed off the walls.

"Saves time," Sal said. "No trying to find campsites, and we'll be back on the road first thing in the morning."

Charlie raised an eyebrow. "Worth jail time?"

"All part of the adventure."

Tino smiled with pride; his big brother always thought things through.

They reached a large cell housing over a dozen detainees.

"Home sweet home, boys."

"Excuse me, sir," Tino said, "do you have cells for two?"

"Oh," Charlie said. "You must be talking about the luxury suites. Sorry, but they're all taken."

Glances from the D-unit drifted their way.

Olive-green woolen blankets lay over cots framed in angle iron, and arranged in several lines with narrow aisles between. A five-foot-high panel, a foot off the floor, offered privacy to whomever used the toilet that was butted up against the back wall.

Charlie inserted a key into the lock plate. He opened the door of iron bars. Tino stepped in, eyes shifting nervously.

Clang! The door slammed shut behind them. Odors: stale urine, cigarette smoke, alcohol breath.

A pint-size man, a good ten years older than Sal, who seemed thin enough to fit between the bars, sat on the cot nearest the door. He smiled sadly at Sal and Tino.

Charlie faded down the hall as he switched off banks of overhead lights.

"Look for adjoining cots," Sal said under his breath.

An inmate, toothless and disheveled, in soiled clothes and high-top black and white tennis shoes, stood at a cot mumbling.

Two stone-faced Indians in jeans and new cowboy shirts huddled in a corner, turned to check out the two new detainees. The taller, thinner of the Indians had his hair braided into two black snakes that rested on either side of his chest. A scar ran from eyebrow to mid-cheek, his shirt torn at the shoulder and blotted with dried blood. His chubby partner wore a turquoise pendant around his neck, and his matted hair hung like stiff wires around the pockmarks on his face. Their glazed eyes gave them away as drunks.

Sal nudged Tino toward a couple of cots in front of the toilet privacy panel. The small man with the sad smile nodded as they passed.

"*Buenas noches,*" he said.

"*Buenas,*" Sal answered just over a whisper.

Tino kept focused on the cots praying that no one would talk to him as he passed.

A towering, heavy-chested white man in a faded black cowboy style shirt, frayed at the neck, leaned against the crossbars of the cell. Thick stubble covered his face. He seemed too young to have such deep creases and leathery skin. His upper lip curved in where there had been front teeth. A blurred tattoo covered the big man's heavy forearm.

Tino couldn't tell if the tattoo was a tiger or a naked lady.

Big-Man noticed Tino eyeing him and winked. Tino nodded, not sure if Big-Man was being friendly or inviting him to share a bunk for the night.

The brothers sat on the cots and untied their boots.

Tino lay back and covered himself with the blanket despite the warm and stuffy conditions—the less exposure the better.

Snoring soon filled the room. Tino fell into a tired sleep. He woke hours into the night when the Chubby Indian rose from his cot. Tino kept a wary eye on him as he shuffled in soft whispers to the toilet. The Indian's pee splashed the floor before hitting toilet water. Tino couldn't relax until Chubby was back on his cot.

MOST OF THE DETAINEES were up in the morning by the time Charlie arrived pushing a steel food tower.

Tino overheard Chubby Indian. "You got a couple of good ones in on the motherfuckers at the Horn last night before they cuffed you."

Scarface cackled.

"Ugh, ugh." Grunting from the toilet. A pair of thin ankles with pants piled on top of well-worn tennis shoes were behind the privacy panel. Another grunt, and, "Ah."

"Eggs benedict and truffles," Charlie announced.

Men formed a line by the hall. No one challenged Big-Man's lack of etiquette when he cut to the front. Charlie spooned scrambled eggs, fried potatoes, strips of bacon, and a piece of toast without butter onto a metal plate and handed it to Big-Man through the portal cut into the bars.

Sal and Tino waited to be served until last. "Well, lookie here," Charlie said handing Tino a plate. "I plumb forgot the garnish."

Tino chuckled quietly.

Charlie wheeled the cart away.

The chow was cold, glistened with grease and tasted as bad as it looked, but hungry men aren't finicky. He ate it all.

"Food was better last time," Scarface said to Chubby.

Tino looked over at them.

"What're you looking at?" Scarface said.

"Nothing."

He stared menacingly into Tino's eyes.. "You calling me nothin'?"

"Yes, sir, I-I mean, no."

"What're you in for? Butt-fucking a steer?" Chubby Indian laughed wickedly. Someone pressed against Tino's shoulder. It was Sal glaring at the Indians.

Chubby lowered his plate and wrapped his hand around a spoon, stem pointed at Sal.

Scarface's upper lip rose in a snarl.

All eyes were on the Indians and the two new detainees. A brawl was about to break out.

Tino shook with fear—eyes large and scared.

Scarface leaned toward them.

"Leave 'em alone," Big-Man's voice boomed through the room. "He's just a kid. Now leave 'em the fuck alone."

"Better watch your mouth," Scarface said weakly, but his face said it all; don't mess with Big-Man.

Charlie rolled a cart for bussing dishes to the cell. "Settle down, boys. Getting tough will just get you into more trouble. Much as I love you all, I'd rather you weren't visiting." He unlocked the door. "Caballero, Caballero, come on out."

Tino made a beeline for the hall, and didn't feel safe until the door slammed shut behind them. They followed Charlie down the hall and out a door to the front desk. "Nice adventure?"

An officer handed them the clasp envelopes. "Make sure that all of your items are there."

Charlie punched a timecard and accompanied the two out into the cool morning. "Y'all come back and see us, won't you?" he said and headed for a bus stop bench at the curb. "But I wouldn't blame you if you took another offer."

"Yeah, sure," Tino said.

"It wasn't exactly Ma's *chorizo con huevos*," Sal said, "but it was a free meal."

Tino grabbed his crotch "*Aquí tengo tu* stupid free meal."

Sal burst out laughing. "*¿Qué?* You didn't like my money and time saving idea?"

Tino growled, "No more damn jails."

Sal laughed all the more.

6.

A Cathedral

SAL AND *TINO* RUMMAGED THROUGH their gear in the jail parking lot, hunting for jackets to wear against the cool morning air.

Sal dug out toothpaste. "Get your brush."

"Forgot to bring one."

"You're not going an entire month without brushing, Chico."

They crossed the street to a Rexall drugstore where Tino bought a brush and a postcard that Sal insisted he send Father Mooney as a thank you for the loan. They rode to a city park and found a water faucet on the wall of a maintenance shed.

Tino squeezed toothpaste on his new brush.

Sal made lather with a bar of soap, wiped it on his face, and shaved using his bike mirror. He rinsed and patted his face dry with his sweatshirt. "How's your neck?"

"Like I got stabbed."

Sal looked annoyed, probably anxious to get back to traveling.

"Jeez, I'm sorry I'm hurting."

Sal found the rubbing alcohol, unscrewed the cap, and poured a small pool into his palm.

"Boy," Tino said, wincing with Sal working his fingers deep into his neck and shoulders. "I hope our run-in with those guys in the jail is the worst thing that happens to us on this trip."

"Forget about it. Let's go."

They reached Williams and pulled up to a 7-11 store. Tino kept an eye on the bikes while Sal shopped. He exited with a family-size bag of Fritos corn chips and a bottle of Dad's Old Fashioned Root Beer for Tino and a Dr. Pepper for himself.

"Those rough Indian guys in the jail saw you were afraid," Sal said, crunching on chips. "If anything like that happens again, don't show fear."

Tino wiped soda from his mouth with his shirtsleeve. "They weren't messing around."

"Listen to me, Chico. It's okay to be scared. Just don't let the other guy know it. You're muscular. Use it to your advantage. If something like that happens again, puff up and keep repeating to yourself, 'Don't be afraid.' You can talk yourself into anything."

"You and your mind-over-matter stuff."

Sal poked a finger against Tino's chest. "If they know you're afraid, you're done for. Never—show—a bully—fear. Got it? Bullies are cowards and they'll back down if you stand up to them."

"And if they don't?"

"Then let your anger take over and give 'em all you got."

"But…"

Sal stashed their trash into a trashcan and hopped on the Hawk.

"C'mon," he said, "got something to show you." Sal was good at coming up with fun surprises for his siblings—trips to parks, to museums or to the ocean for beach parties.

Sal led the way to state Highway 64 North. They soon came across the first sign: GRAND CANYON 50 MILES.

Bitchen! Tino thought.

The forty-minute ride took them through a forest of Ponderosa pines, the road gently dappled with filtered sunlight. The cool and clear morning air gave Tino renewed energy.

They stopped at a kiosk manned by U.S. Park Service rangers wearing Smokey the Bear hats. Sal paid the entry fee. Sal and Tino rode around a hill, up a rise, into a long, sweeping bend where an otherworldly landscape unfurled before them.

"*Hijole*," Tino whispered. Walls of crusted and eroded layers of rock and compressed soils in horizontal tiers rose hundreds of feet from out of the canyon. Wide chasms spanned forever. The alien-like formations reminded him of pictures he'd seen in science books of how other planets might look.

They parked at a vista point and walked to a waist-high wall at the canyon's rim. Blinding-white masses of clouds against a deep blue sky caused Tino to squint. He peered over the wall. The Colorado River, a long, thin, jade-green snake, zigzagged through the base of the canyon.

"If there weren't rangers around, I'd throw a rock out as far as I could," Tino said.

"We'd never hear it hit bottom."

A gray-bearded ranger, wearing shorts, a tan uniform shirt, and horn rim glasses motioned sightseers to gather.

"Welcome to one of the great natural wonders of the world. You'll notice that the air is free of smog. We're aware that you folks from Los Angeles aren't used to it, so if you pass out, we'll put your head under an exhaust pipe until you come to."

The docent waited for the laughter to subside before lecturing on the canyon's geological and social history.

Hundreds of tourists passed in cars, many towing trailers, some riding in buses, others on bicycles. Hikers trekked down trails into the canyon.

The brothers continued on after the lecture and rode to several vista points. Tino sat on his bike restless at each stop, as ever-curious and studious Sal had to read every stupid plaque and brochure.

They reached the North Rim observation point in the soft dusk, sat on the bikes and stared trancelike at shafts of sunlight filtering through a mass of dark clouds huddled over the canyon. A blinding flash of lightning bolted into the gorge. A thunderous percussion followed, vibrating Rocinante under Tino. A gentle rain began falling. Rays of sun transformed the droplets into bits of gold. The sun eased into the earth, radiating an orange-red aura that faded to a single ember, leaving scarlet-red clouds against a purple-blue sky. Tino envisioned an Apache on a spotted horse, arms raised in praise of the Great Spirit. He spoke solemnly. "I get what the Indian girl at the ice cream shop meant about this place; feels like a cathedral."

7.

A Primal Scream

S AL AND TINO RODE in the dark-gray of dusk from the North Rim observation point to a campground, hoping for a campsite, but none were left.

"We just need a spot to lay our bags for the night," Sal said to the ranger. "We'll sleep anywhere, by a bathroom or a trash bin, and we'll leave early."

"If I make an exception for you, then guess what the next guy's going to want?"

"Yes, of course," Sal said and motioned Tino to leave. He pulled over around a bend and grinned slyly. "Did you see that dirt road chained off back there?"

Tino nodded uneasily.

"It's probably for emergency vehicles. What do you say we ride around the posts and camp up in the hills?"

"It's off limits. That's why it's chained—Darn it, Sal!" Worried,Tino chased after. What if they get caught? They could wind up in jail with the steer butt-fucker brothers again.

They rode around the posts, up uneven rutty trails, to the crest of a hill and dismounted in a clearing in the chaparral.

Sal unhooked the bungee cords securing his sleeping bag. "Getting one over on them more than makes up for the lack of amenities out here."

"*Ay tú*, Mr. College Degrees. *¿Qué son* 'amenities'?"

Sal laughed. "You know. Showers, toilets, stuff like that. We'll lay our bags under the shrubbery to shade us from the sunrise."

Tino took his sleeping bag from his bike. "You, of all people, shouldn't be breaking laws."

"Just because I'm a priest, doesn't mean I can't have a little fun once in a while. Besides, we're not hurting anything."

"Gotta admit," Tino said. "This is pretty cool."

Sal gathered dry leaves and formed mattress pads.

Tino crawled into his bag. "This is the best, riding bikes with you, seeing cool stuff. I always heard kids in school talk about where they went on vacations: Lake Tahoe, Yellowstone, Yosemite. Now I can say that I've been to the Grand Canyon."

Sal nodded. "I know what you mean. We never had real vacations. It's always been about survival for us. The only thing that came close was going to visit family in Mexico. Get some shuteye. We've got a lot to see tomorrow."

Tino wiggled forming the dry leaves under him to his body's contours. "This is comfortable."

"The Sheraton couldn't be much better," Sal said and turned to his side.

Tino lay back thinking of his big brother. At twenty-nine, Sal was ten years older than Tino. Sal was also the eldest of the seven children and *el consentido*, the favored son.

Sal entered the seminary straight out of high school, and was ordained a priest after eight years of study. People addressed him as "Father Caballero." His present assignment was as chaplain of Mercy Catholic Hospital in San Diego. He said Mass, heard confessions, gave Holy Communion and anointed the dying.

Sal, at five-feet seven inches tall, was slighter of frame than Tino and his twin brother Val. In a litter, Sal would've been the runt. His younger brothers stood at five-feet nine. Sal more than made up for his small size with Spartan-like attributes— hardy, able to survive on little, loved testing his limits. Two years ago he and a friend had three-speed bicycles shipped to Canada to ride back to San Diego. The friend got saddle sores and flew home. If Sal had any discomfort, no one ever knew. He pushed hard and beat his scheduled arrival by a day.

Sal snored softly.

"Thanks for planning this trip and for waiting for me to catch up to you," Tino whispered. A person needs to say thanks even if it isn't always heard.

Late into the night, Tino dreamed that he was at home ready to leave on the trip but Pa had him by the wrist. "You're registering for college." Tino struggled but couldn't break Pa's iron grip. Tino was drawn up from the depths of his dream. Sal had reached over and grabbed his arm, with a finger to his lips.

Sal rose to his hands and knees. Tino narrowed his eyes trying to make out Sal's movements in the dark. Sal leaned forward to take a step but froze. On the other side of Sal's bike was a large, cat-like animal.

Tino shook to his core.

Sal and the animal locked eyes.

"Hiiissss."

It felt as though a hand had Tino by the throat, choking out breath. He was about to witness Sal be torn apart by a beast of the wild.

"Hiiissss," The animal hissed louder and deeper.

Do I run so at least one of us survives?

Deadly silence. The animal was about to pounce.

"Yeeaahh!"

Tino bounded a foot off the ground with Sal's earsplitting scream. The animal bolted scattering dry leaves. Sal's scream echoed through the hills. Sal breathed heavily, his chest expanded and contracted. He reached and turned on his bike's headlight. A few low-lying branches and a small patch of dry weeds on the ground appeared. He whispered, "Turn on your light."

Tino rose slowly and stepped cautiously toward his bike. He felt around for the light switch ready to be attacked.

He flicked the switch.

Nothing.

"C'mon, hit it!" Sal whispered.

"I did."

"Toggle the switch!"

"*Le estoy switchillando ¡pero nada!* (I'm toggling it, but nothing!) The fuse must have burned out again."

"Did you put in the right one?"

"I put in the one the kid at the dealership told me to!"

Sal whispered so loudly that he may as well have been yelling. "You talked to a kid? Why didn't you talk to a grown mechanic?"

"Don't tell me who to talk to."

"Are you toggling the right switch?"

"*¡Nomas ay un fucking switch!*"

"Watch your mouth!"

"We're about to get eaten alive and you're worried about…"

"Let's get the hell out!" Sal yelled.

They flew into their pants, jackets, and boots untied and without socks, stuffed their gear into the sleeping bags, piled them onto the bike seats, hopped on, and took off.

The eroded bumpy patches of the road slowed their retreat. Tino followed close behind Sal, depending on Sal's headlight. He slid on loose grit and skidded into Sal.

"Watch it!" Sal yelled over his shoulder.

"Sorry."

It felt an eternity before they reached the road. Tino expected that at any second a mountain lion would jump out of the dark, and Sal ahead of him would never know.

Bam! Rocinante hit something on the road. "Fuuuck!" Tino screamed.

The headlight blinked on.

The hour-long ride to Williams felt endless. They pulled into a motel. The first few letters of the red neon welcome sign flittered like a fly struggling in a spider's web.

Tino dismounted. "Your scream scared the crap out of me."

Sal stared in a daze before he broke out laughing. "That came from a primal place, all right." He then walked off heading for the motel office.

"What's so funny?" Tino yelled behind Sal. "I suppose I shouldn't have shown fear of that bully mountain lion." Sal snorted laughing and disappeared into the dark.

8.

Red Earth

A TUG ON TINO'S FOOT early the next morning woke him up. He groaned and opened his eyes, puffy with sleep. "All ready?"

"Lots to see before we catch up with the guys. Come on, I'll treat breakfast."

"Some consolation for almost getting me eaten alive last night."

"Do you want breakfast or not?"

"All right, but I'm taking a shower first."

"I'll call Ma while you're getting ready," Sal said at the door. "Take your time, but hurry up."

"*Chíngate, menso.* (Screw yourself, jerk.)"

A half hour later they were sitting at a roadside diner next to the motel. Tino chopped bacon with his fork and mixed it with the hash browned potatoes and egg yolk on his plate.

Sal took a spiral notepad from his shirt pocket and set it on the table.

"What's that?"

"Travel log. Lots to write about."

"No kidding," Tino said. "Grand Canyon, cutthroats in the jail, mountain lions. How'd you know the lion was there last night?"

"I got up to pee. When I got back in my bag I heard shuffling and thought it was a ranger, but I didn't hear an engine or see a flashlight beam. I figured it was an animal and hoped it was anything but a meat-eater."

Tino ran a napkin across his mouth. "I about crapped when it hissed."

Sal picked up his cup of tea chuckling, "Me too."

Tino dabbed egg yolk with toast. "I was so scared I couldn't move. What if you hadn't been there? *Chingado hombre*, you stood up to a lion and scared it away."

"More of a instinctual reaction I guess."

"God, I hope that's the worst thing that happens to us on this trip."

"Forget about it."

They headed east toward New Mexico on the grandfather of all highways, Route 66.

DON'T MISS THE AMAZING METEOR CRATER CREATED 50,000 YEARS AGO, read a highway sign, the next read, METEOR CRATER A WONDER OF THE WORLD – JUST AHEAD, and then METEOR CRATER, NEXT EXIT. Moments after, TURN BACK – YOU'VE MISSED METEOR CRATER!

They rode through Winslow, the Painted Desert, Holbrook and past the Petrified Forest. "No forest, just a crummy field of rock," Tino noted later.

"Welcome to New Mexico, the Land of Enchantment," read the sign at the state line. They stopped in Gallup for a stretch and sodas and continued on riding through the countryside where the skies, like Arizona's, were clear and deep blue. But there was less here: less traffic, fewer towns, fewer people. Tino scanned the vast solitude of the high desert, unchanged since the glaciers receded from the Ice Age. A lonely dirt road wound its way up to a chain of snow-capped mountains where a river emerged and struggled its way across the plain. New Mexico's ancient gray landscape had long since lost its green youth, its skin now powdery dry, its hair, thirsty grey bush.

A roadrunner appeared out of the chaparral and sprinted along the roadside, its spiked crown jetting back and forth, its feet moving in a blur. The two bikers made a wide turn around the desert bird. The roadrunner stopped, made a one-eighty, and darted off in the opposite direction.

A horseman wearing a cowboy hat, faded jeans, and well-worn, heavy leather chaps rode through the bush up ahead alongside the highway. A handful of steer meandered to his front.

Sal waved getting Tino's attention, pointed toward the horseman and slowed. Tino followed him off the road to the horseman.

The horseman tugged on the reins as they neared and signaled them to stop. The brothers braked and cut the engines. The cattle stopped and lowered their heads to nibble. The horse flapped its lips.

"Don't need your motorbikes spooking the cattle." A coiled lasso hung from the saddle next to a Winchester rifle holstered in a leather scabbard.

"Excuse us," Sal said.

"You can walk on over if you got something to say."

"Good afternoon," Sal said setting out his kickstand with the heel of his boot.

The horseman tipped his hat. "Lo." His voice had a soft, worn tone. His face was toughened by decades of hard weather, crow's feet at the corners of his eyes, sideburns streaked with gray. A bit of his deep bronze-colored skin showed from between a long-sleeve tan shirt and leather gloves. He stacked his hands on the pommel of his saddle.

"You boys ain't from around here, are ya?" He had an ease about him as if he were where he was fated to be and was at peace with it.

"California," Sal said. "Ever been there?"

"Tucson's furthest west I been. Go there for the rodeos."

"We've got an uncle who lives just south of the border in Sonora. He's a rancher like you, and he goes to rodeos in Tucson."

"You don't say. I probably seen him there. I've met some fine folks from Sonora.

"You live close by?" Tino asked.

The horseman pointed his chin to the west. "Wife and I got a ranch. Been running it by ourselves since our boy, Buck, went off to college."

"What's he studying?" Sal asked.

"Wants to be a lawyer. Says he wants to fight for our people's rights. You ever hear of a fella named Russell Means?"

"Yes, of course," Sal said. "He's made the news. He started the American Indian Movement and has quite a following."

"Buck saw him give a talk and got inspired. Says he wants to join Russell. Lot of movements going on these days, people protesting against the war, Negroes in the South demonstrating for equal rights, even the women are at it. Ain't an easy thing to do, I told Buck, fighting for people's rights. But gotta admit, I'm proud he's aiming to do it."

Sal nodded. "Going to college sounds better than getting drafted and winding up in Vietnam."

"Another reason I'm glad he's getting schooled. We've lost some boys off the reservation to the war. Tragic. They put on nice funerals for 'em, twenty-one-gun salute and all."

"A good friend of mine is serving there now," Tino said.

"I think half the country's got a boy over there," the horseman said. "I saw my share of fighting in the Second War. Served in the South Pacific."

Sal nodded. "We've had men in the family who have served in wars since the Civil War, and one served in the South Pacific."

"No fooling? We may have crossed paths. Small world, they say. Army used us Navajos to transmit over the radio. Japanese never did understand us. We were proud to be able to contribute like that. Got my fill of war, even if it had to be done. But I just can't see much good coming out of this war."

The horse shifted his weight and flicked his ears sending a small swarm of flies lifting into the air.

"We miss Buck, but he needs to make his own way in the world. Needs to learn to survive on his own, like I did."

"You mean by learning to be a rancher?" Tino said.

"Wish it'd been that easy." The rancher pointed to a mountain range. "They'd be the Sangre de Cristos. My father took me halfway up on my nineteenth birthday. Gave me a knapsack and knife, told me to make it back home—said it'd take me three days. His father did the same to him. 'Bout time you're manned,' he said. I was young, strong, and not a little foolish. Thought I'd show him just what kind of man I was and make it home in half the time he figured. I walked the first day and halfway through the night. I learned what it is to be hungry, thirsty, and tired. Second day I decided I'd better slow down a little if I was gonna make it back in decent shape."

"Flop. Flop." A steer had raised its tail and dropped globs of manure.

"So how'd you make it back from the mountains?" Tino asked.

"Dug into a dry streambed 'til I hit water. Ate wild onions, chokecherry, purslane, cactus apples, pretty much anything I could get my hands on. I ran down an old jackrabbit. He could hardly run anymore. Made a fire and ate him. Toughest meat I'd ever had." The rancher chuckled. "But I made it home a half day early."

"I'll bet your father was proud of you," Tino said.

"Didn't say it outright, but he treated me like the rest of the men on the reservation after that. Felt good."

"I wish my father would treat me more like a man," Tino said.

The rancher chuckled. "You seem like a good boy. Give him a little time. He'll come around."

Sal neared the rancher, offering his hand. "We need to hit the road. We've got to catch up with friends. Nice meeting you."

The rancher pulled off a glove and extended his deep brown hand. "Same here."

"May I ask you your name?" Tino said.

"Red Earth. But most folks call me by my Christian name, Floyd."

"I like Red Earth better."

9.

King of the Road

SAL AND TINO CAME TO A LONELY TOWN of single-story, worn-out wooden structures that possessed the desolate visage of a Western ghost town. A handful of citizens walked in a slow, tired gait under storefront overhangs. The sidewalks were made of worn-out wooden planks. An old man in a cowboy hat leaned his chair against a structure with a sagging roof. A sign over his head read SALOON. They pulled into a Texaco gas station at the end of the town. An attendant sat inside, paging through a magazine. He glanced up at the bikers riding in, then turned back to the magazine.

Sal and Tino steered across the cracked tarmac stained with long ago oil spills. A vehicle repair stall housed an antique dust-covered car with running boards. The gas pumps, once red, were now blistered and faded pale pink.

Tino leaned Rocinante on his kickstand and made for the bathroom to the rear of the gas station massaging his butt, aching from hours of sitting. The doorknob was missing; the room smelled of old dirt. The toilet was rust-stained from water heavy in iron. He found a wrinkly *Playboy* magazine dated February 1967 and leafed through it. He decided to urinate outside under a mesquite tree. A horned toad appeared from around the tree trunk. It stopped and gave Tino the evil eye. He kept it at bay with his stream. He returned to see Sal walking back from a phone booth at the corner of the lot.

"Ma said that Gary and Patrick had called her. We're meeting up with them tomorrow morning at ten at the Amarillo Public Library."

"Cool," Tino said. "It'll be good seeing the guys."

SAL AND TINO HAD RIDDEN through Albuquerque by early afternoon and were back in open country. Tino considered Red Earth's journey into manhood. He had to fight through his fear and hunger to make it home from the mountains and prove himself to his father, and after that he treated Red Earth like the rest of the men on the reservation.

Sal's brake light blinked on. He pulled over and pointed up the road. A cloud of dust had risen over the bush. Dozens of horses, led by a brilliant stallion, appeared from the chaparral. His dark brown coat gleamed. His mane waved behind him like a proud flag.

"Wonder who they belong to?" Tino said, his eyes locked on the herd.

"Wild horses. Never thought I'd be lucky enough to see one, let alone an entire herd. Listen to their hoof beats." The mustangs' heavy and deep clops filled the air as they trotted across the road and into the bush.

"Wish I was one of them," Tino said.

Sal started his bike. "I'm just glad that they're still around."

An hour into the ride they came on a biker squatted next to a gleaming candy-apple red chopper with a teardrop gas tank, its chrome accessories reflecting the sun.

Sal and Tino pulled alongside. "How're you doing?" Sal said peeling off his wire-rim sunglasses.

The biker rose from inspecting the engine. "Been a hell of a lot better."

His windblown jet black hair covered the nape of his neck—his eyes dark, clear, and alert, hard jaw, as if chiseled from stone, Levis faded, black T-shirt tight against his tall, muscular frame. His boots were scuffed and stained with oil. Steel buckles ran across the instep just below the cuffs.

"Can't believe I forgot to pack a plug socket."

"I've got one!" Tino said, hopping off his bike.

"Where're you headed?" Sal asked.

"Lubbock, Texas."

"Have you been on the road long?"

"Since Tucson."

"Got it!" Tino said taking the socket out of his tool kit.

"Right on, man!" The biker said and motioned Tino to toss it over. He caught it, snapped it onto a ratchet, set it on a spark plug, broke it loose, and cranked. The biker had a tattoo of a cobra on his forearm, its mouth open wide revealing two sharp fangs and a forked tongue curling out.

"Where're you dudes going?"

"We're meeting friends in Amarillo," Sal said.

The biker finished installing the new plug then reached for a shop rag on his bike seat. He wiped his hands and Tino's socket and gave it back. "Thanks, man."

"Mind if we ride along with you?" Tino said.

"Not at all. Always nice riding with other dudes. Breaks the monotony. Plus the troopers think twice about pulling you over when there's more than one of us."

He mounted the chopper and gave the kick-starter a hard jump. The bike blasted loud as thunder and settled to a deep, ominous rumble—a rodeo bull snorting before the gate opens. He put a heel to the kickstand, retracted it, and pulled onto the road, leaning back against a sissy bar.

Tino followed, wondering how much tattoos of cobras cost. They rode through the afternoon and pulled into Santa Rosa, New Mexico. Sal offered to treat dinner. The biker gladly accepted and suggested a nearby restaurant.

The air conditioning in Jodie's Steak House offered relief from the heat. A waitress fluttered her eyelashes at the biker and led them to a booth trailing a wake of perfume. Her dark hair was cut into the latest style, the "shag."

Sal and Tino sat opposite the biker. The waitress jotted down their orders and left.

"You got a bitchen bike," Tino said, trying to keep his enthusiasm in check. "Is that sissy bar comfortable?"

"Too comfortable. Fell asleep one night. Goddamn near killed myself."

Tino laughed as much over the biker's mishap as at his ease in cussing unabashedly in public.

"How long you been riding?" Tino asked.

"My old man gave me a hand-me-down when I turned sixteen."

"Wow. You must really like riding."

"Don't think much about liking it or not. Feel caged up when I'm in a car, and at ease when I'm on my bike."

Sal nodded. "I've really been enjoying the freedom of biking. Mind if I ask what you do for a living?"

"Mechanic. Fuckin' good one too. I'll fix anything that runs on gas, lawn mowers to giant-ass trucks."

"Did your dad teach you mechanics?" Tino asked.

"Sheeit, my old man could've taught me something if he'd been around."

"Did he have to travel for work?" Sal asked.

"Ha! That's a good one. The Okie son of a bitch was an outlaw."

"He was from Oklahoma?" Sal asked.

"Yeah, why?"

"I thought that from the color of your skin, you might have a little Mexican blood like us."

"Pa was white as a ghost. But my ma was a full-blooded Yaqui."

"Your father was an outlaw?" Tino asked.

"Dealing drugs and dodging the heat."

"The what?"

"The heat man, you know, the law, cops."

"I kinda knew that," Tino said.

"How'd you learn to be a mechanic?" Sal asked.

"In the pen."

Cool!

"Must've been tough on you," Sal said.

"Tougher on ma. She was a real churchgoer. She didn't want me to be like Pa so she put me in Catholic mission schools, figuring that the priests and nuns would straighten me out. Didn't work. But doing time sure did."

"We're Catholic too," Tino said.

"No kidding? I was an altar boy, learned the Latin prayers and all that shit."

Tino squirmed over the biker saying prayers and shit in the same sentence.

"How does a nice guy like you wind up in prison?" Sal asked.

"You want to know what I did, right?"

"I apologize. It's none of my business," Sal said.

"I like you, so I won't take it personal," the biker said.

He then turned to Tino. "My P.O. said I should tell my story to young dudes like you. It's good for you to hear about a bad kid straightening out his act."

"P.O.?" Tino asked.

"Probation officer, a babysitter for cons. I was about your age when I got mixed up with a couple of dudes who introduced me to heroin. Wound up with a monkey on my back."

Tino looked to Sal for an explanation but Sal looked just as puzzled.

"Monkey, man! Having a monkey on your back means getting hooked on drugs." He pointed to Tino. "Don't fuck with that shit. It'll get the better of you. I don't care what you think. 'I can handle it,' I kept telling myself. Next thing I knew it had me by the throat." The biker picked up his glass of water and drank.

Tino leaned into him hungry for more.

"We were doing junk one night." The biker shook his head at their clueless expressions. "Junk—heroin. Don't you dudes know nothing? What are you, priests?"

"Yes," Sal said.

"You're shittin' me."

"No, I'm not shittin' ya."

Tino laughed.

"And here I been cussin' up a storm in front of you."

Sal sighed. "A drawback with being a priest is that people don't feel that they can be themselves around me. But I'm on vacation. So fuck it."

Tino and the biker laughed hard, drawing annoyed glances.

"You're all right, Father."

"Please, it's Sal."

"If there were more priests like you there'd be a lot more people going to church. I was in the middle of something?"

Tino straightened. "You had junk on your back."

"Ha! I see you're paying attention."

Tino nodded. "So what happened?"

"We ran out of heroin and money, so we staked out a house for a break-in. The windows were dark." He looked to Sal. "I swear, Father Sal, we thought that nobody was home."

"Please, it's Sal."

"We broke in and searched around for stuff to fence, but an old man came out of a bedroom. He got scared—real scared—and started yelling. I had to gag him. 'We're not going to hurt you,' I kept telling him but he died of a heart attack right there in front of me."

The waitress appeared with large plates of food. One in each hand and a third balanced on her forearm. "Let me know if I can get you anything else," she said looking into the biker's eyes.

"Yeah, sure," the biker said and took his knife and fork and cut into his steak.

Tino squirmed, anxious to hear more. "So what happened after the old man died?"

The biker talked as he ate. "A detective came around asking what I knew about the burglary. He saw that I was nervous, and the next thing I knew, I was sitting in a room with detectives asking a lot of hard questions. They said that I'd do life if I didn't come clean." The biker raised his chin to swallow.

"So, did you 'come clean'?" Tino asked.

"Spilled everything."

"How long were you in for? And what was prison like?"

Sal raised a hand. "That's enough."

"It's okay, Father Sal. Been too long since I've gotten this out. It's like I'm confessing, ha! Anyhow, I got the lightest sentence because I was young and hadn't had a felony. I served eight of twenty years. It might've been the best thing for me. I'd been getting into bad habits, hanging with young dumb dudes who were as mixed up as me. Now I'm the best mechanic around. Got a good woman too, Sharon. She says if I get into trouble again, I better hope that the cops find me first."

"We appreciate you sharing your story," Sal said. "It's inspiring."

"It's happened to a lot of dudes. Details might change a little, but it ain't new. You'd a thought getting sentenced would've scared me enough to go straight, but the first thing I did when I got in prison was to join a gang." He tapped the tattoo of the cobra on his forearm. "This was my initiation. Black was the only color of an ink pen that my cellie had. Anywhere else you'd get a paint job with decent colors."

Sal looked at Tino, Tino looked at Sal; both shrugged their shoulders.

"Paint job, it's prison talk for tattoos. You guys crack me up, but in a good way, a real good way."

"We live a pretty sheltered life," Sal said. "Our community is very Catholic and very conservative."

"Looks like it's worked out good for you. You're not the types who get into trouble."

"Our Pa's like your wife Sharon," Tino said. "You don't want to get in trouble with him around."

"I wish my Pa would've cared enough to raise me like that. I thought it'd be cool to be an outlaw like him, but I learned that cons will turn on each other in nothing flat, even dudes sworn into gangs. They'll rat each other out if it means getting out sooner or better treatment from the guards. One dude ratted out another for a pack of smokes."

"Jeez!" Tino said.

"Do you have a shop?" Sal asked.

"Yup. Judges who want to give young offenders a second chance send them to me for a job, and I got two rules for them when they show up. If you come in to work loaded on any-thing—alcohol, dope, or whatever—you get your final pay-check on the spot. Second rule: payday's Monday. Give kids dough on Friday and the next thing you know they're out sniffing around for a good time. Some of the guys I've trained have gone on to work for the best car agencies in the state."

"Who minds the shop while you're gone?" Sal said.

"Fernando, Mexican dude, my right hand man, been with me from the start, going on twelve years. Having him lets me take time off. Summertime, I hook up with a club of bikers who are on the mend like me. I'm meeting up with them now.

We're touring the Grand Canyon, Lake Mead, and the Pueblo Cliff Dwellings. Last year we rode to Canada. In the winter Sharon and I go to some place that she picks out. Works good." He pushed back from the table. The waitress came with the check. Sal reached for his wallet and handed her a twenty.

"Thanks, for the meal," the biker said. "I'm much obliged. Next time the treat'll be on me."

"You're good people," the biker said in the parking lot and shook their hands. He mounted and kick-started his bike. The world around them filled with its reverberating thunder.

"Hey!" Sal yelled. "We never got your name."

The biker squeezed the hand brake, put a boot on the ground, and leaned into them. "Rex, Rex Camino. See you on the road." He gave a two-finger salute and pulled into the street. The chrome mufflers reflected the soft reddish hue of dusk. He rode off leaning against the sissy bar.

"Bitchen guy," Tino said and yawned. "Shouldn't we find a place to sleep for the night?"

"Not until we get into Texas."

"Come on Sal. My neck's killing me."

"I'll rub you down later."

They rode from the restaurant to a near-by service station. When Sal finished pumping gas, he reached for his wallet.

"Crap!"

"Now what?"

Sal tapped his pockets in a panic. "My wallet!"

"God, you're always losing stuff! Maybe you left it on the table at the restaurant. Get your brown *nalgas* back there before somebody takes it."

Sal jumped on his bike. "Wait here!" he said and raced out.

"Wait here?" Tino said. "Where else am I going to wait?" He paid for the gas, used the bathroom and rode to the curb.

Sal rode back, relief on his face. "Waitress had it at the cash register. Somebody found it."

"It's always something with you: wallet, keys, an important paper you need right away. Good thing your dick's attached."

Two hours into the ride Tino shook his head trying to keep awake; neck muscles screaming. Would Sal take the next off-ramp? No. Damn, how about the next one?

Tino wasn't able to read a sign they passed later, but he was able to make out "Texas" in large black letters. Sal, mercifully, took the following exit off of the highway and found a spot in feral shrubbery to sleep, but decided that it wasn't well enough hidden from state troopers who would make them move. Tino followed Sal onto a narrow uneven dusty road that cut through spindly bush. Their headlights lit up the powdery chaparral on either side of them. Sal stopped and pointed down into a sandy arroyo. "There's the spot."

Minutes later they were crawling into their sleeping bags.

"We saw a lot of places today, met great people, and still logged over 500 miles," Sal said.

"Wonder if there're mountain lions around here," Tino said.

"Don't think about it." Sal pointed into the night sky. "Check out the stars."

Tino gazed up, hands under his head. "Sky's almost white with them."

"That's why it's called The Milky Way."

"Do you suppose it looked the same to the cowboys a hundred years ago?"

"It's the same sky that the cowboys and *vaqueros* saw," Sal said.

"Who?"

"*Ay*, don't you know anything about your *cultura*? Mexican vaqueros, the original cowboys. They roamed here centuries before the gringos. You never read about that in our history books."

Tino spoke in a quiet voice. "The Grand Canyon was beautiful and sacred like the Indian girl at the ice cream shop said. It's so much bigger and beautiful than what I'd imagined. And New Mexico was so open and still. Instead of The Land of Enchantment, it ought to be called The Land of Echoes."

"Good one, Chico. Did you notice that there were more Indians and Mexicans there than white people? Nice to be in the majority for a change."

"Sal, you told the Indian cowboy we met today that someone in our family served in the Civil War. What do you know about that?"

"Ma told me about her Scottish grandfather, John Thomson, when I was a kid. He served as a Yankee and was killed in the Civil War. Didn't you know that?"

"I knew that we had a great-grandfather who was Scottish, but I never heard about him being a soldier. Ma told me about it just before I left to catch up with you in Flagstaff."

"Why would that even come up?" Sal said.

"Ma's old Uncle, our Tio Nene," Tino said. "He called her from Mexico and he asked how you were doing. She told him that you had left on a trip around the country. Nene said that there's family folklore that Great-grandpa John Thomson's name could be on a monument in Bath, Maine. Nene said that the Thomson family had migrated there. He said that John was killed in Virginia around Fredericksburg."

"Interesting," Sal said.

Tino continued. "Nene asked that if we get close enough to Maine that we go and see if the monument exists, and if it does to take a picture of it."

"I don't see how we'll be able to do that, Chico. I've only got four weeks of vacation time and we've got over seven thousand miles to cover. I've got the route planned out to the inch and the schedule to the second. Our destination is New York and Maine is way north of there, impossible to fit it in. And besides, like Tio Nene said, it's only family folklore. Most likely nothing more than wishful thinking."

"Seems like we should at least try."

Leaves shuffling underfoot and a dark mass on four short legs with some type of weird armor ran out of the dark and over Tino's bag.

"*¡Ay cabrón!*"

The animal scurried past and disappeared back into the bush.

"Armadillo," Sal said, rock in hand.

Tino put his hand to his heart. "*Qué susto*. What if there's a mountain lion after that thing? We'd look a lot tastier. Maybe we ought to sleep in a town park or something."

Sal tossed the rock aside and got back into his bag.

Tino lay back keeping an eye out and thinking of Rex Camino. How would Tino manage to live an independent life like Rex's? It'd be so cool to dress any way he wanted, talk any way he wanted and ride a bitchen chopper. Hell, Tino could even get a cool tattoo of a cobra.

10.

Miss Dorie Mae's

"TIME TO GET GOING, CHICO." Sal's voice broke the morning quiet.

Tino pulled the bag from his face, sighed, and said in a frog-like voice. "What time's it?"

Sal hopped on a leg putting on his pants.

"Just past six."

Tino crawled out of his bag. "Hurry here, hurry there."

"Lots to do in life."

"Can you at least tone it down a little?"

"Sure," Sal said. He sat on a washed-out tree trunk to put on his boots and whistled an annoyingly perky tune.

Tino picked up his pants lying alongside his sleeping bag. A small, black, furry hand dropped from a pant leg to the ground.

"*¡Ay, chingado!*" he yelled tossing his pants and throwing his hands into the air. A tarantula stood defiantly in front of Tino as if saying, "Go ahead and try something."

Sal walked over and squatted in front of the giant spider. "Beautiful specimen."

"That hairy monster almost eats me alive and you say 'Beautiful'?"

"Relax, they're harmless to us."

The tarantula meandered off.

Tino carefully picked up his pants and dangled them.

Sal and Tino bumped up the side of the arroyo to the road, reached the highway, and rode for an hour to Wildorado, Texas.

Tino put a foot to the ground at a stop sign and leaned toward Sal. "I'm hungry."

Sal nodded, and continued through the intersection and stopped along the sidewalk. "Excuse me, sir," he said to a man in a white cowboy hat. The hat's headband was dark brown with sweat-dried dirt. "Know where we can get breakfast?"

The man pointed down the road. "Ain't but a skinny piece from here. Miss Dorie Mae's, y'all git you the best breakfast anywhares." The color of the man's teeth matched his hat's headband.

Sal and Tino pulled up to an aging wood frame, two-story farmhouse converted into a diner surrounded by a dusty picket fence. A sign nailed on the rickety gate confirmed they were in the right place: MISS DORIE MAE'S. A rangy, thirsty rambling rose supported the worn out arbor.

A long-distance truck driver parked his rig among others in a dirt lot across the road. He slid out of the truck and headed for the eatery.

"Good morning," Sal said.

The trucker acknowledged Sal with a grunt. The brothers followed him through the gate and upstairs to the porch. The trucker opened the screen door, stepped in, and pulled the door closed behind him.

Tino spoke under his breath. "He could've left it open."

A dozen patrons chatted among the smells of coffee and breakfast fare. A thin blue cloud of cigarette smoke hovered overhead. A middle-aged man in a baseball cap and plaid cowboy shirt sitting at the counter, coffee cup in hand, set a suspicious eye on Sal and Tino.

A tall pot-bellied cook worked a spatula over a grill behind a set of swinging doors. Twangy music came from a static-plagued radio. A woman with a heavy Southern accent sang about the day her mama gave a piece of her mind to the Harper Valley PTA.

A woman with platinum blonde hair teased out to the size of a football helmet was at the register. She laid her cigarette in an ashtray on the counter and rang up a tab. Two large meat hook-like curls hugged her cheeks. A pink waitress outfit and a food-stained, lace-lined apron strained to contain her bulges. "What say, Chad?" she said to the man who'd entered in front of Sal and Tino. "Anything new?"

"Same ole, Miss Dorie Mae. What I want to know is do you still love me?"

"Why, hell yeah, sugar."

Tino smiled. He'd only heard people talk with such accents in movies.

The woman looked the two brothers up and down. "Find you a seat."

Sal nodded. "Thank you, ma'am." They sat at the only unoccupied table. It teetered. Sal took a napkin from the dispenser, folded it, and shimmed the short leg. The paper menus, pressed between bottles of ketchup and mustard, were wrinkled and food stained.

Three men at a neighboring table flipped coins and laughed or cussed when they won or lost the money that had each put into the pot.

A boy of about ten, with curly brown hair and a full-moon face rusty with freckles, came through the door. "Hey, Miss Dorie Mae, do yuh still love me?"

"Why, you know ah do, Junebug."

She stepped to Sal and Tino, took a notepad from the pouch in her apron, and pulled a pencil out of her hair. "Whatchya want?" she said stiffly.

"A Trucker Pancake Combo and a glass of milk, please," Tino said.

"And I'd like oatmeal, toast, and a cup of tea, ma'am," Sal said.

"Well you got manners anyway."

Tino scanned the room. Balls of dust in the corners and bits of dried food sprinkled the floor around nicked table and chair legs. Pinned to the wall behind the cash register were glossy black and white photos of men standing next to large fallen game animals or holding big fish.

Naugahide seat covers on the counter's swivel stools were shiny, having been buffed by patrons' rears for decades. One stool had a small, sharp bulge where a spring was struggling to find daylight.

The woman picked up a coffee pot from the Bunn-o-Matic and made a round topping off cups. Men at another table chatted over their plates. "Did you all see that ole high school running back? Boy's outta Vega. Hershel's the name. It's a sight the way he jukes and jags, and fast? Boy's quicker'n a hiccup's all I'm saying."

"But the damn coach be giving him the ball too much. The whole defense was ganging up on him. By the fourth quarter, he had 'bout as much chance as a grasshopper in a henhouse."

The cook pushed through the kitchen doors with two large platters piled with food and set them on the table.

"Thank you," Sal said.

The cook left without responding.

Steam rose from Tino's plate of giant pancakes, three of the thickest slices of bacon he had ever seen, scrambled eggs, and a mound of what reminded him of the coarse *masa* that

Ma prepared for making tamales. He barely managed to finish the food.

"Five dollars and twenty-six cents," the woman said at the cash register.

Sal handed her a ten.

"You have a very nice place, ma'am," Tino said.

"Well, we sure ain't gonna make no fancy-ass magazines, but food is all what counts around here. Where you boys out of?"

"San Diego, California," Sal answered.

She struck a match and put a cigarette to her lips. "Y'all take a wrong turn er what?" The cigarette danced between her lips as she talked.

"I've taken wrong turns before," Sal said, "but this time I meant to come this way."

"You gonna be here a while?"

"Just passing through on our way to Amarillo."

"Y'all ain't some o' those ole Hell's Angels motorcycle gang we hear about, are ya?"

"No, ma'am. They're much bigger and fatter than us. So are their motorcycles. 'Hogs' they call 'em."

"Who they callin' hawgs?" she said amused. "They selves or they motor scooters? Well, no matter, Hell's Angels er not, you welcome here anytime."

"Well, thank you very much, ma'am. We'll stop in on our way back."

"That'll be just fine with me. And you makin' me feel like a ole dried-up milk cow the way you be calling me 'ma'am.' Call me Miss Dorie Mae, like the rest of Texas."

"Or hot honey-biscuit buns, like rest of us," a patron shouted. The place broke up; hee-haw laughter came from the kitchen.

"Chadwick! Mind your manners or I'll put lumps the size o' bull nuts upside your head!"

"Ain't like he don't got it comin', Miss Dorie Mae," said his table partner.

Sal and Tino left with contented bellies and mounted the bikes, ready to go, when Miss Dorie Mae's voice rang out.

"You might be needing your change, darlin.' " She stood on the porch waving a few bills.

Sal jogged over. "Thank you for your honesty."

"Don't make no mind about it. I didn't think much of you when ya you walked in, but I can tell you been raised by a God-fearing momma, and you're fine boys."

"Thank you, ma'am I mean Miss Dorie Mae."

"You got it, sugar."

Sal returned and started the Hawk. Tino had to hit Rocinante's kick-starter several times before the engine woke up.

"What's wrong?" Sal asked.

"Heck if I know. He's been acting up."

"Crap," Sal said. "I suppose we should get it checked out even if it'll cost us travel time."

"Not yet. Maybe it'll go away. That's how Pa deals with engine trouble. He ignores it. It either goes away, or the car dies, and he has to get the *'hijo de la chingada'* fixed."

"Ha! That's Pa, all right. Let's see how it holds up today."

They arrived in Amarillo just before 10 a.m., and the day was already uncomfortably warm.

11.

A Tiny Island Surrounded by the Sea

"K EEP AN EYE OUT FOR THE GUYS," Sal said when they parked in front of the Amarillo library. "I'm going into the library to take a leak."

Tino stretched his arms and neck and realized that the soreness had lessened considerably. He jogged up and down along the curb to get his blood flowing.

"It's well past ten and no guys," Sal said when he returned. "What's taking them?"

"Probably Gary. He's never on time," Tino said. He looked up and down the street. "Hey! Here they come."

Even at a distance it was obvious that Gary was leading. He rode tall in the saddle like cowboy heroes. Gary was fair-skinned, handsome, just shy of six feet tall, and powerfully built, having worked out with weights through high school. Girls nicknamed him, "Zeus."

Gary had a melancholy air about him due in part, to his parent's divorce when he was a boy. His relationship with his stepmother was a cold war of sorts that flared into hostility on occasion, with Gary coming out the loser. One clash ended with her yanking his record player from his bedroom and flinging it onto the concrete patio, destroying it. She later gifted him a new one. "Wish I had a family like yours," Gary had once said to Tino. "You like each other."

Gary had bought a new Honda motorcycle with a 350-cc engine. He called his bike "the Rookie." Sal and Tino's bikes were equipped with oversize gas tanks and gear ratios designed for sustained high-speed travel. Gary's bike was designed for urban travel with a lower gear ratio and smaller gas tank. Fortunately, its engine was big enough to handle the 7,000-mile plus trip.

Patrick, riding behind Gary, stood at five-foot eight and weighed just under one hundred and fifty pounds. His small size, milky-white Irish skin, and curly red hair belied his toughness. Sean Kelly, a feared bully and a head taller than Patrick, picked a fight with Patrick. They met after school behind the gym. A handful of boys circled them. Patrick bounced side-to-side ducking and reflecting blows, while landing solid punches, frustrating Sean. Sean charged Patrick in a rage. Patrick sidestepped and landed a solid hit on the jaw, knocking Sean face first onto the ground. Patrick jumped on his back and hit him again and again, pounding his face against the asphalt. The guys who had been cheering Patrick on went silent. Patrick, demon possessed, screamed and cussed as he pounded away.

"You're gonna kill him!" somebody yelled. Tino and Gary wrestled Patrick off Sean. Sean wound up with a broken jaw, Patrick a broken bone in his hand.

Patrick divulged later that his father had been a boxer in Ireland and forced Patrick and his brothers to box with him. When drinking, he'd beat his sons mercilessly, saying it was for their own good.

Patrick rode "Peewee," a 175-cc Honda. When Sal questioned him about attempting the trip with such a small engine, Patrick, a good mechanic, assured Sal that he'd make it work.

Gary and Patrick rode up with fat cigars clenched between their teeth.

Tino laughed, raising his hand in a high-five. Patrick slapped it hard.

"Jeez, take it easy, dude," Tino said, shaking out the sting.

"Good to see you guys," Sal said.

"Ooh, sheeeit, man," Gary said eyeing Rocinante. "This be one badass bike."

"Sheeit yeah, mofo," Tino said snapping his fingers and strutting around his bike like a rooster, mimicking the black kids in his neighborhood.

Patrick threw the cigar to the curb, spit, and dug out a pack of Juicy Fruit gum from his pocket, unwrapped two sticks, rolled them into one and tossed them into his mouth. "Your bike's dee-lux, man. Tachometer, dual exhaust pipes, even a fifth gear to really haul ass."

Tino beamed.

Sal hopped on his bike, started it, and revved the engine. "Let's hit it, muchachos!"

Patrick threw his fist into the air. "Let's go for it!"

Two teenage girls, wearing short-shorts and tank-top T-shirts, stared at the four bikers riding down the street. Tino gunned his engine. Rocinante's tailpipes roared drawing the girl's attention to him. He rode tall.

On the highway, he realized that they weren't going to be traveling as fast as Sal and he had been. Peewee's small engine, after lugging Patrick's weight and gear, was barely managing sixty-five, undoubtedly frustrating Sal.

A half hour into the ride Rocinante began misfiring and slowed to a crawl.

Tino signaled for Sal and Patrick to keep on, and Gary to follow him. Rocinante sputtered along to a repair garage.

"What's wrong?" Gary hollered.

"Crap, it's time to get the *hijo de la chingada* fixed."

"The what?"

A short man, fat as a sumo wrestler and wearing blue overalls, had his head ducked under the hood of a new Chevy pickup in a repair bay. The truck's radio blared Jerry Lee Lewis's piano-pounding tune "Great Balls of Fire."

Tino and Gary pulled up behind the truck.

The mechanic backed out from under the hood. "What cain I do for ya'll?"

Tino's forehead furrowed with worry. "Bike's acting up, and I need to get back on the road quick."

"Almost finished with this here. I get to you right off." The mechanic ducked back under the hood.

"Thanks," Tino yelled, then turned to Gary. "I hope it's not going to take a shitload of money and a long time to fix."

"No kidding," Gary said. "By the way, are you still on for joining the Marines with me after the trip?"

"Hell yes, man. Our dads are going to be so proud of us."

Gary grinned. "That's gonna be so bitchen. Have you told your dad about it yet?"

"No. I've only told Val. I can't keep nothing from him."

"What'd Val say about it?"

"That I was crazy. Said they'd send me straight to Vietnam. I told Val that if I didn't join the Marines, I'd get drafted into the Army and wind up a grunt, like the Marquez twins."

"Robert and Gilbert Marquez got drafted?"

"Yeah," Tino said. "Gilbert came by the house looking really sharp in his Army uniform. He said that he'd just gotten orders to serve in Vietnam. My Pa put his hands on Gilbert's shoulders and said that he was proud of him. Tino looked to the ground and spoke softly. "Pa's never done anything even close to that to me."

"And my dad thinks I'm a coward for not going out for varsity football," Gary said. "But we're going to show them. Marines aren't cowards."

"I could get killed in the war, like my granddad," Tino said grimly.

"Who?"

"My great-grandfather died in the Civil War. I'll bet that he died a hero and that his father was really proud of him. If I don't make it back, I hope that at least I die a hero, like him and that my dad will be proud of me too. Better to die a hero than a bum and a shame to the family."

Gary punched Tino in the shoulder. "We're not getting fuckin' killed! Marines are the best-trained fighters in the world. Besides, we'll be together. We'll watch out for each other. You'll see."

The mechanic walked out of the garage, blew his nose using a shop rag and nodded toward Tino's bike. "Nice thing 'bout these Hondas is they real reliable." He wiped sweat from his round face with the snot rag. "450 cc's will get you around pretty good. Name's Raymond, but mostly they call me Ray." He had gaps between some teeth and a couple of leaners.

Tino offered his hand. "Good meeting you." The thin slivers of Ray's fingernails that weren't chewed to nubs were black with grease.

"It's been sputtering. And today I couldn't keep up with the guys."

Another mechanic, tall, thin, with squinty eyes, joined them.

"This here's Cooter," Ray said.

"Pretty unique name," Gary said laughing.

"His proper name be Carter, but Cooter fit him better." A tattoo of an anchor with "USN" inscribed over it covered Cooter's forearm.

"I'll fetch my tools right quick," Ray said.

Tino breathed a sigh of relief. "Thanks a lot." He put a hand in between his legs. "I gotta take a whiz, bad, Gare."

Tino came on two water fountains on the side of the garage, one a bit lower. *For kids, nice.* A sign on the wall read, "White." An arrow pointed to a bathroom door. A second sign read "Colored." An arrow pointed to a door farther back. *Holy shit!* He thought of a photo he'd seen in a magazine of a lynched Negro. White people milled about as if at a hunting party admiring the prize kill. A chill ran down Tino's spine, despite the heat.

"Only a clogged fuel filter," Gary said on Tino's return.

"Fixed already? Outta sight, man!"

Ray, sitting on the ground next to the bike, held up the fuel filter, the size of his plump thumb.

Cooter tapped Ray's shoulder. "Tell you what, ole Ray's got smart hands for fixin'."

"Aw," Ray said, uneasy with the praise. "Ain't a whole lot to it. Problems are mostly no spark or no fuel. You had plenty a spark, but not gittin' enough fuel." He rose with a grunt. "Where you boys headed?"

"New York," Gary said. "Started in California."

"Heavens to mercy!" Cooter said. "You mighty ambitious."

Tino went for his wallet. "What do I owe you?"

Raymond raised a hand. "I can't charge ya. Wasn't much to it. Besides I ain't got motorbike parts to sell you."

"Well, thank you very much, Ray."

What could their opinions be regarding race relations Tino wondered, recalling segregated bathrooms. They didn't seem like the racist types. "What do you think about the Negroes demonstrating, Ray?" Tino asked.

"Can't says I blames 'em. I'd be doing the same thing."

"Really? So do you think they should have the same rights as white people?"

"Why, hell yeah, same's anybody."

"You think they should be able to vote?"

"I think niggahs should be able to put in one of they own to have say-so over they own kind."

Cooter nodded. "They ought to have the same problems as us whites with our politicians, who be praying in the pews on Sundee, then come Mondee they be dickin' the housemaid."

Tino snorted a laugh.

"We got them Separate-but-Equal laws here," Raymond said. "But ain't nothin' equal about 'em. Niggah schools ain't never been taken care of worth a shit. Now, I wouldn't be sayin' as much in the town square for certain people to be hearing, but it's my opinion. And you know what they say about opinions."

"No, what?"

"They're like assholes. Everybody's got one, just some are louder and smellier'n others."

Tino and Gary burst out laughing.

"You think whites and blacks should be able to marry?" Tino said. Ray and Cooter looked at him as if he had just broken every one of the Ten Commandments.

Ray stepped to a water nozzle for filling radiators and poured a spot of water into his greasy palm. He unscrewed Rocinante's dipstick and allowed a drop of oil to fall in the small pool.

The oil floated like a tiny island surrounded by the sea. "They just don't mix."

"Never have and never will," Cooter said. "It's just the way of it. God made black people and white people each to be with their own kind. Otherwise He'd a made us all the same."

"You've given me a lot to think about," Tino said.

Ray pointed down the street. "The Honda store ain't but three blocks away. You have yourselves a fine trip."

Tino and Gary mounted and started the bikes. "Thanks a lot," Tino said ready to roll out, but Cooter signaled them to stop. They hit their brakes and leaned toward him.

"What's the last thing a fly sees when it hits a windshield?"

"What?"

"His asshole!"

Tino pulled into the street, laughing. An oncoming driver slammed on his brakes to keep from running into him. The driver leaned on his horn. Tino glanced apologetically at him, hit the gas, and fishtailed, tires squealing. Ray and Cooter howled.

"Clogged fuel filter," Tino said, pulling up to Sal and Patrick in the parking lot of ABRAHAM LINCOLN HIGH SCHOOL FOR COLOREDS.

"Clogged filter," Patrick said. "I should've thought of that. That's why it sputtered under a load."

"Let's get to Dallas," Sal said, anxious to make up time.

Tino rode through the parking lot. Potholes covered the asphalt like a bad case of smallpox. He stopped to scan the school's complex: paint faded and chipped; windows cracked, broken, or missing. A rain gutter hung like a broken limb from a roof.

Separate but equal?

12.

Your Bike's a Stud

Sal, Tino, Gary, and Patrick rode out of Amarillo passing fields of cotton. Black men, women, and children dragged large cloth bags, filling them with the snow-like crop. The field workers lifted bulging bags to men on flatbed trucks. They emptied the bags into large bins. Spider-web-like bits of escaped cotton had been blown onto wild shrubbery and barbed wire fencing that paralleled the road.

Patrick pulled alongside Sal and pointed to his gas tank. Sal gave a thumbs up in an A-Okay, and rode to a Flying 'A' service station.

An attendant with "Pie" stitched over his breast pocket greeted the four. "How y'all doing?" His olive-green uniform shirt was clean and starched, his pants ironed with sharp creases. Pie's shining hair was streaked silver at the temples, nary a single strand out of place.

"Doing good," Tino answered.

A small cross, tattooed between Pie's forefinger and thumb, looked like a faded blue inkblot against his dark skin. The tattoo was a signature marking of a *Pachuco*, a cool-dude subculture of Mexican Americans.

Pachucos kept their cars immaculately clean and lowered so they barely cleared the street. They used pomade to keep their hair in place, and they ironed creases into their pants, be they slacks, khakis or jeans. Pachuca girlfriends also tattooed crosses on their hands and peroxided their black hair, turning it rusty brown.

Pachucos were prideful and super macho. Whenever groups crossed paths there would be strutting and fighting.

Ma Caballero insisted on raising her children outside the barrios. She would not have them influenced by *'esos fachosos'* (those showoffs) who mixed English and Spanish so that neither language was spoken properly.

"*Ustedes son un* motorcycle club?" Pie asked in a Texan drawl.

Patrick unwrapped two sticks of gum. "We're Sal and the So-Cal Mofos."

"We're just friends touring the country," Sal said.

"Well, ain't that something. Are you all a Mexicano?"

Sal set the gas nozzle in his tank and squeezed the lever. "My parents were born in Mexico, so I'm Mexican-American, though I hear people saying *Chicano* these days."

"Call me Chicano," Pie said. "Or Mexican-American, or Mexicano, or Tex-Mex, but don't nobody better call me *un pinche*, Greaser." He raised his fists, crouched, and bobbed side to side as if in a boxing match. "1952 Golden Glove champ in my weight division, *ese*." He threw a few air jabs.

"I always did want to do something like what you all are doing, riding around free and easy, *tu sabes*? Hey, if you'll give me a *minuto*, I'll buy me a *moto* and come along with you all."

Sal finished pumping gas and hung the hose. "*¡Simón qué sí, ese!* Then we would look *como un* motorcycle gang."

Pie smiled, displaying a set of large and straight white teeth. "*¡Órale!* You're all right, *ese*."

Sal pointed down the frontage road lying straight and long on the Texas plain. "Anybody have the guts to race me?"

"Hell, yeah!" Gary said.

"*Qué loco, moco* (How crazy, booger)," Pie said.

"Not fair," Patrick protested. "You guys have bigger engines than me. I'll do it, but only with a head start."

"You got it," Sal said. "We'll line up in the road on either side of the center divider. The distance will be ten telephone poles. Losers buy the winner a soda. Pat, you'll get five seconds before we come after you."

A young, tall, and thin man wearing grimy jeans and a T-shirt with a pack of cigarettes wrapped up in a sleeve, walked out of the gas station. He raised his chin at Sal. "*¿Quiúbole, carnal?* (Whats up, brother?) I'm *El Faról*."

"*Quiubo*," Sal said.

Pie approached El Faról, looked up at him, and raised his fists.

"*Órale guey* (Let's go you dumb ox)," El Faról said crouching like a boxer. The two bobbed, juked, and jabbed around each other's heads.

Pie faked haymaker punches. "Pie, *el tigre del* ring, has El Faról against the ropes!"

"*Pero* (But), what's this?" El Faról said landing an imaginary uppercut. "El Faról is making a comeback even though the *pinche piojo* (damned head lice) is hitting him below the belt in the *huevos* (balls)."

"*¡Óye!* (Hey!)" Sal shouted, laughing. "We need you to give the signal."

Pie lowered his fists. "*Simón* (Sure–slang). I'll finish him off later with one good *putazo* (big fucking hit). Hey, which one of you is going to win?"

"I'm not as heavy as any of them, " Sal said. "My engine will put its muscle into speed instead of carrying the extra weight."

"All's I need is the five-second head start," Patrick said.

Gary leaned forward, ready to go. "My new 350's quicker than any of them."

Pie pointed his chin at Tino. "*¿Y tu?*"

Tino patted Rocinante and smiled.

Pie elbowed El Faról. "I'll bet you *una Pexsi qué el* Sal wins. Like he says, his engine don't got to work so hard, carrying so much *nalga.*"

"You're on, *guey*. I say the 350's going to take 'em. It's *nuevecita* (new), and don't got the miles like *los otros* (the others.)"

The four bikers lined up, two on either side of the road.

"Pat will take off when you yell go," Sal said. "Say it again in five seconds."

Pie raised his hand.

The racers leaned forward, revving their engines. Rocinante's tailpipes were loudest. Birds in nearby trees got spooked and burst into the air in a mass of feathers and wings.

"Go!"

Peewee burned rubber. His front wheel lifted high off of the ground.

"One thousand and one, one thousand and two," Tino counted. "He's already in second gear. Five seconds was too much."

"Go!"

"*¡Ándale!*" Sal screamed, releasing the clutch and getting a jump on Gary and Tino. Gary bolted.

Rocinante's back tire skidded on grit. "Damn it!" Tino yelled shooting out a foot to keep from falling over. The rear tire grabbed. Screech!

Everyone pulled away, shrinking in Tino's field of vision. Sal gained on Patrick; Gary gained on both. Patrick, in the lead, had shifted into fourth. Tino shifted into second. "C'mon boy," Tino said, shifting into third.

Gary passed Patrick at pole six, and Sal at pole seven.

"We're gaining on them, Roci! Let's show 'em what we got!" Tino said, shifting into fourth and flooring it. Air pushed hard against Tino, pulling his hair straight back. The asphalt below passed in a blur—broken white lines of the road, mere dots. He flew past Patrick, then Sal. Gary's bike, the Rookie, was maxed out, his quickness no longer an advantage.

Rocinante's speedometer hit ninety-seven and climbing as he rocketed past the Rookie between poles nine and ten.

Tino flew through the finish line. "Yeah, baby!" He hit the brakes, skidded to a stop, let out the kickstand, and leaned back to clean his fingernails. Gary sped past. Sal and Patrick had given up and coasted in.

Tino yawned. "Thought you dudes would never show."

"Your bike's a stud!" Gary said.

"I'll take an RC Cola from Pat, a Dad's Old Fashioned Root Beer from Gary, and a Nehi Orange from my bro. Been a pleasure doing business with you gentlemen."

"Let's hit the road!" Sal said.

Tino glanced back at the service station. Pie and El Faról were ducking and bobbing, throwing air punches. "*Pinche raza*," he said cracking up.

13.

Texas Justice

T HE REALITY OF RIDING IN THE HEAT for long, tedious
hours had returned by early afternoon. The traffic
lessened considerably after they passed Wichita Falls, and
the multi-lane Highway 287 had shriveled into a scrawny
two-lane country road.

The four passed a tired, wooden sign reading BOWIE, one
of many backwater towns of north-central Texas—if one can
call a gas station, burger stand, Baptist church, post office,
laundromat, and general store a town. The structures surrounded a small park with sick-looking yellow grass. In the
center of the park stood a stone monument to the frontiers-
man, Jim Bowie. Modest wood-frame houses, many in need
of paint, lay scattered along dusty side roads, most without
fences or defined yards.

A few citizens, going about their business, laid weary eyes
on the bikers pulling into the park.

Sal pointed to the laundromat. "This'd be a good time to
wash clothes."

Tino and Patrick volunteered to do the wash and wrapped
everyone's soiled laundry into T-shirts. They bought a box

91

of detergent and a quart bottle of bleach at the general store. Patrick picked up packs of gum and a soda for Tino, making good on losing the race to him. At the laundromat they loaded white clothes in one washer, colors in another.

Tino started reading directions on the box of detergent, but Patrick snatched the box away. "Just do it," he said and emptied half the box into each washer and the bottle of bleach in with the whites.

"That was fun racing today," Tino said.

"Man, your bike kicked our asses good!" Patrick said.

"I bought the bike from Mr. Gray, the English Lit teacher."

"I saw him riding it in Balboa Park last summer," Patrick said. "Old man Gray said that it sat in his garage most of the time and that he never really opened it up." Patrick mimicked Nigel Gray's British accent. " 'I enjoy trotting along with the breeze on the machine.' That bike's a stallion, it needs to fuckin' run wild."

Tino looked at two women sorting laundry on a nearby counter. They glared at him and Patrick. One of the women, with a bandana covering her hair rollers, that were size of toilet paper inserts, caught a fly in midair with a swoosh of her hand and slapped it against her hip. It fell to the floor spinning in desperate circles.

She squashed it.

Tino elbowed Patrick. "I wouldn't cuss so loud."

Patrick answered in a loud whisper. "Who cares? We'll be outta here soon anyway."

Tino gave up. "What're you going to do now that we've graduated?"

"Try out for the Green Berets, man. Gary says that you're joining the Marines together."

"I don't want to get drafted and wind up a grunt," Tino said. "And the uniform is deluxe. I can't wait for my dad to—"

"Ha! Ha!" Patrick laughed and pointed. Mounds of suds were spewing onto the floor from the washer with the bleach.

Tino jumped to shut down the washer and transferred the clothes to another. He felt eyes on him.

"You worry too much," Patrick said on the way back to the park.

"You shouldn't cuss so loud when there're people around."

"You're such a pussy."

"*Pinche guero.*"

"What's that mean?"

They dropped the damp laundry on a bench. Tino shook a T-shirt and laid it on the grass.

Patrick hung a pair of socks on the monument.

"What the heck are you doing, Pat?"

"They'll dry faster up here from the heat coming off the stone."

"It's not a good—"

"How many times do I have to tell you? We'll be out of here before anybody has a chance to do anything. Jesus, you're driving me fucking nuts!"

Patrick set his briefs over the inscription of Bowie's name. He was right about the hot stone: the clothes dried in minutes.

A man driving a rusting pickup truck with gun racks in the rear window stuck his head out. "That ain't a goddamn clothesline!" he yelled and sped off.

Patrick shrugged "hell with him." He took a wad of gum from his mouth and stuck it to the base of the monument.

"Pat!"

Patrick busted up, unwrapped two new sticks, and flung the wrappers toward a trashcan, missing the container by a foot. He went for his toolkit.

"Think you could figure out what's wrong with my headlight?" Tino said. "It turned off on me. I changed the fuse and it was okay, but I couldn't get it to work later, and then last night it worked just fine."

Patrick pressed the lead wire between his thumb and forefinger and followed it along the frame. "Aha! I can feel that it's frayed and the insulation's worn through. The wire's been shorting out when it shifts, and it grounds out on the frame. That's why it's been intermittent. I'll wrap it with electrical tape. You should replace the whole wire when you get home."

Sal walked up, sipping from a bottle of Dr. Pepper. "There're artifacts on display at the rear of the general store about Jim Bowie. He's quite the local hero."

Gary pulled up on his bike, with a long fat watermelon standing on end leaning up against his bare chest and held in place by a bungee cord hooked to his belt loops.

"Great idea!" Patrick said. He fished out a long and heavy hunting knife from his gear. "Give it to me and I'll cut it up." Patrick laid the melon on the grass and cut it into quarters.

Tino sank his teeth into the slice of watermelon that looked like a big red smile. "Man that's good. Perfect in this heat."

Sal inhaled deeply and spit out a seed that landed five paces off. Gary launched one just beyond. And the contest was on. The four ate watermelon and rocketed seeds.

Three state patrol cars with large black stars on their doors rode into town and formed a half circle corralling the bikes between the park and the shoulder of the road. The door of the lead car opened. A shiny black boot landed on the pavement. A massive barrel-chested lawman in a tan uniform and mirrored sunglasses emerged from the car, his face shadowed by a broad, white cowboy hat. The other lawmen exited their cars, slamming the doors behind them.

The giant approached Sal. "I sees all you all from Califonya."

"Yes, sir. Is there a problem, officer?"

"Ya'll got them goddamn war protesters out there, hippies and such, don't wanna cut they hair or wash up, smoking loco weed, taking all kind a drugs. Girls be burning up they brassieres, boys burning they draft cards and running off to Canada to keep from serving their country. White trash cowards, is what I think."

Tino trembled with fear.

"Y'all had trouble with your niggras few years ago in Los Angelees, burning up the city. Had to send in the National Guard. 'Round here if they gets uppity on us we just shoots 'em. You got no respect out that way, that's the problem. You got no respect for anything."

His backups leaned against their cars, hands at rest on their revolvers.

"Where you boys headed?"

"Dallas," Sal answered.

The lawman stepped up to Sal, swallowing Sal in his shadow. Sal stood his ground and looked up into the lawman's dark glasses. "We haven't done anything wrong, officer, and we'd like to get to Dallas."

The lawman stared menacingly into Sal's face. "You best not give me any lip, boah. Y'all was reported vandalizin' the laundry-mat and defacing Jimmy Bowie's shrine. You done come to the wrong place to raise hell."

A handful of townspeople had gathered by the monument to witness the interrogation of the filthy bikers. Tino recognized the man in the pickup truck with the gun racks standing to the front.

"You been here a good while, ain't ya?" The lawman said.

"I have no idea what you're talking about," Sal answered. "We've done nothing of the sort and—"

"Damn liar!" hollered the laundromat woman with the big hair rollers.

Sal looked confused. "I don't know what you're getting at, officer. Please tell me what you think we did."

"You deaf, boy? I just told you. Vandalizin' the laundry-mat and defacing the monument."

"No, you're wrong—"

"Liar!" yelled gun racks. "Give 'em some Texas justice."

The gathering had grown to at least a dozen—some muttering angrily.

The lawman raised a hand, demonstrating that he was in charge.

"We haven't vandalized anything, sir," Sal said.

Tino spoke weakly. "We put too much soap in the washers. Suds spilled on the floor. We're sorry."

"Well, you sure laughed about it," shouted big hair rolls.

"Wasn't funny," Patrick said in a small voice.

Sal glared at his little brother. "Did you think it was funny?"

"No."

"Did you clean up the mess?"

"No."

"Why not?"

"We didn't have anything to clean with."

"That's no excuse. Ma and Pa would not be happy with you right now. Did you deface the monument?"

"We hung clothes on it to dry," Patrick said, his face downturned.

"Anything else?"

"No," Tino said, praying that no one saw Patrick stick his gum on the monument. "We meant no disrespect."

Sal turned to the lawman. "Officer, I hope spilling suds on the floor and some foolish boys hanging clothes on a monument would not be taken as vandalism."

"Hanging your nasty-ass clothes on a shrine is defacing enough for me, and you jobless bums dressed up all raggedy and comin' to Texas thinking you can do whatever you please—"

Sal stiffened. "You're wrong there, sir! I am not a bum! I have a very good job. I'm on vacation, and this is the way I choose to dress. If you're ever in San Diego, stop in at Mercy Hospital and ask for Salvador Caballero, and you'll see just what kind of job I have."

The lawman leaned back, surprised. "Well, you'll have to talk to the magistrate." He nodded to a slightly hunched white-haired man dressed in a gray suit and string tie standing in front of the crowd. "Would you mind steppin' over here for a minute, Mister Travis?"

The old man looked at Sal dismissively. "I heard plenty enough. Y'all can pay a tin dollar fine for vandalizin' or spend the night in jail."

Sal pleaded his case. "Sir, we're good citizens. We meant no harm and—"

"I can make it another tin dollars for not wearing your motor-scooter helmets, if you keeps it up."

"They're not required in all states, sir, and we didn't know we had to wear helmets in Texas."

"Tin dollars or jail. Is all up to you."

Sal slumped his shoulders and reached for his wallet.

"You ought to make 'em pull down they pants and whip they asses," yelled hair rollers.

Laughter.

"You can get you a receipt for the fine at the post office up to five o'clock," the magistrate said. He walked off with Sal's bill in hand.

Sal spoke softly to Tino and the guys. "Ride out slowly."

The deputy nearest Tino grinned mean. "I'd get my raggedy ass back to Califonya if I was you."

The four mounted and started their bikes.

"You all come back an see us, you hear?" hollered hair rollers.

More laughter.

Sal, Tino, and the guys slowly slinked out of town like banished felons. Sal picked up speed as soon as they were out of sight of Bowie and rode for most of an hour before stopping at a Mobil station in Decatur. Sal stared hard at Tino. "I could buy enough gas to get to New York with that money. I can understand not knowing how much soap to use, but leaving a mess and hanging clothes on a monument? ¡*Válgame dios que tonteria, Chico!* (God almighty what foolishness, kid.)"

Tino's cheeks burned with embarrassment. "Why didn't you tell them you're a priest? It would've saved a lot of hassle."

Sal glared at him. "I didn't take my orders to catch breaks. And just because Catholic priests are respected where we come from doesn't mean they are down here. Those lawmen were Texas Rangers."

"So?"

Sal smacked his fist against his palm. "They were organized to kill Mexicans!"

"What?"

Sal unscrewed the gas cap and shoved the nozzle into the tank. "Most of the people here were Mexican Nationals after the war with Mexico, and Texans felt threatened. The Rangers were formed to harass, kill, and scare us off. What they refuse to accept is that we belong here." Sal didn't notice that the gas tank was near full. Tino pointed to it but Sal was on a roll. "We were here long before them, and have every right to be here. And those *mensos* think they can push me around? ¡*Qué se chingen!* (they can go and screw themselves)"

"Sal!" Tino yelled and pointed. Gas overflowed and spilled onto the engine producing toxic steam. Sal yanked out the nozzle, spraying a mist of gasoline over Patrick.

Patrick jumped back. "Hey!"

"¡*Híjole!* Sorry, *muchacho*," Sal said hanging the nozzle. He grabbed paper towels from the dispenser, dipped them in the water for windshields and patted Patrick's clothes.

Patrick stepped away. "It's okay, man."

"Weren't you scared of the big cop, Sal?" Tino asked. "I thought he was going to lay into you."

"What did I tell you in Flagstaff after our run-in with those jailbirds?"

"Don't show bullies fear."

"Good. That's what all that posturing was about. He was bullying. But then he called me a 'bum.' I don't have to take that crap from anybody. I only paid the fine because it wasn't worth losing a day fighting it. Texas justice, humph! Let's go."

Tino followed his older brother onto the road, bursting with pride.

14.

A Night in Dallas

THE RUSH-HOUR TRAFFIC into Dallas was a miserable, hot crawl, the air thick with exhaust fumes. Sal led them off the highway to a downtown motel where they rented a room for Sal and Tino, another for Gary and Patrick. "Meet out here after cleaning up," Sal said, "and we'll look for a place to eat."

LANDRY'S HOUSE OF RIBS was a five-minute walk from the motel. A cool wave of air, carrying the aroma of barbecue engulfed them as they entered through the tall glass doors. The dining room was filled with loud chatter and people dressed in Western-style clothes. Hat racks seemed to bow under the weight of cowboy hats in all sizes and colors. A life-size black and white picture of Tom Landry, the revered coach of the Dallas Cowboys, in his trademark suit and Fedora, occupied a wall in the reception area. The photo was taken during a game—on the sidelines, Landry is talking to his quarterback, Don Meredith.

A young waitress in blue jeans, silver cowboy-style blouse, white vest and hat greeted Sal, Tino, and the guys. "Haya doin'?" Her nametag read "Bobbie-Jo."

She sat them at a table made of shellacked mesquite wood and took their drink orders. She walked off, her blond ponytail bouncing cheerfully behind her.

"Cowboy chicks are foxy," Gary said.

"Yeah," Patrick said. "And Texas Rangers are dicks."

Tino and Gary cracked up. Sal leaned forward and spoke softly. "Not a good idea to use foul language so loudly in here. God-fearing Baptists might not be too bashful about letting us know how they feel about it. We've been through enough for one day."

"Jesus, I don't want to blow it again," Patrick said.

"Unless you're praying, I wouldn't use Jesus' name either."

"Son of a bitch, you're right," Patrick said in a loud whisper, keeping his pals laughing.

Sal shook his head. "*Ay, como eres travieso.* (You're so mischievous)"

"Is that good?"

The waitress returned with a tray carrying tall tumblers filled with ice and soda. She set the drinks on the table, tucked the tray under her arm, and jotted down their orders.

"Well, I'll tell you what," she said. "You boys 'bout to have the best darn barbecue y'all ever going to eat."

"Right on," Tino said.

The waitress winked at Tino and walked off.

"Hanging our clothes on that crummy monument wasn't a big deal and the Rangers knew it," Patrick said. "They only hassled us because we're from California."

Gary looked to Tino. "We should've told them that we're joining the Marines to fight Communists so jerks like them can have the freedom to hassle guys like us."

Tino cringed at Gary divulging their plan, knowing that Sal would have a problem with his taking such a risk.

"You're what?" Sal said.

"Somebody's got to stop the Commies," Gary said. "If they take Vietnam, then Thailand will fall, then Cambodia, and Laos, and it'll keep going until we're the only free country left."

"Ah, yes, the Domino Theory," Sal said. He turned to Tino. "How much thought have you given to enlisting?"

Tino didn't want to have to defend his decision in front of his friends, and tried to steer the conversation away. "I still think the Rangers were wrong."

Sal let it go. "Wouldn't you be offended if Southern guys hung their clothes on a statue of John Steinbeck or Luther Burbank?"

Patrick leaned forward. "Fuckin' A right, I would," he said busting up his friends.

Sal covered his face. "You're incorrigible. "

"Boy," Tino said. "I hope our run-in with that mob is the worst thing that happens to us on this trip."

"You guys go on to your room," Patrick said back at the motel. "There's still enough daylight for me to give the bikes a quick check over."

"You're a real asset to us," Sal said.

TINO KICK-STARTED HIS BIKE at eight the next morning ready to leave with Sal and the guys. He dropped the transmission into first, gave it gas, and released the clutch. Rocinante didn't move. "Aw, crap!"

"Now what?" Sal said.

Tino shifted into neutral, back into gear, and accelerated. Still nothing.

"Damn it!" he said, hopping off to check the engine. "I don't even know what to look for." He caught Gary and Patrick out of the corner of his eye, hiding laughter.

"All right, what's up?"

Patrick reached into his tool bag and held Rocinante's drive-chain over his head like a trophy.

"Did you see the look on Tino's face?" Gary said, laughing.

"Real funny, Pat," Tino said.

Sal forced a smile.

Patrick had the drive-chain on in moments. The four pulled out and headed for the first state of the Deep South, named after France's King Louis and Queen Ana.

15.

Louisiana

THREE HOURS INTO THE RIDE, Sal and crew passed a small, nondescript black-and-white sign with block lettering reading, CADDO PARISH.

The thirsty, late-summer gray chaparral of West and Central Texas had evolved into fuller foliage. Dusty soils of the semi-arid regions became darker and richer, the air heavy and sticky. They stopped at an Esso station on the outskirts of Shreveport.

Sal and Tino rolled to a pump island behind a mid-'50s Chevrolet sedan. A tall, lean Negro man in dark slacks, white dress shirt and black bow tie exited the car and took the gas nozzle.

"Not so fast there, boy." A short, middle-age attendant, with fat pink cheeks and a turned-up nose that exposed a set of dark tunnels for nostrils appeared from behind the pump. "Strom" was stitched over his uniform's breast pocket. He nodded toward the brothers "Show some respect," he said. His gums were sick purple.

The Negro man tightened his jaw, and offered Sal the hose.

"That's okay," Sal said. "Go ahead."

"You were here first," Tino said.

Strom tapped Sal's tire with his shoe. "I sees you boys are outta California."

"Yes, we sure are," Sal answered.

A leer smile spread across Strom's face. "Lots o' pussy out there."

"We've got lots of puppies too," Tino said.

Sal busted up. The Negro man bit his lip to keep from laughing.

"Go on," Strom said. "Get your gas before this here boy does."

The Negro then cradled the hose in his hands, as if pleading Sal to accept it.

The brothers got it. Things could get dicey if Sal didn't accept. "Well, thank you. That's very gracious of you."

Relief on the Negro man's face.

A new, long white Cadillac, driven by a white man in a white suit, pulled into another island.

Strom grabbed a squeegee and made for the car. "Get that windshield for you, sir?"

The Negro man spoke to Sal in a hushed tone. "I'm afraid it's just the way things are done down here." His voice was smooth as felt, and his eyes glistened deep black. The bridge of his nose was flat against his face, his graying goatee neatly trimmed. "We're working to change things down here, but for the time being it'll save trouble if we go along with it."

Sal offered his hand to the man, "Salvador Caballero."

Tino listened in as he filled the bikes.

The man took Sal's hand. "Frederick Washington. Pleasure to make your acquaintance."

"My training as a Catholic priest dictates that I treat people with respect; black, white, rich, poor."

The man chuckled. "And here I had you pegged for motorcycle gangsters. Do I call you Reverend or Father?"

"No, please, it's Sal. I'm on vacation. May I ask what you do for a living?"

"Trained as a lawyer, graduated Fisk in '53."

"Well," Sal said. "Between the two of us, we've got the law and the church covered."

Frederick chuckled.

"I'm sorry for the trouble you folks have had over all these years," Sal said.

"Thank you, but I'm used to it. I learned to keep my cool under fire in Europe in the second war. I've since learned to fight with law books. We'll win this war too. It's just a matter of time. Besides, we're not in the struggle alone. There are a lot of fine folks working with us: white, black, Northerners and Southerners. The opposition's lost. They just don't know it yet."

"I think that the entire world is on your side."

"Thank you. It helps hearing an encouraging word."

Tino finished filling the tanks and handed Frederick the hose. He excused himself, and pushed his bike to the rear of the station, where he found bathrooms with black and white doorknobs. He later joined Gary and Patrick waiting at the road. Sal and Frederick exchanged a bill for coins outside the gas station office before Frederick entered.

"He's a good man," Sal said joining the guys.

"I've never heard you tell someone that you're a priest," Tino said.

"I normally keep it to myself, but I felt simpatico with him."

"How so?"

"We're both minorities who've found some success in this society. His road's been much harder, considering what he's had to face."

"Why did you trade money?"

He didn't have the exact amount. He said he got short-changed by a white clerk once and when he called him on it, the clerk accused him of trying to steal from him and threatened to call the police.

"That's really fucked up," Patrick said.

"Been a pleasure," Frederick said in a loud voice. He stood by his car. "Hope to see you again."

Tino waved. Sal raised a thumb in an A-Okay.

"What do you say we take country roads south and tour the Bayou country," Sal said.

"Hell yeah," Patrick said. "Getting off the highway means I won't have to keep my engine maxed out all of the time trying to keep up with everybody. It's hard on the bike."

Over the next four hours they rode south through the parishes of Bossier, De Soto, Sabine, Beauregard, and Calcasieu. The vegetation thickened—the heat and humidity, tormenting.

They reached Lake Charles and headed east, riding through Jefferson Davis, Acadia, and Lafayette parishes. Gary veered off the road and ran through a mass of pale-green spider-web-like Spanish moss hanging from tree branches clear to the ground. A large piece broke off and fluttered behind him like a ragged cape.

Three heavyset black women sat in a tight circle on the porch of a shack, its walls sun-bleached gray. They stitched, with thread and needle, a quilt draped over their laps joining them as one. A dog lay at their feet. Chickens pecked along the roadside.

They rolled into a small rural town with a handful of modest businesses. Tino motioned to his mouth. Sal nodded and pulled in front of Leroy's BBQ.

"Did you see the women sewing back there at that shack?" Tino said.

Gary stretched his hands over his head. "I think that was a shanty."

"I wonder if it even had plumbing or electricity," Patrick said.

Sal did a deep knee bend. "It reminded me of some of the labor camps we lived in before the twins were born."

"Were we that poor?" Tino asked.

"Close. Real tough times for the family."

The porch creaked under their feet as they headed for the screen door. The aroma of sweet barbecue made Tino's head spin with want. Picnic tables lined three across and four deep filled the room. The floorboards were worn smooth. The lunch hour had passed, and the roadside diner seemed lonely for company.

A short, heavy-chested, light-skinned, balding Negro man, with alert green eyes and rosy cheeks, stood behind a long stainless steel counter stirring the contents of an iron pot big enough to hold a small pig. The man's head seemed too small for his protruding belly, thick arms, and bear-like torso.

"You boys makes yo selves right at home. Ole Leroy be fixin' whatever ya you like, long as it be ribs."

"Looks like we came to the right place," Tino said.

"Well you's bout to find out it's your lucky day, sho'nuff. Ain't nobody cooks ribs like Ole Leroy. Dat be a fact, and Leroy be me!"

He slid a stainless steel platter out of a tall and wide refrigerator and peeled back the tin foil revealing slabs of ribs with deep red sauce.

Etta James's voice rose softly from a radio on a counter, singing that she'd rather be blind than to see her lover walk away.

Leroy tapped the radio lovingly. "Oh, you sing it so sweet, baby girl."

Tino picked the table closest to Leroy. Leroy set hefty plastic glasses filled with ice cubes and a gallon-size pitcher of sweet iced tea on a tray and carried it to their table.

"Drinks all you please."

Limes sliced in half floated in the dark brew. He returned to the counter and talked as he prepared their meal.

"One o' the secrets is to put your ribs in sauce a day before you heats 'em up. Second is sauce. Barbecue without good sauce jus ain't barbecue, simple as dat. When I was young like you boys, I work for ole King Crisco. The best sauce man ever lived in Louisiana. Ole King-C, he put me to slicin' an choppin.' He don't want me to be learnin' his secrets, no sir. But I study his ingredients and how much a-dis and how much a-dat he be mixin' in. King-C, he look to see if I be spyin.' But I put my head down and chop away like I don't have a care about nothin' he be doin. He go back to makin' sauce and I look up to studying him. He look up. I look down." Leroy pantomimed his furtive movements.

"And that be the way how I come to learn his sauce making. Ole King-C, he be dead for some time now, but I got what I need. And this be the way of it."

The screen door squeaked open. A skinny light-skinned, gray-bearded Negro man in well-worn blue overalls entered.

Leroy smiled broadly. "Twigs, the bess shit-man in Louisiana! Whaz goin' on, brother?"

"Workin' hard, man." Twigs spoke slow and easy.

Leroy wiped his hands on his apron. "This be my friend, Roscoe Pamieé, but we just call his skinny-ass self 'Twigs.'"

Sal nodded. "I can tell Leroy knows what he's doing when it comes to ribs."

"Oh, he sho enough do," said Twigs, his beard bouncing with his jaw. "But some white folk, they be too proud to come into a black man's 'stablishment, no matter that he be a mulatto, like me. But that don't mean nothing to some people, is why they send somebody else to get some o' Leroy's fine ribs for them."

"Have you seen that happen?" Tino asked.

"Seen it? Sheeit, I done it! I be fixin' the white lady's leaking faucet some time back. She be married to that fat-ass lawyer who work at the Parish courthouse." Twigs put his hands on his hips and mimicked a snob. "'Oh my, what that is, that be smellin' so good?' So I tells her, 'I give you a piece of the truth, ma'am. That sweet smell be comin' from ole Leroy's. You can smell his sauce all over this town. I mean to say, Leroy's sauce, that smell is loud! Would you be wantin' me to git you some o those fine ribs, ma'am?'" Twigs sang in a lilt, "Ooh my, dat be lovely."

All laughed at the mini drama.

Leroy reached under the counter and brought up a wrinkly brown paper bag wrapping a bottle. He unscrewed the cap, raised it to his lips, and gulped. He wiped his mouth with a dishtowel and handed the bag to Twigs.

"These ribs are the best!" Tino said with a mouthful.

"And they're not real greasy," Sal said.

"The sauce isn't too spicy and it's sweet and tart at the same time," Patrick said.

"I'm not sure which I like better, Leroy," Tino said, "your stories or the ribs."

"Oh, it be the ribs, all right," Twigs said, raising the bag in a toast to Leroy.

"You can say that again," Patrick said.

Twigs lowered the bottle. "It be the ribs, all right."

Patrick laughed. "I didn't mean for you—"

"Jus fuckin' with ya, boy."

Tino elbowed Patrick, "Dumb ass."

Leroy slid out a platter with a wiggling glob of clear gelatin from the refrigerator. Suspended in the football-size mass were bits of animal flesh. "You might like to take a bit o' my headcheese. It be real fine on French bread."

"Thank you, but we don't have spare room," Sal said. "We'll try it on our way back."

"It be your loss," Twigs said.

Sal collected money from Tino and the guys and paid the tab.

A black mid-'40s flatbed truck with balding tires and a cracked windshield was parked next to the bikes. On the bed, was a black 2,500-gallon tank with a cartoon drawing of a man in overalls. He held a hose in one hand and a sandwich in the other. The inscription read,

"ROSCOE PAMIEÉ'S SEPTIC SERVICE - IT MIGHT BE SHIT TO YOU, BUT IT'S MY BREAD AND BUTTER."

"We need to head north if we're going to make it back by dark," Sal said.

They rode over bridges that spanned slow-moving, brackish streams, along swamps, and through a forest, the air sweetened with cypress. Tree branches formed a canopy over the road, blocking sunlight, and giving the feel of dusk.

Leroy's iced tea had worked its way through Tino's system and he needed to go. Maybe Sal would pull over soon for a pit stop, but a half hour later they were still hard at it. Each bounce in the road stabbed at Tino's sated bladder. He pulled up next to Sal, raised a finger and signaled for Sal and the guys to keep going.

Sal nodded. Tino hit the brakes, parked and rushed into the dense bush. He reached a bayou, pulled down his zipper with a trembling hand, closed his eyes, and the sweet release began. He counted his breaths to take his mind off the pain. His stream splashing into the water went on for twenty-two breaths; the pressure slowly eased.

"Ahh."

He opened his eyes. On the opposite side of the bayou was a decrepit mansion with the air of fallen splendor. A sign, hanging askew on the tall entry doors read, CONDEMNED.

Wild vines and vegetation had long since strangled Doric columns that supported the sagging roof of the porch and conquered the grounds. Towering magnolia trees hadn't been cared for in a lifetime. Raised flowerbeds, overrun by weeds, flanked each side of the moss-covered cobblestone entry.

Sharp movement over the water. A white egret, in the shallows of the bayou, had speared a fish and held it quivering at the end of its beak.

A duck flew low overhead. Its feet dropped as it landed on the water. A set of dark jaws with rows of pointed teeth appeared from out of the depths, snapped shut on the duck, and disappeared in a swirl of water. The egret escaped into the blue.

Tino zipped up, made a fast retreat to Rocinante, and sped off. What kind of monster got the poor duck? The answer soon came when he passed a yellow road sign with the black silhouette of an alligator. He raced to Sal and the guys. Over the next three hours they rode through woodlands, over waterways, passed the towns of Vidalia and Ferriday, and reached Tallulah, in the northeast corner of the state where they headed east.

16.

A Three-Legged Mutt

TALL STEEL TOWERS OF A BRIDGE loomed above treetops. Curious since they weren't approaching a city. Tino and company came to a wide body of mud-brown water. A sign read, MISSISSIPPI RIVER.

Rocinante's tires hummed on the steel grating of the half-mile long bridge. Wide barges, laden with cargo, navigated slowly on the water below.

Tino stared at the river—more fresh water than he had ever seen in one place. He followed Sal off the end of the bridge onto a narrow dirt road toward the river. They pulled over and parked on dry, packed silt.

Tired of riding, Tino tried to plant a seed on the walk to the riverbank. "Great spot for camping, huh Sal?"

Sal sat on a small dusty rise to take off his boots. "I want to say I waded in the Mighty Mississippi."

The four walked on tender feet through knee-high weeds. The silt softened with moisture as they neared the bank.

They stepped into the muddy water. "Feels good in this heat," Tino said.

Sal squatted on his haunches, his butt barely clearing the water. "We've just crossed the third largest river in the world, and we're over half way across the continent."

"Cool," Tino said.

Gary and Patrick slogged upstream looking for a spot to pee out of the view of traffic on the bridge.

"You were home from the seminary on summer vacation once, and you took Val and me to get library cards," Tino said as he squatted next to Sal.

"Sure, I remember. You guys checked out *The Adventures of Tom Sawyer* and *Huckleberry Finn*, right?"

"Yeah. Mr. Gray, the man I bought the bike from, was my American Lit teacher. He explained to us how Mark Twain used the river to represent time passing. Huck matured as he rafted downstream and became a man."

Sal grinned. "Nice analysis, Chico."

"We're on a river too," Tino said. "It's a river of asphalt."

"Ha, good one!"

Tino beamed. For the first time, he was the teacher. "Maybe we're becoming men as we travel it."

"I'm twenty-nine," Sal said. "If I'm not a man yet, I may never make it."

The guys sloshed back. "There're two boys back there," Gary said pointing upstream. "They were swinging from a rope tied to a tree branch and plunging into the river buck naked."

"Ha! Right on," Tino said. He raised his arms in a long slow stretch. "Set up camp, Sal?"

Sal rose to his feet and headed for the bank. "Not yet."

"Jeez, Sal."

"Don't you ever get tired?" Patrick said. "I'm about ready to crash out for the night.

"If we're going to make the trip during my vacation time, we've got to stay on schedule." Sal searched out a map from his gear. "We'll continue on Route 80 to Morton where there're campgrounds. It's only seventy-five miles away. We may not make it by nightfall, but we'll make good headway, even after touring the bayou country."

"Only seventy-five miles away," Tino smirked.

They rode through Vicksburg in late afternoon and came to a dirt road in a wrecked neighborhood. Old tires, broken toys, beer, and soda bottles—labels sun-bleached and peeling—littered the roadside. A lonely rusting refrigerator sat in a yard. In another, a '30s vintage pickup truck, stripped of wheels, doors, and fenders sat on wood blocks. Dry weeds waved on a hot breeze where there once was a windshield. A chicken with a rooster in hot pursuit ran down the road.

A middle-age white man in threadbare pants and soiled undershirt stood on a sagging porch, staring at the bikers passing the house. Sal threw his hand into the air in a friendly wave. The man stared, stone faced. A three-legged mutt bolted off the porch, barking and snarling. The man grinned—dark gaps between teeth.

The dog headed for Tino. He raised his boot and reared back hard catching it under the jaw. It yelped, flipped into the air, and landed on the road in a swirl of dust. The four made haste out of the neighborhood and rode until dusk, when they pulled to a pump island at a gas station.

Patrick dismounted and slapped Tino on the back. "That was cool, dude. The dog was going to get you, but you got him."

"It was either him or me."

Two men strolling along the road caught Tino's eye—one, a thin, pasty-white, middle-aged, cadaverous looking individual; the other, Tino's age, trim at the waist, muscular, white-blonde hair in a military-style crew cut and dressed in a T-shirt with green Army camouflage pants. He elbowed Pasty-White, and they strolled over stopping in front of Sal and Tino's bikes. Gary and Patrick had parked behind them.

"How ya'll doin'?" Pasty-White said. Overhead fluorescent lights blinked on, brightening the dim light of dusk.

"Name's Cal." He patted the young stud's shoulder. "This'd be Brotha."

All nodded.

Across Brother's T-shirt was a drawing of a human skull, a bullet hole between the eyes; above it, M-1 rifles forming an X. The inscription read "One Less Gook."

"Looks like you been travelin' for a good spell," Cal said.

"California," Tino said. "Going to New York."

Brother raised his eyebrows. "Well, fuck me runnin'!"

These men looked like Southern racists out of a movie. Deeply curious to hear their opinions, Tino tossed a little bait. "I understand you have a lot of Negroes here, but I don't see many around."

Cal spit a stream of tobacco juice into the street. "Cuz it ain't 'niggah-day.'"

"Ain't what?"

"Niggah-day, man! Is when coons can come to town and do they shoppin' and what have you. But they know they better not get caught 'round here after dark."

Brother sniggered.

Intrigued, Tino pressed on. "Have you had much trouble with them?"

Two attendants walked out of a repair bay, one of medium height and build, the other short and muscular. Both wore crew cuts.

"They's been gettin' a little uppity lately," Cal said, "what with all they gotdamn protestin'. Gotta string one up in de niggah tree every now and then to keep 'em in line. Just ask de Revren' Mahhtin Luthuh King Joonyah." He pronounced the name with mocked reverence. "Tell you what, ole Jimmy Ray up theah in Tennessee give that boy what he got comin'."

Fiendish laughter from Cal, Brother, and the short, muscular attendant.

None of the bikers laughed.

"Y'all ain't niggah lovers, are ya?" Cal said with a hard look. A shred of wet tobacco seeped out of his mouth onto his lower lip. Cal wiped it with his long bony fingers.

Tino froze with fear. Sal pressed up against his shoulder glaring at Cal and Brother. "We don't dislike people who've done nothing wrong to us," Sal said.

"I get it," Brother said, staring at Sal. "Y'all are niggah lovahs. You look half niggah yaself."

Tino tightened his bladder to keep from going in his pants.

"Mostly Mexican," Sal said. "But you look one hundred percent Mississippi jackass."

"Ha!" Patrick laughed.

Brother quaked with rage and kicked the Hawk's front tire, jolting it.

Tino sprang, spearing his shoulder into Brother's abdomen.

"Oomph!" Brother doubled over.

Tino wrapped his arms around thighs, lifted and drove Brother to the ground. His head hit the concrete floor with a sickening thud. Brother's fingers, digging at Tino's back, went limp. His eyes rolled back in his head and closed.

The short muscular attendant went for Tino.

"Crack!" Gary's huge fist smashed into his jaw. The attendant's head snapped back, knees buckled, and he dropped.

Sal grabbed his canteen by the strap and spun it over his head. "All right!" he screamed, eyes on fire. "Who's next?"

Gary glared, his fists at the ready.

Patrick appeared next to Gary, in a crouch and leading with his hunting knife; the long blade gleaming under the lights. Cal and the last standing man stepped back.

Tino rose to his feet and stared down at Brother wondering if he'd killed Brother, but his eyes opened. "What happened?" he said, his words slurred. He rolled over to his chest and rose unsteadily to his feet. He took a wobbly step toward Tino and stood nose to nose. Brother reeked of body odor.

Tino didn't flinch. *Don't show fear. Don't show fear.*

Brother stared menacingly into Tino's eyes. Tino held. Brother blinked. Brother stepped back and squatted, putting his hands to his temples. "Oh mah head."

"Ain't no use in callin' these boys names, Brotha," an attendant said. "Jus cause they see things different, they's got a right to their opinions."

Brother growled. "Shut ya damn mouth."

Sal lowered the canteen. "I'd get him to a doctor."

Brother walked unevenly toward the station office, hands pressed tight to his temples. "This ain't over."

A thread of blood oozed down Brother's neck, staining his shirt.

The short muscular attendant rose, ran his forearm across his bloody mouth and glared at the bikers. He pointed a stiff finger at Gary. "We gonna have us a big time later. Jus you wait an see."

The four mounted and started their bikes. Patrick revved Peewee's engine. It gave a pathetic whine and spewed a small puff of smoke.

Tino led them out and stopped when they were out of sight of Cal and Brother. "They're most likely rounding up some guys and coming after us. We need find a place to lay low for the night."

"Then what?" Patrick said.

"Get out before dawn."

A mile out, Tino turned onto a dirt road that led up a hill into woods. They passed a complex of dilapidated wooden structures. Dozens of vehicles surrounded a large old barn at the far end. The barn's windows emanated a golden glow into the darkness.

Tino rode to the crest of the hill. "We should be safe enough here until we slip out."

"You kicked Brother's ass good," Gary said, parking next to Tino.

Tino unhooked the bungee cords from his sleeping bag. "I didn't kick his ass. I pulled a wrestling move on him and he hit his head. If it would've been a real fight, he probably would've killed me."

"Naw, man," Patrick said. "You could've taken him. You're strong. I saw how Coach worked you guys out on the wrestling team."

"Wrestling wouldn't be much help in an all-out street fight. I never would've tried taking on such a big guy, but I lost it when he went after Sal. I wish Coach could've seen me though. I could hear him. Shoulder to abdomen! Hands around thighs! Lift! Drive! Drive! Drive! He would have been proud."

Sal put an arm around Tino's shoulders. "I'm proud of you, *hermano* (brother). I'll have you next to me in a tight spot anytime. You held your ground against a tough bully who was doing his best to intimidate you." A wave of emotion welled up in Tino's chest with his big brother's praise.

"Thanks for taking out the guy who came after me, Gary," Tino said.

Patrick elbowed Gary. "You popped him good, man."

"Why do they hate black people so much?" Tino said.

"Cal and Brother were okay until they realized that we didn't hate niggers like them," Patrick said. "I mean I don't hate 'em all. There's good ones and bad ones, like anyone else."

"I'd rather we didn't use that word," Sal said.

"I don't mean anything by it."

"I gotta take a leak," Tino said. He walked off and relieved himself by a tree overlooking the road. A sheriff's cruiser appeared creeping along the road. The stark-white beam of its spotlight cut through the night as if its passengers were searching for something. The passenger in the sheriff's car wore a camouflage T-shirt and had a bloodstained bandage wrapped around his head. A rickety pickup truck with a burned out headlight, looking like a Cyclops, followed close behind. Tino ducked back and then peered around the tree trunk. Three men sat in the cab of the truck. At least a half dozen stood on the bed, bats and clubs at the ready. The short muscular attendant that Gary had decked, stood leaning his chest against the cab of the truck, looking ahead scanning the roadsides—a rope coiled around his shoulder.

Dark fear engulfed Tino. He leaned against the tree to steady himself, head spinning. He kept an eye on the cruiser and truck until they went up and over a rise.

"Brother and a gang are hunting us," Tino said, interrupting Sal and the guys' grim conversation.

Scared stares.

"How do you know?" Sal said.

"I saw Brother with a truckload of guys following a sheriff's car, searching the sides of the road."

"Son of a bitch," Patrick whispered. "Did they see you?"

"No."

"How many were there?" Sal asked.

"At least ten."

"We're going to have to leave long before sunlight," Sal said.

Patrick stood up. "I say that we go into the woods and find tree branches in case we have to fight 'em tonight."

The four went in with flashlights. Back at camp Tino tore twigs off of his branch and practiced attacking with it. Patrick took his hunting knife and sharpened the ends of everyone's branches into sharp points.

Tino unrolled his sleeping bag with a sense of doom. Sheriff's Deputies must be on alert, anxious to avenge Brother, who had been viciously attacked by a biker gang out of California. When they tried to sneak out, even one at a time, a sheriff would surely catch sight of one of them setting off a series of events that would end at Cal and Brother's 'niggah tree.'

Tino turned a fearful ear toward the sound of a vehicle approaching below. The hum of the engine grew, peaked, and faded as it passed. He sighed in relief.

Upbeat piano music, singing and hands clapping in rhythm rose from down the hill.

"Some kind of church service," Sal said. "It must be coming from one of those old buildings we passed on the way up."

"They sound happy," Tino said.

"I'll bet it's a black Southern church service," Sal said. "I'd like to go and check it out."

"Jeez, Sal," Tino said. "Why do you have to be so curious all the time? What if those guys see you?"

"The buildings are halfway up the hill. I don't think that they can be seen from the road."

Gary stuck his branch into the ground. "I'm not going anywhere."

"Me neither," Patrick said.

"I don't want you to go alone, Sal," Tino said.

"I don't need protection, but I'd like to have you along." Tino looked to the guys. "I'll scream if we need help."

17.

Sunday's a-comin'!

THE DRIVE-CHAINS RATTLED SOFTLY on their sprockets as Sal and Tino coasted their motorcycles downhill. They came on the dilapidated wooden buildings and parked. F. Douglas School, was painted over the entrance to a one-room schoolhouse, barely visible in the darkness.

The music and singing that they had heard came from the large barn at the far end of the handful of buildings.

They came to the next structure. MARION'S HARDWARE AND GENERAL STORE, painted on its facade. They crept up and peeked through a window. A naked, low-wattage light bulb, hanging by a single wire from the ceiling cast a shadowy light over the expansive room. Stoves, ringer washers, refrigerators, and farm tools: hoes, axes, shovels, and pitchforks occupied most of the floor space. Lines of gunnysacks, bulging with what appeared to be grains and root crops, leaned against the walls. A counter for serving customers stretched the length of the front of the room. Behind the counter were shelves stacked with supplies.

Sal spoke in a low voice. "Let's go see the service."

"Whoo!" An owl, perched in a tall, dark fir tree, pierced the intruders with a hard stare. They continued on to the barn. The walls seemed to vibrate with music. Sal pointed out a cross erected on the roof. They passed lines of vehicles and stopped between a shiny royal blue '58 Buick Century convertible with gleaming white upholstery and a beat-up, black, two-ton flatbed truck with sideboards of splintered plywood concealing its cargo. The odor of chicken manure, and a hen's nervous cluck gave it away.

They peered over the Buick's hood through a window. Negro men in suits, and women in dresses and hats, some with meshed veils covering their eyes, filled the pews. An overflow crowd lined the walls. Everyone bounced, singing and clapping their hands in rhythm. A heavyset man in a deep red robe faced the gathered. His silver-white hair reflected the overhead lights turning his hair into a halo. To his side at a piano, a thin, wiry man, his fingers tickling the ivories.

"Good evening, Father Caballero."

Standing behind Sal and Tino, his graying goatee upturned in a smile, was tall, lean Frederick Washington, the man they had met earlier at the gas station.

Sal put a hand over his heart. "You scared the devil out of me."

Tino leaned against the chicken truck breathing deeply.

Frederick chuckled. "I suppose if I'm going to scare someone, it's best at the devil's expense."

"We're camping nearby and heard the music," Sal said. "We wanted to see the service. Are you a member of this congregation?"

"Yes. Our little barn-church has more spirit than any church I've ever attended, even in larger parishes. And don't worry about eavesdropping. I assure you, no offense will be taken."

"What do you mean?"'

"You and your brother." Frederick's forehead furrowed as he gestured toward Tino. "I apologize, but I don't know that I got your name."

"Tino, sir."

"Happy to know you. Reverend Coffey, our pastor, asked me to invite the two men outside to join us."

"But how'd he know we—"

"The Reverend has the gift of the sixth sense."

"We're not very well dressed."

"It's a safe bet that Our Lord's followers weren't well dressed, either, and I promise to keep your being a priest to myself."

Sal looked to Tino. Tino shrugged.

"Shall we?" Frederick ushered them to the tall barn door and slid it open. Music stopped. The cavernous room quieted. All eyes turned to Frederick and the two young men, scruffy as bums. Women fanned their faces; men used their hats. Two boys in the loft lying on bales looked down on the service. Tino smiled at them. They smiled back, their big white teeth shone against their black skin.

Reverend Coffey's baritone voice filled the room. "Welcome, brothers."

Frederick patted his guests' shoulders. "Fine men. I met them at a service station this afternoon. The attendant ordered me to allow Mr. Caballero to pump his gasoline before me even though I had gotten there first. But Mr. Caballero refused and only relented on my insistence. The attendant didn't know what to make of it."

Applause.

Tino shifted with unease.

A gangly, bearded man, sitting in a pew next to the brothers, said something to the man next to him. They stepped out of the pew and offered them their seats.

"No, thank you," they said simultaneously, having been raised to give up chairs, not accept them.

"You showed kindness to one of our brothers, a stranger to you," the Reverend said. "Now allow strangers to return the favor. For whatever ye shall sow, so shall ye reap."

"Amen!" A woman's voice rang out. "Tell it like it is, Reverend!"

Sal bowed in a gesture of thanks and elbowed Tino into the pew. Tino wound up next to a man a head taller than him, dressed in a dirt-colored well-worn suit, jacket stretched tight across his massive chest and shoulders.

Reverend Coffey raised his hands drawing attention to himself. "Brothers and sisters, we all have trials. No one is immune from them. You all have trials, and the Good Lord knows I have had my share. He sees fit to send them, not so much to test our wills, but to temper us for this arduous journey called life."

A man hollered, "Oh yes, Reverend!"

The Reverend closed his eyes. "We have trials that at times seem so heavy that a team of oxen could not pull them along. We, as a people, have a great burden to bear for our Shepherd. Brother Martin has been taken from us at the hand of an assassin.

"When I am faced with such trials—when the load feels too much for me to bear—I see Brother Jesus. I see him praying mightily in the Garden of Gethsemane. Do you think He realizes that it is over for Him?" The Reverend panned the room. "Yes, brothers and sisters. He realizes it is over for Him. For He knows that the centurions are at hand. He can all but hear their footsteps approaching. He knows that they are coming to take Him away, to be whipped like a slave, to be cursed at and spat upon like the vilest of criminals, and that He will be tortured until His soul departs His mortal body. I see Him so afraid, so taken by despair, that instead of sweat, blood seeps from the pores of his brow."

The Reverend continued in a hushed tone. "And why? It's because it's Friday. But I tell you," his voice rose "Sunday's a comin'. It's Friday and Jesus is a prayin' and Peter is a sleepin'. Judas is betrayin' but I tell you, Sunday's a comin'.

"It's Friday, and Pilate is struggling, the Sanhedrin is conspiring, the crowd is vilified; they don't even know that Sunday's a comin.'"

"Well, pastor," said a woman. "Well, well, well."

Reverend's voice grew stronger. "It's Friday and the disciples are runnin' in every direction like sheep without their shepherd, Mary's cryin', Peter's denyin', but they don't know that Sunday's a comin.'"

The congregation stirred with sporadic cheering and clapping.

The Reverend, feeding off the congregation's vibe, raised his voice and picked up his tempo.

"Oh, it's Friday, and the Romans they beat my Jesus, they robe Him in scarlet, they crown Him with thorns, and Jesus is walkin' to Calvary, His blood drippin', His body's stumblin' and His spirit's burdened, but that's because it's Friday."

"Keep goin' pastor! Keep goin'!"

"Today it's Friday and the world is winnin' people are sinnin', and evil's grinnin'. The soldiers nail my Savior's hands to the cross. They nail my Savior's feet to the cross. They raise him up between condemned criminals because it's Friday, and the disciples are questioning, 'What has happened to our King?' And the Pharisees are celebrating that their scheming has been achieved.

"It's Friday. He's hanging on the cross, feeling forsaken by his Father, left alone and filled with doubt because it's Friday! But what?" The Reverend pointed to the congregation.

"Sunday's a comin!" They cheered and laughed and raised hands into the air.

"It's Friday and the temple veil is ripped from top to bottom the earth is shakin', the rocks splittin'.

The Reverend quieted and spoke in a somber and defeated tone. "It's Friday and the earth trembles, the sky grows dark, my King yields his spirit and hope is lost; and death has won, sin has conquered, and Satan's laughin'. Jesus is buried, a soldier stands guard, and a rock is rolled into place. And people are saying, 'As things have been, so they shall always be. You can't change a thing.' And Satan's doing his little jig saying, 'The world is mine!'"

The Reverend's face sparkled with beads of sweat. His eyes closed for a moment before they slowly opened. "Friday!" he roared

"Sunday's a comin'!" the members of the barn-church screamed, and erupted with cheers and riotous laughter.

The piano man hit the keys. The congregation rose to its feet bouncing and hugging in joyous victory. The giant next to Tino embraced him and lifted him a foot off the ground. Something popped in Tino's spine.

Reverend Coffey raised his hands and waited until the congregation quieted.

"When those trials come, my brothers and sisters, no matter how ominous, no matter how heavy, they will always be followed by a sweet and blessed Sunday."

He looked to a tall, heavyset woman sitting in the front. "Sister Sarah, take us home." She stood and made her way to the Reverend. He gave a nod to the piano man, "Brother Reginald."

Reginald wiped his face with a handkerchief and played a sweet and tender tune. Sister Sarah swayed from side to side, waiting for the music to come around. She dabbed her forehead with a hanky and sang. Her powerful voice filled the barn-church. The song ended with the final verses: "He promised us deliverance, oh brothers and sisters, yes indeed.

He promised deliverance. Our sorrows be but a while, but our freedom, oh brothers and sisters, shall be forever more, sweet Lord, our freedom shall be forever more."

The service came to an end.

Well-wishers surrounded Sal and Tino, standing in the aisle, shaking their hands, and welcoming them. The giant who had been next to Tino, brought a woman forward. "I's Benjamin," he said, offering his massive hand.

"Pleased to meet you," Tino said and offered his hand. Benjamin's hand swallowed Tino's. He expected it to be crushed, but Benjamin was gentle.

"This be Miss Lizzie," Benjamin said. Lizzie was a bit shorter than Tino, but could have been twice his weight. Her dress barely contained her bulging breasts and hips.

He offered his hand. But still brimming with the spirit of the sermon, Lizzie wrapped her hot damp arms around Tino and squeezed him breathless. "You was kind to a black man. May it be returned a hundredfold, baby."

"Thank you, ma'am."

"You's good men," Benjamin said. "What be your names?"

"I'm Tino." He pointed to Sal, engaged in conversation with a parishioner. "He's my big brother, Sal."

Benjamin laughed. "You bigger'n him, but he's your big brotha!"

Lizzie winked at Tino and licked sweat from her upper lip. "You come back an' see us anytime, baby."

"Yes, ma'am."

"You so fine with your yes sirs, and yes ma'ams. You sweet as molasses."

Frederick's voice came from behind. "I see you've met Benjamin and Miss Lizzie, Mr. Tino."

"Yes, sir."

Frederick reached for Sal's arm. "Excuse me for the interruption, but Reverend would like to meet you and Mr. Tino."

"I'd be honored," Sal said.

Benjamin and Lizzie followed them to the front. "Thank you for your graciousness with Mr. Frederick today," Reverend Coffey said and offered his hand.

Sal took it. "Just trying to live the word, Reverend."

"You sound like a minister."

Sal glanced at Frederick.

Frederick winked.

Sal bowed. "Father Salvador Caballero at your service."

Frederick chuckled.

"Well, my, my," Lizzie said. "A preacher man, and dressed like this."

The Reverend scratched his head. "And just how did you manage getting your bishop's permission to tour about on a motorbike and dressed, how shall I say it. Casually?"

"Simple, I didn't ask for permission."

Reverend Coffey's laughter bounced off the barn-church's walls and ceiling.

Sal continued, "A priest in the diocese bought a motorcycle some years back. The bishop got wind of it and made him get rid of the bike, so I figured I had better keep mum if I was going to pull off this trip." Sal narrowed his eyes and spoke in a mocked threat. "So none of you had better snitch on me."

"Well, Father Caballero," Reverend Coffey said, "if you're found out, it won't be because of me. And how is your touring going?"

"Interesting," Sal said.

Tino shook his head. "Too interesting."

Frederick raised an eyebrow. "How so?"

Sal told them of their run-in with Cal and Brother. Everyone knew of them. Cal had been implicated in the brutal killing of a Negro however; the sheriff's investigation found the death to be accidental.

Reverend Coffey ushered the group to his office located behind the altar. He had them form a circle and join hands. "Lord," he prayed, "we ask Your help in this time of trial. Infuse us with Your wisdom. Help us to deliver our brothers from harm. And though we walk in the valley of death, we fear no evil for You are our shepherd."

"Now," the Reverend said, "we need to get these gentlemen away from here quickly and unseen. The question is how?"

"We're planning on leaving before dawn," Sal said.

"The sheriff will undoubtedly have an alert out claiming you assaulted Brother," Frederick said. "You won't be safe until you're out of Mississippi."

The group stood in an uneasy silence.

Lizzie raised her head. "I gots it. My man can do it!"

The Reverend furrowed his brow. "How so?"

"He sneaks the boys to Alabama in his truck."

The Reverend put a hand to his chin. "Ben's truck is certainly big enough to fit four men and motorbikes. The bed is hidden from view by the siding."

"You men were by Ben's truck when I found you," Frederick said.

Benjamin spoke nervously. "It be the one with the chickens."

Reverend Coffey read Benjamin's face. "Brother Ben, are you right with this?"

"I wouldn't want you to take such a chance on our behalf," Sal said.

Lizzie leaned her head against Benjamin's chest. "You fine with it, ain't you baby?" Benjamin nodded weakly.

Lizzie rose to her toes, pulled Benjamin's head down, and kissed him. "I's so proud of my man."

Logistics were discussed and a plan was hatched.

"WHAT IN THE HELL TOOK YOU GUYS SO LONG?" Gary said when they showed up.

"You were only going to take a quick look," Patrick said. "We thought you were lynched."

"Sorry," Sal said. "They invited us to join the service. Get to sleep; we're getting up early."

Tino turned in and stared into the starry night, the day's events roiling through his mind; the inexplicable hate that Cal and Brother had for Negroes. And how bad the barn-church people had it here, and yet they were filled with goodness and celebrated with such joy. He drifted off imagining himself worshiping in the barn-church, singing and clapping his hands in rhythm.

18.

Out of Pharaoh's Egypt

T INO LAY IN RESTIVE SLEEP before dawn when he heard dry leaves rustling. "They're coming!"

Gary and Patrick jumped out of their bags, branches in hand.

Sal walked out of the woods, pulling up his pants zipper.

"Ay, Sal!" Tino said breathing hard. "You scared the *mierda* out of me."

"Sorry," Sal said, stifling laughter. "Glad you're on your toes. Time to get to the church."

"Church?" Gary said.

"What're we going to do?" Patrick said. "Pray our way out of this mess?"

"Trust us," Tino said. "We need to go, and now."

They packed hastily and coasted the bikes down the hill to the complex in the predawn. Tino could barely make out the three figures at the barn-church in the dim light: tall, lean Frederick, round Reverend Coffey with his gleaming white hair, and Goliath-like Benjamin, next to his truck with its four-foot high sideboards surrounding the bed. One sideboard was off and leaning against a rear fender.

"Who are they?" Patrick asked.

"Yeah," Gary said.

"Met them last night," Sal said.

Tino pushed his bike toward the church. "Just follow us."

"Good morning, Mr. Tino," Frederick said. "These must be the other men on your trip."

"Gary and Pat," Tino said. "And we can't thank you enough for doing this for us."

Frederick nodded toward Benjamin. "Thank him."

"You're taking an awfully big chance," Sal said.

Frederick patted Sal on the shoulder. "White folks took great chances on our behalf with the Underground Railroad."

"I wish there was a way that we could pay you back," Tino said and held out a few folded bills. "Please accept a little gas money." Sal reached for his wallet, but Benjamin raised a hand.

"It already be taken care of, suh."

"This is too much," Tino said. His voice broke with emotion, "and please don't call me sir."

"It's the Lord's work," Reverend Coffey said. "We are but His instruments."

"We best get the motorbikes loaded," Benjamin said. "We's got a bit of a ride since I be sneakin' round back roads." He lifted Rocinante with a grunt and set him on the truck.

"Whoa!" Gary said. "I'd never be able to lift that bike by myself."

Frederick chuckled. "I'm glad Ben's on our side."

Benjamin loaded the other bikes and pointed to a coil of rope on the truck. "Best to tie 'em up so's they don't be movin' around." Patrick climbed onto the bed of the truck and got to it.

Sal handed Reverend Coffey, Frederick, and Benjamin slips of paper. "This is an invitation to California. We'll show you around."

"You can show gratitude by helping those in need whenever you're afforded the opportunity," the Reverend said.

"Yes, of course," Sal said climbing on board with Gary. "It's what we're called to do, right? I've learned more about love from you folks since last night than I did in eight years of study in the seminary."

"Oh, that remind me," Benjamin said. He went to the cab and returned with a shopping bag and handed it to Tino. "Miss Lizzie send this along for y'all."

Tino peered in. "My God, food, and a lot of it. Please thank her."

Benjamin nodded and set the sideboard onto the truck, hiding his passengers from view, and secured the latch. He climbed into the cab. The truck rocked with Benjamin's weight. He turned the key but the engine only groaned. He tried again and again.

The cab door opened and the hood squeaked open.

Tino, Sal, and the guys passed nervous glances. What if the truck didn't start?

There were several taps against the engine before the hood slammed shut. This time the engine cranked.

Bang!

Backfire; loud as a rifle shot. The truck started and trembled like an old man. Gears ground, tires rolled. The bikes and sideboards shook as they bumped downhill.

They sat on the hard-packed chicken manure with their backs against the cab. The air smelled of exhaust. The sun cleared the horizon, sending a needle of sunlight through a slit between boards and onto Rocinante's spokes. They gleamed for a second, yet it felt as if time had slowed, and as if at any moment, this scheme would unravel and all would come to a horrific end.

They reached the asphalt road, and the ride became smooth.

"How'd you work this out?" Patrick asked Tino.

"We met them at the service last night and told them what happened with Cal and Brother afterward, and they came up with this plan."

"God bless 'em," Gary said.

Tino stood in a crouch to keep below the sideboards and peered out a slit. Were there any clues of where they were in relation to the state line. Fruitless, all he could see was the uneven tar-patched road, the blur of green shrubbery, and the miserable shacks of the poor. He gave up and sank to sit with the others.

Tino opened the bag that Lizzie had sent—what appeared to be sandwiches wrapped in paper napkins and two quart-size canning jars with a drink containing slices of lemon. He took a jar and sandwich and passed the bag. Wrapped in the napkin was a square of cornbread cut in half, spread with mayonnaise and filled with fried pork rinds.

Tino washed down a bite of sandwich with a drink from the jar. "Lemonade's sweet, like my Ma makes it." He ate a second sandwich and leaned back against the cab, tired from stress and lack of sound sleep. The rhythmic rocking and drone of the engine lulled him to sleep. He dreamed that he and Rocinante were speeding toward the cliff at the end of the world. Hitting the brakes did no good. Rocinante headed straight toward the cliff.

A screaming siren wrenched him awake, and the truck slowed.

Tino crawled to the rear and peered out. "Sheriff! Up against the sides, away from gaps!"

Sal: "Crap!"

Gary: "Shit!"

Patrick: "We're fucked!"

The truck stopped. Doors opened and slammed shut. Benjamin met the sheriff at the side of the truck, scarcely an arm's length away from Tino.

"Where ya goin', boy?"

"A-Alabama, suh."

"You know your license plate expired?"

"No, suh."

"How's come you let it expire?"

"Don't take it much off the farm, suh."

"Ain't legal to be driving 'round without a rear bumper either, an' you got a tire bald as a newborn. Don't you know you risking public safety with this piece a shit on the road? Whatchya hauling?"

"F-furniture, suh."

"Furniture?"

"Yes suh, for my boss. He, he be moving to Alabama."

"Why you so nervous? Let's have a little look-see."

"The boss, he say, don't show nobody, suh."

The sheriff peered in, casting a sharp slice of his shadow on the floor between boards. "You hauling clothes too? I see boots in there."

"Yes, suh. Boss's clothes and furniture."

"You tellin' the truth, boy?"

Silence.

"I'd think that any straight-thinking coon wouldn't be straying so far from the lair. You ain't lying to me, are you, boy?"

"No, sir. Boss, he say don't show nobody."

The sound of steel sliding against leather. The shadow of the sheriff's arm rising. Clack. A revolver cocked.

"You nothing but a goddamn lying nigger. World be better off without lying black-asses like you. Open up."

"Y-yes, suh."

Crunch, crunch, crunch. Gravel underfoot to the rear of the truck. Snap. A latch turned. The sideboard vibrated as Benjamin shimmied it up.

"APB, APB, all units, 10-31, armed robbery in progress. Deputy wounded, Mississippi State Bank, Meridian." The anxious voice of a dispatcher blared over the radio. "10-31 in progress, all units respond immediately, Mississippi State Bank, Meridian, deputy wounded."

Boots landed on gravel as the sheriff ran back to his car. "Get your black-ass back to your farm." Door slammed. Siren wailed. Tires squealed.

Tino closed his eyes. "*Hijo.*"

Sal leaned against a sideboard for support. "That was too close, Ben,"

"I's nervous for a bit, suhs."

Gary slid to the floor. "I thought we were dead. If we would've tried to run for it, we'd get shot in the back. If we stayed, we woulda been lynched."

Benjamin started the engine, jammed the transmission into gear, and drove out onto the road. The ten-minute ride to the state line felt interminable. Benjamin pulled to the side and stopped. He walked to the rear and removed a sideboard.

"We's here, suhs."

Patrick untied the bikes.

"I'm sorry for the terrible scare, and for the way the sheriff treated you," Tino said.

"Prejudice, just a piece of life down here. The South would be better off to be shut of it. You good men and all, and I be pleased to help you, but just the same, I be glad to get my black-ass home."

Laughter.

"Reverend Coffey, he say we to pray for people like the sheriff. He say they minds be confused. But it do feel right getting one over on people like the sheriff."

"Please thank Lizzie for the food," Tino said.

"Sure will, Mister Tino."

"I'll never forget you," Tino hollered, pulling away.

"You been delivered like the Israelites out of Pharaoh's Egypt. May the Good Lord guide your path."

Benjamin's truck vibrated in Rocinante's rearview mirror and shrank as Benjamin and Tino rode away from each other. *God bless Benjamin*, Tino thought. *God bless them all.*

19.

"I mean, how much trouble could I get into?"

WELCOME TO ALABAMA—HEART OF DIXIE—GEORGE C. WALLACE—GOVERNOR. The billboard on Highway 80 East at the state line welcomed visitors. American and Confederate flags hung at the top of each corner of the billboard.

Tino kept a nervous eye on his rearview mirror expecting to see the truckload of vigilantes.

They raced through Cuba and Bellamy. Sal pulled over on the outskirts of Demopolis.

"You guys go on," he said. "I'm going to Florida for a day. I'll meet you tomorrow at noon at the post office in downtown Columbus."

"You're kidding, right?" Tino said.

"Calm down. We're in no danger."

"Why're you going to Florida?"

"I promised a friend from the seminary that I'd stop in."

"Can't we go with—"

"I'm not bringing a crowd. You'll be fine. Just be careful."

"But—"

Sal took off.

Tino spit, disgusted. "I hope he's right about not being in danger. And why're older people always saying stupid stuff like that? 'Be careful.' I'm not a fucking kid. I mean, how much trouble could I get into?"

Patrick smirked "If you're not a 'kid', then why don't you cuss in front of him?"

"Because he's a priest and my big brother, Pat. That's why. Besides I cuss in Spanish in front of him. So *chingete pendejo.*"

"I don't know what that means," Patrick said rummaging through his gear, "but I'll bet it's not good." He found his hunting knife, tucked it in his belt, and covered it with his shirttail. "If those assholes show, I'm taking some with me."

"Let's get the hell outta here," Tino said.

"I need gas," Patrick said sheepishly.

"Jesus Christ!" Gary said. "My bladder holds more piss than your tank holds gas."

At the gas station, Tino tapped Peewee's tire with his foot. "I wish it could go faster. If those guys show up we'll never outrun them."

"The rings are wearing out," Patrick said. "The engine's losing compression. It's getting harder to keep up. You guys take my gear so Peewee will run faster. I've got some nylon rope. I'll tie the bikes together and you guys can pull me after Peewee's maxed out."

"Bitchen idea!" Gary said.

"Go!" Patrick yelled when they pulled onto the road. Gary pulled out a hair faster than Tino. Peewee jerked toward Gary. Tino hit the gas to compensate. Peewee lunged in his direction. Patrick lost control and fell.

"Shit! Next time pull at the same time!" The rope whipped up and down as they tried to coordinate timing. Patrick jerked side to side and over he went. The plan was abandoned after a third fall and they hadn't progressed a quarter mile.

Tino's fear and tension eased the farther they got away from Mississippi. Traffic lessened and they rode three abreast. Tino leaned gracefully side-to-side swaying his bike. Gary and Patrick joined in. The three friends laughed as they swayed in unison in a ballet until—Splat! Splat! Splat! Sting! Sting! Ow! Ow!—they rode into a swarm of bees.

Tino swatted at the bees that had stuck to his shirt, stinging his stomach and chest. He lost control and ran into Patrick. Patrick veered off the road and fell.

Tino and Gary pulled over and ran toward Patrick throwing off their shirts peppered with live, angry bees.

Gary stopped to right Peewee. Tino continued to Patrick.

"I smacked myself good," Patrick said, massaging his hip.

Gary walked up pushing Peewee. "I thought you were going to bite it bad, Pat."

"So did I. But I saw loose dirt off of the road and jumped for it."

They stared at one another dazed before Tino broke out laughing at the absurdity of what had happened.

Gary said, busting up. "That was fucked up! Stings hurt like mofos!"

Patrick checked Peewee. "Brake lever's twisted, but it'll work. Left mirror's broken off, and he's scratched up pretty good, but he can still go. Coulda been worse."

They rode for an hour and stopped at Ray's Food Center, a family-owned grocery store constructed of cinderblock.

Tino dismounted. "You guys see the sign a mile back?"

"Camping and fishing ahead," Patrick said.

Gary let out his kickstand. "Bet there're showers there. We should stay there tonight."

Tino guarded the bikes while the guys bought the makings for bologna sandwiches for lunch and chili beans and franks for dinner. They sat under a shade tree adjacent to the store talking and eating.

Patrick drank from his soda, washing down the last of his sandwich. He pointed to an orchard abutting the rear of the store. "Peaches," he said. He stood and strolled casually to the rear of the store and disappeared from view. Moments later, tree branches in the orchard began shaking.

Tino laughed. "God, he's ballsy."

"Whoa!" Gary said and pointed to the ground. A spider at their feet dragged a cricket into a hole. "Trapdoor spider. My dad showed me one when I was a kid. The spider digs out a hole, makes a trap door, and waits until dinner walks by. It ambushes and hits it with venom. Its prey doesn't stand a chance." Gary lifted a flap to the opening with a twig and let it drop shut.

"Pretty harsh," Tino said. "But kind of cool too."

Patrick appeared with an armload of golden peaches and laid them on the ground.

Juice ran down Tino's chin with the first bite. "Damn, that's sweet." The fruit disappeared in minutes.

The three lay back and gazed into the sky.

"Didn't sleep worth a shit last night," Tino said. I thought those assholes were going to show up. God, I hope our run-in with them is the worst thing that happens on this trip."

"Clouds look like mashed potatoes," Gary said.

"More like tits," Patrick said making his friends laugh.

"It sure was cool staying at your place when we were in grammar school, Pat," Gary said, "and checking out your dad's *Playboys*."

"I liked it all right," Tino said. "But frustrating as hell. I got really horny with nowhere to park my boner."

"Did you ever jack off after?" Patrick asked.

"I tried, but nothing came out."

"Ha! Ha! You didn't wax the helmet long enough, fool."

They laughed with glee.

"Isn't jacking-off a sin?" Tino said.

"Hell, yeah," Gary said, "that's why I confessed it."

"I wouldn't have the balls to confess to yanking the hose," Tino said.

"Better than dying with a mortal sin on your soul and burning in hell."

"What'd Father say?"

"'It is not a good practice, lad,'" Gary, said mimicking Father McGuinn's Irish brogue. "'It may lead to worse habits.' I thought that was kind of lame. But then he said, 'Would you be wanting boys to be masturbating to pictures if they were of your girlfriend?' He had me there. It made me feel even guiltier every time I did it after that. The next time I went to confession I asked him if it was a sin for pagans to look at pictures and yank."

"Good one!" Patrick said. "What'd he say to that?"

"'People who haven't been exposed to the truth don't know better. It's our duty to live in accordance with our moral code. It isn't easy at times, but the eternal reward will be worth every second of foregoing momentary pleasures.'"

"I'm going to have a lot of momentary pleasures when I get married and screw anytime I want," Tino said. "Don't know if I can hold out that long. I get horny every time I see a chick."

"I'm going to fuck my wife all night long," Patrick said. "And in the morning I'm going to hold up Mr. Stiffy and say, 'Look who's up, honey.'"

Tino and Gary lost it laughing.

"I'm going to fucking fuck her before and after breakfast, lunch and dinner," Gary said. "And there'll be dessert!"

Tino snorted. "Stop! You're fuckin' killin' me!"

"It's not fair having to be moral," Gary said. "Wish I didn't know the Truth."

Tino lay quietly, considering the advantages of paganism.

Drained from their trials over the past few days, they sank into sleep.

The sun lay low in the sky when Tino awoke hours later with a stiff back, "Hey, we better get to the campground."

The guys sat up yawning, stretching, and rubbing sleep from their eyes.

"Damn," Patrick said. "How long were we out for?"

"GOOD DAY OF RIDING," Tino said at a campsite in the dim light of dusk.

Patrick walked with a limp and tossed his sleeping bag to one side of the fire-pit. He pointed at Tino and laughed. "You should've seen the look on your face when we bumped bikes."

"Me? You turned whiter than your sorry white Irish ass already is. Toss me your canteens. I'll fill 'em up while you guys get dinner going."

Tino followed signs to the bathrooms, looking for a water tap. Silver splinters of moonlight filtered through treetops onto the ground. The night was peaceful, free of traffic and the endless drone of engines. He passed by a middle-aged couple sitting on folding chairs. Flames from their campfire reflected off an aluminum trailer. The aroma of frying fish surrounded the campsite. They wore matching golf shirts and plaid Bermuda shorts. The man said something that made the woman laugh. Tino looked longingly at them; would the day ever come when he would find what they had? A long, stable and loving relationship. At a second campsite, kids sat around a fire-pit talking and giggling reminding Tino of fun outings with his brothers and sisters.

Tino took a knee at a faucet on a shower room wall. He set a canteen under the faucet and opened the tap.

"Aren't you one of the guys on the motorcycles?"

A pair of woman's low-top red tennis shoes stood at the base of the bathroom wall. Tino looked up her smooth legs, past her Levi cutoffs, past her sleeveless scarlet red blouse, and to her face.

Her thin lips glowed deep red from an application of lipstick. The flames of a nearby campfire danced in her dark eyes. Eyebrows, elegant arches, shining black hair reached past her shoulders in waves. A mysterious black beauty mark stood out against her cheek.

Wow!

20.

Louise

"**U**M, WHAT?"

"I asked if you're one of the guys on the motorcycles?"

"Sure am, but how'd you know?"

"Saw you ride in. Where're you from and where're you headed?"

"West Coast, California, where San Diego is, the San Diego that's in California." Tino was sounding like an idiot. He knew it and needed to calm down.

"All that way?"

"Yeah, on our way to New York."

"Wow."

The canteen that Tino was holding under the spigit overflowed. Tino fumbled turning off the tap. He raised the canteen. "Drink?" *Stupid!*

"No thank you," she said laughing and offered her hand. "I'm Louise."

"Tino." Her grip was surprisingly strong. "It's short for Augustino, Augustino Caballero."

"Augustus the Horseman. Beautiful."

"I never thought of my name as beautiful, and how do you know what it means?"

"I teach high school Spanish. We don't realize nice things about ourselves. It's hard for us to see them. *¿Eres Español?*"

"*Soy Mexicano. Mis padres nacieron en Mexico*, but all the kids were born here."

"*Entonces tu eres México-Americano.* That would explain that nice tan of yours. We gringos spend hours in the sun trying to get what you have naturally. You're lucky."

"First my name is beautiful, now I'm lucky to have my skin. I could get to like you."

"And a sense of humor too."

"My color comes from Pa. He's got a lot of Mexican-Indian blood but my Ma's fair because her grandfather, John, was from Scotland. That's why I'm not so dark. Some of the kids in the family are lighter, some darker. Funny how that works."

"I'm an only child. I've often thought how much fun it must be to have a big family."

"It's fun until you have to use the only bathroom in the house."

She laughed and said, "Are you busy later?"

"Me? Oh, no, not really. I mean I'm going to eat hot dogs and chili beans with the guys, and go to bed, unless, I mean, I wouldn't mind—"

"Why don't you meet me at the lake after you've cleaned up and eaten?" She gestured toward a boating dock, its sun-bleached planks reflecting moonlight. "You're a nice guy. I'd enjoy talking with you."

"That'd be bitchin!" Tino covered his mouth. "Oops."

"God, you're cute. It's a date then. *Hasta pronto, Señor Caballero.*"

"What time?"

"Like I said, after you've cleaned up." She walked off, disappearing into the night.

Tino ran toward camp, lightheaded with the possibilities. *Outta sight!* A real fox wanted to spend time with him. But, what kind of time? Sal wasn't around, so he wouldn't find out if something happened. Not even the guys had to know. It'd be just like them to pull a prank. What if she wanted to do it? Tino would have to confess it. Was it a sin even thinking about it?

The guys had a healthy fire burning by the time Tino returned. He found a change of clothes, hurried to the showers, and was soon at the table wolfing down a chili dog. Gary and Patrick chatted companionably about rock concerts they'd been to.

"The Doors did a boss concert at the Community Concourse," Patrick said, "but I don't think anybody could top Santana when he played Balboa Stadium."

"I'm going for a stroll," Tino said tossing his paper plate into the fire.

"Mind if I tag along?" Gary said.

"Yeah, I would. I need to do some thinking."

Confused looks.

"What? Can't a guy have a little time to himself? Jeez."

"Easy," Gary said. "I'm cool with it."

Patrick shrugged and turned back to Gary. "Linda Ronstadt with the Stone Ponies played at the arena with The Turtles. They put on a fun show, and there was so much smoke at the Jefferson Airplane concert, you got stoned just breathing."

"Ha!"

Tino broke into a jog when he was out of sight of the guys, but no Louise at the lake. He strolled to the end of the dock and sat, dangling his feet over the water.

What in the hell was he doing here? He gazed over the lake. Nothing could come of this. He'd be back on the road in the morning. Was she a tease? She was probably laughing at him right now. Maybe it was best that she didn't show.

"*Buenas noches, Augustino.*"

"Jesus!" he said with a start. "You've got the strangest way of just appearing."

"Didn't mean to startle you. Mind if I sit?" She set a thigh against his.

Tino's heart pounded hard in his chest. "How'd you learn Spanish?" he asked trying his damndest to keep cool.

"Got my Masters in it and I lived in Mexico for a year afterward."

"Why'd you choose Spanish?"

"I love the culture, *y español es así como tocando música* (Spanish is like playing music). God created Spanish because He needed a suitable language for poetry."

"That's cool. I've never thought of it like that."

"It's because you grew up with Spanish. Your language is beautiful."

"Where're you from?"

"Saint Louis, sorry to say."

"You don't like it there?"

"It's a nice enough place. Maybe I've just got too much history there."

"Are you on vacation?"

She laughed a bitter laugh. "If you can call towing a trailer to Florida for a friend who's dying of cancer a vacation. This is the closest I've come to a vacation in a long time. My husband's too busy saving souls."

Husband? Shit! "He saves souls?"

"Baptist minister."

"Boy, do I know how you feel. My Ma is super religious. She prays when good things happen, when bad things happen prays when she's happy, when she's sad. Her cure for everything is prayer, prayer and Mentholatum. She sticks that crap in every possible orifice."

"Oh my God! You make me snort."

"Ma made us go to Catholic schools, and when we get sick she puts a holy card of a saint under our pillow; and when someone in the family leaves on a trip she blesses them asking God, the saints, and our ancestors to watch over us. Ancestors! A little weird, no?"

"I think it's sweet. Did she bless you when you left on this trip?"

"Yes, I got her holy hex."

"I saw people invoking their ancestors when I lived in Mexico," Louise said. "I think that they had a way of communicating with them somehow. It makes more sense to me praying to ancestors who were at least blood relatives, rather than saints who aren't."

"Maybe I'm just tired of going to church for this and that. Seems like it never ends."

"Aren't you just sick of it?" Louise said.

"Fuck, yes! Oops."

She nudged him. "Just because I'm a minister's wife doesn't mean— Oh, fuck, fuck, fuck."

Tino busted up. "I like you. I like you a lot."

"I like you too. It's nice being myself and not the obedient pastor's wife. Jonah has to play the role of the good pastor, and his family be damned if we get in the way of *that!*"

"So, why'd you marry him?"

"He wasn't always like that. I met him when he was in the seminary. He was normal then and loved kidding around. Jonah once did an impression of an old pastor wearing nothing but a cleric's shirt and a jockstrap. I wet myself laughing.

At first we spent a lot of time together having fun, but now his time's been taken by a constant stream of church functions. It's too much. The spark in his eye has been snuffed out by so many demands." Louise looked ready to cry.

"I wasn't raised religious, but I loved him and promised I'd try. His mother says that I'm not dedicated enough. She's never accepted me. She says we're not 'cut from the same cloth.' She got angry when I said that our son should be able to choose whether or not he wanted to become a minister.

"And Jonah's changed over the years. He wasn't meant for the religious life. I tried talking to him about it, but he says I'm wrong. He's become bitter and controlling."

Moonlight reflected off a tear on her cheek. "I told him that I needed to take the trailer to Florida. He said it wouldn't look proper for his wife to be traveling alone, and that he had to put his foot down. But it wasn't him talking. It was his mother. She's possessed him! 'I'm taking that fucking trailer by myself!' I said."

Tino's jaw dropped. "You cussed at a minister?"

She wiped her cheek and chuckled. "You should've seen the shock. And he thinks I'm going to help him minister in Mexico. I'm not going to spread that crap among those beautiful people."

Tino listened intently, intrigued by her take on religion.

"My dear friend asked me to take her the trailer so she can travel while she still has the strength. And my husband's main concern is what the sheep might think about me traveling alone. I'm not taking it anymore."

"Didn't he want to come with you?"

"Yes, but only because he knew that I wasn't backing down. 'I'm going by myself,' I told him. 'We'll talk when I'm ready.'"

"You really don't care what people think?"

"Not anymore. I was happier before this church life, and I'm not going to live the rest of my days putting on a show." Her voice broke. "Who knows how long we have to live."

Tino put an arm around her shoulders. "I know what you mean. In school they said we are to be 'beacons in the world,' and joyous because we belong to the 'one true faith.' But sometimes I'm not joyous, and I don't want to be a beacon. I don't want to convert the world. Wow, I can't believe I just said that."

She patted his hand. "You're smart. Listen to yourself. You don't need anyone telling you right from wrong. Do you think God wants people who are too messed up to realize they're unhappy putting on a show in His name? Or would He rather that we simply be who we are?"

A heron flew low overhead, fanning the air.

"I'm sorry for laying all of this on you," Louise said. "*Pobrecito*, (poor guy) you're on a wonderful trip. You don't need to be brought down by my problems."

"I like hearing them, especially when it comes to church."

She laid a soft kiss on his cheek. He slid his hand between his legs embarrassed over the rise in his pants.

"I'd like to have some fun," she said.

"So would I!"

"I'd love a ride on your motorcycle."

"Oh, sure. Hell, I'll take you clear to New York, if you want."

"You're the sweetest. I'll wait for you here."

He didn't move, hoping for another kiss.

She giggled and pushed him. "Go!"

Tino sprang to his feet. "Be right back!"

21.

Lola

TINO RAN TO CAMP. The guys were lying over their sleeping bags, idly talking. Gary poked embers in the fire pit with a stick.

Tino jumped on his bike and hit the kick-starter.

"What the hell?" Patrick said sitting up.

"Tell you later!"

Louise clapped her hands, excited as a kid, when Tino pulled up. "This is so exciting!" She hopped on landing with a bounce. She leaned into him wrapping her arms around his chest and pressing her breasts against his back. "What fun!"

They rode away from the campgrounds along the lakeshore. Warm air streamed through their hair.

Louise spread her arms. "Faster!"

He hit the gas. Rocinante lunged.

"Whoa!" she yelled, grabbing Tino's shirt to keep from sliding off. She squeezed him tight.

Wonderful arousal.

They coasted to a stop opposite the campground under the broad canopy of an oak tree. Campfires reflected off the lake.

She rested her chin on his shoulder. "Ooh," she whispered, absorbing the timeless and mesmerizing sight of fire mirrored off water.

She hopped off and in a single move pulled off her blouse and threw it to the base of the tree. "Let's swim!"

A dizzy, exciting rush.

Louise stripped to her bra and panties. "What're you waiting for?" she said and ran into the lake laughing and splashing water.

Tino fumbled while undressing, greatly relieved that she intended for them to swim in their underwear. He hopped on one foot stepping out of his pants and walked backwards into the lake hiding his erection. The water cooled his body from a day of riding in the sun.

"Race you to the diving platform," Louise said and was off. Her back was broad, shoulders strong, her strokes fast and deep. Much as he tried, Tino couldn't catch up to her. They reached the platform panting and climbed on.

She leaned over to wring out her dark hair. Water splashed onto the platform. "Don't you love swimming?"

"I mostly body surf," Tino said staring at her hair sparkling silver with moonlight.

"What's body surfing?"

"If you catch an ocean wave just right, you glide along the surface, and the water rushes all around you. Great feeling."

"Must be nice living by the ocean."

"I've never thought about it, but yes, it is."

He lay on his back to keep from looking at her bra and panties all but transparent against her wet skin.

Louise stood, staring down at him. She got to her knees, slid onto him and kissed him long and slow. His heart pounded so hard he wondered if she could feel it. She ran her fingers through his hair.

Water lapped against the platform. Ripples, like small rolling mounds, went gliding across the lake, each carrying a piece of the moon.

She rolled off. "All right, darling boy, time to get back before something regrettable happens." She stood and pulled on his hand, helping him to his feet. They swam back side by side.

Tino stole glances of her patting herself dry and dressing.

On the return ride, he leaned his head back, pressing his cheek agonst hers. "I want to ride forever with you." She tightened her embrace. He rode slowly, stretching their time together.

"Would you like to see the trailer?" she said at her campsite.

"Yes, I really would!"

She led him up the steps into the long and wide trailer. She pointed to a padded bench at a table. "Have a seat." She took bottles of beer from a small refrigerator and popped off the caps. "I've decided I'm going back to the life I knew before I met Jonah, which means having a drink once in a while." She poured beer into glasses, handed one over, and sat with him. He trembled with excitement as he raised the glass to his lips.

"There's a freedom being on the road," Louise said. "No one to answer to. Gives a person time to think. I could get used to this kind of life."

"God, you're beautiful."

She took the glass from his hand, set it on the table, and kissed him spreading her lips and squirming her tongue against his—another rise in his pants. His hand trembled as he eased it onto her breast. To his amazement, she just kept kissing him. He ran his hand under her blouse and tried getting under her bra but it was tight against her skin. He squeezed a finger under and felt a small lump. *Nipple!* His head spun. He pulsated in his pants, once, twice, three times. *My God!*

She cooed into his ear. "Have you ever had sex with a woman?"

Sure. Sex here, sex there, sex, sex all the time with the sex.

"No, I've never done it. I made out with a girlfriend, but we never went all the way. I've really wanted to."

She put a hand to his lips. "Shush. Shall we take care of your little problem?"

"I thought you didn't want anything regrettable to happen."

"This won't be regrettable."

She took his hand and led him to a bed at the rear of the trailer. "*Quítate la ropa* (Take off your clothes)," she said with no hint of embarrassment. She undressed at the end of the bed, with her back to him.

He slipped out of his pants and slid between the covers.

She turned and walked toward him. Tino's eyes were fixed on the small dark patch between her legs and her swaying breasts. She pulled back the covers and broke out laughing.

He shot his hands over the tent pitched in his boxer shorts. "What?"

"My, you're modest. If you're going to find out what it's about then you're going to have to show some skin."

She pulled off his shorts and flung them over her shoulder. He'd never felt more vulnerable.

She cuddled next to him. "*Qué cuerpo tan bonito.*"

"I never thought of my body as anything special."

"You're muscular and handsome, you know that. Don't you?"

"I've got a big nose."

"It gives your face character. Doesn't always work that way. You're lucky. Women would kill to have your dark eyes and thick, wavy, brown hair."

"Really?"

"Yes, 'really,' " she said studying him. "Have you ever seen the statue of David?"

"In books."

"Your body's like his."

"I like your body too," Tino said. "I like it a whole lot."

"*Pero que mi esposo se sentiera lo mismo.* (I wish that my husband felt the same.) He wants me to look like women in magazines."

"Your body's perfect and I've never felt for anyone the way I feel about you. You're beautiful, beautiful in every way."

She lay over him kissing him again and again. She ran her tongue across his neck, held his manhood, and gently stroked. Tino's head spun round and round. She rolled onto her back and tugged to get him on her.

"I don't want to get pregnant. When you feel yourself coming, pull out."

He nodded nervously and tried to enter her but couldn't find the spot. She took hold of his manhood and guided him. Her inside was moist, warm, welcoming.

She gyrated slowly and moaned. "Mm, oooh, mmm." She began moving faster. "Oh! Oh my God!" Harder. Louder. Her thick legs and strong hips bounced him one way and the other. Harder, louder, faster. "Oh God! Oh!" she yelled. Bounce. Bounce. His body slammed against hers. Bounce. Bounce. He wrapped his arms around her neck just to stay onboard. "Oh yes! Oh my God! Oh yes! Oh Jesus! Pull before you come!"

"Okay," he said into her ear.

She screamed "Oh, oh God! Pull before you come! Pull before you come!"

"All right! All right!" he said, afraid neighboring campers would kick the door down and beat the shit out of him, thinking there was a murder going on. The pulsations were coming. He didn't want to pull out. But at the last second, he did.

She shuddered and the ride came to a sudden end.

He went to roll off, but she dug her nails into his back. "Don't move. Enjoy this for a moment. Men are always in such a hurry. Just stay with me."

"I thought I was hurting you."

"Oh no, quite the opposite. My goodness, I needed that. It's been too long since I've felt like this."

"Whoa," Tino whispered. "I just made love to a woman."

She raked her fingernails across his back. "Feel good?"

"More than just good. A lot more."

"You can get off me now."

She lay on her back looking at the ceiling. "I need more from life. I'm going to demand that Jonah choose; the church or me. The good little pastor's wife is no more. He's going to make love to me like a man who lusts after his woman, or he can go screw himself. I declare Good-Girl Louise is dead."

She sat up. "From here on I. Am. Lola!"

"Did I do that?"

"Ha! Ha! No, it wasn't our little session. I did it. I made up my mind I was going to stand up, and by God, I did!"

"Little session? This was no little session, for me."

"You have a ways to go in the lovemaking department, darling boy."

"I've never done it before."

"You'll be fine. You're sweet and handsome. You'll find a good woman to be happy with, you'll see."

"I'm not feeling too sweet right now. I don't know how you can do this with me and think about getting back with your husband. I'm in love with you."

"Dear one, I'm afraid you're confusing a roll in the hay with love. You don't know me well enough. Love takes time."

"I want to love you, Louise."

"No more Louise. It's Lola."

"Okay, I want to be with Lola, forever. This feels so right, but I've sinned, adultery no less, and with the wife of a man of God!"

"He's no man of God! And so be it if this is a sin. No more guilt."

"Don't you believe in what we've been taught?"

"I'm not sure what I believe anymore, but I'm damn sure I don't believe in letting fear or guilt rule my life."

"I wish I could live like that."

"You'll figure it out."

"We've committed a big sin and could burn in hell forever if it's not forgiven."

She reared back and slapped him hard across the face.

Shock.

"Did making love to me feel like a sin?"

Tino massaged his jaw.

"Answer. Did it feel like a sin?"

"No, I liked it. I liked it a whole lot. It's all so confusing."

"Did you hurt anyone?"

"I don't think so."

"No. You did not."

"What about your husband?"

"Okay, I've cheated a little, but goddamn it, he's as much to blame."

"We've cheated on him."

"He'll never know."

"God does."

She reared back.

He ducked.

"Listen to me," she said, lowering her hand. "You need to get off that path. I've been on it for too long. It leads nowhere."

"It's the only one I know."

"Don't be afraid to try another. I was free before I married him, and I'm not going back."

Tino looked at her with want: want of her, want of her strength.

"*Eres buena persona, Augustino.* If you want to be free, you'll have to learn not to be afraid. Freedom and fear don't mix."

She looked more beautiful, more desirable, yet a nagging dread lingered. "I've always lived in fear, fear of sinning, fear of God, fear of going to Hell, fear of my father."

"You poor, poor boy." She laid her hands on his cheeks, kissed him and pulled him back onto the bed. This time he wasn't nervous and didn't need help entering her. She moved slower, moaned gently. He released his seed deep inside her.

Tino pushed up to look into her face. Her hair lay in sensual dark waves against the white linen, her dark eyes imprisoning his, her elegant beauty mark, a small dark isle against her white skin.

"I've never felt so close to anyone," Tino said. "I want to be with you."

"You are."

"For good."

"It sounds wonderful, but how would it be after a few days, a week, a month? Maybe not so much fun."

"I'll never get tired of you."

"You're sweet. Your parents did a good job raising you."

"Don't talk to me like a fucking kid!"

"Good. You stood strong. And sorry for sounding condescending, but lifelong commitments can't be made so easily."

"How do you know? Can't we at least try?"

She nudged him in the chest getting him off of her, and rolled out of bed. "Tell you what. I'll give you my friend's address in Florida. If you still feel the same after you get home, write me and we'll talk."

"I'll write you the day I get back."

"If I'm not lucky enough to get you," she said outside at the bike, "then some fortunate woman will. Good bye for now."

Tino rode away from the love of his life, empty. Maybe he should abandon the trip and go back to Lola and talk her into letting him go to Florida. Not realistic. Sal would find him. He'd have to wait.

Gary and Patrick lay still as corpses in their sleeping bags. Tino had no idea what time it was, but it was late, very late. He crawled into his bag. A bird's call echoed in the dark and lonely night.

22.

And Then There Were Two

SUNLIGHT SHONE THROUGH THE TREES onto Tino's face. He opened his eyes and tried to piece together what had happened and where he was. The fire pit smoldered. *Did I make love to a mature and beautiful woman last night? A magical dream?* No. His jaw ached from Lola's slap. And yes, he made love to Lola, beautiful Lola. It didn't seem right that a loser like him could have had such a magical experience.

Had she left the campground?

Maybe there's time enough to find her and make love once more before I have to leave. Have to leave, have to...

"Holy shit! We're gonna be late to meet Sal! Get up!"

Gary groaned from his sleeping bag. "What're you yelling about?"

"We're supposed to meet Sal at noon!"

Patrick rolled out of his bag, his curly red hair matted from sleep. "What time did you get in?"

Tino hopped from leg to leg getting into his pants. "Get your asses moving!"

Gary sat up. "Where were you last night dude? We waited and waited."

"I got laid."

"I know you got in late. What time was it?"

"Laid, Gary. Laid!"

"By a woman?"

"No, a donkey. Yes, a woman. I'm not into donkeys like you, and now's not the time to talk about it. I'm going to be in trouble with Sal."

Patrick stood and massaged his hip. "Aw, come on. You're not going to keep this to yourself."

"Sal's going to be pissed off about us being late, and I'm the one who's going to hear about it."

"Ha!" Patrick laughed walking to his bike with a slight limp. "Tino gave a chick his fat hog."

"She's not just a chick," Tino said, mounting Rocinante. "So you can go screw yourself, *pinche bolillo.*"

"Is that good?"

"Gare! Move!"

"I'm not even going to brush my damn teeth!" Gary said, loading his gear.

They raced out of the campground to the road. Tino cursed Peewee. He had maxed out at 63 on the highway. It felt like forever before the Columbus skyline came into view. Tino asked directions to the post office from a cabbie parked outside a downtown hotel. His stomach turned when he saw Sal pacing the sidewalk.

"I called Ma, wondering if you guys had had an accident," Sal said.

"Sorry," Tino said wondering if his face had changed after having had sex.

Patrick jumped off Peewee and pulled up his shirt, showing the reddish-pink dots against his pale-white skin from the bee stings. "We were attacked by a huge swarm of bees!" Tino and Gary raised their shirts.

Patrick walked toward Sal, exaggerating the limp in his gait. "I wrecked and messed up my leg. And look at my bike!"

"Dang," Sal said. "Looks like you're lucky to be alive!"

Patrick sneaked Tino a sly smile. Tino winked.

"You guys gotta be careful," Sal said. He then pointed to a diner across the street. "I thought we could eat there. But a sign in the window said 'White trade only.'"

Patrick spit toward the diner. "We got stuff to make sandwiches."

"I passed a city park where we can eat," Sal said.

They sat on grass in the shade of a towering magnolia when Patrick made a surprise announcement. "The long haul and high rpms are too much for my bike. I've decided to go to Chicago where I have relatives. I can ask if you guys can come along if you want to take it easy for a few days."

"I'll keep you company," Gary said. "I wouldn't mind taking a break from so much riding and sleeping on the ground."

"I'm sticking to my plan," Sal said. "*¿Y tu hermano?*"

"I want to go with you," Tino said.

"Good. We'll stay in touch by calling Ma," Sal said to the guys.

"You mean like we did early in the trip when we met in Texas?" Gary said.

"Exactly, and we'll meet up on the way back somewhere west of the Mississippi."

Patrick mounted Peewee. "Scrape off the carbon buildup on your plugs; bikes'll run smoother and you'll save a little on gas. And tighten the drive-chains every thousand miles." He and Gary pulled out.

"See you guys," Tino yelled behind them. Peewee trailed a thin plume of smoke.

"Let's get to it," Sal said. "We're way off schedule."

Tino kept focused on Gary and Patrick, afraid that Sal would read something on his face, but Sal wasted no time and rode off. They kept a steady pace of just over the highway limit. Tino rode wearily from a lack of sound sleep, consumed by his night with Lola and burdened by committing adultery.

Could it have been fated that they were to meet? Was it mere coincidence that two people from different parts of the country, traveling in different directions, just happened to cross paths and make the deepest of connections? If there was such a thing as soul mates, then Lola and he must be, and he was speeding away from her.

Sal pressed on, and on. Time crawled by, the drone of the engine, hypnotic, the road, endless.

Sal pulled into a restaurant in North Charleston at sunset, after six hours of hard riding.

"How're you doing?" Sal asked in an upbeat mood, likely happy with their progress.

Tino stared at his feet. "Okay."

"What's wrong?"

"Tired, haven't been sleeping much."

"How about I treat you to a good dinner?"

"Sounds good," Tino said halfheartedly.

Sal asked for a table where they could keep an eye on the bikes. Tino ordered his meal and went to the bathroom. He took his time so as not to have to face Sal. He studied his face in the mirror. Did he look different? Sal was writing in his travel log when Tino returned. The waitress walked up with a plate in each hand: burger and fries for Tino, fried chicken and mashed potatoes for Sal.

Tino ate slowly with a distant look in his eyes. Would he ever see Lola's beautiful face again?

"You haven't eaten half of your meal. Aren't you hungry?" Sal asked.

Silence.

"You sick?"

"No."

"We haven't eaten since this afternoon. You should be chowing down."

Tino's head dropped.

Sal set his fork down. "Okay, what's up?"

"I met a woman at a campground yesterday."

"And?"

"I liked her a lot, and we spent time together."

"So?"

"I mean we *really* spent time together, and it was hard leaving her." His temples throbbed.

"Are you saying what I think you're saying?" Sal's words hovered over the table like a storm about to unleash its fury.

"Yeah, *we did it.*"

Sal stood, wiped his mouth, went to the cash register, and paid the tab.

Tino walked out and gazed up at the moon, distant and cold. He made ready to mount, but Sal grabbed his arm, spun him around, and shoved hard. Tino slammed into Rocinante; they fell as one to the pavement.

Sal stood over him, panting. "You disrespected her, *cabrón!* Oh, what's the damn use?" His words dripped with disgust.

A feeble "Sorry," escaped Tino's lips.

Sal had disciplined his brothers on occasion, but aside from a backhand to the chest he had never attacked.

Sal mounted and rode off. Tino righted Rocinante and chased after. They rode past signs for Fort Sumter National Monument, South Carolina, but Sal took the route toward Folly Beach.

Tino rode, lost in the unforgiving darkness, the illumination of his headlight infinitesimal in the eternal black night. *Am I the bad seed in the family? Lola had to be wrong about living the way you want.* Mysterious, tiny, flickering lights floating over a field distracted him from his troubled musing.

Hundreds of them hovered over the ground like sparks, but without fire.

Sal and Tino rode up the cobblestone roadway of an ancient arched bridge constructed of large stones. Tino turned his attention from the road to the sparkling field and back to the road. Below him, countless exquisite glistening diamonds dove and darted around each other in the warm humid air. *Fireflies!* He slowed looking on the wondrous sight, wishing that Sal would stop to get a good look.

Tino's wish was more than granted. A galaxy of the flying gems descended on them as if a kind wizard had allowed the two mortals passage into his realm. Hundreds of tiny lights blinked on and off as they flew up and over and around them, engulfing them in a gentle, golden aura. Sal stopped at the crest of the bridge. Tino pulled alongside, cut his light, and carefully removed his helmet so as not to startle the delicate luminescent pixies. The brothers sat on the bikes as the twinkling procession passed, bathing them in the soft glow, as if baptizing the brothers into their fantastical domain. Tino reached out and cupped one in his hands. He separated his thumbs just enough to peer in. The sprite had two small antennae and several legs on either side of its oblong body. It sparked on and off from the back half. It felt wrong to hold so precious a being captive. He opened his hands, allowing her to join her sisters in their aerial ballet.

The glowing, hallowed cluster meandered off in a radiant mass, drifting about in their untroubled world and bringing light into the hard night, leaving Tino a gift of peace. The orbiting swarm rose as one into a tree and settled, adorning its branches—sequins on a princess' gown.

Again in the dark, Sal and Tino started their bikes. Tino wiped a tear from his cheek, and followed Sal down to the other side.

THEY PULLED INTO A PARKING LOT IN FOLLY BEACH, SECURED the bikes with Tino's cable and padlock, and toted their gear over beach sand. The familiar smell of the ocean's salt air and the sound of waves pounding against the shore comforted Tino, reminding him of his home by the sea. They dropped their sleeping bags close enough to the shore to see the foam of the shore break, made white in the moonlight.

Tino knelt and unrolled his bag. "I'm sorry, Sal."

Sal squatted on his hams. "When Ma and her sister, our Aunt Eva, left the ranch to attend school in Hermosillo, Grandma told Ma to keep an eye on Eva because she had a wild side, sneaking off with boys at any opportunity. Eva wound up getting pregnant and had a child out of wedlock. She was ostracized from the family. That's why you've never met her. Grandma blamed Ma. And Ma and Eva will never reconcile because Eva died last year. How do you think Ma would feel if she found out what you did?"

"I know it was wrong," Tino said suffocating with guilt, "but I fell in love with her. I didn't plan to do it. It just sort of happened."

"It just sort of happened?"

"Please don't be like that, Sal."

"How old is she?"

"Around your age."

"Well, if you're going to do it with a strange woman, it may as well be with one who's out for a good time and not one who'll take you seriously."

"She wouldn't do it with just anybody. She's a good person involved in a church."

"What the hell? Is she a nun?"

"No, she's married to a minister." The more he tried explaining, the worse it got.

"Boy! This just gets better, doesn't it? If you think we had trouble with those men in Mississippi, it's nothing compared to what her husband would rightfully do to you if he found out about your little tryst and came after you."

"You don't understand. She's left him."

"They're still married! Don't you exercise any self-control? Dogs go sniffing around looking for anything that'll satisfy them."

"I don't give a shit!" Tino screamed. "I'm not a fucking kid and I'm tired of being pushed around. I've had it with being compared to you. I'm sorry if I'm not perfect like you." He curled his hands into fists, ready if Sal came at him again.

Sal looked away and ran his hand over his dark, curly hair. "Hermano, sex is serious business. You hear hippies talk about 'free love,' but it's not so easy. Emotions are powerful forces that can't be taken lightly. Do you remember Odysseus and the isle of the sirens, and what happened when the sirens sang and lured sailors to their island?"

"Their ships were smashed against the rocks and the sailors drowned."

"Exactly. Homer used the sirens to represent so much of what we're seduced by: sex, alcohol, drugs, money. They can destroy us. If we're not careful, we could wind up like those sailors.

"You're almost a man. Learn to be responsible like one. I would hope that Ma and Pa raised a better son than the one who made a really bad decision last night. And think of the woman—if she really cares for you, how empty she must be feeling."

"I want to be with her so bad it hurts."

"See the entanglements? Learn from this. You're playing with forces that you don't understand. Did you get her phone number or address?"

"Yes, I'm going to write her when I get home."

Sal dropped to his knees and evened out his sleeping bag. "I don't see how this could work. You never know, of course, but everything is working against it. She's older. You live thousands of miles apart, different religions, different cultures really, and you don't know each other except for being together for one lousy night." Sal fished out his toothbrush. "Did she at least have a condom for you to use?"

Tino flushed. "She told me to pull out before I came."

"It's still taking a big chance. If you ever do that again, at least cover that thing of yours. All you need is a kid you can't support. Suppose she gets pregnant and you never see her again. She'll either get an abortion, or she'll give birth to another fatherless kid, like there aren't enough already." Sal's hand vibrated in a blur when he brushed teeth.

Tino slinked into his bag. He would show Sal. Tino would show them all. He would get together with Lola. And if she was pregnant, then they'd have to make a life together. But would Ma and Pa kick him out of the family? To hell with it. Let 'em. If Lola's pregnant he would marry her and he would be a good and faithful husband and father.

The sea's cool breath fanned Tino's face. Lying on the sand was a welcome change from sleeping on the ground.

Lola, beautiful Lola, her eyes, her lips, her black beauty mark that stood out against her cheek. Tino wrapped his hand around his member and gently stroked. The pulsations came, and they felt so good, so right.

23.

Lord's Gift

THE SUN ROSE, WARMING THE SAND FLIES and giving them the energy to fly and feast on the decaying seaweed that had washed ashore.

A fly crawled across Tino's cheek. He raised his hand from out of his sleeping bag and brushed at it. It buzzed off and landed on his ear. He swiped at it. Another crawled over his forehead. He sat up. Hundreds of flies were zigzagging over seaweed lying in heaps on the beach.

He looked out over the ocean and yawned. Waves swelled, crested, and crashed. Water from the shore break rushed forward. The water ebbed back into the sea. A wooden pier's long stilt-like legs carried the deck a thousand feet into the ocean. A solitary man held a fishing pole over the railing.

Palm trees dotted the sandy landscape. Their tall, slender trunks soared overhead and were crowned by wide, fan-like leaves. Tall, green needles of coastal grasses grew in waist-high clusters over white sand dunes.

Sal, lying wrapped in his sleeping bag, looked like one of Ma's bean burritos.

A fly landed on Sal's nose. His hand appeared from inside his bag and brushed it off.

"Morning," Tino said.

"Hey," Sal said, his sleepy voice cracking.

Tino dropped to his knees to roll up his sleeping bag as they prepared to leave. "Look out over the water and tell me if you notice something odd."

Sal looked out and said, "Like what?"

"The sun rose over the ocean."

"You're right, it is a little weird."

"And that's the Atlantic," Tino said. "We've made it clear to the other side of the continent."

"Ha! You're right."

They packed up the gear and trekked over the sand to the bikes.

"We're just over six hundred miles from Washington D.C.," Sal said.

Tino mounted Rocinante. "We should be able to make it there by tomorrow."

Varoom!

Sal kick-started his bike. "We're going to push and make it by tonight."

"*¡Me mates!* (You're killing me!)"

On the ride out they passed a sign at an entrance path to the shore: BEACH AND SEASIDE – WHITES ONLY.

They rode the highway passing fields of an unfamiliar crop, its leaves as long as a man's arm and half as wide. Beat-up wooden sheds stood alongside the fields. What could it be? Tino came upon a billboard of a cowboy along the highway, a coiled rope in one hand, a cigarette in the other. "Come to where the flavor is."

The day was clear and mildly warm with low humidity and a gentle wind at their backs. The South Carolina hills, deep green with shrubbery and expansive trees, made for a ride that would rival one through Eden. Even so Tino was in for it. They were not going to stop until they reached the nation's capital. Tino's positive energy would have long been exhausted by dusk, and Sal would press on. But that torment was for later. For now it was, "Good Day Sunshine."

What a day to have Lola sitting behind him with her arms wrapped tightly around him.

How would he ever support her without a good-paying job? Fate's cards were stacked against him. He'd always been a poor student, and forget about holding down a job. He recalled Pa's reaction when he got fired from McDonald's.

"For Christ sakes, you can't even flip hamburgers!"

What about Rex, the biker from New Mexico? He hires guys like me who have a hard time making it in the normal world.

Tino just figured out the rest of his life. He would learn to be a mechanic from Rex and ride motorcycles with him and his biker friends, but first things first. Tino would join the Marines, earn Pa's respect, become an ace mechanic and marry Lola. Tino's day brightened all the more.

Rocinante began slowing down. Tino hit the accelerator but he continued slowing.

Sal, riding alongside, yelled over, "What're you doing?"

Tino gave a hopeless look, rolled to a stop and checked the engine.

"Crap," Tino said. "The drive chain fell off. Pat must not have put it back on right after his prank. It's got to be lying back there somewhere."

Sal shook his head. "Dang."

Tino looked after Sal riding away slowly with an eye on the road. He stopped a quarter mile away and picked up the snake-like chain.

Sal rode back. "Master link's missing. I hope there's a dealership in the town that we passed. Be back as soon as I can."

He rode off and passed a converted school bus painted the colors of a rainbow.

"Magic Bus," was written in elaborate cursive lettering occupying the space above the windshield. The driver pulled over and smiled at Tino. His bright white teeth were surrounded by a mass of untamed whiskers; a broad beard hung to the middle of his chest. A leather strap tied around his head kept his shoulder-length hair from his face. Grace Slick's voice bellowed from an eight-track tape deck. "When the truth is found to be lies."

The hippie slid out of the driver's seat onto the side of the road. "Having trouble, brother?" His bone-white collarless shirt with puffy long sleeves hung over gray corduroys, pant legs tucked into tan suede boots adorned with tassels that dangled as he walked.

"Nothing my brother and I can't fix," Tino said, feeling odd talking to a guy dressed like a wild gypsy. "He went to get a part. But thanks for stopping."

"We are called to serve, brother," Tassel Boots said. "Too bad about your ride, man."

The double doors of the bus swung open. A pretty young woman descended the steps, her milk-white skin a stark contrast to her shining dark eyes, and hair that hung long and straight to her waist. Her deep blue blouse fit snugly over her slim figure, moccasins barely visible beneath her brown skirt that gently swept the floor. She seemed to hover over the ground like a saint that Tino had once seen in a religious movie. A thin silver ribbon entwined with tiny dried yellow flowers rested on the crown of her head halo-like. She drifted to Tassel Boots and put her cheek on his shoulder.

"Been on the road long?" Tassel Boots asked.

"Since California."

"Wow, far out, man!"

Tino nodded toward the bus. "How's it traveling in that?"

"Groovy, man. Got everything we need."

The Saint spoke gently. "Would ya'll like to trip out on it?"

"Sure, I'd love to see it."

"Go on," Tassel Boots said and headed toward the rear of the bus. "Gotta get something."

Tino followed the Saint into the bus. The dull-sweet odor of incense hung in the air. A petite girl, who couldn't have been much past fifteen, sat on a rocking chair behind the driver's seat sewing a brightly colored patch of a mushroom to the cuff of a pair of faded jeans.

"My baby sister, Dawn," the Saint said. The girl gave him a cursory smile and continued stitching.

"Dawn's fixin' Lord's pants."

"Lord?"

"Our man."

"Interesting name," Tino said, thinking it profane.

The Saint stared into his face with her piercing doe-like eyes. "He be a most interesting man." She leaned into Tino and cooed, "I'm Snow."

His loins percolated. "Nice name," he said, nervous over her advances.

Snow extended her hand in a broad stroke, inviting Tino to admire the world they had created inside.

A portable camping stove sat on a narrow counter. Hand-thrown ceramic plates and cups filled a small sink. He reached down to run a hand over a large, soft, tan hide on the floor. Blankets and pillows in blue and green paisley patterns lay tangled over a mattress to the rear. A tambourine sat by a guitar case that leaned against one side of the bus. Covering the ceiling in glittering gold and outlined in deep blue was a peace symbol *IT IS POSSIBLE* written in deep purple over it.

"This is really beautiful," Tino said.

"Life's beautiful," Snow said inches from his face. Why was she coming on to him? Wasn't she afraid that her man, Lord, would see them?

Lord entered the bus carrying a small leather pouch. "You digging our ride, man?"

"It's pretty bitchen," Tino said.

Lord went to the counter next to the sink, took a pack of rolling papers from his shirt pocket, and peeled one out. He set it flat on the counter, opened the pouch, and tapped on it. A leafy green material sprinkled onto the paper.

"Is that marijuana?"

"It sure ain't tobacco." Lord rolled the paper and ran the edge across his tongue, twisted the ends, and looked up at Tino. "Care to partake?"

Tino stared open mouthed. "Um, no thanks. I'm not into dope."

"How do you know? Ever try it?"

"No."

"Well?"

"Marijuana leads to harder drugs."

"Naw, brother, that's the man's message. It just ain't so. How do you get high?"

"Beer, when I can get it."

"This ain't nearly as hard on you as that shit; alcohol'll kill you. I've done every drug that there is, and alcohol was the hardest on my body. Felt like I got a beating after drinking." He raised his eyebrows. "Come on, what do you say?"

"You're right. I don't know what marijuana's like. Well, what the heck."

"Well, all right, man!" Lord said with a king-size grin.

Snow giggled and clapped her hands. "Beautiful!"

"Why're you so happy about me getting high?" Tino asked.

"Cause you're converting on over to the lat," she said.

"Lat? What's *lat*?"

"You know, like lat bulb."

Lord struck a match against the counter and lit up. He sucked slow and hard; his face grew red. He held his breath and handed the joint to Tino.

Tino brought it to his lips. "What do you mean 'converting to the light?'" He imitated Lord and sucked hard. The smoke tore at his lungs. He coughed and hacked. The hippies burst into laughter. He passed the joint to Snow. She took a small hit and handed it to Dawn.

"Ever hear of Timothy Leary and his church?" Lord asked.

"Sure," Tino said, coughing. "He's the drug addict who keeps getting busted."

"Not an addict, man! A researcher, a researcher in psychedelic therapy at Harvard University. A teacher with a new and beautiful message, like Jesus. Leary has seen the light that all men—"

Snow raised a finger. "And women."

"That all men *and* women seek. We're going to San Francisco. I've wanted to go there since I heard about the Summer of Love. After that we're joining a commune and Leary's church, "The League for Spiritual Discovery." We live his mantra: turn on, tune in, and drop out. Lysergic acid diethylamide is the church's sacrament."

"Lysergic what?"

"Lysergic acid diethylamide. L-S-D, man."

"They're using LSD as communion? Give me a break!"

"You don't understand. It isn't just a drug. It's a portal. A portal to the other side, a way to see, you know? A way to really and truly see, man."

Lord went to the glove compartment, and took out a small yellow box reading "Kodak Film." He removed the small gray canister, peeled off the lid and tapped out what appeared to be tiny pieces cut from shiny black film. He reached to the floor, picked up a *National Geographic* magazine and tore out a page with a photograph of an ancient Mayan temple. Using a razor blade, he cut a small square out of the page that had the glyph of a stylized snake. He set a fleck on the paper and formed a small packet around it. "God forbade Adam and Eve to eat of the forbidden fruit."

"He didn't want them to take LSD?"

Snow sniggered.

"You need to understand something," Lord said. "LSD has the same effect as mushrooms."

"Mushrooms? What do they have to do with anything?" Tino's speech slowed from the effects of the marijuana. Another effect was an intense focus. Tino studied Lord's big white teeth, whiskers, and lips as he talked.

"Not just mushrooms," Lord said, "psilocybin mushrooms. They expand our minds in ways we could never imagine, as does LSD. It was the first time in my life that I could see, that I could really and truly see. It wasn't LSD Adam and Eve weren't supposed to eat, but psilocybin. It helped them to understand so much more than their mortal minds ever could on their own."

Lord took Tino's hand and placed the packet containing the tiny black fleck in his palm and wrapped Tino's fingers around it. "Take the trip when you're in a mellow mood, and where you feel safe. Don't let it get wet, or it'll lose its power."

"You mean this isn't a piece of film, but LSD?"

"A chemist figured out a way to make it look like film. The pigs never suspect. Beautiful, ain't it?"

"Is it like getting drunk?"

"Naw man, nothing like that."

"So what's it like?"

"A psychedelic trip. The ride on the way up is intense. Jittery. Some people don't like it, but if your head's in the right place it's outta sight. You'll peak maybe an hour into it and see as never before. Colors, a fluid and malleable world in which everything and nothing is real."

"Like in Alice in Wonderland?"

"Never thought about it like that, but yeah, it's Wonderland, Mr. Toad's wild ride and Oz all into one. After you peak, there's a beautiful and peaceful ride down."

Tino stared at the packet in the palm of his hand, intensely curious about the drug's supernatural powers and equally affected by a dark, ominous sense that he should not accept Lord's gift. He put the packet in his coin pocket, planning to toss it when he got back on the road.

"It's cool how you hide this from the cops. But how do you hide the pot? Don't you get pulled over and searched? Especially riding around in this bus."

"Major hassle, man. It's another reason we're going to California where it's mellower. The heat's pulled us over a few times. They search the inside of the bus, but never under it. And I've got stuff to sell sealed in cans with Campbell's soup labels and it's mm, mm good!"

Dawn and Snow giggled.

"It's going to be groovy when we all get to Californee," Snow said. "Is it as mellow as they all say it be?"

"I don't know. It's just home to me," Tino said, feeling a tinge of envy. The hippies were living a life of total freedom, one he could hardly imagine. "You're lucky. My folks would never let me live like this. What do yours say about it?"

"My once-self was named Jethro Cornelius Taylor III. And Jethro was born to a rich and confused father who married a rich and confused Southern belle. He got into politics, and he votes to keep 'the nigras in their place,' as he says, and supports dropping napalm and Agent Orange in Vietnam. And the government thinks I'm going to register for the draft. Ha! I reject that life, all of it, even to the name given to me by my parents, who are no less than agents of an oppressive society. I am Lord! And Lord has discovered that love and peace are the way. Make love, not war."

Snow and Dawn gazed on him with admiration. He took an alligator clip from his pocket and pinched what was left of the joint.

"And you?" Tino said, turning to Snow and Dawn. "Aren't your folks worried about you?"

Dawn turned away. Snow looked pained. "We be the last of sixteen young-uns of the fambly what live in the West Virginie Mountains. Momma dances with snakes and drinks poison as her worship, and pap drinks his shine. When he commences to drinkin' that devil water he gets to talking, saying we be his property to do whatever he pleases with it. Most of us have gone off to live with neighbors or hitched up with somebody to our likin' or just done disappeared like me and Dawn."

"That's sad," Tino said, "very sad." He took the clip with the roach from Lord and stared at it. "This makes me feel relaxed. I wish I could always feel this way."

"You're a good dude," Lord said. "Come with us. Every day's a holiday, no hassles, just peace, love, and insight."

"It's possible," Snow said. "This laff's a whole lot more to my likin'. A free laff to live and do what I want, when I want." She held him with her eyes and brushed her breasts against him. "Do y'all believe in free love?"

Tino throbbed with naked lust. "Sounds wonderful."

"I'd surely like to fuck ya'll, right now."

Lord laid a hand on Tino's shoulder. "You can have privacy with Snow, or all of us can have a love-in."

"I couldn't do that."

Lord reached for Dawn's hand to help her from the chair. "Say no more, brother. Everything in our world is free of hassle, free in every way."

Snow touched the rise in Tino's crotch. "What do you say that we have ourselves a beautiful time."

He trembled. "I'd really like to, but I'm in love with some-one."

Snow's dark eyes flooded with tears. "And ya'll want to be true to her. That's beautiful, real beautiful."

"Come with us," Lord said. "Shed the skin of your oppressed life for a new and free life, a life to get high when you want, make love when you want."

Snow gently petted Tino's cheek with the back of her hand. "I'd surely like that."

Tino's head spun with the unimaginable possibilities. Getting high and having sex anytime he wanted, no school, no church. "Boy, I'd surely—" Movement to the rear of the bus. He looked out.

Framed in the rear window was small, dark-skinned Sal racing toward them.

"It's my brother!" The hippies looked out the window.

"He wouldn't be cool with this?" Lord said.

"Cool with this? He's a Catholic priest!"

"Wow. Major bummer, man."

"He's okay with people doing whatever they want. But no way with me getting high."

Lord and Snow ushered Tino out.

Sal pulled up and narrowed his eyes. "How're you folks doing?"

Tino tried to sound normal. "Doing good." He pointed to the bus. "It's really cool inside."

Lord stepped forward and raised his palm in the greeting of an American Indian. "I. Am. Lord."

Sal pursed his lips to keep from laughing, but a snort escaped sounding like a polite little fart. "Lord? I've been wait-ing a long time to meet you."

Lord puffed up. "It's my enlightened name."

"Interesting. Why Lord?"

"Because I Lord over myself. I am the 'I am, who am,' of my life and of my destiny. I reject the culture of consumption that destroys the spirit of men."

"And women," Snow said.

"You're a deep thinker."

Lord stared hard at Sal. "I have learned to see."

Tino, sensing a pissing contest between alpha males, intervened. "He stopped to help me."

Sal softened. "Okay, it's appreciated." He took a small plastic bag from his pocket. "Master link," he said and went for his tools.

Lord hugged Tino. "Have a safe trip, man. It was real meeting you." He turned to Sal. "You got a good brother."

"Yeah, thanks."

Snow blew Tino a kiss. "I'd surely love seeing ya in Californee."

Tino watched them board and waved as they rode by. "Make Love Not War," read their bumper sticker.

"You made quite an impression on them."

"I guess so," Tino said. They sure say 'beautiful' a lot. I wonder if they're really as happy as they're making out to be."

"Hard to say. My guess is that they're trying to convince themselves as much as anybody else that they've found the way."

"Say," Tino said. "You wouldn't have something to eat stashed in your gear, would you?"

"Hungry?"

"Kind of. I feel like something sweet and chocolaty."

"Well forget about eating for now. We've got a crap-load of time to make up." Sal fired up his engine and hit the road with a vengeance.

Tino followed, craving rocky road ice cream.

24.

A Hard Row to Hoe

Tino, stoned on marijuana, looked up ahead at Sal leaning forward in his shorts, dark hairy legs, boots covering his ankles, and riding at a manic pace. He always rode leaning forward to minimize wind resistance, doing anything to gain an iota of time. But Sal, inexplicably, began slowing down and continued until he came to a stop.

"Dang! I knew that I was low on gas and planned to stop at the next gas station."

"It's cool, man," Tino said. "I'll go get you some." He pulled away singing "They call me mellow yellow."

Tino rode north to an Amoco gas station on the outskirts of Charleston. He noticed a candy machine in the office next to the counter and strolled in. "Ooh," he whispered, "Nestlé Crunch." He dropped in a nickel and pulled the knob. He took the candy bar out of the tray and peeled off the wrapper, salivating. Tino closed his eyes, and bit deep into crispy chocolate. It made sweet love with his palate. He put the rest in his shirt pocket. Better not keep Sal waiting.

He borrowed a gallon gas can and headed back to Sal.

Sal emptied the gas can into his tank. "I'll follow you to the station, and step on it."

Tino checked his mirror. Sal was right on his tail. Tino wasn't going to go any faster, so Sal might as well mellow out.

They topped off their tanks at the gas station and were ready to roll, but Sal said, "Crap, I hate killing more time, but I really gotta go." He jogged around to the bathroom.

Tino reached for the Crunch bar and finished it, savoring every bite. And where was Sal? He should have returned.

Tino leaned back and studied the lines of his palm.

Sal jogged back around and hopped on the Hawk. "A man and his kid beat me to the bathroom. Took 'em forever to come out. ¡*Vamonos!*"

"You really need to take it a little slower, dude."

Sal looked at his brother askew. "We're losing time and you want to slow down. What's gotten into you?"

"Too much hurrying. Not good, dude."

"And what's with this 'dude,' stuff?"

"Let's just go, man."

Tino followed Sal hour after hour, losing any semblance of time.

Riding. Riding. Riding.

What would it be like to live like the hippies? Wander the country at a sane pace instead of with Mister, damn-the-torpedoes, full-steam-ahead Sal.

Riding, riding, eternal fucking, riding.

They crossed into North Carolina deep in the night, passing buildings and neighborhoods, all dark and asleep. Sal finally stopped on the shoulder of the highway and pointed down into a dry flood-control channel. They coasted down to the bottom.

"We'll lay the bikes down here, hike up the berm, sleep in the shrubbery, and hit it at first light."

Sigh. "Whatever."

Eighteen-wheeler monsters roared by, vibrating the ground making it hard to fall asleep. Tino drifted off thinking of beautiful and strong Lola—strong in body, strong in mind. *I wish we were together right now inside my bag.*

"Two-forty, two-forty, code eleven-eighty-three. Route 17, one mile north of Ahoskie Over." A female dispatcher's voice blared into the night waking Tino.

Sal was peering out of the shrubbery toward the highway. Emergency lights of a state trooper's cruiser spun around, piercing red light through the shrubbery.

Sal glanced back and whispered, "Stay here."

"Where in the hell would I go?"

Sal eased down the channel with cat-like stealth.

A trooper scanning the area with a flashlight turned with a start when Sal appeared. The trooper drew his revolver.

Tino sucked in his breath.

Sal raised his hands. The trooper stood stiff, gun hand extended at the ready. Sal and the trooper spoke for a moment, and the trooper holstered his gun.

"Jesus," Tino said.

Sal returned. "A trucker saw our bikes lying in the ditch and called in. They thought that we had crashed and had been thrown from the bikes."

"I about crapped when he pulled his gun."

"Scared me too. He's the big-shot type. He said if my gang showed up he'd have dozens of heavily armed men here in minutes. I told him there was no gang. He said he'd run us in if we didn't leave pronto."

Sal and Tino were once again on the highway. The ambulance that the trooper had likely called and forgotten to cancel passed them and pulled up to the scene where nothing had happened.

They merged onto a frontage road and stopped at an office building with a sprawling lawn.

"Take it easy riding over the grass," Sal said. "I don't want to mess it up. No one should know that we were here when they arrive to work in the morning."

"Yeah sure, easy on the grass."

They laid their bags over the grass next to the bikes.

The soft lawn was much better to sleep over. Tino was out in moments and slept soundly until the automatic sprinkler system started.

"Fuck!"

They flew out of their bags, stuffed their clothes into them, set them on the seats, fired up the engines, and raced out flinging wet mud onto windows.

Tino shivered with cold riding in his T-shirt and boxer shorts. They parked off a dirt road under a broad oak tree skirted with shrubs and crawled in on hands and knees under the shrubbery, dragging their dampened bags behind them.

"We'll sleep in a little in the morning," Sal said.

"Shitting wonderful."

Sal laughed. "Can anything else go wrong?"

Tino fell into fitful sleep.

"Cock-a-doodle-do," a rooster crowed in the distance. Tino rustled in his bag. Another cock-a-doodle-do. A nearby rooster answered, "Cock-a-doodle-do."

Son of a bitch.

And the macho duel began.

"Cock-a-doodle-do, I'll kick your ass!"

"Cock-a-doodle-do, come on over, fucker."

Tino drifted off yet again and slept until he felt a shove to his shoulder at dawn.

"Wake up."

Tino didn't move.

A harder shove. "Wake up Hermano!"

"¡Ay, como friegas! (How you bother!)" Tino said, exasperated and ready to throw a punch. "What do you want?"

"We're in poison ivy. We need to get out."

"*¡No me digas!* (Don't tell me!)"

"I hope we didn't rub up against it when we crawled in," Sal said.

"WE NEED TO WASH OFF ANY OIL that might have gotten on us," Sal instructed in a gas station bathroom in Tar Heel, North Carolina. They scrubbed faces, hands and arms using copious amounts of the coarse pink powdered-soap from the dispenser.

"We've had a heck of a time riding through the South," Tino said.

"What do you mean?"

"We almost got eaten by a mountain lion, hassled by the Texas Rangers and barely escaped being lynched. I hope that I've experienced the worst that'll happen on the trip. I can't imagine worse."

Sal pulled down on the cloth of the rotating towel dispenser to wipe his face and hands. "Think positive. The best is ahead."

Tino grabbed his crotch. "*Aquí tengo tu* positive thinking."

Part 2

Blood

25.

The Bloodiest Landscape in North America

SAL AND TINO ENTERED a Winn-Dixie grocery store outside Richmond, Virginia, in midmorning. Tino pointed a curious finger at a breaded tube-like food in a steaming red sauce.

"What's that?" he asked the Negro clerk serving hot foods in the deli department.

"Chitlins, young man."

"Looks to me like some kind of macaroni."

The clerk chuckled. "I suppose you could call it Southern macaroni."

Moments later Sal and Tino were outside next to their bikes. Tino stabbed the noodle-like fare with a plastic fork and gave it a try.

"Good. Kind of chewy like *menudo*." He held out the container.

Sal forked out a portion. "It's not bad. So what're chitlins?" he asked.

"Beats me. Guy in the store said they're Southern macaroni."

Sal wiped red grease off of his lips. "Fredericksburg, the battleground site where our great-grandpa was probably killed is on the way to Washington D. C. We should take a quick look and get back on schedule."

THEY ARRIVED IN FREDERICKSBURG after an hour's ride and crossed a bridge over the Rappahannock River to the site.

"Welcome to the battleground known as The Bloodiest Landscape in North America," said a short middle-age woman wearing a U.S. Park Service uniform. Her nameplate read Martha Farmer.

"The battles over Fredericksburg took place on several fronts December 11 to 15, 1862. Even though the Confederates were greatly outnumbered, these engagements were the most lopsided victories of the war for the South. While they suffered some five thousand casualties, the Union lost over twice that. The battle at Marye's Heights was the bloodiest." She pointed to a long wide grassy plain with a stone wall at the foot of low-lying hills.

"The Yankees had to advance 500 yards across the plain in order to engage the three thousand Rebels who were dug in behind the wall. As you can see, the wall was over 40 feet higher than the plain. General Lee could not have had a better defensive position.

"Batteries of cannons on the hillsides behind them provided almost complete coverage of the plain. Edward Alexander, the Confederate artillery commander said, 'A chicken could not live on that field when we open on it.'

"General Ambrose Burnsides, the Union commander, gambled on an ill-fated strategy of trying to overrun the Rebels. But barrages of musket and cannon fire cut down wave after wave of Union charges."

Tino listened intently, envisioning the battle.

"The carnage continued through the afternoon as assault after assault was fended off. Burnsides, seeing a disaster unfolding before him, called for his elite fighting forces, the Irish Brigades. They were made up of Irish and Scottish immigrants who had recently come to America to escape famine and the economic depressions in their countries. The brigades fought with great courage, wanting to prove themselves to their new country.

"The final assaults launched by the Irish and Scots attested to their valor. Even as they fell in staggering numbers, they continued to advance. The Southerners thought themselves the bravest fighters, but on this day, they gained a new respect for their Northern rivals.

"The Irish brigades managed to get within 50 yards of the wall, closer than any of the other attempts, but realized they were not going to breach the enemy line and finally retreated rather than die needlessly. Firsthand accounts say that the field looked as though it had been carpeted in blue from so many uniforms of fallen Yankees. The wounded lay moaning, begging for water, and calling for loved ones throughout the afternoon and the long, cold December night.

"The next morning, a nineteen-year-old Confederate, Sergeant Richard Kirkland, who had defended the wall, couldn't bear hearing the pitiful cries any longer; he collected canteens from fellow soldiers and took water to the wounded. Kirkland became known as The Angel of Marye's Heights. There's a statue of him in Fredericksburg giving aid to a dying soldier."

"Did he survive the war?" Tino asked.

"He died in battle the following year. His last words were, 'I am done for. You can do me no good. Save yourselves and please tell my pa I died right.' I wish the story had a happier ending, but to soften it would not honor the experience of the soldiers—and the battlefield, baptized in the blood of so many men."

"It's so beautiful and peaceful here," Tino said. "Hard to believe that such a bloody battle happened."

He rode, consumed by the story and remembering that the Irish Brigades were made up of Irish and Scottish Immigrants and that they were elite forces who fought bravely. Tino's grandpa was Scottish. He must have served in those brigades and charged across the field. Could he have been one of wounded who lay suffering through the cold all night long?

And what did Kirkland mean by "save yourselves?" Was he telling soldiers to leave the war?

Tino recalled the hippie's bumper sticker: "Make love. Not war." Maybe he should try to live like the hippies. Live in peace, make love, and get high whenever he wanted. He sank his finger into his coin pocket and felt the packet with the LSD.

Lord had told him to take it when he was in a mellow mood. But there was no mellow with Sal around.

If I took the LSD now, it'd make this ride a lot more interesting, and maybe I'd be over it by the time Sal called it a day. Or should I toss it?

They merged onto a four-lane highway, heavy with traffic and exhaust fumes. They rode onto a long bridge that spanned the Potomac River, and led to Washington D.C.

26.

Columbia Heights

S AL AND TINO STROLLED BY THE WHITE HOUSE and Capitol Building, took a lap around the pool of the Washington Monument and stood at Lincoln's feet in his memorial building.

"I want to see something," Sal said in late afternoon.

Tino followed Sal north through the city wondering what he had in mind. Fire-damaged buildings began to appear, some under repair, others hollowed-out shells. Long black fingers of residue reached up the walls where fire had burned out windows. Ragged drapes fluttered from a deserted apartment building. Broken glass lay strewn along the roadside.

They parked in front of the Columbia Heights Market. "What the heck happened here?" Tino asked, looking at an empty lot with piles of scorched lumber, blackened metal, and appliances lying like the charred remains of dead animals.

"Riots after Martin Luther King Jr. was assassinated in April. I wanted to see it for myself." Sal gestured with his chin at a laundromat next door to the market. "Let's get some laundry soap."

Discarded candy wrappers, cigarette butts, and shattered beer bottles lay on a patch of ground where a tree once stood in front of the market. All that remained was a lonely stump.

Tino found the detergent and met Sal at the sales counter.

"Good afternoon, young gents," said a short, balding clerk. "Visiting The District?"

Sal set a new spiral notebook on the counter. "Yes, sir. Looks like you folks been cleaning up."

"Yup," the clerk said. "Got a ways to go yet."

"Were you here when it happened?" Tino asked.

"Got out soon as I heard King was shot. I knew what was coming. Years of pent-up frustration were going to blow. And did it ever. Total chaos. Thousands of them rioting and looting, and the police couldn't control them. Johnson called in the troops. Rioters got to within a couple of blocks of the White House, for crying out loud. National Guard set up a machine gun on the steps of the Capitol Building."

"Holy cow!" Tino said.

"Mayor stopped gun and alcohol sales. People threw rocks and bottles at the police and firemen and pretty much anything that wasn't nailed down. Reports said a thousand buildings were torched. Smoke everywhere, even drifted into the nice parts of town. Seemed like the whole world was on fire." The clerk shook his head as if he could hardly believe his own account.

"Was your store damaged?" Tino asked.

The clerk pointed to the wall-size glass pane facing the street. "Got a new one with the insurance money. When they came through, they took every bit of food. What's that tell you? They were hungry! Shouldn't be in this country. King was just trying to get them what the rest of us have, no good reason to off him like that."

"Aren't you afraid of getting robbed?" Tino said. "Especially after that?"

"Been here thirty years, never had a problem. I've got Negro customers who've been coming in since the day I opened. Now their kids buy here."

"Thank you for sharing your story with us," Sal said.

"Like I say, they only want a piece of the pie, and there's plenty enough to go 'round."

"EVERYBODY SHOULD SEE THE CAPITAL," Tino said from his bed in their motel room that night.

Sal looked up from writing in his travel log. "So many beautiful statues, government buildings, and gardens."

"And so different from the neighborhoods where the riots happened," Tino said.

Sal licked his finger, turned a page of his log, and continued writing.

Tino switched off his lamp; his thoughts turned to beautiful Lola.

SAL AND TINO RODE THROUGH Pennsylvania's Amish country the next morning and toured historic sites of Philadelphia. They headed north in late afternoon and pulled over at a viewing area at the George Washington Bridge spanning the Hudson River. They shut down the bikes and dismounted to take in the metropolis across the river. The solid bank of buildings made it look like a colossal walled city.

"We made it!" Tino said. "We made it from San Diego clear to New York City!"

Sal stared at his brother for a moment. A victorious grin spread over his face, "Yeah, we did it!" He laughed and started dancing a jig.

"Ha! Ha! You can't dance worth a crap!"

27.

The City

Sal, the Hawk, Tino, and Rocinante rode the George Washington Bridge triumphantly over the Hudson River and were soon on a different kind of river; a river of asphalt that ran through towering canyons of concrete skyscrapers. They were insignificant specks in flowing and receding rushes of taxis, trucks, buses, and cars controlled by green, amber, and red traffic lights. The constant rolling din of the nonstop hustle echoed off the towering walls of Manhattan's buildings, block after block after block. The sidewalks were alive with people; those on business quick-stepped it around those who strolled.

Tino jumped with a start at a traffic stop when a bicycle messenger whizzed past him.

The light changed to green, and a delivery van made a sudden jerk toward the messenger as he passed, causing the messenger to fall. "Asshole!" he yelled. He was up in a heart-beat peddling hard, and he reached the van at a stoplight. He knocked the van's side mirror askew as he passed.

"Asshole!" the driver yelled and jumped out of his van to realign the mirror.

The traffic light turned green. A cab driver behind the van leaned on his horn and stuck his head out of the cab. "Move it, fucknuts!" The van driver sneered, ready to go after the cabbie, but a line of cars behind them created a chorus of blaring horns.

Sal and Tino rode the epic streets of New York into early evening. Neon signs in various windows blinked on: UPTOWN STEAKHOUSE, O'GRADY'S PUB, GOOD EATS, OPEN 24 HRS.

Sal waved for Tino's attention and pointed to a restaurant. Glowing red letters, written in Chinese-like characters, read SUN LUCK GOURMET RESTAURANT.

Tino nodded and followed Sal to a nearby Amoco gas station, where they changed into their cleanest clothes. Sal looked oddly funny in long pants.

They rode to a parking garage where a tall, muscular attendant in blue coveralls sat in a booth paging through a magazine, a busty woman in a nightie on its cover. The attendant had the top two buttons to his coveralls undone, showing a mass of black chest hair and a thin gold chain with a religious medal. New York Yankee World Series Pennants from 1961 and 1962 were pinned to the back wall of the booth, along with black and white glossy photos: Joe DiMaggio at bat, Joe Namath ready to take a snap and Rocky Marciano standing over an opponent sprawled out on the mat.

"Hey, ha ya doin'?" The attendant said. He gestured toward their license plates. "You mean ta tell me that you drove these things all the way from California?" His words shot out fast as machine-gun fire.

"We sure did," Tino answered.

"Tell you what, youse guys can put your bikes in one space instead a two. Saves you a little dough that way. Name's Vinnie by the way." He extended his huge hairy hand.

"Well, thank you very much, Vinnie," Sal said. "This is a nice welcome to New York. I've heard New Yorkers can be a little testy. You're not living up to that."

"Testy? Tell it like it is. Some of us are real jerks, but just shine them on, and if one gets too pushy just say, 'Hey asshole, fuget about it.' Fuget about it, asshole, is all you got to say. They'll back right off." He looked curiously at Sal. "What are you, by the ways?"

"What am I?"

"You know, are you Eyetalians? You looks a little Eyetalian to me."

"Oh, I see. No. Not Italians. Mexicans. Our parents were born in Mexico."

"You talk Spanish like Pee Ahs?"

"Pee Ahs?"

"Pee Ahs, Puerto Ricans."

"Oh yes, of course. PRs, like in *West Side Story*, right? We speak Spanish, but it's a little different than what you're used to."

"Never seen me a Mexican before, and you sure don't look like no Pee Ah. Hey, nice meeting youse guys. Lotsa luck to you."

"Did that palooka talk fast enough for youse?" Sal said, out on the sidewalk.

"Fuget about it, asshole."

THE RESTAURANT'S TABLES WERE SET with scarlet tablecloths, folded white linen napkins, silverware, and chopsticks tucked in paper sleeves. Red lanterns adorned with golden tassels hung from the ceiling and emitted a soft glow.

The hostess, a petite Asian woman with long, shining black hair, wore a silky jade-green dress that hugged her slender body. She smiled. "May I help you, sirs?"

"Table for two, please," Sal said.

"So sorry, sirs. Must have coat and tie for dinner."

Tino ached for food. The luring aromas coming from the kitchen made it nearly unbearable.

Sal smiled awkwardly. "Oh yes, yes of course, coats and ties."

The brothers made for the door, sorely disappointed.

She spoke behind them. "You are traveling, yes?"

Sal turned. "Yes. We're on a long trip. Started in California."

"Very long. Please to wait for minute, sirs." She walked into the kitchen.

"Maybe take out," Tino said.

She returned. "We can offer you side room, if you like."

"Bitchen!" Tino said, drawing a glare from Sal.

"That would be great," Sal said.

She led them to a nook off the dining room and had a waitress attend to them. The hostess dropped in during their meal and caught Sal trying his hand at chopsticks. He dropped one, picked it up, and held it by the wrong end. She turned away trying to hide her giggling.

Tino, eating in big bites, was oblivious to anything but the exotic and aromatic foods. He'd never eaten meats prepared with almonds and cashews and mixed with amber sauces that were both tart and sweet, or vegetables mixed with rice, egg, and bits of chicken. He'd never had noodles in broths containing small wafers of beef. He picked up a small plate with a yellow paste. "Mustard?"

"Don't know," Sal said. "Try it."

Tino poured a spoonful on an eggroll and tossed it into his mouth.

"Ay! Ay! Ay!" The paste burned like acid fire. He gulped water. "Doesn't help! ¡Hijo! ¡Hijo!" His face reddened, eyes watered. He drank more.

The hostess appeared. "What wrong?"

Tino fanned his mouth and pointed to the yellow paste.

The hostess hurried to the kitchen and returned with a glass of milk and bread. She emptied a packet of sugar into the milk, mixed it, and handed it to Tino with the bread. "Eat, drink."

He stuffed his mouth and drank. He breathed deeply and wiped his tears and sweat. "That was harsh."

"So sorry, you no understand Chinese mustard."

Tino stared sharply at Sal. "Did you know?"

"No."

"Well, why're you laughing, *menso*?"

"You enjoy dinner?" the hostess asked.

Tino pushed from the table. "Except for the hot stuff, it was the best."

"So happy you like."

Sal reached for his wallet. "Thank you for serving us."

The hostess directed a waitress to pack the leftovers and led Sal and Tino to the cash register. "There are many Chinese in San Francisco, yes?"

Sal laid a ten on the counter. "Oh, yes. There's a big Chinatown, and all the signs are written in Chinese."

"You show me San Francisco one day?"

"Who, me?" Sal said. "Yeah, yeah sure."

"Please to wait one moment." She walked into the kitchen.

Tino spoke softly into Sal's ear. "She was hitting on you, *ese* dude!"

"Think so?"

"Yes, Sal, and she's a real fox."

"Fuget about it, asshole."

The hostess returned with two large bags. "You leftovers."

Sal took the bags. "Maybe I can pay you to teach me to use chopsticks."

She giggled and reached behind the cash register and handed Sal a business card. "When you show me Chinatown?"

"Yes, of course. *Y qué bonita eres.*"

The hostess looked confused. "What that mean?"

"You're a nice lady, a very nice lady."

She smiled shyly. "You come back, yes?"

Sal motioned Tino toward the door. "We will."

VINNIE POINTED OUT SAL AND TINO to a man standing at the garage booth. "These the Mexican fellas I's telling you about, Joey."

"Hey, ha you doin'?" Joey said. "Yeah, Vinnie, it's just like ya say, the little one looks Eyetalian, what with the skin and dark, curly hair."

Sal nodded. "Thank you for the compliment, and nice meeting you."

"Hey, you's pretty funny. I's never thought of calling somebody Eyetalian like it was a compliment."

"Any culture that can claim such greats as Michelangelo and Leonardo De Vinci, not to mention a line of popes, is certainly worthy."

Joey pointed to the picture of Rocky Marciano. "Speaking of the greats, you can't forget about the greatest heavyweight that ever lived."

"What about Muhammad Ali?" Tino said.

"I ain't never going to call that nigger Muhammad Ali. His name's Cassius Clay."

Tino winced at the racial slur.

"Clay couldn't last tree rounds with the Brockton Blockbuster."

"My father thinks so too," Tino said. "But it's a fight we'll never see. Rocky's been retired too long. Neither of them has ever lost a championship fight."

"I'm glad that they stripped Clay of his title for refusing to serve in the army," Vinnie said.

"He had it coming," Joey said.

"Have you served?" Tino asked.

"I's got a bum knee."

"Me too," Vinnie said.

Tino laughed inside. "Nice meeting you guys."

Sal reached into his pocket at the parking stall.

"Crap!"

Tino groaned. "Now what?"

Sal tapped his pockets in a panic. "My key!"

"God, you're always losing stuff!"

"I can't imagine where it could be!"

"*Ay, pero como eres, menso,*" Tino said, preparing to help Sal search for the key, but noticed that it was still in the ignition and pointed it out.

Sal sighed in relief.

"I'm going to tie it to your dick."

Sal started his bike laughing.

Tino would normally want to call it a day, but the rich food, kindness of the hostess, and the hour-plus break from riding took the edge off. And the city was throbbing. A group of young men and women dressed in sparkling shirts and bell-bottom pants filed out of a taxicab and made a beeline for a nightclub across the street.

"Dance to the Music," by Sly and the Family Stone blared onto the street.

"Hey!" Sal yelled. "Got something to show you."

"*¡Ándale!*" Tino said, ready for adventure.

"*Sígueme* (follow me)," Sal said.

They stopped at a red light on the way. A disheveled black woman who was crossing the street, mumbling angrily to herself, noticed Tino and approached him.

"You wanna start sumthin'? Go ahead, mutha fuckah, start some shit!"

Tino turned Rocinante's front tire toward her and gunned the engine. Tailpipes roared. She drew back and continued on her way mumbling. He looked after her. How did she manage her feral existence in such hostile territory? Drivers behind the two bikers leaned on their horns as soon as the light changed.

"Hey! Fuget abat it, assholes!" Sal yelled. Tino raced after laughing. They stopped at 47th and Broadway. Thousands of marquee lights illuminated the street for blocks: *Hello Dolly*, *The Music Man*, *Hair*, *Oh Calcutta*. A chauffeur in a black cap, suit, and white gloves opened the rear door of a limousine. Lights reflected off the car's hood and tinted windows. A man in a tuxedo and a bejeweled woman in a sparkling gown stepped out.

They made a second pass through Broadway. Sal turned left onto 50th Street, and they rode five blocks to a street paralleling the river. An endless string of headlights from cars crossing a bridge, reflected off the water. Sal pointed toward a set of ballpark light standards; probably one of the only spots in the city where they could get away with sleeping outdoors. They wheeled the bikes into a massive hedge along the outer wall of the field.

"Hope we're not rousted by some cop in the middle of the night," Tino said, brushing teeth.

"I'll just say 'fuget abat it, asshole.'"

"Great idea *menso*. I can't believe how big New York is. Ten downtown San Diego's could fit in this place, and there'd still be room."

Sal crawled into his bag. "Population's seven million. San Diego's just over a half million. Hard to imagine this was once forests and Indian tribes."

Tino lay back. Few stars were bright enough to pierce the smog. "We've done a lot of stuff today. Saw the Amish farms and the people in horse-drawn carriages, saw where the government was born in Independence Hall, ate Philly cheese steak sandwiches, rode through New Jersey, and now we're in one of the greatest cities in the world."

"That *is* a lot," Sal said. "How're you holding up?"

"What do you mean?"

"A lot of hard riding."

"So?"

"So, just wondering how you're feeling."

"Okay, I guess. A little tired, but I'm handling it." Tino sensed something behind the questioning.

"You know that woman you spent time with down South?"

"Lola," he said, surprised by the question.

"Do you ever think of her?"

"Everyday, why?"

Sal lay back and stared up into the blackness. "What was it like?"

"Like?"

"Come on, you know. What was it like being with her?"

"I've never, ever felt so close to someone, not Ma, not Val, girlfriends, nobody."

"That strong?"

"Stronger. I'm constantly thinking about her. I want to go back and be with her for good. Have you ever wondered what it'd be like to be with a woman?"

"Of course, but I made a vow."

Tino didn't offer more and was relieved that Sal left it at that. The din of traffic faded in his ear. He lay back, imagining a life with Lola. The two of them lying on a couch in their own home, watching TV, then making love.

HONKING HORNS AND REVVING CAR ENGINES from the morning commute awoke Tino. Sunlight struggling through an obese layer of smog, created by countless vehicles on the roads, arriving and departing jet liners, tugboats, ships in the harbors, and industry smokestacks gave the world a rusty hue. New York was too big for its own good.

Tino yawned, rubbed his eyes, and looked over to Sal. He lay with his back to Tino. "You awake?"

"Yup," Sal said, rolled over, and stretched his arms. "We're invited to Paul Gill's parents' home in New Hampshire so we can rest up for a couple of days."

"Right on!" Tino said. Tino knew and liked Sal's friend, Father Paul. They were ordained as priests in the same class.

"Hey!" Tino said. "We'll be closer to Bath, Maine. We'll be able to make a trip up there to see if there's a monument with grandpa's name on it."

"We'll be closer alright," Sal said. "But our stay with the Gills will knock the crap out of my schedule."

"But you said that we'll be staying for a few days, we can fit a trip to Bath, no?"

"I didn't say a few days I said a couple as in two. We'll need some time off from traveling, and we'll also need to do maintenance on the bikes, and who knows what Paul has planned out for us."

"Please, Sal, I really want to find out if there's a monument."

"We'll see."

"Whenever I hear 'we'll see,' it never happens."

"Forget about it for now, hermano. Let's concentrate on how much of New York City we can get in today before we head out."

They rode the labyrinths of New York: Madison Avenue, The Bronx, Brooklyn, Harlem, by "the house that Ruth built," Yankee Stadium, through Central Park, and the Empire State Building, the tallest building in the world. They ferried across the harbor to the Statue of Liberty, entered it at its base and climbed 354 stairs to the portals of her crown, where they scanned the City's skyline, the harbor, and Ellis Island. They ate hotdogs in late afternoon at Nathan's on Coney Island.

"Ready to head to Father Paul's?" Sal said.

"Yup. It'll be nice getting out of heavy traffic, sleeping in a bed and having some home-cooked food."

They joined a crush of commuter traffic leaving the city and entered a tunnel that burrowed under a body of water. Headlights blinked on, and the rumble of hundreds of vehicles echoed off the walls. The tunnel continued on and on. Tino had the sensation that it was closing in on him.

Concentrated exhaust fumes from leaded gasoline stung his eyes and left a sinister taste in the back of his throat. Nausea. He gave Sal an incredulous look as if asking *Does the tunnel ever end?* He put a hand over his mouth and nose.

A speck of daylight in the distance appeared. Tino signaled Sal, and sped off. Sal followed Tino passing cars on the right and left, close enough to touch. Horns blared at the brazen bikers. The feeble ray of light grew steadily—and finally, a burst of clean air and glorious sunlight.

They pulled over onto the narrow shoulder of the road. Tino breathed deeply, clearing his lungs. He rinsed the sting from his eyes with water from his canteen.

Sal spit. "Let's go. I want to make the Gill's before dark."

"The odor's stuck in my nose," Tino said. "No more damn tunnels." Sal laughed and coughed.

They rode through Connecticut and Massachusetts, passing highway exits for Yale, Harvard, Salem, Plymouth Rock, and Cape Cod. They skirted around Boston and crossed the state line into New Hampshire after sunset. Sal stopped at a supermarket in Manchester.

"Can't wait to get there," Tino said. "Hope they live close by."

"Too late to be showing up at someone's doorstep."

Sal bought bananas and milk.

They rode around the parking lot to the rear of the store. Sal took large squares of flattened cardboard out of a trash bin and stacked them for beds.

28.

The Gills

Vroom! Vroom! An engine revving loud and rude awoke Tino in the overcast, gray dawn. He peered out of his sleeping bag to see a truck's front tires and grill. Vroom! Vroom!

Sal and Tino had blocked a trash truck from getting to the trash dumpster.

The driver nervously tapped his thumbs against the steering wheel. "Sorry!" Tino yelled.

The brothers tossed their boots to the side, and threw on their shirts and pants. They heaved the sheets of cardboard they had slept on into the dumpster. The driver gave a "sorry, but just doing my job," shrug. Tino nodded knowingly. The driver rolled his truck forward, inserted the steel prongs of the lifting mechanism into the dumpster slots. The engine roared, the dumpster rose into the air, and emptied it into the truck's hopper.

The driver nodded and backed out.

"We'll park the bikes in the front parking lot and change into our cleanest clothes in the store bathroom before heading for the Gill's," Sal said.

The packet of LSD slipped out of Tino's pocket onto the floor when he changed clothes. He shot a sideways glance at Sal as he threw out his foot to hide it. Sal was busy hopping into his pants. Tino got to a knee to tie his bootlace and stashed the packet.

They pulled up to the Gill's home, a two-story, wood-framed bungalow located in a working-class neighborhood and scaled several stairs to the sunroom door, its walls made up of glass panes. In the center of the room sat a rattan patio set in a semicircle around a coffee table. Throughout the room were houseplants: coleus, impatiens, wandering Jews, spider plants. Pots sat on waist-high pedestals; others hung from the ceiling by cords of braided jute. Pairs of goulashes sat next to the front door of the house under cold weather gear hanging from wall hooks.

Sal rang the doorbell. Paul and his parents appeared with warm welcoming smiles and walked through the sunroom.

Paul hugged Sal and stepped back. "Ma, Dad, meet men without faults." Mr. and Mrs. Gill were middle-aged, short, and stout.

Paul's father offered his hand. "Claude Gill." His rose-colored cheeks were full—nose plump, shiny scalp free of hair.

Paul's mother put a hand to her breast. "Marie. I've heard so much about you Father Caballero."

"No, please, it's just Sal, we can't spend the next two days being so formal."

Mr. Gill winked at Tino and offered his hand. "Do we call you acolyte? Or is Tino alright?"

Tino chuckled. "Just Tino, I haven't been an alter boy for a few years."

Mrs. Gill held the door open. "Please come in. Let's sit in the kitchen where it's cozy."

Wainscoting, painted white, lined the parlor walls. Portions of the hardwood floor not covered by rugs reflected the light from a brass floor lamp that sat next to a padded armchair with an ottoman. Long-ago photographs of people in hats, dresses, suits, and ties lined the hall. Tino caught the aroma of baking pastry as they filed through a hall toward the kitchen. Everyone except Mrs. Gill sat at the table covered by a red and white checkered tablecloth. She made for the oven, took a stick match from a drawer and glanced back. "I understand your parents were born in Mexico."

"Yes, ma'am," Sal said. "Ma's from Hermosillo in the Sonoran Desert south of Arizona. Pa was born in Mazatlán, a fishing port on the Pacific Coast, south of the Tropic of Cancer."

Mr. Gill slid an ashtray sitting in the center of the table to him and took a pack of Kent cigarettes from his shirt pocket, tapped one out, and lit up.

Mrs. Gill struck the match, turned a knob, and held the match to a burner. "South of the Tropic of Cancer how exotic." A flame burst open and settled to a blue glow. She set a teakettle on the burner, turned and walked to the table. "Paul tells me that you have an identical twin brother. I've heard twins can read each other's minds and feel each other's pain. Is that so?"

"I only feel it when he gives me a good one upside the head."

Mr. Gill chuckled and coughed out smoke. "It must be fun mixing up people."

"Even Ma," Sal said. "When they were newborns, she put a small gold chain around one of their necks to tell them apart."

"I can't imagine," Mrs. Gill said. "You must have a story or two of confusing people."

"Yeah!" Tino said, enjoying the attention. "We pulled a really good one once with our friends, Robert and Gilbert Marquez. They're identical twins like us."

Mr. Gill dropped his cigarette into the ashtray. "Holy smokes! You mean you and your brother are friends with another set of identical twins?"

"Yes sir. We met in grammar school when we were in first grade and they were in second. We grew up together until we moved out of the neighborhood. Sometimes we all played together, other times Gilbert and I went one way, and Robert and Val went another. It was really hot one day and Gilbert and I were sitting on the porch when here come Robert and Val eating snow cones. Those cold cones looked good, so Gilbert and I went to get some too with money we'd made selling newspapers on street corners. By the time we got back Robert and Val had finished theirs and went back for another one. Pretty soon they came running back.

'Free snow cones! Free snow cones!'"

The teakettle whistled, shooting a funnel of steam into the air. Mrs. Gill went to the stove, keeping an ear turned toward Tino.

"'There's no such thing as free snow cones,' I said, thinking that they were trying to fool us. They said that the snow cone lady said, 'Boy, you two sure like snow cones.' They laughed and explained that they had twin brothers who had bought some too, but she didn't believe them. 'If you can prove it, I'll give all of you a free one.' You should have seen the look on her face when the four of us came running up to her shop."

Mr. Gill's belly bounced with laughter.

"That's a wonderful story," Mrs. Gill said, setting a tray with the teapot and a bowl of honey on the table. "Are you still friends with them?"

"Yes, ma'am. We were always together until we moved. They just got drafted into the Army after graduating high school last year. Gilbert came by to visit just before I left for this trip to to tell us that he got orders to serve in Vietnam."

"I'll pray for him," Mrs. Gill said. She set a basket of cinnamon rolls on the table. Tino reached for one.

"Paul tells me you've just graduated," Mrs. Gill said. "Are you going to college?"

Tino swelled with pride. "No, ma'am. I'm joining the Marines and hope to see Gilbert in Vietnam."

Mrs. Gill's face dropped. "You may want to know something about this dreadful war before you join."

Tino squirmed. Why wasn't she proud of him?

Mr. Gill grumbled. "Ellsberg's exposed it all. They're lying about this shitting war!"

Mrs. Gill jumped with a start. "Claude Gill!"

Paul covered his mouth holding laughter. Mr. Gill furrowed his forehead. "I may be Catholic, my love. But I'm also a man." He looked to Sal as if looking for help.

Sal laughed. "No offense taken. My father uses descriptive language, and he even does it bilingually!"

Mr. Gill wheezed a chuckle.

"I've been hearing a lot of accents on our trip," Sal said. "I detect a slight one with you folks. It's a new one to me."

"Maybe a little French," Mr. Gill said. "We come from Quebec. 'Frogs,' the Americans call us. The 'Quebecans' proposed building a bridge across Lake Champlain to the United States. What do you think the Americans said? 'Let the frogs swim.' Ha!"

"I understand that it doesn't rain much in California," Mrs. Gill said. "I'd love to live where it doesn't rain quite so much as it does here."

"Where does your water come from if it doesn't rain?" Mr. Gill said.

"The Sierra Nevada mountain range," Sal said. "Water's channeled hundreds of miles to us in Southern California. The Mexican government complains that we're not leaving enough in the rivers that flow into their country. Southern California get less than a foot of rain a year. And Northern Mexico gets even less than that."

Mr. Gill raised his eyebrows. "Less than a foot a year? We haven't had rain in two weeks, and it's darn near a drought.

And Mexicans should get their fair share. They otta be pissed off at us."

Mrs. Gill jerked when she kicked her husband under the table.

Mr. Gill winced. "I'm just saying we shouldn't push around our neighbors. It just ain't right, ya know? The Canadians don't like our factory smoke drifting into their territory and coming down with rain causing all kinds of problems."

"Acid rain," Sal said. "I've read about it. It's killing their fish and defoliating forests. They're working on filtering systems for factory smokestacks."

Tino reached for a second roll. "And I heard that the world is warming up because we're putting so much smoke in the air. It could get hot enough to melt the poles and flood everything."

Mr. Gill snorted a laugh. "Well, that's a new one on me," Tino's face flushed red.

Sal came to his rescue. "I've read about it in news magazines. It's called the Greenhouse Effect. Scientists say that since the Industrial Revolution we've burned more coal, gasoline, and timber than ever before. The smoke and gases are getting trapped in the atmosphere, causing a rise in temperature. But I don't think we'll be floating off any time soon."

"What do you say I show you around Manchester?" Paul suggested.

"Fine idea," Mrs. Gill said. "Escape before Claude gets into politics."

"You're giving the impression that I'm opinionated, dear." Mrs. Gill crossed her arms. "John and Bobby Kennedy, Martin Luther King, Jr., and George Wallace."

Mr. Gill's face tightened up. "Two good ones are killed! And the racist son-of-a-bitch governor of Alabama is allowed to run for president. The very idea!"

Mrs. Gill covered her face. "I rest my case."

Sal turned to Paul. "What do you say we tour your beautiful city?"

Mrs. Gill pointed toward the door. "Escape!"

THE GILLS LOOKED ON AS SAL AND TINO worked on the bikes in the driveway later that afternoon.

"Where you boys headed to next?" Mr. Gill asked.

Tino squeezed drops of eighty-weight oil onto Rocinante's drive chain. "I want to ride up to Bath in Maine. Our Ma said that there might be a monument to the soldiers who died there in the Civil War, and that her grandfather's name might be on it. There's still time, no?"

"I was hoping that I could take Sal and you on a tour of the diocese cathedral and bishop's chancery when you're done working on the bikes," Paul said. "Besides Bath is a couple of hours drive north of here. Who knows how much time it'll take to search out the monument if it even exits and then come back, it'd be awfully late."

"I wouldn't want you to miss out on dinner," Mrs. Gill said.

Tino's face dropped with disappointment.

"Not to worry," Paul said. "We have tomorrow. I'll be glad to take you fellas up."

"Sure," Sal said. "And I'll pay for gas."

"The hell ya say," Mr. Gill said. "Save your money. You got a long way to go yet."

"I appreciate the offer but—"

"I ain't hearing another word about it."

Mrs. Gill stomped her foot, ending further debate. "The frog has croaked!"

"Cool!" Tino said. "I can't wait for morning to come."

Sal, Tino, and the Gills sat in the living room after dinner watching the news on television. "The President has ordered an additional ten thousand troops to Vietnam," Walter Cronkite said from his CBS news desk.

Mr. Gill put down his glass tumbler of whiskey, his neck veins bulging. "This goddamned war's a waste of the treasury and young men's lives!"

Mrs. Gill turned an angry eye. "Claude Jean Gill, enough!"

Mr. Gill spoke weakly. "I'm just saying, dear, that the money would be better spent on Johnson's Great Society Programs helping the poor. Why is there always plenty of money to kill, but never enough to help people down on their luck?"

Sal and the Gills got into a discussion about the war and the economy. Tino stayed fixed on the television. "Thousands of protesters and police clashed last night at the Democratic Convention in Chicago," Cronkite said. "National Guard troops with fixed bayonets supported helmeted police wielding billy clubs.

"Among the antiwar groups are Vietnam veterans, The Women's Strike Force for Peace, Bobby Seale with his Black Panther Party, Tom Hayden with the Students for a Democratic Society. Earlier this week radicals Abbie Hoffman, Jerry Rubin, and the Youth International Party, known as 'Yippies,' staged a peaceful demonstration billed as the Festival of Life. Police disrupted the event."

Tino looked on as cops went at protesters. Camera lights lit the scene. Police beat and dragged demonstrators off. He leaned closer to the TV. A camera close up caught a cop laying a stick on a guy's back.

Holy shit, it's Gary!

Tino looked to Sal and the Gills—all locked in discussion. Back on the screen, the cop dragged Gary off.

What's he doing there, and where's Pat?

Cronkite continued, "In other news. New York's Radical Women organization is planning to protest the Miss America Beauty Pageant, saying that it's exploitive of women."

Mr. Gill slapped his arm chair, "Johnson signs the Civil Rights Act, the greatest piece of legislation in a generation, then he escalates the war! Hope, then all dashed to hell."

Mrs. Gill rose from the sofa. "I think we've heard enough politics for one day. Mrs. Duvalier sent over a rhubarb pie for us and our guests. I'm going to serve it up. If you don't mind your tongue, Claude, you'll only be watching the rest of us enjoy it."

Paul laughed "He was just hitting his stride, Ma." Mr. Gill smiled at his wife as she walked past him and then frowned as she made her way to the kitchen.

Tino lay in bed later, haunted by Gary's episode. Did he have money for bail? Was he hurt? Tino decided to keep it to himself. Why burden Sal with it. He'd find out in due time.

Best to think about grandpa John, a real war hero. If I get killed in Vietnam. Maybe there'll be a monument with my name on it and Pa will see it.

29.

Hopeless

Disaster for Tino—not only was the late afternoon tour of the New Hampshire Diocese Cathedral and Chancery boring for him, but an aide of Bishop Primeau approached Paul and Sal to inform them that the bishop had heard of a California motorcycle priest visiting the Gills, and while the bishop's schedule did not allow him to meet Sal that same day he invited him for a visit the next morning and then to a monthly luncheon at a downtown hotel attended by local higher-ups in the church and politicos.

Seeing that this latest turn of events could mean that the planned drive to Bath was in serious jeopardy, Tino pleaded his case for making the trip on their drive home to the Gills house. He leaned forward from the back seat and rested his arms on the front seat. "Is it really so important for you to go meet the bishop tomorrow? Can't you make up an excuse? I mean you've met other bishops. Their getups are the same, it's only the faces that changes. Right?"

Paul laughed as he drove.

Sal in the passenger's seat leaned his back against the door and faced Tino. "I know that you want to go look for the monument hermano, but I need to meet the bishop."

"Why?"

"I need to feel him out. I have to see if he's the type who'll keep my riding a motorcycle to himself, or if he's the kind who'll snitch on me."

Tino knew better than to question Sal's decisions, but he had to try. This might be the only opportunity in his lifetime to see if there was a monument honoring his great-grandfather.

"Hey, I know what I can do," He said. "I'll go up tomorrow by myself when you and Paul are with the bishop."

"You're not going by yourself, Sal said sharply. "I'm not going to be wondering if you've gotten lost or in a wreck, now drop it."

"Hopeless," Tino whispered and threw himself against the seat angry enough to cry.

Paul glanced in his rearview mirror. "You might just be chasing windmills."

Tino didn't answer.

He lay in bed that night in the guest bedroom that he shared with Sal. Sal sat, pillows against his back, making an entry into his travel log. Tino may never find out if the monument honoring his grandfather exited. There had to be a way, even if Sal forbad him to ride up to Bath by himself. There had to be a way.

30.

An Ancestor

Sal and Paul left for the chancery just past nine o'clock the next morning.

Tino walked from the breakfast table to Rocinante parked in the driveway. "What do you think? Do we go anyway? I came on this trip after Pa told me not to. Now I want to go after Sal told me not to. If I did it'd really piss him off."

The screen kitchen door squeaked open. Tino turned to see Mr. Gill. "Whatchya gonna do today now that your big brother's gone?"

Tino gave a blank stare for a second and then smiled. "I think that I'd like to go to Bath and look for the monument."

Mr. Gill reached into his shirt pocket for a cigarette. "Do you know how to get there?"

Tino gave Mr. Gill his sad dog eyes and spoke wishfully. "No, sir, I don't but I'll find it somehow."

"Hell, son, I ain't doing nothing today how about we go up together?"

"That'd be great, sir. I'll get Sal's helmet for you, so you can ride on the back of my bike."

"Ha! We'll go in my car."

Tino threw out a little more bait hoping for more. "I looked for Sal's camera after he left so that I could take a picture if I found the monument, but he must've taken it with him."

"I'll bring my Polaroid, so if we take a picture we'll have a photo on the spot."

"Gee, Mr. Gill, that's swell, real swell."

Mr. Gill laughed again.

Mr. Gill turned on the headlights and windshield wipers of his 1960 aqua blue Pontiac Bonneville against the fog dampening U.S. Highway 1, a narrow two-lane route that hugged the irregular coastline.

"I saw a sign on our way here for Salem," Tino said. "Do you know anything about the witch trials?"

"What do you want to know?"

"Were witches burned at the stake?"

"Hanged mostly. Some died in prison. They put large rocks on one's chest until her lungs collapsed and she suffocated."

"Do you know anything about any one in particular?"

"Bridget Bishop was notorious. She owned a tavern, played shuffleboard with men, and wasn't afraid to stand up for herself, even to men. It's said that she dressed provocatively. That must have riled the religious women and probably led her to being accused of witchcraft. People have claimed to have seen apparitions of women who were executed."

"Bridget Bishop?"

"Not sure about her specifically. But once those kind of stories start, people begin seeing all sorts of things, like headless horsemen riding through the countryside at night." The fog had lifted by the time they reached Bath, but a low gray ceiling remained.

Mr. Gill drove to the Bath Chamber of Commerce Office and asked if there was a monument to the Civil War dead.

"Sure is, Mister," a woman clerk said.

Tino's head spun with a rush.

The clerk took a pencil sticking out of her hair wrapped in a tight bun, and drew the route from her office to the location. "It's at the intersection of Centre and High Streets, can't miss it."

"There it is!" Tino said pointing from the car to a gray stone monument located across the street from the Sagadahoc County Courthouse, a circa1800s red brick building.

A black Civil War-era cannon, mounted on a concrete foundation, sat in front of a handful of steps leading to the square base of the cenotaph. A stone column rose from its center with an eagle perched at its apex. An inscription etched into one side read:

HONOR THE BRAVE
ERECTED BY THE CITY OF BATH
A.D. 1867
AND DEDICATED TO
THE MEMORY OF THE SONS
WHO DIED THAT THE NATION MIGHT LIVE

The names of the war dead were listed on the remaining three sides.

"What's your grandfather's name?" Mr. Gill asked.

"John Thomson."

Tino took one side to search for the name, Mr. Gill took another. Tino read, "George F. Trull, Frank J. Tracy, John S. Thomson. Here he is!"

"Great!" Mr. Gill said and walked around.

Tino ran his fingers over each letter of his grandfather's name. Strange sensations crept over him. Cheer? Cry? He felt weak and leaned against the monument. His great-grandfather existed. A monument honoring his sacrifice to the country existed. Sorrow. Pride. Tino's chest welled up. Tears welled up at the corners of his eyes.

Mr. Gill had stepped back into the street and snapped a shot. Tino pulled a napkin from his back pocket and pretended to blow his nose but wiped his eyes. He walked to Mr. Gill and looked on in anticipation as Mr. Gill ripped the glossy-wet photo paper from the camera. He fanned it to dry the paper and hurry the photo to develop.

Tino craned his neck. "Can I see?"

Mr. Gill chuckled. "Patience is a virtue, son. Here take it." He handed over the photo. "Hold it at arms length." Tino stared at the glossy paper. First to emerge from milky-white photo was the black canon, then the dark tree trunks and canopy, and finally the monument, its spire rising majestically toward heaven.

"Wow," Tino said solemnly. "This is so cool."

"Not a bad shot, eh?" Mr. Gill said taking an envelope from his pocket. He handed it to Tino. "I brought this to protect the picture."

"My Ma said that Great-grandpa died in Fredericksburg," Tino said on the ride home.

"Yeah?"

"The park ranger said that the Irish Brigades were the Union Army's elite forces because they fought so bravely. The brigades were made up of Irish and Scots. My great-grandpa had to have been one of them. The ranger said that when the Irish Brigades charged that they got closer to the wall that the rebels were defending than any other of the brigades. She said thousands of Union soldiers were killed. The wounded and lay on the battlefield, moaning and begging for water all night long. I wonder if my grandpa was one of them."

"It's certainly possible."

I'll bet that he was really brave and that his father was proud of him for being a hero.

Mr. Gill rolled down the window and threw out a cigarette. He sat silent for a moment then said. "I would guess that

his father would have rather had a live son than a dead hero."
He turned a corner in his neighborhood and headed for the
driveway. Tino trembled. Paul and Sal were standing in the
front yard talking. Would Sal lay into him?

Mr. Gill pulled in and parked.

Tino emerged from the car and spoke casually. "Hey Paul
and Sal."

"Where you been?" Sal asked. Sal's suspicion palpable.

"Bath." Mr. Gill said shutting the car door behind him.

Sal stared hard Tino. "I asked you not to go there."

"You said for me not go alone."

"And he didn't go alone," Mr. Gill said. "I insisted on taking
him up, and really, it was no trouble at all." Mr. Gill patted
Tino's shoulder. "He's a fine young man. Why don't you show
your brother what we found?"

Tino stepped toward Sal and raised the envelope that he
had held all the way home. He opened the flap, took out the
photo, and raised it.

"Holy smokes," Sal whispered, "It exists."

"I saw great-grandpa's name."

Mr. Gill's belly bounced with laughter. "Not bad for a day's
work, eh?"

"Boy," Sal said. "Good news on both fronts. I can trust that
the bishop will keep my riding a motorcycle to himself and
Ma is going to be thrilled that we found the monument."

"What do you mean, 'we'?" Tino said.

Mr. Gill laughed all the more.

31.

"Go West Young Man"

T HE CAT WAS OUT OF THE BAG, word was out in the parish that a couple of Californians riding motorcycles were staying at the Gills, and one a priest!

The Gills hosted a potluck dinner, offering friends and family a chance to meet the "motorcycle priest" on his last night in Manchester.

Paul had brought holy vestments from the church to celebrate Mass in the Gills' living room that night. Tino beamed, proud of Sal co-celebrating Mass in the dining room. When Tino's turn came to receive Holy Communion, he closed his eyes, raised his head, and opened his mouth. Sal lifted a host from the chalice and said, "Corpus Christi." He placed the sacred host on Tino's tongue. The host was tasteless and dissolved in his mouth.

Dinner followed Mass, and since it was Friday, eating meat was forbidden for Catholics. The dinner spread covering the dining room table included fried fish, baked fish, fish sticks, tuna casserole, tuna salad, and various colors of Jell-O, one with walnuts and whipped cream.

In the kitchen on a counter sat a large, ice-filled bowl with tongs; bottles of liquor, mixers, and wine.

Maurice, Paul's brother-in-law, a little man wearing big black framed horn-rimmed glasses with thick lenses that made him look like a small rodent with glasses approached Sal. "Father Caballero, I hear that out there in California there are movie stars all over the place. You know any?"

Everyone listened in. "I graduated high school with a man named Victor Buono. He started acting at the Old Globe Theater in San Diego, made it to Hollywood, and landed major roles in films, one with Frank Sinatra and Ursula Andress."

"Ursula Andress! Ain't she the actress who's always taking off her clothes in the movies? Hey, maybe I'll go to that Globe place and make my way up to kissing her in the movies!"

Laughter.

Sal fielded questions about their trip and life in California— its beaches, sunny weather, and the hippie migration there. Mr. Gill nudged Tino with an elbow and jerked his head toward the kitchen. Tino followed wondering what Mr. Gill was up to.

The kitchen was empty of people. Mr. Gill nodded toward a counter with two shot glasses filled to the brim with whiskey. "You don't have to," Mr. Gill said. "But if you're anything like I was at your age, you wouldn't mind joining me in a taste."

"Cool!" Tino said.

Mr. Gill chuckled and handed Tino a glass. "Not a word to the Misses."

They tapped glasses, and down the hatch. The liquor burned Tino's throat. He choked and coughed.

Mr. Gill patted his back. "Easy, son. You'll get the hang of it."

Tino engaged people in pleasant head-spinning and humorous conversation the rest of the night.

People left in pairs and family units, bidding good night to their hosts and the motorcycle priest.

Tino spoke from bed in their bedroom later. "It's been nice sleeping in a bed and eating home cooking. But I'm ready to get back on the road. I'll be glad when morning comes."

"Me too, hermano."

"I want to get inland where there's sun," Tino said. "It's been overcast since we got here. No wonder everyone here is so white."

"It's a different culture, all right."

Tino rolled to his side and started floating off when he heard scratching against an outside wall of the house. The curtains fluttered on a cold breeze. Moonlight made dim by ghostly gray fog, cast shadows of thin gnarled tree branches swaying against the wall. He pulled the covers over his head and covered his eyes, afraid of seeing Bridget Bishop. Another cold gust, curtains fluttered again. Scratch. Scratch. Tree branches or a bony hand?

"Go west, young man!" Mr. Gill's voice rang out from the hall in the morning.

Mrs. Gill had a scrambled egg breakfast ready. "It's been a true joy having you stay with us," Mrs. Gill said at the table.

"It's been great for me," Tino said, spreading strawberry jam on toast. "I didn't realize how tired I was. And I got to work on Rocinante too."

"Who?" Paul asked.

"My bike's name."

Mr. Gill laid down his napkin and pushed back from the table amused. He reached into his shirt pocket for a cigarette. "Wasn't Don Quixote's horse a nag?"

"He's no nag to me," Tino said forking the last of his egg into his mouth.

"He beat my bike and the other two on our trip in a race," Sal said. "It wasn't even close."

In the driveway, Mrs. Gill handed Sal a sack lunch.

"You folks have been very generous with us," Sal said packing the sack in his gear. "You need to come out and see us, so that we can return the favor."

"You're good men," Mr. Gill said. He caught Tino's eye and winked. "Drink plenty of liquids."

Tino laughed. "Sure will."

"¡*Ánnndale!*" Sal yelled, hit the gas, and sped off.

OVERCAST SKIES CLEARED THE FARTHER INLAND that they rode. At times the sunshine was brilliant and leaf-dappled, when filtered through the forests of maple, tamarack, white bark birch, beech, and aspen trees. The late summer landscape was on the verge of erupting into autumn color. Tino came around a bend to see a tree turning blood red; other trees, in gold and crimson, dotted the rolling hills. The roar of their engines echoed in the covered bridges that spanned streams of clear water.

They ascended the Green Mountains of Appalachia in Vermont, crested at Sherburne Pass and, started the descent.

I got as far away from home as possible. Now I'm on my way back. Hard to believe I've come so far.

They rode through Rutland, Vermont, crossed into western New York State, and pulled over in a wooded area. They sat with their backs against a black locust tree to have lunch.

Sal handed over a fat sandwich wrapped in wax paper from the sack.

"This sure beats cold cuts with mayo on bread," Tino said and bit into the double decker meatloaf sandwich layered with homegrown tomatoes, lettuce, and sweet onion.

"I wanted to get going earlier this morning," Sal said.

"I could tell," Tino said, amused. "You kept checking your watch at breakfast."

Sal continued. "We're about five hours from Niagara Falls. I'd hate to miss it, but if we stop in, it'll knock us further off schedule. What do you want to do?"

"Let's get there quick as we can, ride a little longer afterward, and make up a lot of time tomorrow. We'll leave early in the morning, burn up the highways, and ride late."

Sal laughed. "I hoped you'd figure it out."

Tino drank from his canteen. "You wanted me to come up with the plan that you already had in mind."

Sal laughed. "So you're not as *pendejo* as I thought you were!"

"*Chíngate, menso.*"

Hours later they were standing on a platform a stone's throw from Horseshoe Falls.

Staggering volumes of water cascaded over the cliffs, sounding like a continuous explosion. A massive column of mist rose high into the air from the center of the falls' arc.

Sal and Tino walked a footbridge over the Niagara River into Canada and returned to join tourists listening to a docent. "A number of daredevils have ventured over the falls in homemade crafts. Only a few have survived."

Sal whispered into Tino's ear. "Bet I could design one and make it."

"And I bet that you should shut the hell up."

Sal laughed softly. "I'm just saying, someone could design it to get enough oxygen and also be cushioned from collisions with rocks."

"And I'm just saying that you think that you can do anything. And you can't, so just shut up."

Gray clouds had amassed, and a steady drizzle started by the time they returned to the bikes.

"Motel?" Tino said.

"No, it might let up."

"If I get sick, it's going to be your fault."

"Think positive."

Ten minutes into the ride, the drizzle had developed into serious rain. Sal exited the highway and pulled to a motel.

Sal dropped his gear in a corner of their room. "You can have first shot in the bathroom."

"We're living like the gringos," Tino said. "I've never stayed in a motel in my life and now I've stayed in several. I like the free little bars of soap and bottles of shampoo."

He walked into the bathroom and inspected the packet with the LSD. Still dry.

Later, Tino pulled the covers over himself and sighed. The extra long and hard day tomorrow of chasing Sal to make up time would test Tino's mettle.

He fell to sleep and had the dream; the dream that had been haunting him. He's on Rocinante and they are speeding toward the cliff at the end of the world. He hit the brakes in a panic, but to no avail. He leaned hard trying to steer away, but Rocinante held steady. Tino tried to jump off, but he was stuck to the seat. He dragged his heels against the ground. Tino flew over the cliff.

32.

The Trip

"Nooo!" Tino screamed.

"What the heck?" Sal yelled from inside the bathroom.

"I had a harsh dream."

"Hash browns? Is that what you said?" Sal said. "If you want hash browns, you'll have to wait. We need to get to it."

Tino ignored the misunderstanding and lay still, steadying his heart before he rose to check the weather. He drew the shades open—dark skies, steady rain. "It's still raining. We'll get soaked if we try to ride."

"I know," Sal said. "I looked out a bit ago. I also saw a dry cleaner across the street."

"So?"

"Got an idea. Get ready."

"Now what?" Tino said, standing outside under an awning.

"Watch and learn." Sal covered his head with his jacket and jogged through the rain to the cleaners.

A half hour later they were pulling away from the motel lot wearing their helmets with the face shields snapped on, protecting their faces from the rain. They were also wrapped neck to ankle in plastic sheeting—for protecting laundered clothes—held in place by dozens of rubber bands.

Rainwater ran off the plastic in tiny rivulets as they rode toward the highway. Sal had told Tino to spread sheeting over his crotch and bike seat to keep his privates comfy. Great. Leave it to Sal to find a way to beat the elements. The bits of sheeting between the rubber bands whipped in the wind. The sheeting vibrated on the highway at fifty miles an hour; at sixty it began shredding. Cold water seeped onto Tino's clothes and worked its way to his chest, arms and legs. He hoped that Sal would accept that his plan had a major flaw and would pull over at a restaurant to dry off, but Sal charged—sixty-five, seventy.

Tino got the sensation of floating and realized that his tires were hydroplaning on a thin skin of water. He eased off the accelerator to come back into contact with the road. The sheeting was now reduced to tiny bits of vibrating plastic, and he was getting soaked. Rain worked its way around the face shield and dribbled onto Tino's face. The cold spread like an aggressive disease. His only consolation was that drivers couldn't see him through the tinted shield, but Tino still felt the fool.

Rain eased the farther they rode and by late morning the sun ruled the skies, but the chilly air cut like a cold blade.

Sal took an off-ramp and pulled into a laundromat.

"You a sissy?" Tino said, teeth chattering. "I'm only soaked to my *pinche calzones.*"

Sal cracked up. "You can go first."

Tino stood next to a dryer and peeled off his jacket, sweatshirt, and T-shirt. The air warmed his shriveled skin.

Sal remained outside next to his bike, shirtless and fumbling for dry clothes tucked in his gear. A cold gust gave Sal a hard shiver. Tino shook his head, aware that Sal had stayed out there to hide behind his bike so as not to offend the women doing laundry by showing his bare chest. But his bike wasn't hiding squat. The women still had a clear shot at him through the window.

Tino entered the bathroom with his sleeping bag containing dry clothes. He took the packet with the LSD from his pocket and examined it to see if rain had dampened the paper. Lord, the hippie, had warned him to not let the LSD get wet, or it'd 'lose its power.' The packet was slightly moist to the touch. He unfolded it with care. The black flake sat in the center of a photo of a feathered serpent carved on an ancient Mexican temple.

If Tino was going to find out what the drug was about, he'd have to take it now. Rex's warning echoed in his ear, "Don't fuck with that shit. It'll get the best of you." But Rex was talking about heroin. LSD was different, and what if the rain had sapped its strength? Then it wouldn't matter.

Tino stared at what was either a piece of innocuous film or a powerful mind-altering drug. He closed his eyes, raised his head, opened his mouth, and placed the flake on his tongue.

"Corpus Christi."

It dissolved without taste.

"You about done in there?"

"Sorry, Sal. Be right out."

Tino crumbled the paper and tossed it in the trashcan and opened the door. He averted his eyes when he passed Sal.

Tino plucked his sweatshirt out of the dryer. The hot cotton stung his icy skin, but warmed him to his core.

"Under hundred miles today," Sal said at the bikes. "Not nearly enough."

Tino jumped on the kick-starter. Nothing. He tried again, and again.

"Dang," Sal said. "We're not going to have trouble with him, are we?"

Bang! Rocinante started with a backfire. "God, I hope not. Let's go."

Tino rode warm and dry, strong and sure, his spirit soaring. He had put on a set of lined leather gloves that he'd stored at the bottom of his sleeping bag, ideal against the cold. He could take whatever effects the LSD might have on him. The hippie had said that alcohol was the hardest drug he'd ever used. Tino had driven home damn well after nights of drinking. LSD couldn't be worse.

Twenty minutes into the ride Sal pulled off the road and checked a map. He gestured toward a high, dark hill to the west. "Shortcut. We won't be able to do much past fifty by going over the hill, but we'll save a crap-load of time and distance from having to go around it. Let's see how much we can make up."

"*¿Sabes qué?*" Tino said, self-assuredly. "We're going to make up twice the time we've lost!"

"*¡Simón qué sí! (Absolutely!)*," Sal yelled and sped off. Tino tailed him. Tino leaned low, taking curves like a professional motorcycle racer up to the crest of the hill when he began the downward spiral.

It had been quite a while since he had taken the LSD, and nothing. It must've lost its power. The hippie said that by eating it Tino would know what God knows. Maybe it was all a pile of hippie crap.

Sal threw his fist into the air and pulled away. Tino laughed. His darn brother was pushing for more. Sal and the Hawk were smaller and lighter than Tino and Rocinante, allowing them to take the curves faster. What could Sal be thinking? That Tino would have a hard time keeping up? Tino tightened his grip on the handlebars and hit the gas, narrowing the gap between them.

A strange jittery sensation crept over Tino. It felt as though electricity was running through his bowels. Did he need to take a crap? And what was this? There were two Sals and two

Hawks. Tino gave a hard shake of his head. Rocinante's handlebars felt jelly-like, as though bulging between his fingers.

A profound, all-encompassing sense of a singularity with creation consumed him. "I am one with the universe," he whispered. "I am Roci's metal, his metal, my flesh, our vision one. I see the road, the white lines, the clear, beautiful, beautiful blue sky, the dark outline of trees flying by, each leaf its own entity, yet all one."

He kept his eyes locked on Sal and the Hawk, now four, all rotating around and around like a beautiful, wondrous kaleidoscope. The world expanded and contracted, expanded and contracted, in green and gold and red, all vibrating: all a part of Tino. Tino a part of all.

"We are human," he whispered. "We are machine, tree, soil, sky, wind. One."

Sal had disappeared around a long sweeping curve a quarter mile ahead.

Tino narrowed his eyes. "Hold on, Roci."

Faster.

He leaned low into the curve, lower than in any previous curve. He came to a straightaway and still no Sal. Another curve. Faster. Lean lower. A slight vibration; Rocinante's foot peg scrapped against the ground, throwing tiny sparks, the asphalt a blur.

A snake appeared on the road. Tino leaned hard away. His tire edged off the road onto the gravel shoulder.

Going down. It was as if he had left his body and was seeing himself move in slow motion. He raised his leg to keep from getting pinned under the bike. He let go of the handlebars and rolled off.

Rocinante scraped hard and deep over the ground sounding like the screams of a mortally wounded warhorse.

Tino slammed against the earth. His helmet bounced off the ground in deafening bounds. He tumbled chest to side to back—light, shadow, light, shadow. He spread his arms and legs and slid on his back speeding over the ground like a sled down a steep slope.

I soar through the infinite universe forever expanding and contracting, pulsating with life, pulsating with death, in beautiful, beautiful colors.

He smashed head-on into a guardrail. A red bolt of pain struck his neck and spine.

Something wrong, terribly, wrong. Can't breathe. Need to straighten head. Can't breathe. Can't move. Can't...

Tino's body battled furiously to save itself. His frantic movements were soon reduced to intermittent spastic twitches before he settled into a peaceful and final repose. The roiling cloud of dust created by the tumult settled over him like a death shroud.

33.

Hades

THE HEAVENS CONSUMED THE SOUNDS of screaming metal, leaving the world in peace.

Tino found himself on Rocinante continuing their ride down the hill, immersed in a tender, warm light. The stabbing pain that had ripped through him was no more. His mind, in an altered and confused state moments ago, was now lucid. He rode as smoothly over the road as a swan over water. The snake he had avoided running over crawled in front of him. Tino understood that he was to follow. All felt natural and effortless.

A man dressed in deep blue with a musket at his side came into view. His moustache curled over the corners of his mouth, and locks of dark brown hair hung down from under an odd sort of baseball cap. Next to him stood a mailbox with a wood-carving of a rooster on top as if crowing at dawn.

The man, who looked to be Tino's age, lifted the musket by the end of the barrel and brought it down onto a large rock. Chips of metal and wood flew into the air. To his relief, Tino passed him without further incident. He turned back. The man winked with a knowing smile.

Rocinante took the curves with ease and came to a stop at the foot of the hill on the bank of a dark river. In the shallows lay a slug the size of a walrus, its skin slimy, ashen gray and spotted with small brown patches. No mouth, or ears, or eyes. A palpable evil emanated from deep within its mass.

Lola lay on the opposite side of the river, her legs spread, inviting Tino. He throbbed with lust but to reach her, he would have to get by the monstrous slug and cross the river of dark water.

The slug communicated directly from its mind to Tino's. "Come."

Lola held out her arms beckoning him, her breasts, round and full, nipples soft and pink. She touched herself and moaned, "Come, sweet boy."

The slug-monster turned Tino's blood cold. Only Lola's soft body could bring him warmth.

The beast possessed a magnetic force that dragged Tino toward it. Dread. Lust. Dread. The toes of his boots edged into the dark water. Blood seeped from the pores of his brow.

A woman's soft voice, "*Ven, siéntate conmigo.* (Come sit with me.)" A gentle hand guided Tino to reach behind him. He felt Rocinante's fender and held tight. Rocinante tried to pull him away, but skidded on loose gravel and swayed to the side.

The beast's gravely and angry voice: "Come. To. Me."

Rocinante's tire grabbed the road dragging Tino away. He spun around, leaped onto Rocinante's seat, laid his chest against the gas tank, and held tight. Rocinante sped off. Tino's dread dissolved.

Rocinante galloped in a full trot, up the hill to the guard-rail that Tino had slid into.

Confusion.

Tino saw himself lying on the ground motionless. A woman knelt over him, her mouth over his, forcing air into his lungs. She pushed on his chest forcing air out.

"Come back, baby," she said anxiously and again put her mouth over his.

"I'm okay," Tino said, confused over seeing himself bleeding, eyes closed.

He crawled into his body as he had crawled into his sleeping bag over so many nights and felt the pressure of her hands pressing against his chest. Eyes, head, shoulders, legs, all raged with pain.

"Oh," he moaned.

"You're back!" she said, panting. "You want to live. Good boy!"

Her face expanded and contracted in brilliant colors. He lifted his head to shake out the sensations, but she held him at his temples.

"Don't move!"

"Who are you?" He groaned. "Why am I hurting so much? Why is everything moving?"

"You fell and hit your head. You might have a concussion."

"Who are you? Why're you growing and shrinking. Oh God, I hurt."

She stared into his eyes keeping her hands pressed against his temples. "Who's the President?"

"Is this a dream?"

"Not a dream. Stay with me. Answer. Who is the President of the United States?"

"Lyndon Johnson. Jeez, I'm hurting."

"What day of the week is it?"

"Haven't known for a long time. Why is everything moving? What happened?"

"You had a bad fall. You hit your head. I'm here to help you. You've had trauma to the brain." She spread his eyelids. "Dilated. I need to get to a phone and call for an ambulance."

He tried sitting up, but she held him down.

"Why're you doing this to me?"

"We need to get you to a hospital."

"No! No hospital. I'm so confused."

"You rattled your brain. And I can't force you to go, but if you're as bad off as I'm afraid you are, you could die. You're in no condition to be riding motorcycles, understand?"

She pulsated and flashed like a psychedelic lightshow Tino had seen at an acid rock concert.

"I need to check a few things."

"How long's it going to take?" Tino spoke in slow confusion.

"Not long. Move your legs. Good."

She pressed her fingers against his thigh and worked her way down his leg. He jerked at the knee.

"Nasty scrape there," she said, "but there're no broken bones. Can you move your arms? Your forearm looks like red jelly. At least you can still use it. I'm going to help you sit up." She held him with her eyes, slid her hand to the back of his neck, and gently tugged.

"God, it hurts."

"What hurts?"

"Scalp to toenails."

She chuckled. "Can you turn your head side to side?"

"Neck's killing me."

"I'm not surprised. Your head was contorted at a pretty weird angle. I thought you'd broken your neck. Stay here, I'm going to check your spine."

She squatted behind him and inched her fingers along his vertebrae. "Feels like everything's in the right place."

"How come you know so much?"

"Army nurse. Just got back from Vietnam. Spent my time there trying to save guys like you. Lost too many of them. Goddamn waste. Now let's see if we can get you up."

Tino rolled onto his hands and knees and trembled like a traumatized mutt. She took him by the belt and helped him straighten. He teetered.

"Easy!" She put a hand to his chest. Dirt and pebbles rained down from his sweatshirt and pants.

Blood oozed through a film of dirt on the shredded skin of his forearm. The palms of his gloves were tattered. A thread of blood crept down his knee onto his boot.

Why's everything expanding and contracting? What's with all of the colors? I can't let on. She might try and keep me from finishing the trip.

"I've lost a lot of time," Tino said. "I need to get back on the road."

"No way, man. There's not a doctor who'd allow you to get out of a bed, let alone ride a motorcycle. You've had trauma to the brain and possible internal injuries that I'm not picking up. It'll take a while to sort it out."

Tino put his palms to his temples and squatted. "Are you saying the trip's over?"

"You're going to a hospital, honey. Better there than to a morgue. I'm going to a phone and call for an ambulance." She shaded her eyes with her hand to look up and down the road. "Wish I could flag someone down and get them to make the call, but this road's rarely used since the bypass."

"Go on. I'll be okay."

"I shouldn't leave you alone in this condition."

"I've been knocked around harder boxing with my twin brother."

She lit up. "Identical?"

"Oh God, yes, and no, I don't know what he's thinking, and I don't feel it when he gets hurt. But I wish he could take some of this."

"You picked a hell of a time to be funny. I don't have a choice but to leave you while I go for help."

"It's over for me," Tino said.

"I know it must be hard ending your trip, but it's best. I'm going to a phone now. I'll come see you tomorrow in the hospital."

"Just go."

She climbed into her car and lowered the window. "What's your name?"

"Tino."

"It's your lucky day, Tino. I usually take a different route home."

"How was I when you found me?"

"Gone."

"Dead?"

"No heartbeat, not breathing, you were pretty much gone. I wasn't sure you'd come back."

"Jesus."

She leaned forward to turn the key in the ignition. "Stay here, do you understand?"

Tino nodded. She pulled away. Her car seemed to have a tail trailing behind it like a comet's tail. He focused on the trees and turned away. They trailed. The ground, his hand waving, everything had a tail trailing behind it.

His head throbbed with dull, hard pain. He felt a spasm of nausea and leaned over to vomit, but nothing. Why did everything move and trail in bright colors? Was this a symptom of brain damage? He limped in an uneven line to Rocinante. His mount lay bleeding oil out of a nickel-size hole in the crankcase plate. The hand-brake lever was twisted like a licorice vine; gear-shifter, a dangling torn limb, the shattered headlight speckled the ground in a hundred pieces, gas tank and side panels, all marred with deep scratches.

"My fault, Roci. All my damn fault."

34.

The Rooster

THE BITTER WAIL OF A DISTANT SIREN pierced the quiet. *They're coming for me.* All of his planning with Sal and the guys, getting the loan from Father Mooney, and buying Rocinante had been for nothing. He would return home a beaten cur. Pa would say, "You didn't register for college to go on this trip, and you couldn't even finish it. Look at you. You got your ass handed to you. You're even more pathetic than I thought."

"I can't give in," Tino said. "Lola stood up to her husband, and to her mother-in-law, even to her church. Goddamn it. I'm not giving in!"

Tino, legs unsteady, gathered his gear strewn over the ground from where he'd fallen to where Rocinante had rammed into the shrub. He set his sleeping bag, helmet, tool-kit and canteen on the ground next to Roci. A yank on the rear tire—spikes of pain stabbed at Tino's neck, elbows, and knees. He dragged Rocinante out of the shrub an inch. Tino closed his eyes and pulled hard, pulled through pain, through a pulsating world. He clenched his teeth and grunted a cadence, "Pull, and pull, and pull." Rocinante scraped against the ground, bit by bit clearing the shrub. Tino's head spun with the exertion. He dropped to a knee and leaned a hand against the ground to keep from falling.

The siren grew louder.

A breath. He rose slowly and took hold of the handlebar and pulled. Roci started rising, but his weight pulled Tino back down.

Hard pain.

Tino stopped only long enough to allow himself a short cry and then grabbed the handlebar. "Lift," he said, "and lift, and lift," he said in a cadence. Rocinante rose. Tino leaned against him to keep the bike upright. He let out the kickstand and secured the gear onto the back of the seat.

The siren screamed scarlet red; the ambulance couldn't be a mile away.

Tino coached himself. "Put on helmet. Get to road. Mount. Lean forward. Push with feet." They began rolling downhill.

The ambulance rounded a curve and headed up. Rocinante picked up speed.

The ambulance driver and his partner scanned the roadside most likely looking for the accident. Tino avoided eye contact as they passed. He glanced in his mirror. The ambulance continued on, shrinking in Tino's mirror.

Rocinante rolled faster. Tino pushed on the brake pedal to keep at a safe speed.

Sal appeared on his bike riding up the hill and pulled over. Tino pointed downhill and kept coasting. Tino looked into his rearview mirror. Sal made a quick U-turn and raced back pulling alongside. He looked pained, likely because Tino was battered and bleeding.

Tino came on a mailbox covered with moss and lichen, its wood dried and splintered. A weather-beaten wooden rooster sat on top with its beak wide open as if crowing at dawn.

What the? Tino fixed his eye on the rooster as he rode by and veered off onto the bumpy road. He leaned hard to get back onto the asphalt.

Get hold of yourself. Focus on riding. Can't fall again.

Nausea.

Could that have been the mailbox in Tino's dream? He couldn't allow himself to think about it and tried counting to occupy his mind, one, and two, and three, but how could the rooster mailbox have been in his dream and in reality? Where was the man in the uniform? Was he a Yankee soldier?

Had Tino died? Was this the afterlife? If he were dead, he wouldn't have pain or feel the vibration of the engine. What in God's name was happening? *Have I lost my mind!*

Tino came to the foot of the hill and coasted to a stop.

Sal ran up. "You had a really bad fall!"

Tino rubbed his neck. "Well, no shit, Sherlock."

Sal shook his head, holding laughter.

"Just bumps and bruises."

"What do you mean just bumps and bruises? You've been bleeding. And why're you talking funny?"

"I only fell doing fifty trying to catch up to you, bounced around like a pinball and smacked the crap out of my head. You'd talk funny too." Tino struggled to sound normal, afraid that Sal would send him home if he suspected serious injury.

"You've bled on your pants, and your arm's a mess."

"I've bled before."

"Well, I'll have to clean you up." Sal's frustration was palpable.

Tino tried to explain. "A snake came out of nowhere Sal, and I didn't have time to—"

"You were going too fast, *menso!*" Sal said, going for his first aid kit. "If you wouldn't have been, you wouldn't have fallen."

Tino gritted his teeth while Sal tapped his wounds with a moistened cloth. Sal seemed to grow and shrink and radiate a warm golden hue. "You're a good person," Tino said.

"What?"

"You're a good person, Sal, a really good person."

"What're you talking about?"

"I see it, feel it."

Sal dripped alcohol onto a piece of gauze. "Well, we'll see how you feel about me after this." He wiped the alcohol over the jellied flesh of Tino's forearm.

A crimson flash and a blaze of pain. "God!"

"Sorry, but I've got to kill the germs."

Tino saw his blood coursing through the veins in his arm and seeping out the wound. "I'm seeing too much."

"You're what? I think that the knock on your head has done something to you. You need to get checked out in an emergency room."

"No," Tino said steadily.

"Listen, hermano. I've seen it in my work. People are often hurt worse than they realize."

Tino fixed a hard eye on Sal. "And have some doctor admit me to a hospital? The only way I'm going home is on my bike, or in a coffin."

"You're becoming as stubborn as me. Okay, no doctor for now, but if you start feeling odd in any way—"

"I'll tell you, damn it."

Sal laughed "You've got some moxie. If you so much as sneeze I'm taking you in." He made a list in his spiral notebook. Sal started the Hawk. "Remove the damaged parts while I get replacements. I just hope we can get it running again." He sped off.

The muscles of Tino's arm ached when he squeezed the pliers—work awkward, progress frustratingly slow. His mind raced. Did he actually see a Yankee soldier, a monstrous slug,

Lola calling him—or was it all a bad dream? No, not a dream. The rooster mailbox was real. Crazy. But if Sal had seen any of it, then it wouldn't have been a dream.

The head spinning hallucinations lessened to a nuisance, but even so, Tino concentrated on his every move as he worked on Rocinante.

"You're lucky," Sal said on his return. "I got there minutes before they closed."

"I sure don't feel too lucky."

Sal unstrapped a box on the back of the seat. "Let's get to work."

Tino started in on replacing the headlight. "Sal, on our way down the hill, did you see a man in a Civil War uniform standing next to a mailbox with a rooster on it?"

Sal looked up from replacing the crankcase plate. "I probably wouldn't have remembered a mailbox, but some nut in a costume? That would've stuck. Nothing even close, why?"

"I could've sworn that just after I fell I saw a man dressed in a Civil War uniform, standing by a mailbox. I thought I might've imagined it, but then I saw the box when I later coasted downhill. How could I have seen the box before I ever came on it?"

"You sure it wasn't little birds flying in circles over your head?"

"Forget it, Sal."

Tino mounted Rocinante after the replacement parts were installed. He turned the key and hit the starter lever; a spike of pain bolted up his leg but Rocinante's tailpipes thundered.

"¡Si, señor!" Sal yelled and hopped on the Hawk.

"Sorry I cost us so much time, Sal."

"You fell because you weren't paying attention, and not only did we lose even more time than we had saved, but you could've been killed!"

Tino followed Sal onto the road—head bowed.

A feeling of peace embraced Tino, just as the hippie had said would happen. His LSD trip had come to an end and he was now on the gentle downside.

They rode until the sun lay half-face above the horizon. The pain from Tino's injuries gradually intensified. He passed a young tree off the road. It lay with a broken trunk. A driver must have lost control and veered off the road and run it over.

Sal found a park in Erie County and paid the dollar and twenty-five cent fee at the entry.

They parked the bikes in their assigned space under a green canopy of Paper Birch Trees, their chalk-white bark standing out in the dim light after sunset.

They unpacked in silence. Sal found buried in his gear a half-full jar of peanut butter and a partial loaf of bread. The peanut butter was dry having had lost most of its oil. The bread was stale, but free of mold. They ate leaning against their bikes.

Tino drank from his canteen to help him down his dry, pasty meal.

"How're you feeling?" Sal asked.

"Like I just lost a fight with Muhammad Ali."

Sal dug through his gear and found a bottle of aspirin. "Take these for a few days."

Tino readied for bed wondering if Sal would scold him for his carelessness and the big hit to his schedule. But Sal took a conciliatory tone.

"I worked on a construction job once. I was standing on a piece of steel rebar sticking out of a building wall. It was giving under my weight, but so slowly that I thought I was imagining it. By the time I realized that it was bending, it was too late. I slid off and cracked my head on the ground. It was a hard lesson on being aware." Sal's voice sounded nasal and hoarse, the onset of a cold, likely from being bare-chested in the chilly air outside the laundromat that morning.

"I remember," Tino said. "It really shook me up to see you hurt and in the hospital."

"Sal, we really should wear our helmets all the time, not just in the states where they're required. I wouldn't have made it today if I hadn't had mine on."

"I'm always on the lookout. I scan on and off the road, aware of everything around me. That's why I don't fall. Don't think of anything else when you ride. If you would've been focused on riding, you wouldn't have fallen."

"Okay, I'll be more aware, but still, you should wear your helmet."

"Just concentrate on yourself."

"*Pues chúpetet el dedo,*" (Well suck your thumb), Tino said.

He tried lying on his side, but the pain in his hip didn't allow. He turned on his back—neck hurt, knee throbbed. Each time he managed to sleep, a spike of pain rousted him awake. How serious were his injuries? The nurse thought that he'd broken his neck. She said he was "gone" when she found him. If she had taken her regular route home, he'd be dead. Life was so fragile, so very fragile. Tears flooded his eyes.

Deep into the night he dreamed that he was a boy at home looking out a window. A black tornado was sweeping away people in the streets, toppling trees, tearing apart houses and heading his way. Ma sat on her sofa, mending Tino's torn school-uniform shirt with needle and thread. The house moaned and creaked under the wind, but Ma remained calm. "*Ven mijo* (Come son)," she said. "*Siéntate conmigo* (Sit with me)." He sat by her. The house steadied. The tornado dissipated. Tino's fear vanished.

35.

I Do Love the Cabrón

Tino woke to the call of a songbird. Morning sunlight filtered through trees. The aching in his back, neck, and joints allowed little sleep. He rolled to his side and pushed against the ground to ease up.

Sal sat at the campsite table in his shorts and sweatshirt with the sleeves cut to the elbow, writing in his travel log.

"Morning," Tino said.

"Hey, you feeling any better?" Sal said in a raggedy voice.

"Pretty sore, and you don't sound very good."

"Nothing I can't handle. Ready to hit the trail?"

"Why're you even asking, *menso*? If I'm not, you're going to say we're hitting it anyway."

Sal laughed in a hoarse voice and then coughed.

Tino dressed wearily, rolled up his sleeping bag, brushed his teeth, and put on his helmet ready to mount.

"Be aware of everything on and off the road," Sal said.

"Okay, but I still wish you'd wear your helmet."

Tino's forearm muscles ached hard when he squeezed the clutch lever to drop into gear despite the aspirin he had been taking.

They rode highways skirting Buffalo and along Lake Erie's southern shoreline. Aside from Sal's bad cold and Tino's injuries, it was a good day for riding.

The sun shone bright against the deep blue sky, humidity was low, and a soft fresh breeze blew off the lake. They rode the coastline through western New York State, the tip of Pennsylvania, and passed the city of Erie. They crossed into Ohio, skirted around Cleveland, and stopped at a motel in Toledo.

Why was Sal quitting early? They couldn't have logged more than two hundred miles. Could it be because Sal had seen Tino limping and massaging his joints when they'd stopped to eat? Or, was Sal quitting because of his cold? No, Sal the Spartan would never take it easy on himself. He quit early to allow Tino some time to heal.

I do love the cabrón.

Tino trudged into their room and sat on a bed to unlace his boots. "Lake Erie's huge, more like an ocean," he said.

"And it's fresh water. Wish they'd pipe some of it to Southern Cal." The rasp in his voice had worsened.

"Want some of the aspirin you gave me?" Tino said, worried that Sal could bring on a serious condition if he didn't take care.

"Don't need it," Sal said and entered the bathroom.

"Of course you don't, Mr. mind over matter."

Tino laid back to rest before getting ready for bed. The soft mattress and fluffy pillow eased the pain from his injuries.

36.

I Ain't No Tramp

TINO WAS STILL IN HIS CLOTHES the next morning. He was also in the same position as when he had lain down.

"I thought about waking you up last night so you could get ready for bed," Sal said, his voice sounding worse. "But I decided to let you rest."

Tino undressed in the bathroom. He peeled off the blood-stained gauze from his knee and forearm. Water running over the raw skin in the shower stung. Water, pink with blood, circled down the drain.

Sal had the bikes loaded and ready to go by the time Tino dressed.

"I've got less than a week of vacation time left," Sal said in the parking lot. "We've got about 1,900 miles to go as the crow flies. That translates into well over 2,000 in road travel."

"I get it. We're in for a lot of hard riding, right?"

"Look hermano, you're pretty beat up, and I don't want to push you too hard, but—"

"It's okay I'm ready to get home, so quit screwing around and let's get to it."

Sal laughed and coughed.

253

They rode out of Toledo, Ohio, through Indiana, and into Illinois. A freight train rolled across the interminable Midwestern plains. The locomotive pulled an endless string of cars. The tracks ran over the earth's skin like the great dark stitches of a scar. Tino expected Sal to stop at the crossing a quarter mile ahead and allow the train to pass.

"Let's beat it!" Sal yelled and hit the gas.

Red lights flashed, warning bells rang. Sal made it under the crossing arms before they dropped. The engineer tugged on a cord. Horns blared.

Tino pulled up to the crossing. Sal waved frantically, motioning him to ride around the crossing arms, but he shook his head "no." He read Sal's lips and laughed. "Crap!"

Sal hopped off his bike and ran to the tracks fishing a coin from his pocket and set it on the rail. The engineer gave the horn cord a long, angry pull. The train passed with a tremendous iron rumble that vibrated the earth. Diesel engines spewed dark clouds of exhaust into the sun-bathed sky. Clunk-clunk, clunk-clunk, the iron wheels ran over Sal's coin.

Tino cut his engine as the parade, two and a half miles long, continued. Men lounged on the floors of flatcars, some clean-shaven and neatly dressed, others in dirty, torn clothes, their faces dark with stubble.

Tino waved hello. Most didn't notice or ignored him; a few waved back.

Where could these poor guys be going? To a brother's or sister's house hoping for a handout, or maybe to somewhere where they heard there's work.

A man wearing a black-and-white striped trainman's cap sat in the caboose. The ground ceased vibrating and the rumble faded as the train trailed off—red lights stopped flashing, warning bells quieted, crossing arms rose.

Tino rode to Sal. They waited for the line of vehicles to pass them before Sal retrieved his coin from the track. His penny had been flattened to a paper-thin copper wafer the width of the rail.

They came to Hammond, a town southeast of Chicago, and parked in front of a mom-and-pop grocery store. They scaled a handful of wooden steps leading to the entrance. Tino sat on a step, worn smooth by a century of foot traffic. Sal went to a beat-up soda machine and dropped in a dime. He returned to sit with Tino and tipped his bottle of Dr. Pepper toward him, "Drink?"

"Thanks," Tino said, "but I don't want to get your cold."

An early 1960s Volkswagen bus, driven by a gray-haired man, pulled up and parked alongside the motorcycles. An adolescent boy, sporting a Chicago Cubs baseball cap, sat in the passenger's seat. The man and boy exited the van. The man was dressed in khaki pants and shirt with a case for his glasses tucked into the breast pocket. He walked with a slight stoop and held the boy's shoulder for support. They walked to the top of the steps where the man stopped to take a breath.

"Good afternoon, gentlemen," he said.

Tino raised his chin. "Hey."

"A good afternoon to you, sir," Sal answered.

"Sounds like you got quite a cold there, young man. "

"I'm on the mend."

Tino rolled his eyes, *You're sick, pendejo.*

"Take good care of yourself," the old man said. He gestured questioningly at the bloodstained dressing on Tino's forearm.

"Had a fall."

"Looks to me like it was a nasty one." The man turned to the boy. "Well, Hare, shall we see if we can find something for dinner?"

The boy followed the man into the store.

Tino looked after them. "Nice old guy," he said and leaned back. "Ow." A tender spot at the small of his back from his fall was a reminder of his surreal experience that couldn't have happened and yet might have. What if Sal had seen the man in blue or the mailbox with the rooster? Then Tino would have a piece of the weird puzzle.

"Sal, I know I already asked you about this, but please try to remember. On the hill where I fell, you rode up and down several times."

"That again?"

"Please, just hear me out. At any time, did you see a guy in a blue uniform next to a mailbox with a rooster on it?"

"No, nothing even close. Satisfied? You hit your head and imagined it."

"The man smiled at me, like he knew me. And now that I'm thinking of it, he even looked familiar."

Sal grinned. "Hey, I've got it. You were in that TV show, *The Twilight Zone*, and it was Grandpa saying 'fuget about it, asshole.' Ha!"

A tingle ran down Tino's spine. "Say again?"

"Maybe it was Great Grandpa John, who died in Fredericksburg, and he came to tell you to pay attention to your riding, not gawking at mailboxes."

"Son of a bitch," Tino whispered.

"What?"

"Do you suppose someone's ancestor could appear to him?"

"*Ay, hermano, te diste un cabronazo en la maseta. ¡Ya no más!* (You hit your noggin, and nothing more.) So forget about it."

"There're stories in the Bible of saints and angels appearing to people, right? I mean God appeared to Moses—and an angel to Mary. And Jesus appeared to his apostles after he died."

"Okay," Sal said. "The Church recognizes visits from the afterlife, but they don't happen just because some knucklehead wasn't paying attention and fell off a motorcycle."

"But not impossible."

"Okay, nothing's impossible, but this borders on it, or it's just plain nuts. The guy that you saw was going to some historical Civil War event."

A man in dusty work clothes holding a jacket folded over his shoulder in one hand and a beat-up satchel in the other, ambled off the road. His cheeks were covered in gray stubble, face dark from exposure to the sun. He reached the foot of the stairs, removed his Fedora and patted his clothes. "Them your motorbikes?" he said looking toward the brothers.

"Sure are," Sal answered.

"I see you been on the road," the man said.

"Yes," Sal said. "I think that I can say the same about you."

"Was that you boys I saw back at the tracks?"

"Were you one of the men on the flatcars?" Tino asked.

"Yup, I been following the work, riding the rails since the end of winter. Say, you wouldn't have a little spare change on you, would you?"

Sal extended a leg, reached into his pocket, pulled it out. "Here's a good half dollar's worth." He poured the coins into the man's soiled and callused hand.

"Why, that's very kind of you, sir."

"What kind of work do you do?" Sal asked.

"Farm labor. I pruned peach trees in Georgia. Got me a regular stint on a Virginia hog farm. Go back there for a couple of months every year. Then I do the harvest circuit: cotton, tobacco, peanuts. Had me a good run this year on account of so many young fellas off to war. Gives us older stiffs a better shot at work."

"And you're broke?" Tino said.

"Didn't I just say I'm a working man? I ain't penniless like a lowdown tramp. I've always worked for a living, but I don't never spend my earnings. Need to get as much home to Momma and the boys as possible. Now that the harvest is over, the trick is to scratch enough together to take the Greyhound back to Texas. A few more bucks and I can ride home nice and comfortable."

"How long have you been working like this?" Tino asked.

"Longer than you been alive, I imagine. I got regulars who expect me to work for them every year, and I don't never disappoint them."

"Isn't it dangerous carrying around so much money?"

"Well, it sure would be, if I was carrying it. I mean you wouldn't be riding around with a season's worth of earnings in your pocket, would you?"

"So where's your money if you've had a good season?"

"In the bank!" The man said incredulously. "What do you think I do with it? There're too many people out there who'd take it from you. Don't you save your money in a bank?"

"I've never had enough to have an account," Tino said. "So you have bank accounts?"

"Hell, yes. Just 'cause I don't wear fancy-ass suits like city folks don't mean I'm some country bumpkin. A man's got to do what a man's got to do to care for his family. I make enough from the end of winter to the end of summer to meet my financial obligations, with a little extra to squirrel away for when the wife and I get old. I go home at the end of summer and rest up for the next go round."

"You can't get a job where you don't have to travel so much?" Tino asked.

"Tried that but I can't seem to stay put. Drive me crazy having to see the same faces every day pretending I liked it. Got a restless spirit, I suppose. But riding the rails takes too much out of me anymore. Was a time I halfway enjoyed it, but them days are gone. Besides there's too much that can go wrong."

"Like what?" Tino asked.

"Like falling off of the train, for starters. I seen men break legs, arms, get their head split wide open like a ripe melon. I seen a man riding the rails missing a goddamn arm. Sometimes when there're too many tramps and 'bos on the train, they go to tossing everybody off. Then you're really in a fix."

"What's a 'bo?" Tino asked.

"Hobo."

"Oh, sure, a tramp."

The man scowled. "I ain't no damn tramp."

Sal raised a hand. "My brother didn't mean disrespect, sir."

"Well, I s'pose I can't blame you if you don't know nothing about it. Hobos work; tramps don't. Tramps think nothing of stealing damn near anything they can get hold of. Give a tramp his pay, and the next thing you know he's going out drinking and whoring around with it." The man picked up his satchel. "I best be gettin' on my way. I'll be able to catch a bus pretty quick good as my luck's been running. Much obliged for the help."

Sal nodded. "Good luck."

The man tipped his hat and shuffled to the side of the store to a hose faucet. He opened his satchel, took out a razor, a bar of soap and prepared to shave.

"I don't know whether to feel sorry for him because he's begging, or you for maybe getting suckered," Tino said. "What if he's making it all up just to freeload?"

"He seemed honest enough to me, and besides, learning about his work life was worth it. I wish I had his kind of freedom."

"What do you mean?"

"It's not easy doing the same thing day after day."

"You don't like being a priest?"

"Didn't say that. It'd just be nice to have a little more variety. I became a priest because I wanted to help people, but I'm not sure it's the best way. Being a priest gets in the way of really communicating with someone on a personal level. Remember the man we rode with in New Mexico?"

"Rex, the cool biker."

"He's helping the kinds of kids I'd like to help. The type who can't fit in, but Rex does it much more effectively."

"He said that some of the guys he's trained have gotten really good jobs," Tino said. "And by the way, speaking of money, you better save what you have left. Except for a little change, I'm out. I'd have another twenty if that cop in carrot town hadn't ripped me off."

"You did better than I thought you'd do. I was sure you'd have gone through your money before we got to New York, but you've made it clear to Illinois."

"You won't have to worry about me," Tino said. "I'll eat your leftovers."

Sal grabbed his crotch. "*Aquí tengo tu leftovers.*"

"*Ni es bastante para una pinche pulga.* (Not even enough for a damn flea)."

Sal laughed. "Tell you what, I'll cover you for the rest of the trip, and you can pay me back when we get home. I'm just glad we've been able to experience this together. We've seen and done so many things. Things that I could not have imagined."

"You can say that again."

37.

A Monk on the Prairie

TINO SAT ON THE STEPS LEADING to the store in quiet contemplation.

The old man and boy who had entered the store earlier walked out. The boy leaned a bag filled with groceries against his chest using both of his hands. The old man stopped at the steps where Tino and Sal sat. The old man nodded toward the bikes. "According to them license plates, you've come a long way."

"San Diego to New York," Tino said. "Going home."

"Quite a feat! Are you two brothers?"

"Yes, sir," Sal said.

"By the sound of your voice, and the looks of your brother's arm, I'd say that the both of you could benefit from sleeping off the ground and out of the elements for a night. You'd be welcomed to stay out at our place."

Tino sat up. "That'd be great!"

Sal put a hand to his mouth and coughed. "We're fine, but thanks."

Damn it Sal!

"Your voice tells me that you need a good rest. I'm afraid that all I can offer you are cots on the porch, maybe not the best accommodations but at least you'd be off the ground. Name's Harold by the way." He patted the boy's shoulder. "Grandson's named after me. We just call him 'Hare.' Why don't you follow us. We aren't but a mile down the road. It'll be a welcome change for Hare and Corncob to hear somebody besides me yakking at them."

"This is really generous of you," Tino said.

Harold led them onto a gravel road in a rural neighborhood of acre-plus lots. He pulled into the driveway of a two-story wood-frame farmhouse. The mailbox read, PROFESSOR HAROLD STRATTON.

The brothers parked behind the van with a decal of a peace symbol on its rear window.

An expansive vegetable garden stretched from the side yard to the rear. Plump dark red tomatoes peered out from deep green leaves. Rows of onion and garlic plants covered at least a hundred square feet of ground. There were also plants of peppers, zucchini, cucumber, squash and pumpkin. Inch-thick wooden stakes shaped into tepees and standing tall as Tino supported vines of string beans. To the rear of the property was a field of tall, handsome corn stalks.

"Arf! Arf!" A dog barked from inside a screen-enclosed porch. Harold and his grandson dropped from the van, slamming the doors shut behind them and came around. Sal and Tino unstrapped their sleeping bags.

"You have a really nice home," Tino said.

"Been in the family for a good while. You can follow us to the porch."

The dog barked excitedly as they approached. Harold took hold of a handrail at the foot of the steps leading to the porch and pulled himself up. He stopped at the screen door and took a breath before entering.

"Arf! Arf! Arf!" A black and white cocker spaniel mix spun in happy circles.

"He's not the smartest, but he's family," Harold said. He leaned over. "Corncob, sit." The dog obeyed, keeping his attention on his master. "Smile!" The dog's upper lip rose showing his teeth.

The brothers burst into laughter. The dog seemed to appreciate their reaction, stood up, and fanned the air with his tail. Tino dropped to a knee and stroked Corncob's head. The dog licked his hand.

"What do you think of my new porch?" Harold said.

Sal set his sleeping bag down. "Very nice."

"Lost the first one to a tornado a couple years back. I screened this one in. Nice sitting out here on summer evenings without mosquitoes pestering you."

Harold positioned himself in front of a wooden rocker padded with worn, flattened cushions and dropped to the seat. He pointed to wicker chairs at the far end of the porch. "Bring them on up and take a load off." The dog lay on the floor next to him. Hare took a chair by his grandfather.

"Thank you, but we sit on our bikes all day," Sal said massaging his rear. "Feels good standing." Tino leaned a shoulder against the house wall.

"That must've been something," Sal said, "having a tornado come through. I've always wanted to see one."

"Darnedest thing," Harold said. "Porch is the only piece of the house that we lost. Some neighbors weren't so lucky. The twister claimed a house here, a barn there, and scattered debris all over creation. Lifted a tree and sent it through my neighbor's garage. A long-distance truck driver was killed on the highway. He was thrown around in the cab, died from blunt force trauma."

"Didn't seem fair, me coming out relatively well, while others paid a heavy toll. I helped my neighbor fix his garage.

He helped me with the porch. Got 'em fixed with insurance money."

Sal squatted on his hams. "That'd scare me enough to move to California."

"Not moving. I'd never seen a twister before, haven't seen one since. Besides, you folks have earthquakes out there."

"You got me there, Harold. I've felt a few."

"What's it like being in an earthquake?"

"I was in one last year," Tino said. "Pa and I were working in the front yard. I heard a low rumble coming from deep in the ground. It sounded like huge boulders were grinding slow and hard against each other. Then a funny kind of vibration ran up my legs and everything started swaying, like a ride at a carnival. Pa's car in the driveway moved up and down like someone was pushing down on it, and the telephone wires were whipping up and down. I thought they were going to snap."

"Doesn't sound like a carnival ride I'd like to take," Harold said.

"I knew what it was because I'd been in one before, and since I was outside, I knew that I was safe. And then it stopped just like that. It was kind of fun."

"How long did it go for?"

"Reports said less than a half minute, but it felt a lot longer."

"Well, I'll take a twister any day. By the way, you boys are welcome to use the shower."

"Great!" Tino said. "We probably don't smell too good."

Harold chuckled. "Well, I didn't want to say anything."

"Thank you very much," Sal said.

Harold pushed on the arms of the chair, rose, and led them inside. The floors of the dining room were light brown hardwood accented with braided oval rugs. The centerpiece was an oak table with six chairs. An antique sideboard stood against a wall and the wallpaper matched the drapery.

"Looks like your home has had a woman's touch," Sal said.

Harold's eyes saddened. "She was nobody's fool when it came to keeping house."

He pointed to a side room. "That would be my study."

Tino peered in. A brass lamp sat on a wooden roll-top desk with a swivel chair. A small table next to the desk held a typewriter and stacks of papers. An entire wall, floor to ceiling, was dedicated to shelves of books.

Harold opened a set of louvered accordion doors at the end of the hall. "Plenty of towels and shower as long as you like. The well's deep and the pump is new."

"Thank you very much," Tino said.

"When you're done cleaning up, you can join us in the kitchen for some dinner."

"Really, this is too much," Sal said. "We have food."

"I figured that you could use a little home cooking when I first saw you outside the store and bought plenty extra groceries, figuring we'd invite you over—and besides we'd love the company."

"What a good old guy," Tino said. Water from the shower gloriously rained over him.

"His generosity reminds me of Ma and Pa," Sal said looking at himself through the steam in the mirror shaving.

"Funny how you take things for granted," Tino said. "You don't realize how wonderful showers are until you haven't had 'em for a while." Scabs on his knee and forearm had hardened into dark shells. Water running over his wounds and circling the drain carried no tint from blood.

Harold pulled two chairs from the kitchen table and gestured for Sal and Tino to sit.

A half loaf of Roman Meal bread sat on top of a dark brown refrigerator with a chrome handle for opening the door. Its motor hummed in a low buzz. An electric stove matched the fridge in color. Both appliances had a permanent air to them, as if they had occupied their spaces for decades.

Harold ladled broth with cubes of beef, chopped onions, yams, potatoes, string beans, cabbage, and half ears of yellow corn into bowls.

Sal leaned over his bowl and inhaled deeply through his nose.

"Looks like Ma's *caldo*," Tino said, longing for her tortillas.

Harold sat and instructed Hare to fill the bowl on the floor with dog food and bring the cornbread he had made from the oven. Harold uncorked a bottle of dark red wine and tipped the bottle toward Sal, raising an eyebrow.

"Water's fine, thank you."

The only times that Tino had seen Sal drink alcohol were the small amounts of altar wine that Sal drank when saying Mass.

Harold had a swallow. "It's good you're traveling. There's a freedom about it. The best thing I ever did was travel. I hitched rides and even hopped trains."

Corncob finished his bowl of food and settled on the floor at Harold's feet.

Tino huddled over his food and ate like a starving refugee.

Harold wiped his mouth with a napkin and said, "Loved traveling, taught me a lot about myself. I had to make do with little. It's a good thing to learn that you can get by without so much stuff. And you boys are doing it at the right age." He had another drink of wine.

Sal looked over at Hare. "You're the quiet type." The boy looked to his shoes.

"He's been mute since his mother, my daughter, passed away last year."

"I'm awfully sorry," Sal said. "I can't imagine."

Tino looked up from his meal. "What happened?"

"Car accident. She was driving with Hare sitting next to her. A young man in a pickup truck ran a traffic light and slammed into her door. Hare got away with bumps and bruises. Seatbelt probably saved his life. Doesn't seem right. No child should witness a parent die. Specialist says Hare should get over it and talk again, but his father and I are concerned."

Tino connected with the boy. Both relegated to the sidelines: Hare, due to circumstances out of his control; Tino because he could never measure up. "You'll talk when you're ready," Tino said.

Hare smiled weakly and averted his eyes.

"His father drives trucks. Left early this morning with a load bound for Oklahoma. He's a fine, hardworking man. Keeps this place up."

"Our father's a truck driver too," Tino said. "But all his deliveries are in town."

"We've had a run of bad luck. My wife, Angelina, died of cancer a year before my daughter's accident."

"Jeez!" Tino said.

"Met her in Italy after the First War. She didn't speak English. I didn't speak Italian." Harold chuckled at the thought. "But love is love. We never had a problem communicating. There's more than one way to communicate. Don't need to be yakking all the time." He picked up his glass of wine and stared at it. "She got me started on this stuff. I've grown fond of it."

Harold took out his wallet to show them a photo. A handsome young couple, arms around each other, stood smiling in front of a body of water with snow-capped mountains behind, he in an army uniform, she in a white blouse with a knee-length dark skirt. Her black hair covered her shoulders in long thick waves. Harold touched the photo to his lips.

Harold sighed. He looked to Sal. "May I ask what you do when you're not traveling?"

"I work in a hospital tending to the infirm."

"Excellent, must be rewarding." Harold turned to Tino. "You must be graduated from high school, or close to it."

Tino slid his chair from the table. "Yes, sir. Graduated in June."

"Have you thought about what you're going to do?"

Remembering the decal of the peace sign on the van Tino decided not to tell Harold of his plans to join the Marines and nodded toward Sal. "He's advising me to consider all my options."

"Good," Harold said and emptied his glass. "Well, Hare, what do you say we get them some cots?"

"I've slept on cots before," Tino said. "My parents bought some at the army surplus store for my other brother and me."

"It'll be good for you to sleep off the ground," Harold said. "I spent a lot of time sleeping on the ground when I fought in Europe."

"Was it tough?" Tino asked.

"Tough? I did things I never would've thought I could do. Killed. It got to where I hated the boys on the other side. When I came across their dead, I'd bust out their teeth with the butt of my rifle."

Tino covered his mouth.

"It doesn't seem to fit you, Harold," Sal said.

"Like I said, I did things I never would've thought I could do, didn't know that I had it in me. Other boys did the same kinds of things, even the good church-going types."

"You're calling the guys you served with boys," Tino said. "Weren't they men?"

"I was nineteen, some were a little older, some a bit younger—boys to my way of thinking. Both sides were stuck in trenches with the wounded and dying lying between. They called out, begging for help and for water. Hard experiencing that. Couldn't get to them because of the snipers. No one should have to experience that, least of all no one you love. Long as I'm alive, I'm not going to let my grandson experience such horror."

"I can't imagine," Tino said.

"Rats everywhere, feeding on the dead. 'War's hell,' they say, but hell can't be as bad."

"I'm awfully sorry you had to experience that," Sal said.

Didn't seem right I came home and they didn't," Harold spoke distantly. "I wanted to apologize to the German boys I killed, and to their families. Wanted to say sorry to the boys who fought next to me, but didn't come back."

"You don't need to go on," Sal said. "I mean, if it's too hard for you."

"It helps me to get it out every once in a while. Your sins can't be forgiven if you don't confess them."

Harold's breathing became shallow. "We got hit with mustard gas. I saw that yellow cloud coming. I didn't get my mask on in time. Darn stuff smelled like mustard too.

"I studied to try and understand war so I could help end it. Made no sense, countries sending off their young to kill each other. Got my PhD in history and spent a career teaching the young to think for themselves. I got into hot water with the administration when I got arrested for demonstrating against this war.

"They're lying to us about it!" Harold yelled and brought his fist down onto the table vibrating plates and silver. He broke into a coughing fit and pressed one hand on his chest and the other on the table steadying himself. Sal took a newspaper from the counter and fanned Harold's face.

Corncob stood up and wagged his tail. Hare sat quietly.

Harold spread his chest to expand his lungs until his fit eased.

Sal laid the newspaper on the table.

Harold opened his eyes and spoke softly. "The older I get, the worse it gets. Well, you boys need to get some rest. Home's a long way off yet." He pushed up from the table with a soft grunt.

Sal and Tino jumped to his aid.

"Thank you for everything," Tino said.

"A good Samaritan gave me shelter when I was traveling, worn-out and hungry like you boys. I never forgot his kindness to me, a stranger. I could've been a thief or worse. When I thanked him, he told me to do the same for someone else. I realized that, that was the way to make peace in the world. Sow kindness, and kindness will grow like good fruit."

Sal and Tino helped Harold to his bedroom, and then went to the kitchen. Hare sat on a stool looking on while they washed dishes.

Tino rinsed suds off a bowl and handed it to Sal. "Harold saw and even did some pretty harsh stuff in the war."

Sal toweled the bowl and set it in a cupboard. "He learned the importance of peace from the experience. Drawing something good from something so horrendous is a good definition for wisdom. Harold reminds me of an order of monks I met while I was in the seminary. They lived the word of Christ by tending to the sick and feeding the hungry. And they weren't afraid to stand up for the poor, even went to jail defending them. Some of the monks were war veterans. They lived simple yet profoundly important lives."

Tino turned to Hare. "You're lucky to have a grandpa like him." A small victory: Hare smiled shyly while facing Tino.

Sal put away the last dish. "Time to hit the sack."

"I SURE FEEL FOR HIM," Tino said from his cot later that night.

"He's had a pretty rough go of it," Sal answered.

"And it's just Hare, his father, and Harold living here. It's such a big house for so few people. Seems like a waste. It was quiet at dinner, same at the Gills'. At our house everybody's always talking at the same time."

Sal chuckled.

"Seems sad, living in such a quiet house," Tino said.

"We ate in silence in the seminary. I never got used to it. A lot of gringos like the quiet."

"It's natural to talk," Tino said. "Even crickets talk at night."

"YOU BOYS DIDN'T HAVE TO CLEAN UP LAST NIGHT," Harold said, standing with Hare and Corncob in the driveway the next morning.

"Least we could do," Sal said, securing his gear. "Besides, if Ma were here she would've scolded us if we hadn't. Thanks again, I feel cured."

"Careful on them bikes. I don't want to hear about a couple of young bucks who got in an accident riding out of Hammond."

Sal and Tino fired up their engines. Corncob barked and wagged his tail.

"Corncob!" Harold said. "Smile!" The dog showed his teeth making the brothers laugh.

The dog spun around barking.

Hare gave Tino a small wave.

Sal handed Harold a slip of paper. "If you're ever out our way—"

Tino set out the kickstand and dismounted, leaving Rocinante idling while Sal and Harold talked. Tino knelt on a knee and looked Hare in the eye.

"If you and your grandpa come see us, we'll take you to see Disneyland. Deal?"

"Deal," Hare whispered.

Tino stared stunned for a second and then started laughing. "You're all right!"

He hopped on Rocinante. "Ready, Sal?"

"Vamonos!"

Tino rode off looking into his mirror, seeing the grandfather and his grandson waving.

38.

Oops

TINO AND SAL HAD RIDDEN over hills and mountains on the western and eastern sides of the continent, but here, in its center, lay the prairie, flat as a Ma Caballero tortilla— more blue heaven overhead than earth below.

They rode through Joliet, Ottawa, Peru, Genesco, East Moline, Rock Island, and to a bridge that spanned the Mississippi River.

A lifetime had passed since Tino had crossed the great dividing river a thousand miles to the south. Since then he had taken a giant step in conquering his fear by standing up to a big and tough bully. He had made love to a woman, eaten forbidden fruit, died, and risen from the dead.

Tino and Sal passed tracts of land cultivated into measureless farms with small agricultural towns in between. Mechanical monsters consumed swaths of hay, digested and dropped rectangular bales out their rears. The sweet smell of cut hay filled the air. They passed ranches with thousands of head of cattle. The smells of straw and manure were oddly pleasant, sparking a distant memory for Tino of visits to his old *Tio Nene* and his humble *ranchito* in Mexico.

They rode past vast fields of wheat, soybean, corn. In late afternoon, Sal stopped alongside the road at a small rise and cut the engine. Tino pulled up alongside giving him a what's up look. "Let's take a look," Sal said. They stood on their bike seats to find themselves adrift in an ocean of green corn stalks. Tassels, like fine threads of gold, waved on a breeze.

They crossed into Iowa, rode through Des Moines, and stopped at a Chevron gas station in Stuart, a welcome break for Tino. His empty stomach growled like an angry cat. "When're we going to eat?"

"I'm out of money."

But Sal's admission didn't register with Tino. "We need to find a store and get stuff to make sandwiches, right?" Tino said.

Sal reached into his pocket and pulled out a few lonely coins. "This is all I have."

Tino stared into Sal's palm, and the dark truth hit him like a punch in the gut. "We're in deep shit."

Sal laughed as much at Tino's metaphor, as at his dumbfounded expression. "I thought that I had stashed a fifty dollar bill in my wallet just in case, but I must've left it home. Oops."

"How're we going to eat?"

"Not sure. I've got a gas credit card, so we can get gasoline to get us home. But that's it. We'll have to figure something out." Sal jumped on his bike. "No time to waste." He bolted off.

Tino raced after Sal. "Son of a bitch." His motorcycle's speedometer read just below ninety.

Brilliant, Sal, heck, if you go fast enough maybe we'll make it home for dinner.

Sal's brake light blinked on and he rolled to a stop. "Got an idea. I'm going to ride ahead. Don't stop until you reach the next gas station, no matter what." And he was off.

Tino rode, consumed by their ominous state of affairs. He saw a small dead animal lying off the road and slowed. The putrid stench of rotting flesh and hundreds of flies surrounded the remains of an opossum—too far gone to cook over a fire.

A half-mile down the highway Tino came on Sal's bike standing alone on the shoulder of the road alongside a cornfield. Cornstalks in the field were shaking.

Jesus, he's stealing corn!

Tino waited for Sal at the next gas station. He appeared moments later, riding up the highway with his jacket zipped to the top and bulging—the tip of a husk at his neck. He didn't acknowledge his brother, but rode to the rear of the station. Tino waited a couple of minutes before riding back, so as not to be linked with Sal. Tino found him still on his bike ducked behind a trash dumpster.

Sal looked around nervously. "We need to go. I was seen."

"Crap, Sal!"

Tino followed Sal onto a dirt road between cornfields. Sal slowed and rode behind a shed, next to an irrigation channel. "I think we'll be safe enough here for the night."

Tino unloaded his gear in the soft light of dusk. "What if the cops would've caught you? Ma'd be mortified. Pa'd throw a fit, not to mention what the bishop would do to you. I'll do the stealing from now on."

Sal tossed over an ear of corn. "Husk."

Tino stripped off the leaves and bit into the corn. "It's hard and chewy and doesn't taste very good."

"Sorry," Sal said. "I didn't have time to shop in the gourmet section." He pulled out a yellow melon wrapped in a sweatshirt.

"Nice!" Tino said "Where'd that come from?"

Sal hit the melon against the ground, splitting it apart and handed over a piece.

"Vegetable garden in a backyard next to the cornfield. Must've been a hundred melons in a patch. I figured they wouldn't miss one and then went for it. I heard a man yell. He was on the porch of the house a few hundred feet away."

"*Hijo*, what'd you do?"

"I kept my eye on him and backed up into the cornfield. He went into the house. I saw him through a window, dialing a phone."

"*Chingada!* The cops must be looking for us. Don't do this again. I'll do the stealing from now on. There've got to be loads of vegetable gardens and chicken coops between here and home. I can steal eggs, or a chicken that we can cook."

Sal covered his mouth to keep from laughing.

"I'm serious, *menso*."

"Could you kill and cook a chicken?"

Tino waved him off. "Well, your plan stinks."

"I'm glad that you're willing to take chances, but we've got to find another way. Our luck can only hold out for so long before we're caught." Sal went for his sleeping bag and toothbrush. "By the way, when you brush your teeth, don't eat the toothpaste."

"*Ay, que chistoso* (You're a real riot)."

Tino crawled into his bag, remembering a story he had heard in a religion class. Moses had led the Israelites through the wilderness in search of the Promised Land. Their food stocks became depleted, and the people grew hungry. Moses prayed to God and a miracle occurred. Meat fell from heaven, and they found bread lying on the ground. They rejoiced.

39.

Caught!

A N INSECT CRAWLED OVER TINO'S EAR in the morning. He brushed it away. Then the insect tickled his cheek. He opened his eyes to see Sal squatted with a corn husk in hand, using it to tickle Tino's face.

"*¡Ay, como eres menso!*" he said and pushed Sal's knee, causing him to fall and roll onto his back. "If I wasn't so beat up from my accident, I'd give you a pounding."

"You and what army?" Sal said getting to his feet. "Let's see if we can make it through the rest of Iowa, Nebraska, and into Kansas by nightfall."

They rode west on I-80. The dour, gray morning sky was indistinguishable from the gray land at the horizon. They crossed the Missouri River at Council Bluffs in midmorning, and stopped at a 7-11 convenience store on the outskirts of Omaha. Sal walked toward a phone booth. "I'm going to call Ma to see if the guys have called her."

Tino stared into the store at a glass case where glistening hotdog wieners rolled seductively on heated steel rollers.

"Sure enough they called Ma," Sal said walking up.

"Huh?" Tino said distantly; eyes transfixed on the wieners.

"The guys called. They left Pat's uncle's house in Chicago a couple of days ago. They're just ahead of us. We're meeting them at the U.S. Mint in Denver day after tomorrow at 9:00 in the morning."

"Hope they've got something to eat."

"Hungry?"

"Yeah. Should I hit a cornfield and meet up at a gas station?"

"Not yet. I want to get some distance before we go on the hunt."

Tino removed the face shield from his helmet and tucked it into his gear. The air fanned his face as he rode. Weary from fitful sleep and a lack of nourishment, he yawned long and deep. Whap! Something smashed into the back of his throat. He lost and regained control of his bike. *Ow! What in the hell was it?*

Scratching at the back of his throat.

Bug!

He hit the brakes, came to a skidding stop and stood straddling Rocinante. He hacked, trying to dislodge the bug. No movement. If it wasn't going to come up, then it'd have to go down. He tried swallowing, but his mouth was pasty dry.

"What's up?" Sal said, pulling up.

Tino pointed to his mouth, eyes streaming with tears. "Bug!" He opened wide. Sal peered in and depressed his tongue with a finger causing Tino to gag.

Sal ran to his bike for his canteen. "Tilt your head back." He poured. The bug scratched Tino's throat as the flood of water forced it downward. Tino took deep breaths and pounded his fist against his chest.

"Feels like it's stuck; look again."

"I'm sure it went down. It feels like that because of the irritation. Your throat will feel better in a little while, but hey, at least you got something to eat."

"*Chíngate, buey.* (Screw yourself, dumb ox.)"

Sal shook his head laughing. "If it's not one thing, it's another. Let's go."

They came to a town whose name Tino didn't bother to read. They pulled into a shopping mall. Sal stopped at a lawn to one side of a Bank of America. It was past three in the afternoon, so the bank was closed for the day.

"I'm really hungry, Sal. I can ride back to the cornfield that we passed on our way in."

"Got an idea," Sal said. "Wait here." He dropped his bike into gear and rode off.

"Wait here for what?" Tino yelled. "I'm starving, damn it!"

Tino parked Rocinante and sprawled out over the lawn.

What's he going to do? Rob a grocery store? He fell asleep thinking of his Ma's burritos and how he often traded one in grade school for a package of Twinkies or chocolate cupcakes. His classmates devoured the burritos, raving on how good they were.

Tap, tap on Tino's foot. He moaned and rolled to his side, laying his cheek on his hand. Tap. Tap. He opened his eyes to see a set of shiny black shoes and pant cuffs of a dark uniform.

A tall, thin policeman with a neatly trimmed moustache, nightstick in hand, was standing over him. His sunglasses reflected Tino's image.

"No vagrancy," the cop said sternly.

Tino sat up and rubbed his eyes. "Sorry, sir. Just having a little rest before I get back on the road." The cop's cruiser idled behind him with the driver's door open.

"Where're you going?"

"Home, sir."

"Where's home?"

"San Diego, California."

"You like melons?"

Oh no! "Melons, sir?"

"You deaf?"

"No, sir, and yes, I like melons. I like a lot of things, but why them, in particular?"

"Don't play dumb with me. You stole them from a farmer, and he's not happy about it."

"Please, sir, I haven't stolen anything."

"That's what they all say."

Sal rolled in behind the cop. The cop turned to the side, keeping both in sight. He raised his nightstick into a defensive position. "What's going on? How many of you are there?"

"It's just my older brother and me, sir," Tino said. A sense of calm came over Tino with Sal's presence.

"Is there a problem, officer?" Sal said.

"I don't think so, Sal. Somebody stole a melon, and the officer thinks I might have done it."

Sal dismounted. "Officer, I can assure you my brother did not steal a melon."

"Why should I believe either one of you? I'm taking you in for questioning."

"Officer, please," Sal said. "If my brother stole something to eat, it would be because we wouldn't have the money to buy food, but look." Sal reached into a box strapped to the rear of his bike and lifted one of two grease-stained paper bags. He opened it, revealing a big fat hamburger.

Tino stared, his mouth watering.

The cop's eyes shifted from the bag to Sal to the bag. "How do I know you didn't steal them too?"

Tino stood up. "Because officer, my brother's a Catholic priest, and he'd never steal, or allow me to. My twin and I were altar boys at his first Mass."

Sal glared at Tino.

"Priest?" The cop said pointing his nightstick up and down at Sal. "Dressed like that?"

Sal sighed; his hand had been forced. He took out his wallet and showed his ID card with a photo of him in his black priest's suit with a white Roman collar.

"Let me see that." The cop took the card and held it up, matching Sal's face to the photograph. "Reverend Salvador Caballero, Chaplain Mercy Hospital, Diocese of San Diego, California. Well, I'll be damned. Jesus, I mean jeez, father. I don't mean disrespect, and sorry to have been so tough on you. We just never know who we're dealing with."

Sal reached for the card. "You're a good man with a tough job to do."

"Thank you for understanding, Father."

"Please call me Sal. I'm on vacation. It's refreshing being with people who don't know that I'm a priest. I just hope the Bishop doesn't find out I'm dressed like a bum and spending my vacation on a motorcycle."

"Ha! That'd be as bad as when the chief caught me asleep in my cruiser!" The cop looked to Tino. "Hey! I was an altar boy too. Let's see what you got. *Ad Deum qui laelitificat.*"

Tino didn't miss a beat. "*Juventitum meum.*"

"Ha! Great job! Hey, nice meeting you." The cop shook Tino's hand. "And you too, Father. I mean Sal. No, it just doesn't sound right talking to a priest like he's just one of the guys. Boy, your mother must've been proud, seeing all three of her sons on the altar. And twins. Like bookends! Hey, have a safe trip. Hope your bishop doesn't find out. Ha!" The cop climbed into his car and rode off laughing.

"What'd I say to you about not using my being a priest to catch breaks?"

"It wasn't me who forgot the back up money. And you could show a little gratitude. I just saved your holy *nalgas*. (butt cheeks)."

Sal tried to be angry, but snorted trying to hold back a laugh.

Tino grabbed the second bag from Sal's bike and looked in to see a burger, fries, and a large soda. Tino sat on the lawn. He gulped from the soda and stuffed a fistful of fries into his mouth. One got away and fell to the lawn. "How'd you pull this off?" he said, speech muffled.

"Found a burger stand and told the owner about our situation, asked if I could clean up the lot, wash tables, and sweep floors in trade for food. Turned out to be a good guy. He was curious about our trip and about California. 'Lotsa pussy out there.' I told him."

Tino choked on the fries laughing. "Don't get started, *menso*. How do you pull off these *movidas*? (Slick underhanded moves.)"

"Simple. People want to help. You just have to give them the chance."

"You're too much, man."

"No, you are. You handled the cop like a champ."

"I was scared at first, but when you showed up, something happened and I wasn't afraid anymore." Tino was about to bite into the hamburger but stopped. "Hey, wait a minute," he said. "It's Friday. We're not supposed to be eating meat today."

"We're traveling, so it's special circumstance," Sal said, his cheeks bulging with food and eyes laughing.

"Don't make me laugh!" Tino said and turned away. He ate everything, down to the fry that had fallen.

"Let's see how far we can get for the rest of the day," Sal said when they finished eating.

Tino jumped on his bike, threw his fist into the air and yelled. "*¡Ánnndale!*"

"*¡Ánnndale!*"

They rode until dusk. Tino led the way into a farm town, scaled up a secluded bluff and stopped at the crest. Long, tired shadows had consumed the town. Lights blinked on.

Sal lay back with a satisfied look. "We did well today."

"Me? You did well. You got us food."

"And you got us out of this jam. When we started the trip, I wasn't sure if you'd be able to keep up, but you're doing it, and doing it well."

"Thanks, Sal."

Tino gazed up into the infinite firmament—the moon, a thin white sliver, floated in a sparkling sea. A shooting star with a long tail flashed across the sky in a half second. He rolled onto his side with the realization that the world was not a hard, threatening jungle where one was either predator or prey, but a wondrous horn of plenty. There are a lot of good people in the world willing to help you along. He smiled and closed his eyes.

TINO WOKE TO SAL HUMMING and studying a map.

Sal looked over. "*¿Como estas, hermano?*"

"*¿Como estoy?*"

"Your injuries."

"Oh, fine. Not hurting bad at all. Your voice sounds a lot better, Sal."

"My voice?"

"Your cold, *pendejo.*"

"I'm over it."

"You and your mind-over-matter crap. Where are we, by the way? I'm not even sure what state we're in."

"Nebraska. Ready to hit it?"

"Yeah, let's go."

They crossed the state in a southwesterly direction heading for Colorado, and by early afternoon had reached I-70 West into Kansas. Sal pulled into the parking lot of a row of roadside businesses in Goodland—truck stop, diner, shoe repair shop, laundromat, and grocery store. All of the merchants shared a long wood-frame, single-story structure, each with its own façade. Facing the highway on a frontage road was the tall wide screen of a drive-in theater. The marquee read THE GREEN BERETS.

They parked the bikes by the road, away from the string of cars in front of the shops and stores.

Sal reached into his pocket and produced one dime, a nickel, and two pennies. "You got any left?"

Tino had twenty-one cents.

Sal took the coins and headed for the store. He returned and tucked a family-size can of chili beans into his gear. They continued on, riding into the flat monotony. By the end of the day, the terrain had changed into rolling hills, a welcome sight after riding endless miles across the plains. The deep green ridge of a steep mountain range, capped by a craggy, gleaming white crown silhouetted against the evening's purple sky, lay far ahead.

"Look Rocinante, it's the Rockies!"

Tino and Sal rode into Denver, Colorado as the sun met the horizon. INSPIRATION POINT PARK NEXT EXIT read a highway sign. Tino laid his cheek on his hand mimicking sleep. Sal nodded and fell behind to follow.

Tino took the Sheridan Boulevard exit and pulled over moments later at the park entrance. "Park Hours: 9:00 a.m. – Sunset – No Camping."

"I'm not going to argue with you," Tino said when Sal pulled alongside. "I know you'll want to sneak in to hide and sleep, but if we get caught and kicked out in the middle of the night, I'm going to be really ticked off at you."

Sal nodded toward the sun, halfway below the gleaming snowy ridgeline of the Rockies. "It's not sunset yet. So we're not breaking the law."

"Okay, but it says 'No Camping,'" Sal.

"We're just going to sleep—no tents, no campfire, no nothing. Now turn off your headlight."

"If something happens I'm going to be really pissed off at you."

The paved road wound through the park past parking lots adjacent to picnic tables under trees, past a volleyball court over a green lawn and areas left to nature. Sal pulled over and pointed to a massive weeping American elm tree, a hundred feet away. Its branches touched the ground and blocked visibility from the road. They jumped the curb to the elm and puttered through its branches that swept the ground and under the canopy.

"It's like a natural tent under here," Tino said, cutting his engine.

Traffic on the boulevard outside the park decreased, and a chorus of crickets grew louder as the night crept over the mountains like a slow, sure flood.

"Good day of riding," Sal said. "It'll be no sweat making it on time to meet the guys tomorrow."

Tino dropped his sleeping bag on the ground. "It'll be nice not rushing for a change."

Sal rummaged through his gear and found the bag with the can of chili beans he'd bought earlier. Tino looked on as Sal cut the lid off with a can opener and set it on the picnic table.

"I suppose cold beans are better than no beans at all," Tino said.

"Ye of little faith," Sal said. He took a can of Sterno out of the bag.

"Well, if you don't beat all."

Sal pried the lid off of the can of Sterno with a screwdriver, struck a match, and lit the jelly-like fuel.

Sal took the can of chili beans by the rim with a set of pliers and held it over the soft blue flame.

"Any idea how far we are from home?" Tino asked.

"A thousand miles, give or take."

"It'll be good sleeping in my bed, taking showers, and eating Ma's food again."

Sal looked up from holding the chili over the Sterno. "I've really enjoyed this freedom. I like wearing shorts and being a regular person."

"It's always been funny to me," Tino said.

"What?"

"You know, how people treat you as a priest. But you've just been my big brother to me, who's always made me laugh a lot and taken us kids to fun places."

"Like where?"

"Like to the beach to have a beach party for a whole day. You got us building sandcastles or racing each other along the shore, and at night we cooked weenies and marshmallows over the fire pit using clothes hangers. And it was great fun hearing your funny stories about our old uncles in Mexico.

"I remember once I felt like a real hero when you locked the key inside Pa's pickup truck. You had to break a hole in the vent window big enough for me to fit my hand in to unlock the door."

Sal laughed. "You've got a good memory."

The chili steamed and bubbled. Sal set the can on the table and handed Tino a plastic spoon from the bag.

"You're a bigger boy than me. Just leave me a little."

"Thanks," Tino said. He spooned out a small mound of steaming chili and blew on it.

40.

Rocky Mountain Cuisine

Tino led the way into Denver and came across the Foothills Café and pulled in. "I'll go in and see if we can earn some grub."

"You up to asking?" Sal asked.

"If they say 'no,' we'll go somewhere else. Besides, people want to help. You just have to give them the chance."

"Ha! You're getting it."

Diners at tables and booths chatted; silverware tapped against plates, busboys stacked dishes into bins and carted them through swinging kitchen doors. Patsy Cline sang from out of a jukebox about being crazy for loving someone.

A middle-age woman in a white blouse and black pants that hugged her lean figure was at the cash register. The eraser end of a pencil peeked out from her big red hair, stiff with Aqua Net. She held a cigarette to her lips as she talked with a man sitting at the counter on a swivel stool, his belly rolling out of his denim jacket. The greasy remains of his breakfast lay on a plate in front of him.

"Good morning," Tino said to the woman. He didn't smile, figuring it best to look businesslike and not like someone looking to mooch.

She scrutinized him head to foot. "What can I do for you, hon?"

"May I speak with the owner?"

"He ain't here right now," she said, her eyes squinting against the cigarette smoke. "Wha-cha need?"

"My brother and I are on our way home. We ran out of money and are willing to do a lot of work for a little food."

She shot a sideways glance at the man on the stool. He nodded. She scratched her scalp with a gleaming red, claw-like fingernail. "Saw you boys pull in. You aren't some kind of a motorcycle gang, are you?"

"No, ma'am. We're kind of dirty because we've been on the road for a long time, and we're just trying to get home."

"Sure, there's something I'd love you to do for me hon, but you ain't been around near long enough to know how to do it the way it oughtta get done."

"Hell, Grace," the man said, laughing. He wiped his mouth with a napkin. "I been around long enough. Out back or in my truck?"

She let loose a raspy laugh and swatted him on the shoulder and turned back to Tino. "Well, tell your brother that I'll take your offer to do a lot of work for a little food."

She jotted down a list of tasks as she led Tino and Sal through the kitchen and around the property. Over the next hour and a half, the brothers washed, swept, mopped, ripped apart cardboard boxes and hauled trash to a bin at the rear of the restaurant.

When they finished, she walked around with them checking off the items on her list and ended in the kitchen.

"Great job!" she said. "We just might pass the county health inspection this time round."

"Emilio," she said to a tall, slender young man dressed in white and working food on a large grill with a spatula. "Would you bring up a couple of Rocky Mountain Oyster Omelet Combos for these hungry boys?"

"*Si, Señora Grassy.*"

Tino and Sal sat on swivel stools next to Grace at the register after washing up.

She planted her elbows on the counter, rested her chin on her palms and looked into Sal's face.

Tino sneaked a glance at her ample cleavage.

She noticed Tino looking and asked, "Lose something?"

He turned away blushing.

She turned back to Sal—cheeks on palms. "It can't be any too comfortable sitting on that motorbike all day with the wind blowing in your handsome face and curly hair."

Sal laughed uneasily. "You get used to it."

Tino helped himself to another peek.

"And you can't take much with you," she said holding Sal with her eyes. "And even less if you had a honey sitting with her arms wrapped around you nice and tight. You got a sweetheart?"

"Not at the moment," Sal said overdoing laughter. "And I suppose if I had another person riding with me, it'd be in a sidecar."

"Sidecar? If you ain't the funniest. To think you made it all the way to New York. I hear it's big and busy and full of nasty people. That so?"

"It's pretty exciting, all right. But except for a couple of incidents, the New Yorkers were great."

Emilio, the young cook, brought out two steaming platters piled with food and set them on the counter.

"*Mira no mas, que bonito,*" Tino said.

Sal gave Emilio a thumbs-up. "*Gracias, hombre.*"

"*No hay de qué, señor,*" he answered. Light reflected from the gold lining on a front tooth.

Grace straightened. "By God, I'm going to do it someday! I'm going to see the country, but not on a motorbike. I'm taking a car and trailer. A woman needs her things, you know."

A middle-age couple with a teenage boy and girl entered the restaurant. Grace picked up menus and showed them to a table.

Tino wasted no time and devoured everything to the sprig of parsley. He might be uncomfortably full for a while, but he'd be able to go a good stretch without eating.

Grace returned from the Bunn-o-matic, after making a round topping off cups. "You boys enjoyed the food?"

"Yup," Tino said. "And thanks for letting us work for it."

"Well, you sure earned it."

"You called this a Rocky Mountain Oyster Omelet," Tino said. "Where do you get oysters out here?"

"Moose nuts," She said with a mischievous look.

"You're kidding."

"Ha! Ha! Let's just say you've had genuine Rocky Mountain cuisine."

Tino looked to Sal, hoping he would say that she was putting them on, but Sal didn't seem to have a clue.

Grace walked over to the kitchen doors, pushed them open, and peered in. "Emi, the boys liked your oysters!"

"*Si, muy bueno, Señora Grassy.*"

"You've been very kind to us," Sal said, uneasily.

She spoke seductively. "You need a place to stay tonight?"

Holy crap! Tino thought.

"Huh?" Sal said. "Oh yeah, ah, well, it's very kind of you. But we've got an appointment."

"Well, suit yourself handsome, and by the way, the next time you boys stop in we'll treat you to elk testicles under glass." Grace laughed and hacked. She fanned her face with a menu and leaned against the counter steadying herself.

Sal smiled uneasily. "We'll have money next time."

"Hard as you work, and cute as you are, you ain't gonna need money, honey." She stepped to him and kissed him on the cheek.

Tino's mouth dropped open.

"Thank you," Sal said, nudging Tino toward the exit.

She took a pack of cigarettes from her apron pocket, shook one out, pinched it with her lips, and talked from the side of her mouth. "Come back and see me anytime." She lit up and looked after Tino and Sal as they walked out.

Sal shot her an exaggerated wave from his bike.

She blew him a kiss.

Sal threw his head back laughing.

Tino shook his head at how awkward Sal was in dealing with women who showed him interest. *Wish I could have a shot at Grace.*

41.

Dainty White Butterflies

Tino and Sal arrived at the U.S. Mint on Colfax Avenue in Denver; no sign of Gary and Patrick.

"I'm going to Western Union to get the money Ma wired us," Sal said from his bike. "Don't say anything to the guys about us going broke."

"What do we need money for? When we had it we ate peanut butter and jelly; without it, burgers and omelets."

"Ma realized we were broke when I had to call her collect. She's sending us money so she won't worry."

"Sounds like Ma," Tino said. He looked after Sal, riding down the street. Tino stretched and jogged up and down the sidewalk. The guys appeared up the street heading in his direction.

"That thing still running?" Tino said when Patrick pulled up in a trail of smoke.

"Long as I keep pouring oil into it."

"Just about every fucking time we stop," Gary said. "And Jesus, what the hell happened to your bike Tino?"

"Bad fall." Tino held up his forearm, showing the long, wide scab. "I thought it was the end of the trip for me."

"Damn," Patrick said. "You got to be careful." He took a can of oil wrapped in a plastic bag from his gear and removed two bits of oil-soaked paper that plugged the pour holes. "Engine's developed piston slap. Rings are wearing out. I switched to 40 weight and added STP, but it's only helped a little."

All of the bikes were dirty and caked black where the tailpipes were bolted to the engine blocks.

"Hey, *muchachos*," Sal said pulling up on his bike. "It's good to see you. We need to hit the road and get over the mountains today. I don't want to spend the night up here in the cold, and I'd like to visit one of the Pueblo Indian sites in Mesa Verde on the way down."

"Right on!" Gary said. "*National Geographic* did a good spread on them."

"Is there a place for us to crash out for the night?" Patrick asked.

"Not sure. Map says there's a lake close to a town called Cortez. Don't know if there's camping, but we'll make do."

The temperature cooled significantly on the ascent into the Rockies. Sal signaled toward a general store ahead where they could stop to add a layer of clothing. A doe poked her head out from a near solid wall of trees. She stepped into the road. Afraid that she might get hit, Tino gunned his engine making his pipes roar, hoping to scare her back into the woods. But the doe, with a fawn close behind, bolted into the road. The deer crossed Gary's path. He leaned away, but clipped the fawn's rear legs. It fell, jumped up, and darted off. Gary went into a slide. He hit a rise at the parking lot entrance, went airborne, and crash landed on his side in a drainage ditch, his leg pinned under the bike.

Sal, in the lead, didn't notice. Tino and Patrick pulled over and ran to Gary.

"Get it off!" Gary screamed, pushing at the bike.

Tino and Patrick yanked it off him.

Sal ran up. "You okay?"

Gary gasped. "Muffler was on my leg. Burned it," his breath visible in small white puffs in the frigid air.

Sal pulled up Gary's pant leg revealing a patch of bright pink skin on his calf. He removed Gary's boot and examined his leg. "No sign of a broken bone. I'm more concerned with the burn," Sal said. "It could infect if it's bad enough." He wrapped Gary's calf with gauze. "That's about all we can do for now. Got to take a leak. I'll be right back."

Tino helped Gary to his feet. Patrick appeared with his tool kit. He snipped off one of Gary's signal lights that was dangling by a wire.

"Hope your leg's okay, man," Tino said.

Sal returned with a bottle of aspirin and gave it to Gary. "This should help with the pain. Store clerk said that you slid on black ice."

"On what?"

"Frozen water on the asphalt that doesn't thaw because it's in the shadows. Clerk said that *lowlanders* are always sliding off roads up here. One guy slid off the side of a mountain. They found him the next day in his car dead from exposure."

Patrick went to where Gary had slid and stepped into the shadow of the forest. He slipped and fell on his rear.

The day turned gray and colder as they rode on. Exhaust from the bikes formed small white trails. The air cut like a razor, penetrating Tino's clothing. Even with lined leather gloves, his fingers ached, and his body grew stiff from fighting the cold. He remembered visiting a friend in the hospital who had gotten frostbite mountain climbing. His toes had turned black and purple.

"Almost home, almost home," Tino said, his teeth chattering.

At Fremont Pass, he came to fully understand how cold it could get at this altitude. Small pure-white butterflies fluttered against the dark green of the forest. Except that they weren't butterflies but snowflakes gently falling.

Rocinante sputtered.

They wound through the mountains, the gray gradually giving way to clear cerulean skies. A cascading stream ran to the base of the valley and joined other streams to form a river that meandered past a huddle of buildings: post office, general store, sheriff's station. Blue-white smoke rose from chimneys of cabins dotting the mountainsides. A halo-like rainbow appeared and arched over the valley.

Tino rode through S-turns, battling the cold and ever vigilant of the villainous black ice that lurked in the shadows. They topped a pass and began the final descent. The air slowly lost its bite. Their collective spirits rose.

42.

More Than Curios

TINO, SAL, PATRICK, AND GARY PULLED into Mesa Verde National Park in midafternoon. Across the street from the parking lot was a thousand-foot cliff housing a compound of dwellings, some rectangular, others round. One, a tall tower, might have served as a vantage point for spotting arriving allies or hostiles.

Patrick scanned the cliff. "How in the hell did they build that?"

"Great defensive position," Sal said. "Let's go and have a look."

"My ankle's too sore," Gary said. "I'm staying here."

"I'll keep him company," Tino said.

Sal and Patrick crossed the road and scaled a string of steps leading to the site.

"I saw you get busted at the Convention in Chicago, Gare," Tino said at the parking lot.

"No kidding?"

"Yeah, we were staying at Father Paul Gill's in New Hampshire and watched the news one night, and bigger'n shit, there you were, in the middle of everything and getting it from a cop."

"Did Sal see me getting arrested?"

"No, everybody was in a big discussion about the War. How in the hell did you wind up at the convention?"

"We were at Pat's uncle's place. Pat and his cousin Sean and I went to see what was going on. It was really cool. I got to march right next to Abbie Hoffman and Tom Hayden."

"Wow, cool!"

"Sean said that Mayor Daley wasn't going to let the protesters take over the City. He said that Chicago was covered by smoke during the King riots, and Daley wasn't going to let it happen again."

"Sal and I saw burned-up buildings in Washington D. C. that happened after King was killed," Tino said.

Gary continued. "Anyhow we were having a lot of fun demonstrating and chanting. A group of veterans marched and chanted, 'one, two, three, four, we don't want your fuckin' war.' Then the cops came at us, and they weren't messing around. They beat the crap out of people and dragged 'em off. They even roughed up TV newsmen. Everybody was pushing and shoving. I fell and a big cop grabbed me. I didn't resist, but he gave me a good one across the back with his club and dragged me to a paddy wagon."

"Jesus, how'd you get out?"

"There were peace lawyers at the jail. I told mine that I was on vacation and just wanted to see what was going on and that I was about to join the Marines. He got me off as long as I agreed not to come back."

"If you had an arrest record, you wouldn't be able to join up with me," Tino said. "I want to hear more, but I got to take a leak, and bad."

Tino rode his bike to the restroom at the far end of the parking lot. He was leaning Rocinante on his kickstand when movement on the mountainside caught his eye. A majestic bighorn sheep walked out onto an outcropping of boulders. It studied Tino for a moment and meandered off into the bush.

"Beautiful," Tino whispered.

A tourist shop in the design of cliff dwellings sat under the outcropping. A sign read BROKEN ARROW – MORE THAN CURIOS.

43.

Quetzalcoátl

A BELL JINGLED WHEN TINO OPENED THE DOOR.
"Good afternoon, young man." A woman stood behind a glass showcase. Her black and silver hair was woven into twin snakes that rested on either side of her turquoise blouse. Glass shelves in the case held dozens of figurines—one, a shaman in leathers, stooped over in a dance holding a rattle in one hand, a snake in the other.

"Good afternoon, ma'am," Tino answered.

She set a curious eye on him. "You've been on a journey."

"How'd you know?"

"Well, most everyone who comes here is traveling, but you've had a different kind of journey."

Tino looked confused. "Yes, ma'am. We've traveled from California, to New York. We're on our way back home."

"Long in miles, for sure, but maybe long in other ways?"

"Yeah, long and unbelievable."

She came around the showcase, leaned against it, and covered her mouth with a hand. "Maybe more of a pilgrimage?"

"Hmmm, it could've been something like that. I fell off of my bike and hit my head and saw some pretty weird stuff."

"I see," she said. "Go on."

"It's crazy, but I think I saw my great-grandfather, who died a hundred years ago. And I think I saw the devil. I don't know if I imagined it or if it was real. I've been trying to figure out what it all meant, or if it meant anything at all."

"Of course it meant something. But it's rare to have a visit from an ancestor *and* a spirit in one quest. Tell me more about the passage?"

"Passage?"

"How you got there?"

"Got there?"

"Jesus, how'd you hit your head?"

"Oh yeah. Well, I was trying to make up for lost time."

"Tsk, tsk. I've never understood your people talking about 'losing time.' How can one lose what one doesn't understand? But that's a different conversation. Continue."

"I was taking a tight curve on the road when a snake came out of nowhere, crawling in front of me. It was as if it just appeared. I leaned away hard, trying to keep from running it over. I fell with my bike and hit my head, and that's when I started seeing stuff. A nurse found me laid out along the road and resuscitated me. She said that I was 'gone' when she found me. Could I have died and come back?"

"What good luck."

"That the nurse saved me?"

"No, but that you came across a snake on your journey. Snakes are good omens for pilgrims. It may be a guide for you. Lucky you didn't harm it. Great civilizations like the Maya and Aztecs revered the snake. In one ritual, a priest mimicked a snake by shedding skin, symbolizing a rebirth. Quetzalcóatl, a snake with feathers, characterized one of their most important gods, joining the sky and earth in one deity. Brilliant."

"How do you know so much about that stuff?"

"My father was an archeologist. He worked sites in Mexico, and I earned a degree in anthropology. Imagine, an Indian who knows a little bit about something other than whiskey?"

"I didn't mean to say—"

"I'm used to it. Anyhow, Quetzalcoátl was also known as Precious Twin."

"No kidding? I'm a twin!"

"Really? You have some very interesting patterns in your life. The snake is definitely a guide for you."

"But if I would've run it over, I wouldn't have fallen and gotten hurt."

"No pain, no gain, they say. Tell me more about your spiritual quest."

"After I hit my head, I found myself back on my bike, riding down the hill as if I hadn't fallen but was just continuing the trip. The snake I almost ran over led me down the hill."

The woman shifted her weight but kept her attention on Tino. "I'm not surprised."

"On my way down I passed a man. Even though I couldn't have ever met him, I think he was my great-grandfather who was killed in the Civil War. He smiled at me and smashed his rifle as I rode by. Freaked me out. I kept going and stopped at a river. On the other side was a beautiful woman I had met." Tino flushed. "I had made love to her earlier on the trip."

The woman smiled. "My, you've been busy!"

"She called me to her, but she never smiled. And there was this huge and ugly slug, laying in the mud. It started dragging me toward it." Tino shivered. "Was it the devil who was trying to take my soul?"

"My, you had a journey to Mictlan, what the Greeks and Westerners referred to as *Hades*. There's certainly a lot there."

"Could all of that have actually happened? And why wasn't she happy to see me? She kept calling but didn't seem happy to see me. Was it real, a dream?"

"Both."

"What?"

"We are equal measures of the carnal and the spirit, one yin, the other yang. Everything is a dream, everything is real. So your experience was as real as it wasn't."

Tino put his hands to his head.

The woman laughed. "Welcome to a separate reality. The slug, as you call it, was hardly the devil. You must have been in a confused state of mind or it wouldn't have appeared to you as an evil entity. Do you remember what state of mind you were in before your journey?"

"I had taken some LSD a hippie had given me. He said it'd help me to see."

"Ha!" she laughed. "You're the adventurous type. Using a powerful drug disguised as some kind of spiritual elixir certainly explains your confused state of mind. Taking something we can tritely call bad medicine would attempt to claim your soul. The spirit was telling you not to play with forces that you don't understand, forces that can destroy you. That's why it appeared evil. Spirits also come to help us realize our mortality."

"What's so good about that?"

"To realize and accept one's mortality helps us understand the preciousness of life. Too many don't realize something's value until it's gone. Death is just a part of the deal, not something to fret over. Fearing death is a waste of one's allotted time."

"Are you saying that I shouldn't be afraid to die?"

"No, not exactly. I suppose that everyone has some fear of the unknown. Just don't be afraid of death."

"I don't get it."

"Give it some thought. It may take you a little time."

"What was the monster about?"

"It wasn't the spirit that you were struggling against, but your own fears. If you weren't afraid, the spirit would have been a positive entity like a winged stallion that you could've ridden into the glorious blue. Too many people spend their lives being afraid. Those who are able to free themselves of fear find joy."

"What about the woman?"

"Ah, yes, the seductress. You say she was a lover?"

"I met her while I was on my bike trip, and *we did it*. I fell in love with her and want to get back to her bad, real bad."

"The spirit lying on the other side of the river wasn't your lover. She was the embodiment of the bad medicine you had taken, disguised as a pleasurable entity. You have met your own personal siren."

"Like in *The Odyssey*?"

"Ah, so you know a little too. Well, this is extraordinary. In all my years, I have never met someone who has experienced as much as you on a single quest. This makes my day. Thank you for coming in and sharing your story with me."

"No. Thank *you*."

"You are very fortunate. You lost your life, but you were able to get it back, a most extraordinary gift. The experience will bring you a certain measure of wisdom, and at such a young age. Someone with much power has been protecting you."

"My Ma is always praying, asking God, the saints and our ancestors to watch over her kids."

"I might have known. There aren't many forces that can match a mother's love and orations. You're lucky to have her. Heed her instruction. It's worth more than you realize, maybe more than even she realizes. You are also lucky to have had a visit from an ancestor. Some people live their entire lives without such a visit. Others have had the experience but turn a blind eye to it, or they are fearful of it, or don't try to understand."

"I sure want to believe."

"You are in for a good life, young man. Not without trials. We all have them, but you will be fortunate. Someone will always be there for you when you most need help."

"I didn't think I was important enough for spirits or ancestors to bring me messages."

"This not feeling worthy is a common ailment. Get over it. We're all worthy, even if we don't realize it. But the worst burden is fear. Fear is a dark and cold path on this trip of life. Don't allow it to steer you."

Sal's voice rang from outside. "Hey! Let's go!"

"Darn it! That's my older brother."

The woman offered her hand. "You come from ancient and wise cultures. Embrace them."

Tino cupped her hand in both of his. "Thank you so much." He started for the door but she tightened her grip and looked him in the eye. "Your ancestor cares deeply for you. He needs you to understand something. I'm afraid I can't help you with that, but not to worry. It'll come to you when you're ready."

Tino's face fell. "I'm not good at figuring things out."

"Be patient. Learn to see with your mind's eye. You will see his message when you're ready. Now I understand why my cousin Mona couldn't come and take my place today. I was destined to hear your story."

Sal revved his engine. Tino hurried toward the door. "Thanks again, ma'am," he said but stopped to look back at her. "What's the name of your shop, Broken Arrow, mean?"

"It means *peace*. When warring tribes had had enough of bloodshed, they made peace and broke an arrow as a symbol. I wish that our president and his enemies would make peace and do the same."

"Thanks," Tino said. "Thanks an awful lot."

"Don't mention it. Walk in peace. Oh, and try not to lose any more time." Her dark eyes gleamed with humor.

44.

"I Love You Guysh."

TWO-LANE HIGHWAY 160 also served as Cortez's Main Street. A handful of single-story structures sat on either side. A pickup truck bumped its way up a dusty hillside road toward the sun that hung scarcely an inch above the crest.

The four bikers rolled into the town's gas station.

"Don't waste time. We need to make camp before nightfall," Sal said and headed for the bathroom.

"I'm going across the street to the store," Patrick said as soon as Sal was out of earshot.

"You're not going to gas up before going to the store?" Tino asked.

Patrick rode off.

"What in the hell's he up to," Gary said, filling his gas tank while standing astride his bike.

"Don't you need to stretch out a little?" Tino said.

"Ankle hurts too much."

Sal returned from the bathroom and said, "I'm going to make us a good dinner tonight before our final push home."

"Right on!" Gary said. He took out his wallet and handed Sal a couple of bills.

Patrick exited the store with a shopping bag, stashed it in his gear, and rode toward the gas station, passing Sal halfway through the street.

Tino and Gary waited at the side of the road.

Patrick gassed up and made for Tino and Gary as Sal pulled up with a box loaded with groceries strapped to his bike. "Good news," Sal said.

"Someone invited us to dinner?" Tino said.

"And we can poke their daughters?" Patrick said.

"No on both counts. The checker gave me directions to a campground and lake close by. We'll be set by dark."

On the road to the campground, Patrick swerved to run over a small dead animal with black fur, making Gary laugh.

Patrick didn't notice the skunk's white stripe until it was too late. Peewee's tires carried the penetrating stench to the campsite.

"You're going to have to park away from here," Sal said sharply.

Patrick sheepishly rolled Peewee off.

Sal yelled behind him. "And park far enough away so it doesn't bother other campers!"

Gary limped to the picnic table and sat.

Sal took a plastic bag filled with ice from the box of groceries and handed it to Gary. "This and the aspirin I gave you should knock down the pain quite a bit."

"Thanks again, Sal. You're the best, man."

"You'd do the same for me, right?" Sal popped the tab from a can of Dr. Pepper. He took a deep pull and stifled a belch with the back of his hand. "I'm going to look for firewood."

"I'll help," Patrick said.

Tino put a foot on the picnic table seat, rested his hands on his knee and leaned toward Gary. "I got a plan for when we get out of the Marines."

Gary perked up. "Yeah?"

"I met this cool dude in New Mexico named Rex. He rides a bitchen chopper. He also owns a garage and trains young guys to be mechanics. I want us to learn mechanics from him, and then we can ride with him and his biker friends."

Gary laughed. "Right on, man!"

"And get this; he lives close to my aunt and uncle in Tucson, so it'll be easy to find him."

"Outta sight, dude!"

The two friends talked excitedly about their futures.

Sal and Patrick returned with armloads of wood and tossed them at the fire pit. Patrick sat at the table with Tino and Gary.

Sal took the box with groceries from his bike, set it on the table, and took out a roll of aluminum foil, a cube of butter, four fat potatoes, and a butcher-paper package. He tore off a side of the box, ripped it into pieces, and laid them under the heavy cast iron grill piling kindling over the cardboard. He struck a stick match against the concrete fire ring, and lit the pile at the base. Yellow flames and white smoke rose.

He then instructed Tino to wash and coat the potatoes with butter, then wrap them in tinfoil and set them in the pit when there were coals. Sal unwrapped the butcher paper package revealing four thick red steaks.

"Cool!" Gary said.

Sal laid heavier wood over the fire. "Nothing any of you couldn't do."

Tino and Patrick unpacked gear from the bikes and set up camp.

Sal set the steaks on the grill. Fat dripped, causing sparks of flame.

"What a difference in temperature today," Patrick said standing at the fire pit. "I went from freezing my balls off in the mountains to sweating them off in the desert."

Sal laughed. "Well, hold on to 'em. You might need them someday." He looked through his tool bag for a screwdriver and wrapped a T-shirt around his hand for a heat shield. He held the screwdriver over coals to disinfect it and stabbed a foil-wrapped potato. Tino and the guys scrutinized his every move, like dogs watching food bowls being filled.

Sal passed the screwdriver. Each took his turn at taking a potato out of the coals.

Tino peeled back the foil and cut out a wedge of the potato. Steam rose in a slow, seductive dance. He filled the cavity with butter.

Sal tossed a handful of salt and pepper packets that he had pilfered from restaurants on the table.

Gary laughed. "You stole them?"

"Wish that was all he'd stolen," Tino said, drawing a warning glare from Sal. Tino rolled his eyes at the warning to keep a lid on it.

Sal laid the steaks on paper plates. "Chow time, dudes."

"What'd you think of the ruins today, Pat?" Sal asked at the table.

"Blew my mind. The Pueblos built reservoirs, did terrace farming, pretty cool stuff. Guide said that there're a lot more sites around here. Wish we could've spent a whole day there."

The four sat or lay on their sleeping bags around the fire pit talking after dinner.

"Hey Sal," Patrick said, poking a toothpick between his teeth. "What's the hardest about being a priest for you?"

"When I was a parish priest, I didn't like having to raise so much money. It's a relief that I don't have to do fundraising as chaplain at the hospital."

"Anything else?"

"I'm uneasy about people kneeling before me to bless them like I'm some kind of a saint."

Tino grabbed his crotch. "*Aquí tengo tu saint.*"

Sal continued, "Being on this trip is the first time that I've been free of responsibility. And I like being treated like a normal person."

Patrick continued. "So you've had doubts about your vocation?"

"Doesn't everyone question major life decisions? I'll bet there isn't a married person who hasn't wondered if they made the right decision."

"Suppose you're right," Patrick said. "I wanted to be a priest and even went to a seminary high school my freshman year."

"No kidding?" Tino said. "How come I didn't know that?"

"Because I don't talk about it. Some stuff happened."

"Like what?" Gary asked.

"A priest did some stuff to me."

"What kind of stuff?"

Patrick stared into the fire. "He told me to see him in his office after evening services one night. He smiled when I showed up and had me lie on my back over his desk. He pulled down my pants and ran his hands over my hair. He started stroking me. He seemed to be loving and hating it at the same time. 'Nice boy, very nice boy,' he said with the creepiest look on his face. I looked away at an aquarium in his office. I felt his mouth over my..."

Sal, Tino and Gary sat in a sick silence.

Patrick's voice broke with emotion. "The pretty little fish swam round and round."

"Jesus," Tino said.

"Didn't you turn him in?" Gary asked.

"He warned me not to say anything or things would go bad for me, and if I left the school my family would be disgraced in our parish. 'Now, you don't want that, do you, young Patrick?'"

"I said I didn't. 'Good boy,' he said."

"Did he do it again?" Tino asked.

Patrick staring into the fire, nodded his head slowly. "I called the headmaster when I went home for the summer and told him that I didn't think the religious life was for me. I just wanted to be a good priest, like you Sal." Fire reflected off the tears running down Patrick's cheeks.

"I'm so sorry," Sal said.

"I've thought of finding him and cutting off his hands."

"It's hard to believe that something like that could happen," Tino said.

"Word got around of a similar incident when I was in the seminary," Sal said. "The archbishop told us that the Church had ways of dealing with these issues. If you give me his name, I could look into it for you, Pat."

"You guys are the only ones I've ever told. I want to keep it that way."

"Think it over, Pat. Just give me the okay and I'll work with you."

"Thanks, just for listening."

Coals from the fire glowed in the black night. A coyote howled in the distance.

"Let's turn in," Sal said softly. "We've got a long, hot grind ahead of us."

Another howl.

"Think they'll come after us?" Tino said, helping Gary to his feet.

Sal squeezed toothpaste on his brush. "I'm pretty sure that they only eat animals."

Tino lay between his friends and fell asleep until someone shook him. He opened his eyes to see Patrick's face inches from his, motioning him to follow. Tino sighed, but there had to be a good reason for this. He looked to Sal; still as stone.

Patrick led Tino through the scrub brush with a flashlight.

"What's this about?"

"You'll see," Patrick said. They came on a dry streambed. "I saw this spot when I was getting firewood. Check it out." Patrick shone the light on Gary, who was sitting on a felled tree trunk.

"Hey, mofo!" Gary said, laughing. Two six-packs of beer lay at Gary's feet.

"Bitchen! How'd you get them?"

"Cortez," Patrick said. "Drinking age in Colorado is eighteen."

They sat in a triangle. Gary pulled cans from the plastic rings.

"Chug-a-lug," Patrick said. "Ready, set, go!"

Heads tilted back. Hard and fast gulping. Patrick threw his can in the center, and raised his hands in victory. BUUURUP! "Yes, siree!"

Gary finished a beat after.

Tino choked, spewing beer out his mouth and nose. "Stings like hell," he said coughing. Gary and Patrick rolled with laugher.

"Never send a boy to do a man's job," Patrick said.

Tino wiped his eyes.

Gary passed another round. "Hey, dude, tell us about getting laid when we were down in the South."

"It's nobody's business."

"Aw, come on," Patrick said. "You can't keep this to yourself."

Tino set down his beer. "All right, but no wisecracks from either of you. I went to fill the canteens at a water faucet outside a bathroom when I heard a woman's voice. I looked up, and there she was, leaning against the wall, and a real fox. I felt a little nervous, but she turned out to be pretty cool. After we shot the shit for a while she asked me to meet her later."

"You fucking charmer," Patrick said. "It's that smile of yours."

"Melts the chicks, man," Gary said.

"We met at the lake and talked for a while and she said that she'd like a ride on my motorcycle."

"Aha!" Gary said. "So, that's when you came to camp."

"Yeah, and I could feel her tits against my back when we rode around the lake."

"Nice!" Gary said.

"And get this, we swam to the diving platform in our underwear."

Gary smiled big. "Boss!"

Patrick tossed an empty can and peeled another from the plastic rings.

"She started making out with me out there."

Gary put his hand between his legs. "Is that where it happened?"

"No, not yet."

Patrick erupted with a long, deep, vibrating belch.

"When we got back to the bike, she asked me if I wanted to see her trailer."

Gary grinned, "And that's where it happened."

"Yeah, and I can't stop thinking about her."

Patrick gulped beer and wiped his mouth. "Did you see her naked?"

"Everything," Tino said.

Gary laid a hand over his crotch. "Unbelievable."

"I want to spend the rest of my life with her. She's beautiful and intelligent." Tino drained what was left of his beer. Gary peeled off another, but Tino waved it off.

"You're not done, man, are you?" Patrick said, his speech impaired by the alcohol.

"I've got a lot to think about, and I need to keep a clear head."

"What's her name?" Gary asked.

"Lola."

"Dude, I'll ride back with you to wherever Lala is."

"It's Lola, Gare."

"Make your plans with her, and when we get out of the Marines you can learn to be a mechanic, then get the GI Bill and buy a house, and then marry Lala."

"Lola, Gare, Lo-la. And I can't do anything more with her until she takes care of some pretty heavy business."

Patrick opened another can. "Burp. Gulp, gulp. Burp."

"Heavy business?" Gary said.

"She's kind of married."

"Are you fucking kidding me, man? How old is she?"

"Maybe Sal's age."

"Man-o-man. You landed a whopper! Wasn't her husband around?"

"No, she'd left him. My folks and the Church wouldn't like me marrying a divorced woman."

"Well, I don't care," Gary said. "I'll back you up no matter what."

Tino put his arm around Gary's shoulders. "Thanks, man."

Patrick slowly rose to his feet and emptied what was left in his can with one long pull. He teetered on his feet. "I, I love you guysh. BUUURUP!" He opened his arms looking for a hug. "Get up, ju mother fuckersh."

"You're drunk, asshole," Gary said, laughing. He tried to stand but fell over and laughed all the harder.

"I know I'm jurrunk," Patrick said, enunciating each word, "but doeshn't mean I don't love ju." He leaned over, put his hands on his knees, and threw up his dinner.

Tino jumped to his feet and held Patrick up to keep him from toppling. Patrick heaved again. He ran his hand across his mouth.

"You drank too much too fast," Gary said, easing up to his feet. "You going to be okay?" Gary swayed.

"Let's get back," Tino said, grabbing each by his belt. Gary hobbled along on his tender ankle. Patrick staggered to camp and eased down onto his sleeping bag.

Tino quietly helped Gary and Patrick into their bags.

Sal lay motionless.

45.

Road Kill

A DELICATE SKIN OF GRAY ASH lay over the fire pit in the soft blue of the predawn.

"*¿Listos vaqueros?*" Sal said. "Let's see how far we can get before it gets hot."

"I'm ready to go home," Tino said, trying to sound alert despite a slight headache from last night's drinking.

No response from the guys.

"Hey," Sal yelled. "Time to go!"

A weak frog-like voice crept out of Gary's bag. "Okay, Sal."

Tino rolled out of his sleeping bag.

"Just a sec, please." Patrick whimpered, lying in the fetal position.

"We need to get across the Mojave by tonight," Sal said.

Patrick dragged himself out of his bag, found his canteen, gulped water and poured some over his head.

Wisps of clouds, made red by the rising sun, portended a day of violent heat. "Fill your canteens," Sal said and collected trash from last night's dinner. Tino and the guys dressed, slow as slugs.

"Come on, pick it up," Sal said. "What the heck's gotten into you?"

"I thought we were going to get attacked by..." Tino yawned deeply. "...by coyotes; didn't sleep good."

"Me too," Gary said.

"Coyotes," Patrick muttered, loading his gear. He had to hit Peewee's starter several times before the engine started. "It's getting harder. I'm not sure how much longer he's going to hold up. Damn, hope I can finish the trip."

"You'll finish even if we have to tow you back," Sal said.

"Tried that," Gary said, massaging his temples. "Didn't work worth a shit."

THE FOUR BIKERS RODE THROUGH an Indian reservation in Arizona and came upon a '40s vintage black Ford pickup. The truck puttered along leaning to one side. Two heavyset dark-skinned women with full cheeks, wrapped against the cool morning air in blankets woven in geometric patterns, sat with their backs against the truck's cab, facing the bikers. A boy of about ten sat between the women. Sal waved as they passed. The women sat stoically. The boy raised a hand. Tino glanced at the men in the cab.

The driver wore a baseball cap, his hair braided into a ponytail. The passenger wore a cowboy hat, his black hair hanging loose like a horse's mane.

By midmorning the air had turned uncomfortably warm. They rode mile after mile through low-lying scrub brush. Taller Saguaro cacti dotted the landscape. Telephone poles ran along the roadside. Lines rose to insulators at the T-bars and fell in between, rose and fell, rose, fell, pole after pole. The string merged with the horizon into what appeared to be an inviting, shimmering lake.

Tino, despite the heat, rode elated over his plans for his future. He'd earn his father's respect as a Marine, learn to be an ace mechanic with Rex's help, marry Lola, and support her like a real man.

A handful of vultures up ahead tore at a flattened mass of hide and dried blood lying on the road. A set of tall ears, standing erect like two guards at the gate, gave the remains away as a desert hare. A semi-truck ahead of Tino, Sal, and the guys spooked the vultures. They took flight. The truck sped past the hare, its ears bent over in the truck's wake, nearly touching the pavement and rose back up at attention. Patrick howled with laughter. He signaled Gary and they pulled over. Tino stopped to see what they were up to. Sal, in the lead, didn't notice and rode on.

Gary and Patrick rode back past the hare and made a U-turn. They gunned their engines and flew past the hare between them, roaring with laughter when the ears fell and rose as if waving goodbye.

The temperature, by noon, had exceeded one hundred. A line of vehicles up ahead inched along, their brake lights blinking on and off. Sal signaled a slow down. A trooper was in the center of the road directing traffic around an accident.

A pickup with a smashed front end had spun around and stopped, facing in the wrong direction. The driver sat in the truck, hands covering his face.

Tino followed Sal over long black skid marks. Glass fragments sparkled against the black asphalt and crunched under his tires.

Medics in powder blue shirts hurriedly wheeled a man on a gurney into an ambulance. One medic tended to him as the other ran to the front of the car and jumped in. The siren wailed as they sped off.

Tino stared at a blanket covering a dead man lying on the road. The man's arm extended out from under the blanket in a puddle of dark coagulated blood.

A battered, gleaming red motorcycle lay off the road. Tino hit his brakes and put a foot to the ground. He turned, taking a second look at the dead man's arm—a tattoo of a fanged cobra.

Patrick, following Tino, ran into him. "Hey!"

"Move it!" yelled the trooper directing traffic. "It's not a goddamn sideshow."

Tino continued and stopped next to Sal, waiting in the meager shade of a spiny Joshua tree.

A handful of men stood around parked motorcycles on the opposite side of the road from Sal.

Tino, Gary, and Patrick pulled up to Sal. "Kind of makes you think twice about riding bikes, doesn't it?" Sal said.

"That's Rex back there."

"What?"

"The dead guy. He's Rex, the biker we rode with in New Mexico."

"Holy shit," Gary said.

Sal took Tino by the arm. "How do you know it's Rex?"

Tino pointed his chin to the mangled motorcycle. "That's his chopper, and I saw the snake tattoo on his arm."

Sal parked and approached the trooper, spoke with him for a moment before walking to the corpse and looking under the blanket. Sal returned, rummaged through his gear, and found a small stainless steel box. "I hoped that I wasn't going to need this." He returned to Rex and took a long, thin purple ribbon from the box, kissed it, and draped it around his neck. He then peeled back the blanket covering Rex, knelt, and put his thumb into a tin of holy oil. With the oil, Sal made the sign of the cross on Rex's forehead, lips, and chest as he read from a small black book. Sal covered Rex and went to the driver of the truck and had a short conversation with him.

"Thanks for doing that," Tino said on Sal's return.

Sal stashed the box. "Let's go. We're not helping the situation, and we shouldn't be standing around in this heat."

Tino pulled up his T-shirt and wiped the sweat running in small salty rivulets down his face. He rode into the wrathful heat empty—aspirations of a bright future lay like road kill on the blazing asphalt.

46.

Dancing Animals

Tino and the four pulled into an A&W hamburger stand in Tuba City.

Tino swung a leg getting off of his bike and looked to Sal. "Did you learn anything from the cops about what happened to Rex?"

Gary and Patrick dismounted and listened in.

"The trooper told me that Rex was in the lead. The pickup truck ran head on into him. Rex broke his neck, died instantly."

"Jesus," Patrick said.

Sal continued. "The trooper also told me that one of the bikers said that in the old days they would've killed the man driving the truck."

"What about him?" Gary asked.

"Fell asleep at the wheel. He and his wife had separated, and he hadn't been sleeping. He said that an innocent man died because he was driving when he shouldn't have been."

"What could you possibly say to that?" Patrick asked.

"Accidents will always happen. And he needed to forgive himself as God already has."

"Good answer," Gary said.

They ordered hamburgers and sodas and stood inside the air-conditioned eatery.

Patrick wiped a small glob of mayonnaise from his mouth with the back of his hand. "The heat is kicking my butt."

Sal sipped from his drink. "It'll cool off a bit with the elevation in northern Arizona, but when we drop into the Mojave it's really going to cook. It's the lowest point on the continent. Some of the highest temperatures on earth have been registered there. Drink plenty of water. Dehydration can make you weak and even cause people to hallucinate."

Sal stashed his trash in a can. "You guys ready?"

"Let's just get this over," Tino said.

They rode through Williams, Seligman, Dinosaur, Kingman, and Yucca, and the torment began. Tino's sweat evaporated as it came into contact with his clothes, leaving small white ridges of body salts.

The temperature held steady throughout the afternoon. They came to the Colorado River and crossed a bridge into California. Gary and Patrick cheered shooting their fists into the air. Tino was in no mood to celebrate.

There was little traffic. Did locals know better than to venture out in midday? A dust devil lurched across the road. A condor, quiet as the desert, rode a thermal in a slow lethargy. Its wings slid over the desert floor like the black fingers of death. How many life stories of pioneers ended in this burning land of thorns, spines, and jagged crags? Locale names told the story: Furnace Peak, Dante's View, The Devil's Playground, Funeral Peak.

They came on a beautiful and endless landscape of soft, undulating, golden brown sand dunes. Tino caught sight of a sidewinder rattlesnake weaving its way up a dune adjacent to the road. It left behind a pattern of scrawls that looked like the work of an ancient scribe.

Sal stopped at a Safeway store in Blythe at nightfall. "Let's get some sodas and then we'll press on."

Tino slumped his shoulders. "Jeez."

Gary frowned.

"I'm ready to crash out for the night," Patrick said. Small white globs of pasty saliva stuck at the corners of his mouth.

"I'm on a deadline," Sal said. "Besides, the night air won't be as hot.

"Wonderful," Patrick said. "I'll put on my jacket."

LOS ANGELES 220 MILES, read a sign on the outskirts of Blythe.

Despite Sal's assurances, the night air wasn't much cooler. The day's heat, stored in the ground, radiated upward. Tino dropped into neutral and coasted, allowing him to take his canteen and have a drink—but he had forgotten to fill it at the last stop. He had precious little water left and allowed himself a small sip. They hit odd streaks of cold air once in a while that lasted a few seconds, and just as suddenly it turned hot again.

Tino's temples throbbed; he felt dizzy. He began seeing cartoonish figures along the side of the road: bears, horses, and elephants spinning round and round on their hind legs. He shook his head, ran off the road, and hit a small rise sending him airborne. He landed with a bounce. Gary pulled alongside. Tino waved him off. He reached for his canteen and drank the last of his water.

He rode trancelike, his world confined to the reaches of his headlight: the broken white lines on the asphalt, the spindly plants along the roadside, powered in dust. All else, a hot, hopeless treading in a black, searing expanse with no sense of gaining ground or time passing.

The city lights of Indio shone at the horizon. The aura of light grew slowly stronger. Streetlamps came into focus followed by the town. Surely Sal would stop here to sleep, but he continued on, on through Palm Springs and on through

Banning. The road widened into a well-lit highway when they entered San Bernardino. Sal took an exit.

Tino followed, dismayed and disgusted. Were twelve-plus hours of riding through the punishing desert enough, even for Sal the Spartan? Sal found a spot under a stand of eucalyptus trees off a frontage road; the night air was warm, but bearable.

Tino asked Gary for a drink from his canteen. The four prepared for sleep in exhausted silence. Tino laid his bag over layers of soft leaves, the air thick with the scent of eucalyptus. Lola came to mind.

How could he ever support her without learning to be a mechanic? And what if he was killed in the jungles of Vietnam? He would write to her and pray that she would respond.

Part 3

And Over the Cliff

47.

The War Comes Home

THE MORNING COMMUTE INCREASED. The highway grew steadily louder drawing Tino from sleep. Morning sunlight struggling through layers of smog funneled by the topography from Los Angeles to the San Bernardino Valley gave the world a rusty hue. The month-long trip would come to an end today.

Ma would likely be waiting at home with a hearty meal ready for Tino, Sal, and the guys if Gary and Patrick stopped by before going home.

Pa would be sleeping before his graveyard shift. How did Pa do it? Sleep days, work nights—he rarely looked well rested.

Tino's Day of Judgment was at hand. He would have to face Pa after having had disobeyed him by sneaking off to make the trip instead of registering for college with Val.

Sal rose from his sleeping bag and yawned, spreading his arms in a long, wide stretch.

"Morning," Tino said

"Hey, how you doing?" Sal said, rubbing sleep from his face.

"Just thinking."

Sal raised a hand and scratched his underarm. "About what?"

"About Pa."

"What about him?" Sal said, reaching for his pants draped over the Hawk.

Tino sat up, scooted to Rocinante, and leaned against the rear tire. "He's going to be really mad at me."

"What makes you think so?"

"He gave me a direct order to not go on the trip and I did. Pa never gets mad with Val, or you. You walk on water in his eyes."

Sal chuckled. "Oh, come on."

"It's true, Sal. You can do no wrong as far as Ma and Pa are concerned. They listen to you whenever you have something to say."

"Parents often treat the firstborn a little better."

"No, it's more than that. You've been a good son to them. You've always worked hard on projects around the house, got an education, and now you're a priest. And Val's never gotten into as much trouble as me, and except for once, he's always outdone me when we've landed jobs."

Sal squatted on his hams. "Tell me about the time you out-did him."

"It was our first job, going door to door, selling subscriptions to the newspaper."

"Sure, I remember. You guys were in seventh or eighth grade, right?"

"That's right," Tino said. "We had to make up sales pitches to sucker people into buying the paper. I told a lady that my father had died and I was earning money to buy my mother a typewriter so she could bring home extra work from her job as a secretary to support my little brothers and sisters."

Sal raised his eyebrows. "You said what?"

"I know I shouldn't have lied, but my boss loved that I was getting so many orders. It was the only time that I excelled at something. I outsold Val by a lot. In fact, I was one of the top salesmen on our crew. Anyway, at dinner the girls always asked us how we did that day. When I told them that I had gotten eight orders they cheered and clapped. Anything over four orders was considered a good day. Val had only gotten two. The girls laughed good naturedly and said he'd do better next time. Pa didn't even look up from his plate and said, 'Tino's a better liar.'"

Sal winced. "Pa shouldn't have said that about you, but try and give him a break. Do you know that he never knew his own father?"

"Yes, Val and I were alone with him in the car once when we were kids. He always talked about how great his mother was, but never about his father. So I asked him. He looked embarrassed and laughed off my question. It was awkward. I got it that he didn't want to talk about it. I'm sorry about that, but does it give him the right to treat me like crap?"

"No, it doesn't," Sal said. "But at least he's always been there for us. Aunt Mary told me that Pa's father abandoned his family when Pa and his brother and sister were little ones.

"We hit some tough times, especially when we were working the fields. Once when I was around ten, Pa was really down in the mouth. 'I've got five mouths to feed and not a penny in my pocket,' he told me, 'but we're going to make it.' We went to a ranch to ask for work. I think that the rancher read the situation and felt sorry for Pa. He told us that we could comb through a field of broccoli that had been picked, and he'd pay us for whatever remnants the migrant workers had missed. We stooped all day in cold fog, scratching around like chickens for bits and pieces. By the end of the day we had made enough money for Ma to buy stuff to make tortillas and beans and a little ground meat.

"The family's in good shape today because Pa stuck it out with us. I hear a lot of people complain about the most minor inconveniences. You'll never hear it from us because we've known hard times. Talk to Pa. Tell him how you feel about the way he treats you compared to Val and me."

"I'm afraid of him, especially when he gets mad and stares hard into my face. And now I've sneaked behind his back. I'm afraid of what he might do to me when I see him."

"Well then, how about if I go with you? I'll stand with you and back you up."

"Would you really?"

"Sure. We'll do it today."

"Oh, man, thanks, thanks an awful lot."

"Let's get the guys up and hit the road."

THE CLOSER THE FOUR BIKERS GOT to Los Angeles, the heavier the traffic became—the closer to the ocean's marine layer, the cooler the air.

With Sal at his side, Tino would be able to talk to Pa like a man. Like the man Pa wanted Tino to be. But a distant, dark episode with Pa came to mind.

Tino had gotten his usual poor report card in the fourth grade, and he was being bullied at school. His anger and frustration manifested itself by his fighting with his siblings. Pa had warned him over several days to stop. But he made his little sister, Carmen, cry over a piece of candy. Their fighting woke Pa from his midday sleep. He stormed down the hall in his pajamas. Tino froze. Pa stared menacingly into his eyes. "Why do you fight?" he yelled and brought his big, powerful hand down onto Tino's chest, knocking him to the floor. He cried out in terror as his punishment was meted out, one humiliating blow after another.

The Trip

They stopped in Santa Ana for gas. Sal went to a phone booth. A couple of tanned surfers with sun-bleached hair, driving an old Ford station wagon with surfboards on roof racks were at the pumps. Gary talked to them about local surfing spots. Sal returned looking somber.

He mounted the Hawk and turned to Tino. "Bad news, hermano. Gilbert, one of the twins you grew up with, was killed in Vietnam a few days ago."

Tino's head spun. He steadied himself against Rocinante.

"You okay, man?" Patrick asked.

Tino's voice broke with emotion. "Let's go." He rode onto the highway, wiping tears and saying, "Oh Gilbert, oh Gilbert." A procession of memories paraded through his mind: the four twins hustling to earn money to buy candy, selling newspapers on street corners, shaking fruit from trees to sell to neighbors, hunting for empty pop bottles for the deposit money. Val and Tino riding sidesaddle on Robert's and Gilbert's bicycles to the municipal pool, playing football, competing to see who was best at making the others laugh.

How can he be dead? I saw him just before I left. How's Robert? How's he going to go on without the brother that he shared a womb with?

The ocean appeared from around a bend in the highway. The familiar sight of the deep blue and the smell of salt air felt like finding a long-lost friend. The air grew chilly. Sal pulled into a beach parking lot to add clothing.

Tino searched out his sweatshirt in a daze. Tino looked out on the beach, a swirl of activity: a dog sprinting after a soaring Frisbee, children building sandcastles, surfers riding waves, volleyball games.

A good guy was killed in the war, and no one knows.

Shorebirds scurried, pecking at insects in the sand moistened by the rushing and ebbing shore break. Seagulls with their gray wings, white chests, and orange beaks, soared on sea breezes.

"Hey! Let's go!" Sal yelled, jarring Tino from the moment. Sal and the guys were in a line on their bikes ready to leave. Tino threw on his sweatshirt and followed. The four merged onto the Pacific Coast Highway, riding only as fast as smoking and rattling Peewee was able.

They crossed into San Diego County early in the afternoon and passed familiar locales: Camp Pendleton, Oceanside, Carlsbad, Encinitas, Cardiff-by-the-Sea, Del Mar.

48.

Always Aware

THEY ENTERED THE CITY LIMITS. Patrick took the Highway 8 East loop off I-5 to head for his parents' home. He raised a hand releasing gum wrappers like confetti. He kept his hand in the air and gave his friends the finger.

They continued toward Highway 94 where they would ride the final short stretch to Euclid Avenue.

The 94 on-ramp came into view. Sal sped up, riding alongside a semi. The truck, without warning, merged into Sal's lane.

"Look out!" Tino screamed.

Sal leaned hard away from the truck and onto the soft shoulder of the road. The Hawk skidded out of control, before slamming against the ground. Sal raised his hands protecting his head. The Hawk slid away. Sal tumbled like a ragdoll flung across a room. Tino relived his fall, viscerally feeling his body pounding against the ground.

He hit the brakes, pulled over, set out the kickstand, and ran to Sal. Sal sat up slowly, face contorted in pain. He rocked back and forth, supporting his left arm.

"I'll call an ambulance!" Tino said.

"No!" Sal yelled. He doubled over and gasped. "Just need a minute."

Tino's head reeled seeing Sal hurt and vulnerable. Gary ran up.

"Get my bike," Sal said through gritted teeth.

Gary gathered Sal's gear. Tino went for the Hawk, lying in a thicket of dry weeds. He pulled up on the handlebars, righting it, and wheeled it over uneven ground to Sal. Other than a missing mirror, the bike, cushioned by the mass of weeds, appeared to be in pretty decent shape. The Hawk started with the first try.

Sal's face was dark with sweat-soaked dirt. "Help me stand up," he said. Tino and Gary grabbed him by his jacket's shoulders and lifted.

Sal groaned. "Easy, easy."

Tino brushed off Sal's clothes. "I thought you were dead."

Sal, his breathing labored said, "Go on," groan. "Tell Ma and Pa I had to get to work," groan. "I'll call later. Not a word about this," groan.

Tino erupted in anger. "You said you're always aware, so you don't get into accidents! You call this always aware? You didn't stand a chance against that truck. What in the hell were you doing so close to it? And without your helmet! If you get killed by doing something as stupid as that, I'm going to be mad at you, and I won't forgive you!"

Sal hung his head and spoke in a weak voice, "You're right, *hombre.*" He mounted the Hawk. "Please help me with my helmet." Tino set it over his head and tightened the chinstrap.

Sal reached for the handlebars, knuckles scraped raw. He faced the highway active with traffic and rode off.

Tino spit. "He was almost killed, and I would've seen every second of it."

"I've never heard anyone talk to Sal like that," Gary said. "Not even your dad. Oh sheeit, you one badass mofo."

49.

A Bird Escapes

Tino led Gary into the Caballero's driveway. The house looked oddly small.

A handful of nephews and nieces playing in the front yard stopped their hula-hoop contest and ran to Tino and Gary. Four-year-old Vincent bounced and waved excitedly. "Hi Uncle! Hi Gary!" The little cousins quickly made their welcome into a game of chase around the motorcycles.

Ma hurried out the kitchen door, raised a hand, and made the sign of the cross.

"*Gracias por tus oraciones, Ma.*" Tino said. "They got me home."

"*¿Cómo?*"

Tino dismounted. "Your prayers; they saved me."

"*Uno siempre debe orar, ¿no? Y el Salvador?* (One should always pray, no? And Sal?)"

"He went to the hospital. Said he'll call later." Tino pulled off his helmet and picked up five-year-old Ana Marie, cutting short a lap around the bikes.

"Can you give me a ride on your motorcycle, Uncle?" She said panting.

"Sure, tomorrow, after I've rested a little, okay?"

"How about now?"

"Tomorrow, I promise." He set her down, and she led the pack back to the hula-hoops.

"I worry for ju boys," Ma said to Gary. "Are ju hungry, Yerry? I make soup and tortillas."

"That sounds awfully good, Mrs. Caballero. I'm pretty hungry." Gary walked toward the house with a slight limp in his gait.

"Are ju okay?"

"Yes, ma'am. I had a little fall. I'll be fine, grashas."

"*No ees 'grashas,' Yerry, ees gra-ci-as.*" She turned to Tino. "*Y fueron a misa por el viaje?* (Did you go to church on the trip?)"

Tino held open the kitchen door for her. "Sal even said a Mass in New Hampshire at Father Gill's home."

A votive candle in a small red glass in front of a foot-high statue of the Virgin Mary burned on a kitchen counter; the flame a constant reminder to the virgin that she return Ma's sons home safely. A golden halo hung over Mary's head, under her feet a snake that represented the devil who tempted Eve and thus brought sin to the world. The image of the Virgin standing on the snake represented the triumph of good over evil.

The aroma of *sopa de albóndigas*, Mexican meatball soup, filled the kitchen.

"*A iglesia mañana a dar gracias*, (Church tomorrow to give thanks.)" Ma said.

Tino and Gary stood next to the kitchen table, stretching to get the kinks out.

Ma warmed two skillets on the stove and rolled out the balls of tortilla dough.

"*Qué me quentas, Ma*," Tino said. "Anything happen since I've been gone?"

Ma told him of her canary's, little Panchito's, escape because knucklehead Pa had left the front door open when she'd cleaned the birdcage. She couldn't count the times she'd told him to keep doors closed when her canary was out.

She placed raw tortillas on the skillets and flipped them intermittently while she rolled out more. Moments later Ma had a stack wrapped in a dish towel to keep them warm. She ladled two large bowls of soup and set them on the table. "Seet down, Yerry," she said and sat with them. Tino lifted an end of the dish towel, peeled out a steaming flour tortilla, and handed it to Gary. Gary rolled it into a tube and bit half of it off. The two friends ate like starving prisoners, putting away two bowls of soup and a dozen tortillas.

Val burst through the door. "Wow!" he said. "Tino, your hair's gotten long, and you look bigger!"

Tino stood up and hugged Val. Val wrinkled his nose. "You stink!"

Gary pushed away from the table. "He smells fine to me. And thank you for feeding me again, Mrs. Caballero. Please excuse me. I need to get home."

Ma hugged him. "Jour welcome, Yerry. Ju must be tire."

"Yes, ma'am."

Ma picked up the bowls and took them to the sink. Val followed Tino and Gary outdoors to the bikes.

"What's with the limp, Gare?" Val asked.

"Fell. I'm not too bad."

"So, you guys made it clear to New York?"

"Your brothers did."

"Not you?"

Gary started his bike. "Tell you about it later." He rode into the street, and waved behind him.

"Hey, where's Sal?"

Tino crossed his arms and leaned against Rocinante. "A big-ass semi truck ran him off the road an hour ago. He hurt his arm pretty bad. He's getting checked out at the hospital. Sal said to keep quiet about him getting hurt."

"I kept wondering how you guys were doing and what the trip was like."

"Long. Saw the Grand Canyon, Niagara Falls, Statue of Liberty, pretty cool stuff. Hotter than hell in the deserts and froze my ass off in the mountains, and I can't think of anything else right now except for taking a shower and resting up. I need to talk to you about something weird that happened."

"Sure. Hey, can I take your bike for a spin?"

Tino tossed him the key. Val hopped on, started the engine, gunned it, and released the clutch. Rocinante jumped. Val hit the brakes and stopped with a jerk. He smiled sheepishly, and tried again doing everything at a slower pace. He then pulled into the street.

Tino walked back to the kitchen and found Pa at the sink in his pajamas drinking water.

Pa set an angry eye on Tino. His persona, a dark looming cloud, engulfed his son. Tino's palms grew damp, his heart pounded, and Sal, who was going to be here to help him manage Pa, wasn't.

"Didn't I tell you to register for college instead of going on the goddamn trip?"

Pa stared menacingly into Tino's eyes. A mosaic of veins turned the whites of Pa's eyes reddish-pink. Tino smelled stale nicotine and alcohol on his breath.

"What do you want to do, wind up a tramp living in the streets begging for handouts like a *sin vergüenza* (shameless person), and a shame to the family?"

Silence.

"Answer me, is that what you want?"

Fear, Tino's nemesis, laughed wickedly in his ear. Nothing had changed. Tino was still a weak screw-up that Pa kept in his back pocket.

But there was something familiar in Pa's stare. It was the same stare that the Texas Rangers had used to bully him, the same menacing stare that the Indians in the Flagstaff jail had used, the same as Brother's in Mississippi. *Pa's only bullying!*

Tino's fear melted and sank deep into the earth. And rising from the earth and winding up around his legs, winding up his abdomen, up around his chest, and entering his spirit were wondrous sensations, foreign to him. Strength. Clarity. Understanding. Tino's tension dissipated. His face relaxed.

"There's no need to get upset, Pa. You know me better than that. I'd never allow myself to wind up a bum."

"I ought to teach you a lesson!"

"That's what I'm talking about, Pa. You're getting upset over something that isn't worth it. Please have a little faith in me. I'll never be a shame to the family. I just needed a break, and I got it. I'm ready to move on with my life."

Confusion in Pa's eyes. He blinked.

"Sal and I had a chance to do a lot of talking on the trip. He told me about stuff that happened to the family a long time ago."

"What in the hell're you talking about?"

"About the days before I was born. He said there was a time when we were so poor that there was hardly enough money for food. He said that some men abandon their families when the going gets tough like that, but you stuck it out with us. Thank you for that, Pa. Thank you for not abandoning us."

Tears flooded Pa's eyes. He turned his back and put a hand to his face. "Those days are over. Best to forget about them." He went to his bedroom, opened the door, held, and spoke without turning around. "Glad you men are back okay." Pa entered his room and shut the door behind him.

Tino walked out the back door to the patio stunned. *Men?* A soft whistle escaped his lips. He looked out over the canyon that abutted the back yard.

What just happened? Was Tino not showing fear all it took to cause this tectonic shift between Pa and himself? He pounded his fists against his chest. His roar soared through the canyon and around the world.

Freedom. If he spread his arms, he would surely fly.

Then it occurred to Tino that Pa had cried when he was reminded of his Pa abandoning him, and fifty years later, Pa was still suffering the loss. His immense pain from having been abandoned must have led to his anger and bullying, and likely to his drinking to soften that same pain.

Pity, profound pity, welled up in Tino's chest. Tino whispered to himself. "*Pobrecito, mi apá.* (My poor daddy.)" "*Gracias pa, por no abandonarnos.* (Thank you Pa, for not abandoning us.)"

50.

A Comrade Falls

TINO, LOST IN HIS THOUGHTS, gazed into the lower back yard from the patio.

What appeared to be a delicate piece of translucent paper lay on the ground. He walked down the concrete stairs into the backyard and squatted to have a closer look at the oddity. He picked it up with a gentle hand—a near-transparent skin that a snake had crawled out of.

Screeching tires and metal crashing from the street jarred Tino from the examination. He gently placed the skin back on the ground, and then sprinted up through the patio and out the gate to the front yard.

Rocinante lay on the asphalt between two cars, hemorrhaging oil. The nephews were at the curb looking to their Uncle Val in the street, leaning against the car that he had rear-ended.

Ma ran out of the house, screaming at the little ones. "*¡No se mueven, ni un pie en la calle!* (Don't move, not a foot in the street!)"

Tino ran to Val.

The driver of the car behind Val had a hand on his shoulder. "Do you need a doctor?"

"No thank you, sir," Val said.

"Are you sure?" Tino said.

A middle-aged woman in a bright multi-colored, loose-fitting African style blouse got out of the car in front of Val. Gold hoop earrings stood out from under her Afro.

"A cat run right out right in front of me!" she said, clearly shaken. "I had to stop or I woulda run that little baby right over. Please tell me ya'll are all right."

Pa appeared bare-foot and in his pajama shirt with the shirttail hanging out of his work pants. "Are you hurt?"

"I don't think so," Val said.

Pa's concern turned to frustration. He stared hard into Val's eyes. "No more motorcycles for you!"

Val hung his head.

Tino spoke to the woman, still distressed. "Why don't you go and sit in your car until the police come, ma'am."

"Thank you, sir," she said, relieved, and walked toward her car.

Tino waved vehicles around the scene. "I'll direct traffic if you'll call the police, Pa."

Pa headed for the house, grumbling and raking his thick, dark fingers though his graying, thinning hair. "*Hijo de la—*"

"I couldn't stop fast enough," Val said apologetically. I wanted to see if anybody in the house was watching me when I passed, then I heard tires squealing. I didn't have time to stop."

"Jesus, you're lucky," Tino said, waving a car to pass.

Police cars soon swarmed in. A patrolman relieved Tino of directing traffic. Another interviewed Val and the woman.

"Okay, you can wheel the bike off the street. I don't mean to sound like a grumpy old man, but you got to be careful on these things. I see too many young men get hurt and killed on them."

"Yes, sir," Tino said.

They wheeled Rocinante, bleeding oil, down the driveway toward the back of the house.

Trumpets, violins, guitars, and José Alfredo Jimenez's booming voice blared from Pa's bedroom window.

"*La vida no vale nada. Llorando empieza, y llorando se acaba,* (Life is worth nothing. It begins with crying and with crying it ends.)"

When stressed, Pa often took the family's record player into his bedroom and stacked his favorite Mexican albums with the volume turned up. Everyone secretly laughed, knowing he'd be snoring before the first song was half over.

Tino and Val rolled Rocinante to the backyard and into a narrow breezeway between the garage and their bedroom—a boneyard of sorts, where items too good to throw away were stored, but were rarely ever used again.

"I'll get it fixed," Val said.

"It's over," Tino said tenderly running his hand over Rocinante's mangled front fork.

"No, I can get him—"

"He'll never be ridden again."

"I'm really sorry."

"I know you are. See you later."

Val walked off mumbling, "Bet it could be fixed."

51.

To Break a Promise

TINO REACHED FOR THE LAMP in their bedroom that night. "I'm sorry about your bike," Val said from his bed.

"It's for the best that it won't be ridden anymore."

"What do you mean?"

"Pretty stupid riding motorcycles without knowing how."

"Come on, man, I've ridden 'em before."

"Not just you. Me. Sal. Anybody. You heard the cop say that he's seen too many guys getting hurt and killed on motorcycles. I had a bad fall back East. Almost broke my neck. And you could've been killed today. But it still hurts losing my motorcycle. It's like losing a best friend. By the way, I heard about Gilbert today."

"Ma was crying when I came home yesterday," Val said. "'*Mataron al Gilberto*' she said, and then I started crying." Val got to an elbow. "Since I heard about him, I've thought of other guys we've known who've gotten killed or hurt bad in Vietnam."

"Gene, our neighbor from our old neighborhood, was killed, and Nick, the bully across the street, joined the Marines to be like his dad. Then he *accidentally* shot himself in the foot when he was over there. And Hector, the guy who graduated in the class before us, got his legs blown off by a landmine. He could have gone to college on a scholarship to play football."

Val fell silent for a moment. "Are you still going to join the Marines with Gary?"

"I want to keep my promise to him, but I met a lot of good people on the trip who are against the war. An Indian cowboy we met in New Mexico, who fought in World War Two, said he couldn't see much good coming out of this war, and Paul Gill's parents in New Hampshire are really against it, and we met an old man named Harold, a retired college professor in Illinois. He had fought in the World War One. He let us stay with him when we were really tired and beat up. He said that they're lying about the war."

Val nodded. "I've been hearing the same kinds of things."

Tino continued. "Gary told me that he saw injured Vietnam veterans demonstrating against the war at the Democratic Convention in Chicago."

"I thought vets would be for it," Val said.

"I don't know what to think anymore," Tino said. He rose and sat on the edge of his bed to look at Val, barely visible in the dark. "Something really weird happened on the trip."

"What?"

Tino took a breath. How to explain his surreal experience?

"I rode to Bath, Maine. Ma wanted me to look for a monument with her grandpa's name on it."

"She told me that you found it," Val said.

"Did I ever. When I saw his name, I thought about his family and how they must've sacrificed to come here from Scotland only to have one of the sons killed in the war. I don't understand why, but I got choked up, really choked up. Great-grandpa John was our Uncle Nene's father. I don't know if I went nuts, but I think I might have gotten some kind of message from Grandpa John."

"What in the hell are you talking about?"

"I know you're thinking it's nuts, but just listen a minute. We got behind Sal's schedule, and he was determined to make it up"

"Sounds like him, all right."

"He got ahead of me, and I was trying to catch up to him. I fell with my bike and went sliding and hit my head hard against a guardrail. I think I died for a while, and my soul left my body."

"Whoa!"

"And then all of a sudden, I was back on my bike right after I fell as if nothing had happened, like I hadn't crashed. I rode past a man in a Yankee uniform standing by the road."

"You got knocked out and were dreaming."

"Just listen. He was next to an old mailbox with a wooden rooster on top, and as I drove by he smashed his musket over a big rock. I thought about it afterward. Did I dream it, or maybe I was hallucinating from some LSD I had taken that a hippie had given me."

"Jesus! Did Sal find out?"

"No. I'd been curious about what it was like, and I took the LSD and got back on the road. The drug hit me hard. Nothing's real, and yet everything's real."

"What's that supposed to mean?"

"When Sal came back, we fixed my bike and we continued. On my way down the hill, I came across the same mailbox with the same rooster on top."

"The mailbox in your dream?"

"The same one. The mailbox was real, and yet it wasn't real. I saw the mailbox when I was dead or in a weird dream hallucinating, and later in real life. Nothing's real, and everything's real. I tried talking with Sal about it, but he just made fun of me."

"Can you blame him?"

"No. And please keep this to yourself. It's really been eating at me, and you're the only one I can talk to about it."

"Yeah, sure," Val said. "Now, I'm going to sound a little nuts. What if the man you saw was some messenger from God, like we've heard about in religion classes?"

"I wondered about that too, but would God choose someone like me to send a message to?"

"I've heard that He's chosen the most fucked-up types."

"Thanks, man."

"Sorry."

"If it really happened, then it had to have been our great-grandfather, John. He even looked like his son, our old Uncle Nene."

Val raised his hand. "Hold on a minute. How would you know what Uncle Nene looked like when he was young?"

"I went with Ma to the museum of the Seri Indians in Kino Bay the last time we went to visit our family in Hermosillo. Ma pointed out Nene in a black and white photo. He was in a group of the Seris as a young teacher. The Yankee soldier I saw and Nene could've been twins. After he broke his rifle, he smiled and winked at me like he knew me."

"So he recognized you?"

"Must've. Otherwise, why would he have done that? I wouldn't be scared if he showed up right now."

Val shuddered. "Don't freak me out, man."

"And get this. I went into a curio shop in Colorado yesterday and talked with an Indian woman running the place. I told her about my experience. She said I was lucky to have had a visit from an ancestor. She said I would figure out what it all meant with my 'mind's eye.'"

"What's that supposed to mean?"

"I didn't have time to ask her. Sal was in a big-ass hurry to get back on the road."

"Of course," Val said.

"The shop was called Broken Arrow. I asked her what it meant. She said when tribes had had enough of war, they made a peace treaty and broke an arrow as a symbol."

"Peace treaty—war," Val said. "Makes sense."

"What do you mean?"

Val rose and sat on the edge of his bed to face Tino. "Maybe Great-grandpa broke his musket as a sign for you not to go to war."

Tino rolled the thought around in his head. "That's it! I've been beating my brains out trying to figure this out since it happened over two thousand miles ago, and you came up with it just like that!" Tino cupped Val's cheeks in his hands and kissed his forehead.

"Hey! Don't go *maricón* (gay) on me, *menso*."

"Harold, the old war veteran, said anyone who's experienced war wouldn't want anyone else to have to go through it, especially if it's someone you loved, like a grandson. 'War isn't a way to solve problems,' Harold said. Grandpa John was killed in a horrible battle in Fredericksburg, and he doesn't want me to have to go through a similar experience. And you figured it out. You saw his message with your mind's eye just like the Indian woman said I would when I was ready. I wasn't ready, but you were. You answered your own question, or was it my question, or our question? Jeez, maybe there is something with twins reading each other's minds. Hey, do you think if I slapped you I'd feel it?"

"First, you're kissing me, now you want to slap me around. Make up your mind, *pendejo*. So now what?"

"About?"

"About joining the Marines?"

"No."

Val flopped back on his bed. "That's a fucking relief."

Tino took a deep breath. "I'm too tired to go on. I need some serious rest."

"Me too," Val said. "But I want to hear more about the trip. We'll sneak some beer tomorrow and talk, okay?"

"I got laid."

"You got laid? How? Where? Who?"

"Tomorrow."

"Aw, man."

52.

Off the Cliff

T INO LAY IN HIS BED IN A MENTAL HAZE. He needed sleep desperately, but his mind swirled with images: Sal crashing and tumbling out of control, sitting racked with pain and rocking his hurt arm; Pa crying for the loss of his father; Rocinante lying on the road bleeding in the street; the delicate snakeskin he had found in the backyard—an old life shed, a new life born.

It was wonderful having had a long shower and eaten a lot of Ma's food prepared with her love, good to be in his own bed once again, but he didn't belong here anymore.

Where were the comforting aromas of the outdoors; trees, the earth, and composted leaves that were his bed? He could barely hear the crickets singing. They were outside instead of close enough to touch. Tino was no longer looking up with only the stars between heaven and him, because he was now in a cage for human animals called a "house."

Ma's canary had escaped and she was worried about it, but the little bird was now flying as it was meant to be.

I wish Sal would call and say, "Pack up: We're leaving at dawn for a trip around Mexico." I feel like I've been reborn. But everyone at home is still living in their old skins. Ma's worried about whether or not we went to church on the trip, and Pa wants to control me. But Harold's message to love and care for one another is what's most important.

I'm going to do that. I'm going to spend the rest of my life sowing good seeds.

Tino floated off to sleep and dreamed that he was standing and crying over Rocinante, lying mortally wounded on the street. *Can you ever forgive me? You carried me across the continent and back. You brought me back from hell itself, and now you're alone and broken.* Streams of Tino's tears washed over Rocinante.

Rocinante rose—frame whole, chrome gleaming, paint shining. Tino mounted. Rocinante rode him down the street, down the on ramp and onto the highway.

Tino understood that Rocinante was grateful to him, grateful for Tino having liberated him. Because of him, Rocinante had galloped through the grandest cities, along the shores of the greatest lakes, across bridges that spanned the mightiest rivers. On a black night they rode through a galaxy of sublime gleaming pixie-like beings that brought light into the darkness. They rode through green forests with trees so tall, so dense, that they darkened the sun. The two companions trekked a thousand miles across the flatlands, rode over frigid, white-capped mountains and through punishing deserts. Before Tino, Rocinante's existence was the dreadful fate of a caged animal only free to be ridden on dead-end Sunday afternoons. If not for Tino, Rocinante would have spent the rest of his life longing for freedom. Rocinante had no regrets—none—only gratitude and love for Tino.

Rocinante veered off of the highway and raced down a narrow road, the road that led to the cliff at the end of the world. Tino hit the brakes, but to no avail. Rocinante burst into an otherworldly gallop. Air streamed through Tino's hair, streaking it straight back. He held tight. The cliff neared: one hundred feet, fifty, ten, and over into the abyss.

They spiraled downward toward the valley floor far below. Tino resigned himself to their fate. He and his companion would die as one. But Rocinante sprouted great white wings.

Tino threw his head back, laughing, mouth wide open, as he and his winged stallion soared up and up into the glorious blue.

Afterword

The principal characters of *The Trip*, Tino, Sal, Gary, and Patrick, are based on the four young men who took a cross-country motorcycle trip in the summer of 1968—Tim (Patrick), Gerry (Gary), Tony (Sal), and Armando (Tino). The novel is a mix of fact and fiction. For example, *The Trip's* route is factual, but many of the events in the story are creations from the author's twisted mind.

Soon after the trip, Tim bought a Harley Davidson "Sportster" with a big, loud, and powerful 900 cc engine (a far cry from Peewee, Tim's 175 cc Honda). He followed through with his plan to try out for the Army Special Forces as a Green Beret, and made the cut. He was soon involved in a rollover accident during a convoy while on maneuvers in the U.S. and was killed. Armando and Gerry attended his funeral.

Gerry also followed through with his plan and joined the Marine Corps. He served during the war in Vietnam where he was injured by shrapnel from a landmine (the Marine in front of him wasn't so lucky and lost his legs). Gerry recovered from his injures at a military hospital. After an honorable discharge from the Marines, he found employment in the U.S. Post Office and retired following a thirty-year career. Gerry lives in San Diego, California. He fully earned his father's respect.

Shortly after returning from the trip, Tony met with his Bishop saying that he felt that the cleric's life wasn't for him. He eventually received a dispensation from the Vatican and returned to life as a lay Catholic. He married, divorced, remarried, and raised three children, a son from his first marriage, an adopted daughter, and the son of his second wife, Holly. Tony and Holly have been happily married for over 30 years. Tony retired from a career in assisting the children of the disadvantaged in achieving higher educations. He and Holly winter in Baja California, and summer in San Luis Obispo, California. He remains a Spartan.

Armando joined the Air Force shortly after the trip and received a medical discharge after a serious back injury. He married, divorced, remarried, and lives happily with his wife Kathy in Santa Rosa, California. He spends much time writing in his studio perched on the summit of a hill overlooking Santa Rosa. Armando, like Gerry, also managed to earn his father's respect. He bought a new Yamaha Bolt Motorcycle with a 750 cc engine in 2016. The bike's name? What else? Rocinante!

Acknowledgments

Many thanks to the editors who helped me shape the story: Suzanne Sherman, Ana Manwaring, and Margaret (Peg) Alford Pursell, and copy editors Arlene Miller (The Grammar Diva) and Brenda Bellinger.

A very special thanks to Waights Taylor, my publisher, mentor, and friend—more of a brother. He's dogged about getting everything exactly right. His training as an engineer has served him well and is especially beneficial to the writers he accepts for publication through his publishing company, McCaa Books. I have tested his patience with rewrite after rewrite. The biblical character, Job, has nothing on Waights.

To my family and friends who read the manuscript offering their comments, I love you: Michael Matthews, Gerry Yanta, Chuey Otero, John Sutter, Emilio Garcia, Holly Garcia, Tony Garcia, Fernando Garcia, Francisco Vasquez, Elizabeth Kern, Laura Larqué, JJ Wilson, Lennie Moore, Johanna Greenberg, Heather Macleod, Marlene Cullen, Liz Martin, Tina Lus, John Potter, and Waights Taylor.

Many thanks to Breana Marie Eads for creating such a beautiful website for the novel.

Thanks to Moira Hill who created the route map of the trip, Bob McIntyre for the cover photo, and Carlos Gonzalez, the model on the cover.

To the offices of Tony Campolo for granting me permission to use his sermon "It's Friday but Sunday's Coming." I heard a cassette recording of "It's Friday but Sunday's Coming" in the mid 1980s and have never forgotten it. The right spot to fit it into THE TRIP presented itself when the two main characters find themselves in a church service while riding through the South. I called Tony Campolo's office and asked to speak with him, hoping to talk him into allowing me to use the sermon. The young man I spoke with assured me that Tony would not have problem with me using it and that it wouldn't be necessary for me to ask Tony for permission. Thank you Tony, I hope that you like the story. I believe the themes and storyline fit nicely with your beliefs.

About the Author

Armando García-Dávila burst upon the Sonoma County literary world in the latter part of the 1980s. What started as a series of op. ed. pieces he wrote concerning the first Persian Gulf War and the memories of friends killed in the Vietnam War, turned to poetry to express wide ranging thoughts rooted in his Mexican-American/Catholic upbringing. To make clear his humble background, he called himself the "blue-collar" poet.

His poems have been widely published and also found their way into union newsletters and Sunday pulpits. He has read his poetry to immigrant laborers in the vineyards and prisoners in San Quentin.

The Trip, Armando's first novel, took him a decade to write. "I have a new found respect for novel writers," he said. "I heard two different successful authors say that their first novel took them ten years to write. Now I understand why. Penning a long story that holds together and keeps a reader's interest is a formidable task."

Newspaper columnist Ray Holley wrote at the time, "Be sure to check out Armando . . . (while) you still have a chance to see him in an intimate setting before he becomes justly famous for his work."

Armando served as Healdsburg Literary Laureate 2002–2004.